The Grotesquerie Gambit

Jay Palmer

Sequel to:

The Grotesquerie Games

All Books by Jay Palmer

The VIKINGS! Trilogy:
    DeathQuest
    The Mourning Trail
    Quest for Valhalla

The EGYPTIANS! Trilogy:
    SoulQuest
    Song of the Sphinx
    Quest for Osiris

Jeremy Wrecker, Pirate of Land and Sea

The Magic of Play
The Heart of Play

The Grotesquerie Games
The Grotesquerie Gambit

The Seneschal

Viking Son

Viking Daughter

Dracula – Deathless Desire

Souls of Steam

Cover Artist: Jay Palmer

Website: **JayPalmerBooks.com**

Jay Palmer

DEDICATION

To Karen Myers,
she who
tames monsters!

Jay Palmer

Chapter 1
Rompday / Thursday

A New Season of Games ...

"Boys ...!" Martin's mother called. *"Bedtime ...!"*

Martin smiled; he'd been waiting weeks for tonight. He missed his monster teammates, the cheering fans, and even craggy old Grand Wizard Bastile Wraithbone.

It was almost nine; his younger brothers voiced their usual complaints, yet Martin watched the last minute of their TV show calmly, concealing his excitement.

At midnight, Martin would fall out of bed into the realm of monsters ... where he'd helped the Shantdareya Skullcrackers win the Finals of last season's Grotesquerie Games. In four days the new season would begin ... and tonight was Martin's first training.

Soon Martin stood before the sink in his pajamas and brushed his teeth as his mother chased his brothers away from the TV and toward their rooms, shouting at them to hurry and change. Martin finished, then stepped out of the bathroom, and almost walked into his older sister as she ambled down the hallway, her nose in a book.

"Say hello to Murder for me ...," Vicky whispered.

"Stay away from broken airlocks ...," Martin whispered back.

Still reading, Vicky smiled and wandered into the kitchen. She had her own books, a universe of space-elves in sleek, powerful starships fighting the evil Slurks. Yet Martin preferred his own discovery; the monster-world where he was already a hero and fan favorite ... Martin the Magnificent.

Murder Shelling was his favorite teammate, although she wouldn't be able to play again for months. Murder was a Dryad, sturdy as a tree trunk, yet beautiful and deep green ... even her skin and hair. She played as a Small on the Shantdareya Skullcrackers, yet she'd suffered a terrible injury. In the semi-finals of the Grotesquerie Games playoffs, she'd saved Martin's life at great sacrifice; she'd been crushed by a vengeful act of the RatKing Fried Fright ... which had gotten him banned from the league for the whole next season ... with no guarantee he'd return.

His other teammates included Brain Stroker, a huge, fanged ogre, yet not as massive and imposing as Allfed Snitchlock, the strongest troll in the league. Yet ogres were smarter than trolls ... and less likely to eat a teammate by mistake. Their other Bigs were Happy Lostcraft, the proud centaur, and Crusto Fernwalker, the wise, secretive lizardman. His least favorite teammate was Stabbing Kingz, not because he was a greasy ratling, but because he was snarky, pessimistic, and delighted in sarcasm.

Martin couldn't wait to see his friends again, so he kissed his mom good-night, closed his bedroom door, and turned off his light. Then, in the dark, Martin changed out of his pajamas, pulled on his socks, sneakers, jeans, and purple jersey with a large, white thirteen on it. He climbed into bed, leaving his sneakers sticking out the side, hidden by the drape of his bedspread. He closed his eyes and pulled his covers up to his chin, in case his parents peeked in on him while he slept.

Once the games started, he'd be desperate to get enough sleep. School would be starting soon, so he'd need rest whenever he could get it.

"Martin ...!" a chorus of voices cried.

Martin awoke as he fell through midair, then crashed into massive troll palms, each of which were as big as his chest. The green hands set him onto his feet in what was obviously a locker room, but with dull white stone walls; this wasn't the gray locker room he'd always appeared in before. Yet he only had eyes for the monstrous shapes around him.

"Crusto, Snitch, Stabbing ...!" Martin couldn't keep his smile out of his voice. "Where's Murder?"

To answer him, Crusto stepped aside. As green as she was lovely, Murder smiled at him. She was still in her wheelchair, although not covered with bandages and splints as he'd last seen her. He ran to her and clasped her outstretched hand.

"How are you?" Martin asked.

"Healing nicely," Murder smiled, her emerald eyes bright and shining. "The human medicines you gave me helped."

"You look great," Martin said.

"I can even walk ... a little," Murder said.

Martin tried to smile, yet couldn't excise his guilt.

"I still say you shouldn't have ...," Martin lamented.

"My injuries weren't your fault," Murder said. "I'll be able to play again ... by the end of these Local games, I hope. Definitely in the next session, when we start playing the Regionals, at the worst before this season's Finals ... assuming we win these games."

"Is there anything I can do ...?" Martin asked.

"Help us win the Locals," Murder said. "Until I heal, we need you as a Small."

"I'm in ... for the win!" Martin promised.

"We're delighted to hear that," Grand Wizard Bastile Wraithbone said. "We need to start training. We don't want to disgrace last season's honorable Finals' victory by not making it to the Regionals."

"Some teams don't make the Regionals?" Martin asked.

"Most teams never get out of the Locals," Happy Lostcraft said, clip-clopping forward on his four centaur hooves. "You joined us in the first game of the Finals; we'd already won the Regionals, and the Locals before that."

"The Locals should be a breeze, except for the Greasy Golems," Stabbing said. "Last year, we beat the Greasy Golems in the Locals, but lost to them in the Regionals, and only got a wildcard into the Finals."

"In the Regionals, we face the winners of all the Locals ... even those who tie," Murder said. "If we succeed, then we enter the Finals ..."

"Win Locals ...!" Brain Stroker roared, and Snitch grunted loudly.

Martin smiled, looking up at the ogre, Brain, and at the even more-fearsome troll, Snitch.

"We'll win," Martin promised them.

"Hello, Martin," Veils said.

Martin turned around and slightly blushed. Veilscreech Hobbleswoon stood in the doorway, her smile beaming, wearing a purple Skullcracker jersey with an eleven printed in big white numbers. Long, dark hair hid her pale, pointed ears, but otherwise she looked human. Veils was a beautiful dark-elf, only two months younger than him. She'd been too young to play in last season's Grotesquerie Games, but they'd used an aging spell to sneak her in, which let them win the last game of the Finals and the grand prize: the magic staff of Master Grand Wizard Borgias Killoff.

"My birthday was last Rompday!" Veils grinned. "I'm officially a Small ...!"

"That means we have enough Smalls!" Crusto said.

"Yes, but it also means none of you can get hurt,"

Grand Wizard Bastile Wraithbone said. "Again, we have no spare Small."

"What about me ...?" Rude asked.

A light-green man with long pointed ears and a breadstick nose came walking out of the dressing room. Rude Stealing was a goblin, a master of strategy, and their cleverest and most articulate teammate. When one of Grand Wizard Bastile Wraithbone's spells had misfired, Rude had accidentally landed in Martin's bedroom in the human world, from where he'd drawn Martin into the monster world in the middle of their first game of the Finals. Rude looked the same as ever; thin, with thick tufts of hair hanging from his ears, yet his eyes were bright and shining. He walked into the room without crutches or a cane.

"Rude!" Martin smiled. "You're healed!"

"No, he isn't," Grand Wizard Bastile Wraithbone smiled. "If Rude is able to play, then we have three Smalls ... and the Grand Wizard's Council won't let Martin back onto our team."

"I won't be able to play ...?" Rude complained.

"You will," Grand Wizard Bastile Wraithbone assured him. "Once the Grotesquerie Games start, Martin will officially be on our team for the whole season ... hopefully including the Finals!"

"One of us will pretend to have a slight accident ... and then Rude can rejoin the team when we need him," Veils said. "Rude's our secret weapon, a backup in case a Small gets hurt; our surprise the other teams won't be expecting."

"We'll be lucky if no one gets hurt... or killed," Murder said. "Our first game is Marsh Paddle Rider."

At this announcement, everyone sighed.

"What's Marsh Paddle Rider?" Martin asked.

"A disgustingly dirty game," Happy said. "Tell me, Martin; have you ever thrown a lasso?"

Martin followed them outdoors, to the starlit playing field, stunned to see the nightmare before him. These dark-stone stands weren't the ones he'd seen before; they were in a different stadium ... and all the flags around the pitch were purple, the color of the Shantdareya Skullcrackers ... and a scent of brine filled the air.

"Are we on Shantdareya Island?" Martin asked.

"Of course!" Stabbing sneered. "We won the Finals, so we get Home-Team Advantage."

Martin frowned; not growing up on the monster world, he didn't know all the rules. However, as they neared the pitch, the changed venue didn't surprise him most. Between these dark-stone stands stretched a long, rectangular lake ... not of water but of thick mud, murky slime, and reeking, festering goo.

Happy Lostcraft lifted a wooden framework and strapped it over his shoulders like a backpack, but its strong framework upheld no cloth bag. Instead, high atop the backpack frame was affixed a leather saddle ... such as a jockey might ride on the back of a horse.

"Marsh Paddle Rider is a real drag," Stabbing sneered. "Bigs wear raised saddles on their backs, and Smalls have to stay in the saddle without falling off ... while Bigs paddle their way through this muck ... and we lasso enemy Smalls. Once we lasso them, we pull our opponents off their saddles, down into the mud. Then we just hold on; our Bigs drag them across our goal line. Every time we pull an enemy Small across our goal line, we get one point ... two points, if we carry the zombie head when we score."

Martin smiled; he'd made friends with the zombie head in the last Grotesquerie Games. He was a nice guy ... for a living, rotting head without a body.

"That's it?" Martin asked. "We lasso and drag their Smalls across the goal line ... with the zombie head ... and we win ...?"

"It's not that easy," Rude Stealing warned. "Their Smalls will be trying to lasso you, and both teams can score at the same time. That muck is thick, hard to push through, and the biggest Bigs get mired in it, even the strongest." He glanced at Snitch. "Bigs carry wide paddles to help them row through the muck, and there's nothing to hang onto while you're atop a saddle. It's easy to fall off ... even without monsters trying to lasso and pull you down."

"That muck's impossible to swim in," Crusto said, hissing his words through his lizardman's forked tongue. "Even I can't do more than wade."

"Magic lassos make it even worse," Murder said.

"Once their loops close, these lassos don't open until someone lets go of the other end the rope ... or until you cross a goal line. That muck is like quicksand ... Smalls sink over their heads."

"Fouls happen with alarming frequency," Crusto said. "You can't lasso a Big, even by accident. Bigs can't grab a lasso, not even to pull a sinking Small out of the muck. Bigs fight with the padded handgrips of their paddles; if they hit a Small, or another Big, with any other part of the paddle, then they get zapped ... and the Small that's riding atop them suffers, too."

"Ouch ...!" Martin grimaced, remembering how painful zaps were.

"You need to learn how to throw a lasso, how to hold onto a saddle, and how to fall into thick muck without hurting yourself," Veils said. "Getting dragged is equally difficult; you have to keep your eyes clear and your mouth closed."

"That's why Rude's terrible at it," Stabbing laughed. "He can't shut up."

"Purposefully blinding an opponent with mud is also a foul, but it's hard to prove," Rude said, ignoring Stabbing's jibe. "You'll constantly need new lassos, as they get filthy ... like everything does in this game."

"Bigs use their paddles to fling the zombie head to their Smalls," Happy said. "A lot of muck gets tossed up; every player gets coated ... and the refs ... and anyone near the pitch, even inside the front rows of the stands. Last season Evilla got caked ..."

"That was funny!" Murder grinned.

"Yea ...," Stabbing chuckled at Murder. "She had nothing nice to say about you for three games!"

Martin grinned, imagining sexy, fast-talking Evilla getting a face-full of mud.

"When do we begin?" Martin asked.

"Right now," Grand Wizard Bastile Wraithbone said. "Let's start."

Chapter 2
Rompday / Thursday

Into the muck ...

Martin's eyes widened as he saw tall Crusto Fernwalker pick up a paddle and jump halfway into the muck; it sounded like he'd splashed into watery oatmeal. He landed knee-deep, then stood motionless as he slowly sank. When his feet hit bottom, the mud almost reached to his chest, five feet deep, so high it would cover Snitch from his waist down ... and no Small on their team was that tall. To his surprise, Crusto set his paddle in his mouth, bit down to hold it, and paddled with his hands.

"Crusto hates this muck as much as anyone," Veils said, walking up beside Martin. "He prefers clean, clear water. His webbed lizardman hands work better than a paddle, but he'll need to keep his paddle in his hands during the game ... to fight against the other Bigs, and fling the zombie head, which Bigs can't carry."

Brain Stroker and Snitch grabbed paddles from a pile and jumped into the muck with Crusto, splashing mud so widely Veils and Martin ran backwards to keep from getting spattered. However, despite their enormous size and weight, neither landed deeper than their knees. Like Crusto, they slowly sank to their waists. Then they began chasing Crusto, paddling their way through the muck. Using both hands, Crusto stayed a ways ahead of them, circling when he could, but as they converged, he took his paddle from his mouth and held it pointed at them. The top handholds of their paddles were obviously soft, flexible, and bright red. As the neared, they jabbed at each other with their paddles' ends.

Unfortunately, Snitch got over-excited and attacked Brain, trying to wrestle his paddle from him. They had to stop, calm Snitch down, and explain the rules to him again.

Martin liked Snitch, yet he was also scared of him. Allfed Snitchlock was his real name, but that was too long for him to remember, so everyone just called him Snitch. Trolls were the strongest players in the league ... now that giants had been banned. But trolls sometimes forgot the rules, or who their teammates were, or the difference between Smalls and snacks; each team's wizard was careful to feed their trolls before every game.

Grand Wizard Bastile Wraithbone stood on the edge of the pitch, shouting to Snitch, Crusto and Brain joining in his teaching. His purple wizard's robe was already dripping mud, yet he didn't seem bothered at all.

Happy came clip-clopping up beside Murder, Rude,

Veils and Martin, and looked down at them.

"Not getting dirty?" Martin asked.

"Nope," Happy grinned, and he pointed his thumb at the saddle atop his backpack frame. Stabbing was mounted upon it, riding high with ease.

"If you want to get dirty, I could always pee on my saddle," Stabbing sneered at Happy. "I wouldn't be the first Small to do that."

"If I wanted to throw you over those stands, I could," Happy snarled back. "I wouldn't be the first Big to do that, would I?"

"See, Martin ...?" Stabbing laughed, looking down from atop Happy's saddle. "You're going to have fun up here!"

"First he needs to learn to lasso ... on the ground," Murder said firmly, and she held up a tightly braided yellow rope, so stiff it coiled into a perfect circle. "Here, Martin; time to start casting."

"Veils, show him how," Happy said.

Veils stepped forward, lifted the lasso, and flung it up into the air so it began spinning immediately. She twirled it with her hands, so the lasso remained an open circle. She moved the spinning coil down to her side, so her lasso spun vertically, and then she cast.

Stabbing reached out to block her cast, but Happy shuddered, shaking his saddle violently, and Stabbing had to grip with both hands to keep from being flung off. Veil's lasso flew over his head and wrapped tightly around his upper arms, pinning his elbows tightly against his sides.

"Don't pull!" Stabbing wailed. "I won't land on muck here!"

"So ...?" Veils grinned wickedly, but she let go of the lasso. Instantly it loosened from around Stabbing, and with Happy not shaking him, Stabbing easily threw it off.

"That wasn't funny!" Stabbing scolded Happy.

"Martin needed to see a proper lassoing," Happy said.

"He also needs to learn to block!" Stabbing argued.

"Baby steps ... learned in the right order," Happy said.

"I've been a Small for four seasons!" Stabbing argued. "I know better than any Big how Smalls need to train ...!"

Suddenly Happy bolted forward, racing as only his equine body could, galloping far away. Stabbing cried out and clung for dear life, shouting at Happy, when not screaming for his life, as Veils, Murder, and Rude laughed. Happy galloped a wide circle, racing back toward Martin and Veils. Finally he halted so suddenly Stabbing was almost flung to the ground; Stabbing slipped off his saddle and ended up hanging upside-down off Happy's backpack frame with one clawed, hairy foot caught in a stirrup.

"Now ... who gets to say how Martin gets trained ...?" Happy asked.

"*You do ...!*" Stabbing gasped, clutching his chest as if his heart might give out.

"Enough of that!" Murder said. "Martin, take a lasso. Veils, show him ..."

Veils smiled and held out her lasso for Martin to see.

"First, to size your loop, use the maximum amount of rope you can manage," Veils said. "Beginners should start with both hands. Then whip the hand closest to your knotted loop with a slow, even frequency. Crucially, with each rotation of the rope, roll it between your thumb and forefinger to avoid accumulating a twist, which will either bind or undo the braid of your rope. Stiffness is paramount; once you bend it, it's stiffness breaks ... and it'll never spin as easily."

She demonstrated twirling a lasso with practiced ease, and Martin nodded appreciatively.

"Your other hand firmly holds the tail end of the rope, one forefinger loosely wrapped around the coils," Rude said. "When you throw, release the coils entirely. When your loop wraps over your target, pull hard."

Veils stepped back several paces and positioned herself. Martin knew what was coming and stood still as she cast. The yellow rope flew overtop him, and then she pulled hard; Martin stumbled toward her.

Eye-to-eye, they stared at each other ... and finally Veils dropped her rope. The loop around Martin loosened.

"Perhaps you should ... let Martin try," Happy suggested.

Climbing back up onto Happy's saddle, Stabbing

laughed, yet Happy bucked slightly, and he desisted.

The yellow rope was stiffer and rougher than Martin had expected, yet it slid through its tiny loop-knot easily. For several minutes Martin tried every method that didn't work. Veils started to correct him, yet Happy intervened.

"Learning what doesn't work is a valuable experience," Happy said. "Let Martin figure out the basics ... and then help him improve."

Within half an hour, Martin was twirling his lasso with ease, and he could position it horizontally or vertically. Veils began explaining the finer points, how to move it closer or farther away, and the best timing from which he could throw. His first attempts to cast his rope failed utterly. Twice he managed to lasso himself, yet Veils, Rude, Stabbing, and even Happy offered suggestions, and soon his casts looped over Happy's outstretched arm.

At Happy's direction, Veils began dodging about. Even without her arms blocking, Martin found targeting a moving person impossible.

"How do you do this?" Martin demanded. "Anyone can move faster than a cast lasso ...!"

"Excellent observation!" Happy said. "Stabbing, explain."

Happy grabbed Stabbing with his muscular arms and lifted him down with ease. Stabbing picked up a lasso from a pile of them and circled around to Veils' other side. She watched him warily while trying to keep an eye on Martin. Both cast several times, always one after the other, until Veils virtually ran inside Martin's loop while trying to escape from Stabbing's near miss.

"You see ...?" Stabbing said. "The best strategy is teamwork."

"It's worse than that," Veils said. "I'm on my feet and able to move. When you're trapped atop a saddle, fighting to hold on, and trying to watch enemy players on all sides, dodging casts becomes insanely harder."

"Time for your next lesson," Happy said. "How not to fall off ...!"

Happy reached down, picked up Martin, and lifted him high. The saddle looked unnervingly taller when Martin straddled and sat down on it. The saddle had a raised knob in front, which Veils called a horn. Martin had to force his sneakers into the narrow stirrups, and Stabbing explained how to balance his weight, almost as if he were lightly standing in his stirrups, and squeeze his thighs against the wooden frame beneath his saddle to hold on. Martin thought he could manage easily enough, but then Happy took one step forward ... and Martin flailed his arms to keep from falling.

"I was chosen to teach you this for this reason," Happy said. "With four hooves, I have the smoothest gait. You'll be riding on me, but if you have to switch off, you'll find bipedal Bigs harder to hold onto."

Happy walked about for five minutes before he began to trot. Martin bounced and fell off several times, yet Happy was an expert and caught him each time.

Sitting still was impossible; the saddle bounced Martin until he was mostly standing in his stirrups to protect his aching posterior. Whenever Happy leaned into a turn, Martin flailed for balance. It took over an hour before he felt confident sitting up high even with both hands gripping his horn.

"Now comes the hard part," Happy said, and he lifted a lasso up to Martin.

Martin tried to repeat his earlier success with Happy remaining still, yet he spent several minutes just getting his lasso to twirl in place while sitting in the raised saddle. Slowly Happy started again, walking, then trotting, and finally galloping with Martin trying to keep his lasso twirling ... and often failing.

Another long hour passed ... and Murder waved them down.

"Time for a break," Murder said, holding out a bulging waterskin.

Happy assisted Martin down, who felt sore in places where he didn't like feeling anything. Back on the ground, he found walking suddenly difficult ... yet managed well enough. He drank long and deeply. He hadn't realized how thirsty he was ... and then he saw Happy frowning at him.

"Sorry," Martin said, and he lifted the waterskin to Happy.

Happy drank deeply, then returned it to Martin.

"You did well," Murder said. "I think you need a rest. Let's go watch Stabbing and Veils; you can see what this game really looks like."

Happy lifted and carried Murder, in her wheelchair, over the rough ground to the mud-splattered concrete edge of the pitch. Martin walked beside them, proud to be still on the team. However, he began to see closely what he'd only glimpsed from a distance.

While Happy had been training him how to not fall off, Stabbing and Veils had joined the practice on the muddy pitch. Grand Wizard Bastile Wraithbone stood there, beside Crusto, watching the practice, both dripping from gooey splatters. Stabbing rode atop the saddle on Snitch, and Veils rode atop the saddle on Brain. Both were twirling lassos, yet what startled Martin was the amount of mud coating all of them. Each looked as if they'd been wrestling in murky filth.

Snitch and Brain charged at each other ridiculously slowly, using their paddles to plow through the thick muck. As they neared, Stabbing and Veils both cast. Their lassos hit each other, were fouled, and both ropes splashed down.

Snitch shoved his padded paddle-tip at Brain, who twisted as best he could, pinned by the thick mud. His sudden jerk to the side almost dislodged Veils, who flailed and half-fell off her saddle. Brain counter-attacked with his paddle, striking Snitch under his chin. The troll barely moved, yet the blow seemed to have upset his balance; Snitch staggered back, and Stabbing struggled to stay on.

Snitch and Brain traded blows, not strongly enough

to hurt a Big, yet hard enough to off-balance their riders, which seemed to be the main purpose of their fighting.

Stabbing yanked his rope back, coiled it, and threw again while Veils was still struggling to regain her seat. His lasso fell over her, instantly tightened, and Stabbing pulled and wrapped his end of the rope around his horn.

"Back, Snitch!" Stabbing cried. "Back! Back!"

Suddenly Snitch turned and began using his paddle to row away. As Veils shouted at Brain, he tried to keep up with Snitch, but Stabbing kept tightening the rope around the horn of his saddle every time Brain got closer, tightening the rope between them.

Veils was still shouting when their gap momentarily widened and Veils was yanked off her saddle. She fell onto the mud and splashed in, yet only penetrated a few inches. Then she slowly started to sink. Brain quit paddling and reached down to try and scoop her up, but Snitch drug her away, out of his reach, splashing behind him wildly with his paddle, hurling mud at Brain.

Helpless, bound by Stabbing's lasso, and screaming angrily, Veils slid atop the filthy mire toward the goal line, screaming complaints.

"That's how it works," Murder said to Martin. "Watch the nuances; tomorrow you'll be in that muck."

Chapter 3
Smashday / Friday

Slop in the Face ...

"Looking good, Martin," his father said.

Winded from doing push-ups in the backyard, Martin jumped to his feet. He nodded to his father, who walked toward him.

"Son, I admire your dedication, but you know how your mother feels," his father said. "She thinks all sports are too dangerous ..."

"I know," Martin said, still breathless.

"Things may change when you get into high school," his father said. "They have more sports ... like Track and Field, where I may be able to convince your mother ..."

"Thanks," Martin said.

"Until then ... no sports," his father warned. "I don't want you upsetting your mother."

"I won't try out for a single team at school," Martin promised.

At midnight, Martin fell into the strong hands of Brain Stroker.

"Martin Small ...!" Brain said with a smile.

"Brain, good to see you!" Martin said.

Brain lifted Martin up and sniffed him, then set him on his feet.

"Small help us win!" Brain said.

"I will ... if I can," Martin said.

Brain was huge, with mottled skin and large fangs, yet he was usually cheerful. He wasn't good at conversation, so Martin didn't try.

"Shall we go outside ...?" Martin asked.

To his surprise, Brain frowned.

"Mud no fun," Brain said.

"I know," Martin said, even though he hadn't touched it yet. "Let's go join the others."

Everyone was on the pitch. Grand Wizard Bastile Wraithbone was standing beside Murder, who sat in her wheelchair, both badly splattered. Deeply layered in mud, Veils was riding Crusto, Stabbing was riding Snitch, and Rude was riding Happy.

"Watch your backs!" Grand Wizard Bastile Wraithbone shouted at the Bigs. "Don't let anyone circle behind!"

"Hello, Martin," Murder said. "Ready to get dirty?"

"Who thought of this game?" Martin asked.

"Lion Changeling of the Barkrover Bullies," Murder said.

"Figures," Martin scowled, remembering almost

losing to their team in the Finals.

"The Bullies used to have three giants as Bigs, and they were barely hampered by the mud," Murder said. "Sadly, the game stayed even after giants were banned."

"Have any games ever been retired?" Martin asked.

"Only when too many died playing it," Murder grinned.

"Happy, Martin's here!" Grand Wizard Bastile Wraithbone shouted. "Let's get him out there!"

It took almost two minutes for Happy to paddle his way across the murky pool, Rude clinging to the saddle behind his head.

"Good to see you back on the pitch, Rude!" Martin said.

"Feels great!" Rude smiled widely. "Still feels a little stiff ... well, you watched me break my leg ..."

"Falling on me," Martin grinned.

"Martin, you play safely out there," Murder said. "That goop isn't as soft as it looks ... and Smalls have drowned in it."

Rude jovially used Happy's head as a step to reach the dry edge. Happy growled at him, but Rude only laughed. Both were covered in muck and slime.

Martin allowed Happy to lift him, where he sat atop the wet, muddy saddle, feeling its cold moisture soak into his jeans. He forced his sneakers into the stirrups, then braced himself as he'd practiced. However, on land, Happy had shown him speed. In mud, the saddle swayed and jerked precariously in all directions as

Happy paddled in a tight circle to turn around.

"With four legs and his paddle, as his legs are thinner, Happy can dig through mud better than most Bigs," Murder said. "He moves faster than Brain or Snitch."

"Think strategically!" Rude said. "Happy's better speed only works in straight lines! He can't turn quickly! He's too ...!"

Happy flicked his paddle backwards, lightly across the top of the mire ... and a thick splat of mud flew up and struck Rude's face.

Murder, Grand Wizard Bastile Wraithbone, and Martin laughed.

"I can't do that in the game," Happy told Martin.

"No blinding opponents," Martin remembered.

"Glad you're paying attention," Happy said.

Martin looked down and back; Happy's centaur body was long, making spins almost impossible. Out on the pitch, Brain could turn faster than he could push through the mud, but Snitch was slowest because he was so wide. Crusto could rotate at will, and was almost as fast as Happy when paddling ... and excelled him when using both hands.

A sudden jerk almost flung Martin off, and he grabbed his saddle horn with both hands. He found a dirty lasso coiled over the horn, which he hadn't seen because it was as muddy as the saddle.

Martin picked up the lasso and tried to twirl it, but it was so slick with mud he found it difficult. It flung muck in every direction every time it spun.

"Stabbing, no ...!" Veils cried.

Martin looked up to see a muddy yellow rope fly overtop him. Too late he tried to fling it off; it snapped tight as a noose around his chest, pinning his arms to his side, and with a mighty yank ...!

Splash ...!

Yuck ...!

The muck was thick as oatmeal, as wet as soup, yet hard enough to hurt when he landed on it. He was instantly drenched.

"Stabbing, are you insane?" Veils shouted, and cries from the edge of the pitch mirrored her outrage. "Landing safely isn't a skill Martin has learned yet!"

"I thought humans were tough!" Stabbing sneered, leaning over Snitch's huge head to leer at Martin.

Suddenly a lasso dropped over Stabbing and seized him. Veils laughed and wrapped her end of the lasso around her horn, and Crusto took Stabbing on a wild, filthy ride. Around half of the pitch Stabbing was drug across the muck, splashing and struggling, unable to pull free.

Martin tried to watch, but felt himself sinking into the mire, a few inches every second. He tried swimming ... but it didn't work.

"Ummm ... Happy ...?" Martin cried.

Happy's hands reached down and pulled Martin up. He was soaked and dripping.

"Watch Stabbing," Happy said, holding him up so

he could see. "He twists to slide on his back ... to keep mud from splashing onto his face. Only when his eyes are clear can he see any hope of rescue."

"Rescue ...?" Martin asked.

"If an enemy Small has you lassoed, his Big will try to drag you across their goal line," Happy said. "If one of our Smalls can lasso their Small, before they get there, and drag them off their saddle, then you're rescued; their lasso opens once they hit the muck."

Martin looked apprehensively at the mud.

"But ... won't I sink?" Martin asked.

"Eventually you will," Happy said. "However, your Big should be trying to rescue you, in your case, me. Of course, other Bigs will try to block me. Yet this is a dirty game ... in more ways than mud. Their Smalls will try to lasso any Small trying to rescue you."

Still pulling Stabbing, Crusto paddled himself past Happy and Martin, forcing his way through the mud.

"Release!" Veils shouted, and her lasso opened, freeing Stabbing only five feet from Martin.

"Hey ...!" Stabbing started to complain, and then he stretched out both of his arms and legs. "Snitch ...!"

"Watch him, Martin!" Veils shouted. "Wider presence, slower sink!"

Outstretched, Stabbing took up more space and sank slower. Snitch came paddling close, although much slower than Crusto or Happy.

"Poor Snitch," Crusto said. "As he's slower, Snitch will be our reserve Big."

"Doesn't Brain need practice?" Martin asked.

"Yes, but Brain is more likely to remember the rules," Crusto said. "Snitch needs constant reminding."

"Speaking of Brain ...," Happy said, twisting his human torso to look behind.

Brain was using his paddle to wade through the muck, Rude on his saddle.

"Hey ...!" Stabbing shouted, still sinking. "Somebody ...!"

"Snitch is almost here," Veils said. "Besides, you look so natural in mud ...!"

Snitch was still seven feet away when he stopped paddling, bent over, reached out with one long, thick arm, and plucked Stabbing from the mud. He held Stabbing up, looking strangely at him. Stabbing's fur was so coated with mud he looked like a soft, oozing golem.

"It's me!" Stabbing shouted. "I'm your Small! Don't eat me!"

"Snitch, put Stabbing on your saddle," Veils shouted. "Behind your head. Snitch! Lift him up ... behind your head ...!"

Snitch looked puzzled, then lifted Stabbing up onto his head. Stabbing pulled free, clambered onto the bald, mud-covered troll's head, then climbed up onto his saddle. Unlike Happy, Snitch didn't seem to mind his head being used as a step-ladder; Martin wasn't sure if Snitch felt Stabbing's weight, which must've been doubled with all the mud soaked into his fur.

"Martin, watch me," Veils said. "If you can, cling to

your saddle and don't be pulled off; that's best, but it's also difficult. One fast jerk ..." she lunged to one side ... "can pull your opponent off-balance ... or at least pull their lasso from their hands. However, that's unlikely to work. If you're falling, it's best to jump ..."

Veils jumped off her saddle and landed on her feet, yet splashed to her knees ... and all over Crusto.

"See ...?" Veils said, sinking past her knees. "Advantages and disadvantages; I'm sinking faster, so I only do this near my Big. Otherwise ..." Veils flopped onto her back, pulled her feet out, and stretched herself wide like Stabbing had. "This will help me stay afloat until Crusto can get to me. Landing flat sinks less, but your risk of injury is greater. Obviously you don't want to land on your head. You can try to swim, but it won't help much."

"How you fall is most important," Crusto said. "Other Smalls have landed head first; all regretted it. If your head goes under, don't panic; we'll all be rushing to rescue you. Keep a hand or foot up so we can find you."

"No Big can carry two Smalls," Rude said, riding up on Brain's saddle. "If your Big must rescue a Small going under, we jump down so they can ... even if it's Stabbing."

"You've never jumped down for me!" Stabbing complained.

"Even in the worst of times, one must display a modicum of taste," Rude laughed.

"Okay, Martin, prepare yourself," Veils said. "Brain,

take Martin for a swim."

Martin watched Rude twirl a clean lasso with ease, and held still as it flew over him. Its tightening and the yank was expected, and Martin tried to pull his sneakers from his stirrups as he jumped, but he failed, flailed, and managed to splash onto his left shoulder. He frowned, feeling like he'd landed in foul, rotten pancake batter, and it smelled like decaying mold. He wasn't hurt, but almost instantly he felt himself being pulled. Slowly he skimmed helplessly across the slick, soggy mud. He tried to keep his face looking behind him, but the slip-knot of Rude's lasso was on his chest, and kept turning him face-down. While being dragged, staying afloat on the thick muck was easy, but with his arms bound, it was hard to wipe the mud from his eyes.

He twisted, spun, and finally heard a voice beside him.

"Hold your feet out, legs apart!" Veils' voice cried.

Martin complied, digging in with his heels, and instantly he gained control against turning over. On his back, he managed to wipe the mud from his eyes, enough to spy Veils being dragged by Stabbing right beside him. She was also on her back. Behind them paddled Happy and Crusto, easily matching pace with Brain and Snitch.

"Loosen up; don't be stiff," Veils shouted. "Glide ... like you're swimming!"

Martin tried, but it wasn't easy. The thickness of the pool wasn't even. Where they crossed a path previously dug through by a Big, the muck became more watery, and they splashed deeper. Elsewhere the mud was so thick Martin could almost stand on it, although he'd eventually sink.

They spent the whole night practicing. Martin quit using his socks and sneakers, and left them on the cement edge by Murder and Grand Wizard Bastile Wraithbone.

Jumping from a saddle proved easier without shoes. He tried to block the lassos of others, usually failed, and both Rude and Veils let him practice casting at them. Aiming from a saddle was easier than throwing while your target was standing on land, since dodging was harder, and multiple lassos threatened every Small.

Eventually Martin had to go back home. Long before dawn, they all climbed out of the muck and stood, fully-dressed, under a series of clean, outdoor showers not far away. Martin washed off the mud as best he could, even from his coated sneakers, yet he still felt dirty.

As he'd done to rescue the sinking Island of Shantdareya, after last season's Finals, Grand Wizard Bastile Wraithbone raised the magic staff they'd won, the staff of Grand Master Wizard Borgias Killoff, and wiggled his many-ringed fingers. A yellow glow surrounded his hand and then shined upon Martin. When the glow faded, Martin and his clothes were suddenly clean and dry.

"We'll see you tomorrow night," Grand Wizard

Bastile Wraithbone said with a grin, and Martin nodded. The many-ringed fingers wiggled again ...

With a sudden drop, Martin fell onto his bed.

Jay Palmer

Chapter 4
Smiteday / Saturday

The Mess was Best ...

"Martin, play with your brothers today," his mother ordered.

"Sure thing," Martin said.

Martin didn't bother to object. He suspected his mom and dad had discussed him again ... this time without him overhearing. His mom didn't like him exercising so hard ... yet nothing he said was going to change her opinions about 'those dangerous school sports' in which Martin wanted to compete, and arguing would only make her angry. His dad just thought anything that cooled her anger was the best solution.

Blasting zombies, skeletons, and ghouls was fun, and watching them splatter amused Martin. Virtual undead gore sprayed everywhere, yet it wasn't nearly as messy as Marsh Paddle Rider.

Tom, Terry, and Ron were delighted to have a fourth player. Martin understood strategy much better than his younger brothers. He led their quest farther than they'd ever gotten before. Vampire bats came flying at them, and they got extra points for blasting them before they transformed into larger targets. Gaming was far easier than exercising. Besides, Murder insisted Martin take a break from exercising every few days to let his body recover.

Brain caught Martin again, and together they walked out to join the others beside the pitch. Crusto and Happy were fighting to get away; Stabbing was trying to restrain Snitch from chasing them.

"They were practicing ...!" Stabbing shouted at Snitch. "They weren't even hitting you ...!"

"Snitch, don't attack teammates ...!" Grand Wizard Bastile Wraithbone shouted.

"Snitch has trouble with the difference between training and playing," Murder explained. "Crusto and Happy were practicing paddle-poking, and Snitch doesn't like to see his friends get hit."

"Maybe Crusto and Happy should wear yellow and green Flying Munchers' jerseys," Murder suggested.

"I was hoping to save that for Stompday," Grand Wizard Bastile Wraithbone said. "If you show Snitch colors too early he gets bored with them."

"Martin needs training more than Snitch," Murder said.

Ten minutes later, Rude and Snitch headed for the showers. Martin and the others resumed practice; they played a tradeoff, rotating who ganged up upon who.

Martin got better at casting; looping an opponent while they were trying to hang on to a moving mount, and avoiding another Small's casts, felt incredibly easier. However, when Stabbing looped him, Martin seized his lasso and yanked hard; Stabbing was almost pulled off his saddle.

Instantly Veils called for a halt.

"You can't grab another Small's lasso and try to pull it from them," Veils warned Martin. "Referees zap that. Block with your forearms." She had Stabbing cast at her, and demonstrated, ducking one way, and pushing the lasso the other way with one forearm. "You can also block with your lasso; it fouls both ropes, but then they'll have to pull theirs back from a longer distance, while yours is close at hand."

Stabbing cast again, and she demonstrated a lasso-block, twirling her lasso in the path of Stabbing's cast; she regained control of her lasso and started twirling it before Stabbing finished recoiling his. She cast again, and Stabbing had to stop drawing in his rope to block hers with his arm.

"Watch for fakes," Stabbing said. "Good players pretend to cast, hoping you'll block at nothing, and then catch you unprepared."

Once Snitch was calmed down, Rude and Snitch rejoined them, and they spent most of the night practicing. For a change, Martin felt he was almost as good as Veils and Stabbing. Yet soon Rude had to stop; he had to go easy to keep from re-injuring himself.

Murder insisted they take a break, then applauded them as they emerged from the mud. Together they sat on the side of the pitch, resting like tall lumps of dripping, wet dirt.

"My mother would kill me if she saw me this dirty," Martin said.

"Your parents still don't believe in us?" Stabbing asked.

"Few humans do," Martin said.

"The range of intelligence in humans is as wide as it is for monsters," Rude said.

"It's probably for the best," Murder said. "If your mother knew you were playing sports, she wouldn't let you come. How's your sister?"

"She's happily flying spaceships with her elf-friends," Martin said. "When she's not home, of course."

"That sounds dangerous," Murder said.

"It's a balance ...," Martin said. "Ships blow up, but they're a lot cleaner."

"Games played with the mind are usually the most dangerous," Rude said. "Where bigger weapons are used, bigger risks occur."

"Outwitting opponents is the best way to win any game," Crusto said.

"That's what worries me," Murder said. "We're playing games. Vicky is helping space elves fight a war. War is never safe."

"The whole point of war is it isn't safe," Stabbing

said. "Before Heterodox was civilized, our whole world was monster clans fighting wars with each other."

"But we're civilized now," Veils argued.

"Civilization requires solid supports," Happy said. "If you take away the needs of the populace, like food, civilization falls."

"Few things are as dangerous as a failing civilization," Crusto said. "My folk can return to the sea, but the rest of you would be subject to ultimate turmoil."

"Tell your sister we're thinking of her ... and to be careful," Murder said.

"And she can come visit us again anytime," Veils added.

"She wants to come and watch a match, but she's headed off to college soon, so I won't see her as often," Martin said.

"Tell her I ...," Happy said, and then he almost blushed. "Tell her ... we wish her well."

Their conversation paused. Clearly Happy meant more than he was saying, yet Martin knew better than to test the stubbornness of a centaur.

"We almost started a war here after we won the Finals," Stabbing broke the silence. "Many wizards didn't want a human returning to our games."

"The wizard's council went ballistic," Veils said. "Grandfather had to return right after he rescued Shantdareya from sinking into the sea. I think only the fact that he carried the staff of Grand Master Wizard Borgias Killoff allowed Martin to keep playing."

"Grand Wizard Veinlet Prize supported Martin," Murder said. "We don't know why. No one expected it ... as he'd lost to us in the Finals. I think only his support swayed the council."

"Grand Wizard Veinlet Prize was greatly impressed by you, Martin," Happy said. "Despite his loss, he said the monsters of Heterodox could do far worse than to learn from humans."

"He's begun a new practice in Lilliesput," Crusto said. "He's got monsters acting on stages, putting on performances, and he's set up contests for storytellers ... offering valuable jewelry to the winners."

"Why ...?" Stabbing asked. "What good are telling stories ...?"

"Perhaps you should ask Martin," Grand Wizard Bastile Wraithbone said, walking up behind them. "It was Martin who recommended telling stories and putting on plays to Grand Wizard Veinlet Prize."

All his teammates looked shocked and stared at Martin.

"I told you ... he approached me before our last game," Martin said.

"You said he offered you a bribe ...," Veils said.

"We also talked about ... other things," Martin said.

"Like what ...?" Happy asked. "Theater ...?"

"Actually, yes," Martin said. "Also ... books and television."

"We don't have television," Crusto said.

"It comes down to strategy," Martin said. "I've

watched thousands of movies, TV shows, and most importantly, I've read books. By analyzing the themes of countless stories, I'm able to predict many endings."

"Of course," Rude said. "With a broader range of experience, trends become more obvious."

"I've been thinking of opening schools in Shantdareya," Grand Wizard Bastile Wraithbone said. "Televisions won't work here, but the human world enjoys millions of books. We could bring some here without anyone noticing. Few things would open the minds of monsters and enrich our civilization as much as teaching every monster to read."

"You're doing it again," Veils said to Martin, eyeing him closely. "You're changing our world."

"It's a small price to pay for getting to play in your games," Martin said.

"We've got only an hour left before Martin must go home," Grand Wizard Bastile Wraithbone said. "Tomorrow is our last night of practice. Martin, are you ready to play?"

"No," Martin said. "I've got the basics, and I think I know all the rules, but I still don't know who we're playing."

"How does that help?" Stabbing asked.

"Nothing loses a competition as fast as being surprised," Martin said. "Knowing who I'm playing will lessen my surprises."

"We're playing the Flying Munchers ... from the Land of Bogz," Murder said. "Grand Witch Dorkey rules them. She's not very powerful, but she's devilishly clever; she's got brains, heart, and courage."

"Munchers bad," Brain said.

"She's got five Bigs and five Smalls ... and extras if they get hurt," Crusto said. "She never runs out of reserves."

"All her Smalls are Flunkies," Murder said.

"What are Flunkies?" Martin asked.

"Similar to ratlings, only they're half-monkeys," Stabbing said. "They're not as smart as ratlings, but they're incredibly athletic. They do flips and long jumps that would kill most monsters, and they can balance on a rope and never fall."

"They can hold the zombie head in their feet as easily as in their hands," Crusto said. "This lets them cling to saddles extremely well."

"They have small wings ... but flying is a foul ... and they know it," Grand Wizard Bastile Wraithbone said. "Flunkies are devious and relentless. They score lots of goals."

"Flunkies have one weakness," Rude said. "They get angry ... easily."

"Any strategy ideas ...?" Veils asked Martin.

"Perhaps," Martin said. "Let me think about it. What kind of Bigs do they have?"

"Treemen ... all five of them," Happy said. "They're not fast, but they're tough. When a treeman hits another Big with a paddle, their Small feels it ... and often falls off."

"That's why the Flying Munchers have never won a Finals," Grand Wizard Bastile Wraithbone said. "Flunkies and treemen excel on some pitches ... but are awful on others."

"A specialist-team," Martin mused. "Great strengths, but also great weaknesses. No variation. There must be some way to take advantage of that."

"Any you can think of ...?" Crusto asked.

"We'll discuss it tomorrow, before our last practice," Grand Wizard Bastile Wraithbone said. "Martin, if we're done practicing, it won't hurt to let you get a few extra minutes of sleep."

As before, they all showered off as much of the mud as they could, and Martin stood still while Grand Wizard Bastile Wraithbone used magic to fully clean and dry Martin, enough that no trace of mud would smear his bedsheets.

"Sleep well, Martin," Grand Wizard Bastile Wraithbone said. "A well-refreshed mind thinks best."

The yellow glow surrounded Martin.

Chapter 5
Stompday / Sunday

The Mind will Race ...

On the way home from church, Martin noticed Vicky holding her arm strangely, protecting it from anything that might touch it. As they arrived in their living room, she fled into her bedroom, and Martin followed. Vicky's room was mostly her bed surrounded by bookshelves, yet boxes lay piled on the floor; she was packing her clothes for college.

"Problems in Zantheriak ...?" Martin asked.

Vicky glared at him.

"Close the door," she whispered.

Martin stepped in and quietly swung the door shut.

"Our ship was boarded," Vicky said. "I took a laser beam ... almost cut my arm off," Vicky said. "Fortunately, advanced elvish medicine works better than wizard's magic."

Martin frowned but nodded.

"The whole team sends their best and asks you to come visit," Martin said. "Murder said to be careful, and

Happy ... he especially asked me to ... wish you well."

Vicky smiled.

"Give them my thanks," Vicky smiled. "Tell them I'll come when I may. Tell Murder I'll be careful, and ... I don't suppose you'd give Happy a kiss from me ...?"

"Unlikely ...!" Martin glared.

Martin splatted into Brain's hands ... which were already caked with mud.

"Starting early?" Martin asked.

"Yuck game!" Brain growled, wiping the muck from his thick arms.

"We'll be done with it soon," Martin assured him. "We play tomorrow."

Brain grunted, shaking his huge head, which flung dirty water onto Martin and the floor. Martin took Brain's muddy hand and they walked out to the pitch together. However, they stopped at the outdoor showers, where Martin took off and left his socks and sneakers behind.

"No point getting them dirty," Martin said.

Grand Wizard Bastile Wraithbone was standing by the pitch, Murder in her wheelchair beside him, both splattered in mud. Pushing through the muck were Crusto and Happy, who were wearing yellow and green jerseys, and Snitch, who was roaring and chasing both. Stabbing was riding Snitch, Veils on Crusto, and Rude on Happy. Veils and Rude were also wearing yellow and green jerseys ... barely seen under the muck.

"Hello, Martin," Murder said.

Martin smiled at her. He licked his thumb, wiped a space on her green cheek clean of mud, and then he bent over and kissed her.

"That's from Vicky to Happy," Martin said. "Would you mind ...?"

"I'll see he gets it," Murder smiled.

Stabbing wolf-whistled ... and Martin blushed. He glanced to see all the Smalls staring at him, especially Veils.

"Happy, come in!" Grand Wizard Bastile Wraithbone called. "We need Martin to ..."

"Could we have a quick meeting?" Martin asked. "I've been doing some thinking ..."

"Certainly," Grand Wizard Bastile Wraithbone said. "Everyone, come in! Snitch, stop chasing! We're all ... Snitch! Stop! Come here! Snitch ...!"

It took everyone yelling at Snitch to get him to stop, yet he finally got their meaning. They slowly gathered together, the Bigs in the muck paddling their way to the side.

"Listen up!" Grand Wizard Bastile Wraithbone said when they were all together. "Martin has something to say ..."

All eyes fell upon Martin. Veils eyed him darkly with a fixed frown.

"I looked on the internet today," Martin said.

"More research?" Rude asked.

"Yes," Martin said. "On Earth ... the human world

... some people race canoes ... small, narrow boats ..."

"We have canoes," Stabbing said.

"Good," Martin said. "Those racers have made a deep study of rowing, and if we use their methods, our Bigs could move faster."

"How ...?" Crusto and Happy asked at once.

"Paddle deeper, where you can," Martin said. "The deeper you paddle, the stronger resistance you get, so each pull can push you farther."

"That's true in clean water," Crusto said. "Sometimes just forcing the paddle into the muck is challenging."

"It won't work all the time, but you can use it when possible," Martin said, and he pulled a printed sheet of paper out of a pocket, unfolded it, and showed them diagrams of proper rowing motions. All the Bigs, even Snitch, leaned forward to look at it.

"That'll work better as the game proceeds," Happy said. "At first, the muck is pretty even, but as we mix it up, pushing through it, paths become easier to travel."

"Any advice for Smalls?" Stabbing asked.

"Yes," Martin said. "Not for playing; I went online to a site for rodeos, where the best human saddle-riders compete, but all the advice I found was what you already told me, balancing in the stirrups and squeezing the saddle with your thighs. Yet there's a book I read which told about a way one team rattled a championship player on the other team, and I found a song from an old TV show we can use."

"A song ...?" Happy scowled.

"Trust me," Martin said. "This will work."

Martin sang the simple song three times, and all of them joined in by the end of it. He didn't sing the entire song, mostly the chorus, but that was enough. Even Brain managed it, and Snitch grunted the melody.

"Perfect," Martin said. "We'll save it as our weapon ... use it when we need it."

Even when they'd finished singing, Snitch kept grunting the melody, smiling as if he liked it.

Rude tried to dismount the same way as before, using Happy's head as a footstool, but Happy seemed ready for it. He jerked his head forward as Rude stepped, then shoved backwards. With a startled cry, Rude tumbled backwards, landing in the muck. His head went under first, and he came up coated in mire, scraping it from his face.

Everyone laughed, and even Rude seemed amused. He spread out wide, stretching his arms and legs to slow his sinking.

"Please ...?" Rude asked.

Happy's muscular arm reached behind. He grabbed Rude, pushed him under once more, then lifted and tossed him onto shore. Rude landed more muddy than Happy, but he shook it off jovially.

Not wanting to get dunked, Martin waited for Happy to lift him before he climbed up onto the muddy saddle. His bare feet didn't give him as much traction as his sneakers, but the stirrups were too narrow for human shoes; Martin suspected these saddles were sized for kids back on Earth.

They spent the day practicing harder than ever. Veils was vicious, roping him from behind, and Crusto dragged him across the goal line several times. However, Veils seemed so intent upon him that Stabbing rescued Martin four times, lassoing Veils while she was focused on dragging Martin. Whenever she hit the muck, the lasso around Martin loosened; he pushed it off and spread out until Happy could rescue him.

Rude came out on Brain's saddle and joined them. They began a free-for-all, each lassoing anyone who wasn't looking. Despite how slowly the Bigs rowed, keeping track of everyone with mud splashing everywhere and lassos flying in all directions proved impossible ... and there'd be six mounted Smalls on the pitch tomorrow.

When Martin did lasso Veils, she screamed in outrage and struggled, despite what she'd taught him to do while being dragged. However, he never got to score by dragging her across the goal line. Rude was quick to lasso him while he held Veils trapped. Martin tried blocking throws with one arm, but that meant he wasn't holding on to his saddle's horn, which mud made slippery. With only the pressure of his thighs, squeeze as he might, staying atop a Big was like a riding a bucking bronco as they struggled to push through the mire.

Whenever Bigs fought with their red, padded paddle handles, Martin had to use at least one hand to hold on. Each hit was jarring. Twice he simply fell off, unable to stay on his wildly swaying saddle, even when holding tight with both hands. Fortunately he was riding Happy, and if he landed on his equine back, then he could climb up the wooden back-pack frame as if it were a ladder.

Happy claimed that Martin's diagrams about rowing deeper was starting to work, but only after they'd played so long that the pitch was crisscrossed with trails. This gave Martin another idea, yet he held it until after practice.

He was starting to think Veils was furious with him before Grand Wizard Bastile Wraithbone called the end of practice and they slowly gathered together.

"Do we know which side will be our goal?" Martin asked.

"They'll be clearly marked," Happy said. "Our goal will have purple flags around it, and theirs will be yellow and green."

"Are we allowed to practice before the game?" Martin asked.

"Why ...?" Crusto asked.

"Mud is easier to push through once it's broken up," Martin said. "If one of us, like Snitch, were to jump into the pitch before the game, and break up all the muck on their half, then their half would be easier to push through."

"Some might call that cheating," Rude said. "Besides, they'd be able to reach the middle faster. That would keep the game on our half."

"Yes, but we don't score based on where the game is played," Martin said. "When a Small is being dragged through thick muck, the chaser has the advantage. They can plow through the muck in the wake of the other Big. Where the muck is thinner, that advantage is lessened, so scoring is easier."

"Yet the closer you are to the goal line, the quicker you can score, and the less chance of being rescued," Rude said. "Also, Bigs can only rescue by blocking; if a Big grabs a lasso, it's a foul. If two Bigs pull on one Small, they might tear them in half."

"Treemen are strong, but slower than us," Crusto said. "Breaking up their half of the pitch would be a small risk and wouldn't last long. Before halftime, the whole pitch will be loosened."

"We've got all day to talk about it," Stabbing said. "Before the night ends, I'd like to hear that song again."

Martin repeated his song until they could all sing it, and then they headed to the showers. As they showered, he tried to catch Veils' eye, to ask if she was angry at him, yet she seemed outraged when she saw him watching her shower. She turned her back on him and stood under the spray, washing the mud from her long, dark hair, yellow and green jersey, and black jeans.

As Martin stood still, Grand Wizard Bastile Wraithbone repeated his cleaning and drying spell, which felt like a tingly hot air dryer blowing a tiny tornado around him. Every night the cleaning spell seemed to work faster.

"You're getting better at that," Martin said.

"Wielding the staff of Grand Master Wizard Borgias Killoff does have advantages," Grand Wizard Bastile Wraithbone said.

"Don't we get one spell for the season ...?" Martin asked.

"Each team gets one spell for each session of each season," Grand Wizard Bastile Wraithbone said. "The Locals, the Regionals, and the Finals; that's three spells total. Otherwise the games become a contest of magic more than skill. There's also sideline spells, which are mostly healing. Each wizard can cast only one spell per game. In the game where you use your one special spell, you can't cast a healing spell until after the game ends."

"What spells do we have?" Martin asked.

"Many different spells, only this time I hope my target doesn't end up in your bedroom," Grand Wizard Bastile Wraithbone said. "When that spell works, its subject transports to the goal line, no matter where they were originally. It usually gives us an extra score. But we won't be using a special spell tomorrow."

"Why not?" Martin asked.

"There're only two tough teams in our Locals, the Greasy Golems and us," Grand Wizard Bastile Wraithbone said. "Grand Wizard Crass Gopherly will be saving his spell to use against us, and if we can, we must do the same. However, the other teams know they'll never reach the Regionals if they can't beat at least one of us, so they'll be using all their best magic against us."

"That could be troublesome," Martin said.

"It will be," Grand Wizard Bastile Wraithbone promised. "They'll have spells ... and we won't."

Chapter 6
Rompday / Monday

Keep the game going ...

In his backyard, Martin practiced all morning, and then he snuck into his room and took a nap in the afternoon. He felt confident about the game and knew it was a mistake; teams often lost because of over-confidence. He had to stay focused and get as much rest as he could. He napped for several hours, and after dinner, he borrowed another book from his sister, space elves, of course, and went into his room to read it. It was actually a good story and he was enjoying it, yet he fell asleep long before his usual bedtime.

Martin didn't awaken until he smacked into Snitch's huge hands with a loud splat; Snitch was covered in mud, yet none of his other teammates were.

"We did as you suggested," Rude told Martin. "The early crowd was gathering in the stands, and Snitch amused them by playing in the mud ... near their goal line only."

"It can't hurt if it doesn't work," Happy said. "Are you ready to win?"

"I am!" Martin said.

"Martin ...," Murder said, and she leaned forward, pushed against the arms of her wheelchair, and slowly managed to stand all by herself.

"Murder ...!" Martin exclaimed. "That's wonderful!"

"I want to give each of you a hug before the game," Murder said, and she opened her arms wide.

Martin went first, and then each teammate hugged Murder, and she wished them good luck. Seeing what was happening, Snitch pushed to go after Crusto, and Veils went last.

"Now let's get out there and play our best," Grand Wizard Bastile Wraithbone said. "And remember: this is just the first game. We've got a whole Locals tournament to play ... and hopefully win. Don't get hurt!"

Cheers exploded as they opened the locker room doors. Unlike the other stands, where the doors opened in back, this crowd could see when the players emerged. Then a familiar woman's voice spoke over a loudspeaker.

"Here I am, yours truly, your Lady of Lusciousness, your Damsel of Darling Delights, welcoming you to the first match of the three hundred and fifteenth season of the Grotesquerie Games! We've got an amazing challenge coming up for the most spectacular team ever ... which never fails to surprise! Here they come, the winners of last season's Finals, Grand Wizard Bastile Wraithbone leading his marvelous home team, the Shantdareya Skullcrackers!"

"Evilla ...?" Martin asked as the crowd cheered.

"Of course," Stabbing said. "We won the Finals, didn't we?"

Martin frowned; he still didn't know all the nuances of these games ... and that worried him more than anything else.

"And here are his players!" Evilla shouted. "Allfed Snitchlock, the Terrible Troll, and Brain Stroker, that Pain in the Brain for every opponent! Brain is carrying the luscious Murder Shelling; a pity she's in that wheelchair; no treeman is a match for a dryad! We'll check on her later. There's Crusto Fernwalker, whose webbed hands should prove most useful on this pitch, and Happy Lostcraft, the Centaur who Strikes like a Meteor, and Rude Stealing, also on injured reserve, but hoping to be ready to play again soon. Here's Stabbing Kingz, that legendary Ratling of Ruin, and in her first game ever, novice Veilscreech Hobbleswoon, sweet granddaughter of Grand Wizard Bastile Wraithbone, and isn't she pretty ...?"

Veils scowled nastily.

"And here's our most controversial player!" Evilla shouted. "Martin the Magnificent, that Wonder from Another World, back to play again after a fiercely disputed ruling by the Grand Council of Wizards. As you know, Martin is a master-strategist, and we're sure to see some human-based surprises today."

Despite the cheers of the crowd, Martin rolled his eyes and shook his head. He liked Evilla ... he just liked looking at her more than listening to her.

As they reached the edge of the pitch, Martin saw Evilla nearby, on a raised pedestal in front of the stands. She was wearing another dress so tight it could've been painted on; this one was white with black zebra stripes ... and she'd dyed her hair to match. She was entrancingly pretty, yet her personality was obviously fake, exaggerated Hollywood-phony, and Martin didn't trust her at all.

As he watched, Evilla struck a dramatic pose, to which the crowd applauded, and then she threw up a hand with long, scarlet-painted fingernails, directing everyone's attention to the other side of the pitch.

"Here come the visitors!" Evilla cried happily. "From the Land of Bogz, here's the young and vivacious Grand Witch Dorkey! She's quick, clever, and can tap-dance her team out of any tough challenge. And she's got her favorite pet, whom she's never seen without, as always wrapped around her waist: her beloved snake Tutu!"

The crowd cheered while Martin stared at her. Grand Witch Dorkey was indeed young and pretty, with long, curly dark hair, wearing a yellow and green polka-dot robe and carrying a large, pale purse that looked like a straw picnic basket. Around her waist clung a live black snake, thinly dressed in a long sleeve of fluffy pink lace.

"Here's her team, from Bogz, The Flying Munchers!" Evilla shouted. "First are her Flunkies, Sir Green Friskers, her oldest veteran, a Small of nine seasons, who's always the first to face his opponents yet has never once been injured. If there's a door to victory he's sure to open it. And here's Trick-Tok who knows when to wait out his opponents time and time again! Here's Jackal Pumpkinshread; he may be skinny, but he's sharp, and can claw his way into any heart. Look! We've two new novices playing their first game, ragged Scratchwork Whirl and pretty Jelly Ajambi, unknowns ... which means we may see some startling surprises."

Martin had no problem telling the Flunkies apart. Sir Green Friskers looked like a one-man army, taller and more muscular than any other Flunkie, and his long beard and mustache were indeed moss green. Trick-Tok stood stiffly, walking with mechanical motions, marching like a tin soldier with the face of a monkey. Jackal Pumpkinshread was tall and thin, with long arms, and fingers like claws, his hands constantly clenching and unclenching. Scratchwork Whirl was a girl whose torn yellow and green dress, under her jersey, had been repaired so many times she looked like she was wearing a ragged quilt. Jelly Ajambi was truly pretty with green eyes and long green hair, yet she wasn't a dryad; all the Flunkies were covered with short, dark hair, had large eyes, small, bat-like wings, and fuzzy curling tails that stuck out behind them. Jelly Ajambi was the only one smiling, yet Martin thought her expression made her look mischievous rather than playful.

"Before we continue, let's give a heartfelt cheer to last season's saddest players, Ghoulish Cowl and Class Fat," Evilla said. "Their Grotesquerie Game careers were cut short by severe injuries, but we know they're here in spirit. Bless you both; we miss you!"

The crowd applauded respectfully, and Martin wondered how badly those players had been hurt.

"Now, here comes the Forest of Fury!" Evilla shouted. "These are the strongest treemen ever, each and every one a veteran of at least five seasons! Leading them is Princess Bogzma, their leader and team captain. King Ghastoria is walking beside her; he's Princess Bogzma's father, and was team captain before her. Here's King Bury A. Bunny ... no one knows what the 'A' stands for, and few are brave enough to ask. King Cruel is their oldest player, second eldest in the league behind the famous Aunt Honey Peekings, and lastly comes Queen Fried-Lice, who always has an itch for winning!"

Martin couldn't tell which treeman was which, yet they all stood out. Two were obviously girls, one younger and one older; he assumed the younger was the princess and the older was the queen. One tree had white bark like a dogwood, one had grayish-brown bark like a maple, and the last was obviously a redwood ... and he looked especially mean. Each wore matching yellow and green outfits, like a short dress, out of which reached long, bare, branch-like arms. However, none had legs; each had a dozen long tree-roots that stuck out from the bottoms of their trunks, which moved like spider-legs, eerily yet swiftly carrying them forward.

Martin didn't like spiders and shuddered at the sight.

"These are our players ... and these are our teams!" Evilla shouted. "The brave Flying Munchers come to Shantdareya Island to face last season's winners, the Shantdareya Skullcrackers, in what we hope will be our most exciting season ever, the Locals of the three hundred and fifteenth Grotesquerie Games!"

Martin turned around and looked at Evilla, who was drinking in the applause, her face beaming with delight, slowly turning around to wave at every monster in the stands. He scanned the crowd, seeing monsters of all types; ogres, vampires, centaurs, mummies, zombies, and werewolves, creatures of every possible description, yet his eyes always strayed back to Evilla. She seemed to spot Martin looking at her and gave him a little wave, but he only smiled and looked away. The last thing he needed during a game was to be thinking about Evilla.

"Here come our referees!" Evilla shouted, and for the first time, the cheers of the crowd turned to boos and catcalls. No one seemed to like the referees, yet they walked out heedless of the loud sneers, and took their places. Both of these referees were women, one with short blue fur, and the other clearly a vampire dressed mostly in black, holding their wands at the ready.

Martin hated those wands; few experiences hurt as much as getting zapped.

Across the pitch, Martin saw three treemen reach down, pick up their Smalls, and lift them to the saddles, mounted on their back-pack frames. Of the girl trees, only the younger tree was starting. She lifted Jackal Pumpkinshread up to her saddle. The treeman who looked like a maple lifted Sir Green Friskers, and the dogwood lifted Trick-Tok.

As Martin watched, fascinated, he was surprised when Happy suddenly grabbed and lifted him up. He scrambled onto his saddle, which was clean for the first time since they'd begun practicing. He looked across at his fellow Smalls, Veils and Stabbing; this wasn't practice anymore.

"The teams are getting ready," Evilla shouted into her microphone. "I'm so excited ...! There's nothing I like more than jumping into the dirty stuff right away ... and as deeply as possible! While we have a moment, I'm supposed to mention that Pterodactyl Tacos and Root-Fear Moats are your special treats today. So if you're hungry and looking for something to bite, think first of me, Evilla, your friendly Mesmerizer with a Microphone, and then scream out what you want .... to the vendors, I mean! The type of food you want ... no, not my name ..., oh, nevermind! You wonderful, silly things ...!"

Evilla waved and posed for the crowd, smiling brilliant white teeth as they laughed and cheered.

"Looks like the game is about to begin," Evilla shouted into her microphone. "Yes, both referees are raising their wands! And here are our distinguished coaches, Grand Witch Dorkey and Grand Wizard Bastile Wraithbone, both raising their staffs. Stop looking at me now, you naughty monsters! The game's about to start! Here's the starting horn! Let the mayhem begin!"

Crusto splashed into the mud first, Veils on his saddle. Brain jumped in right after him, Stabbing on his saddle. Martin gripped his saddle-horn, squeezing his saddle between his thighs, yet Happy took several steps backwards, then galloped forward, jumping as high and hard as any horse could. He flew over Crusto and Brain, who were slowly sinking into the mud, already trying to paddle forward. Yet Happy splashed far deeper than either; Brain had huge, wide feet, and Crusto's feet were webbed, but Happy's hooves stabbed into the mud like four spears, and his heavy, equine body splashed muck in all directions.

Unable to hold on, Martin tumbled forward off his saddle and fell onto one of Happy's outstretched hands. Happy tossed him backwards ungently, up onto his saddle, and Martin landed with his saddle-horn poking into his stomach. The wind knocked out of him, he righted himself and clung for dear life as his saddle shook with Happy's every movement. Yet Martin managed to regain his seat and stuff his bare feet into his stirrups.

To Martin's horror, another part of his plan instantly went wrong. The zombie head appeared in the middle of the field, floating on the muck. He hadn't known he'd appear there, and at his suggestion, Snitch had broken up the muck on their end. The treewoman in the middle must've seen; she'd jumped into the muck angled toward their side, while Brain, Crusto, and Happy had jumped straight into the middle, Snitch hadn't broken paths and the muck was still thick. While Happy's leap had carried them closer to mid-field than Crusto or Brain, Princess Bogzma came pushing faster through the thinner muck, rushing to reach the zombie head first.

Martin chided himself as he clung tight. Not growing up in the monster world was his biggest weakness. The nuances of these games escaped him until he was in the middle of play, and then it was too late.

As Happy paddled forward, the young treegirl reached the middle, shoved out her paddle, and flicked the zombie head up to the thin man riding atop her saddle and leaning around her leafy head.

"Princess Bogzma captures the zombie head!" Evilla shouted into her microphone. "Jackal Pumpkinshread takes it, and he tosses it behind him to Sir Green Friskers riding King Ghastoria! Good start for the Flying Munchers!"

After entering from the side of the pitch, the treemen had spread out, Princess Bogzma toward the zombie head, and King Ghastoria, the maple carrying Sir Green Friskers, paddled through the thicker muck toward the Skullcrackers goal line, which was decorated in purple flags. The dogwood carrying Trick-Tok pushed toward the Flying Munchers goal line, which was decorated in green and yellow flags. Martin glanced back to see the same; Crusto was carrying Veils toward the Flying Munchers' goal line while Brain was carrying Stabbing toward the Skullcrackers' goal line.

Lassos rose and twirled everywhere. Martin noticed the Flunkies couldn't twirl their lassos overhead without fouling them against the leafy braids of tree-hair branching out from atop their mount's heads. Yet they swapped their twirls behind them, from side to side, with incredible speed. He lifted and spun his lasso, trying to keep an eye on everyone.

The monsters in the stands started to cheer with excitement.

"Jackal Pumpkinshread approaches Martin the Magnificent!" Evilla shouted. "Hold on ... to me! We're about to see the first challenge of Marsh Paddle Rider!"

Jackal Pumpkinshread was no slouch with a lasso. He kept twirling his, first on one side, then on the other. Martin couldn't guess where he'd throw from, so he kept his circling over his head. Suddenly Jackal Pumpkinshread's lasso flew forward but stopped short; Martin fumbled and almost dropped his lasso.

"Jackal Pumpkinshread flummoxes Martin the Magnificent with a fake throw!" Evilla shouted, and the crowds in both stands laughed.

Jackal Pumpkinshread's second throw wasn't a fake. Martin dodged it, then tossed his own lasso, but Jackal Pumpkinshread blocked it with a long, skinny forearm. Both lassos fell to the muck and had to be reeled back, both Smalls swiftly coiling their stiff, now muddy ropes, preparing to throw again. Happy and Princess Bogzma paddled closer, only six feet apart.

As they neared, Princess Bogzma thrust out the red, padded end of her paddle at Happy. She had incredibly long arms and exceeded Happy's reach by more than a foot. Yet her arms were thin and wiry, although flexing with long, taut tendons under tight, rough bark. Happy's arms, while shorter, were bulging with muscles, twice as thick as hers. He blocked her thrusts with ease, knocked aside her padded, red handgrip with the middle of his paddle, and charged closer.

Their conflict shook both saddles, and Martin had to grab onto his saddle-horn to keep from being flung off. He stomped down on one stirrup to the side he was flung to, fighting to stay upright no matter to which side his saddle was leaning.

Jackal Pumpkinshread was just starting to spin his muddy lasso again, which flung brown droplets of muck. Then Happy thrust forward and struck Princess Bogzma's thick chin. Jackal's saddle shook wildly, but he pulled one foot out of his stirrup and used it to grab onto his saddle's edge; Flunkies had feet with long, grasping toes, like a second set of hands, and his small bat-like wings also flapped, helping him maintain balance.

Martin used his upset to finish drawing in and coiling his lasso, which was now wet and slick with mud. Both he and Jackal managed to spin their lassos at the same time, yet they were so close they could almost reach out and loop the other without throwing. However, neither threw, both watching the other intently.

"Martin, behind you ...!" Veils shouted.

A lasso fell over Martin from behind and tightened around his arms. Jackal laughed ... and Martin was pulled off his saddle, managed to jump at the last instant, and splashed onto his feet. Yet he sunk to his knees in mud.

"Sir Green Friskers lassos Martin the Magnificent!" Evilla shouted. "He's got the zombie head! This could be two points ... no, look! Veilscreech Hobbleswoon throws!"

The crowd roared as a lasso fell over Sir Green Friskers and Veils pulled hard. Sir Green Friskers fell to the mud and splashed in shoulder first ... and the zombie head fell from his hands. It splashed in deep beside him, but then the zombie head popped back up five feet away, floating upon the muck.

The lasso around Martin loosened as soon as Sir Green Friskers hit the muck. As he'd practiced, Martin flung off the rope and stretched out to slow his sinking into the slimy goo. Happy grabbed him and tossed him back over his head, and Martin began reeling in his filthy lasso.

Veils wrapped her end of the lasso around her saddle horn, and Crusto spun, then began backtracking his path through the mud, paddling as fast as he could. Sir Green Friskers was drug across the mud, skimming the surface.

King Ghastoria had trouble turning around, needing his paddle to rotate. He could've easily reached down and grabbed Sir Green Friskers, but Bigs couldn't grab a roped player; besides being a foul, teams couldn't win if their Bigs played tug-of-war with their own Smalls.

Jackal tossed his lasso down onto the muddy surface ... and circled it around the zombie head, which it tightened around. He rapidly pulled it in.

Managing to stick both of his feet back in his stirrups, Martin raised his lasso. As fast as he could, he just reached out and looped Jackal Pumpkinshread from the side. Instantly his loop tightened; arms pinned, Jackal frowned, but held onto his saddle with both feet and one hand. Struggling not to drop the zombie head in one hand, Jackal resisted Martin's attempts to yank him off. Beneath them, both of their Bigs dueled with red paddle-ends.

"Princess Bogzma is trying to fight her way past Happy ... to rescue Sir Green Friskers!" Evilla shouted. "Martin has roped Jackal Pumpkinshread, but he's holding onto his saddle and the zombie head! King Bury A. Bunny is trying to make his way to rescue Sir

Green Friskers, but Brain Stroker is moving to block him! It's Trick-Tok versus Stabbing Kingz, both preparing to throw. Trick-Tok wins! Stabbing is down! No! King Bury A. Bunny is abandoning Sir Green Friskers! He's dragging Stabbing Kingz toward the goal line!"

Martin yanked so hard he pulled Jackal Pumpkinshread clean off his saddle, but he toppled as well. Both players and the zombie head fell to the muck. Both lassos released, one around Jackal, the other around the zombie head, which disappeared into the muck and popped up several feet away.

"Jackal Pumpkinshread and Martin the Magnificent both fall ... and the zombie head is loose!" Evilla shouted.

Landing hard on the muck, Martin stretched out ... and felt Jackal's leg kick him. Martin kicked back and Jackal cursed and retaliated.

"Small-fight!" Evilla screamed. "You know what that means ...!"

Z-z-z-z-z-zap!

Pain and yellow light engulfed both Martin and Jackal. Reaching hands of Happy and Princess Bogzma jerked back as the referees delivered lightning bolt-punishments. Martin screamed, which earned him a splash of mud in his mouth, but the pain of this zap didn't equal the agonies of being zapped in the Finals. Both he and Jackal were soaking wet, and the crackling volts illuminated the water just beneath them ... yet the zaps left both of them stunned and groggy.

As the pain retreated, Martin felt Happy pluck him from the mud, and spied Jackal Pumpkinshread being lifted by Princess Bogzma. Both Bigs deposited their Smalls onto their saddles. Neither had a lasso; both had lost grip of them, while being zapped, and they'd sunk into the muck. Dazed and weak, Martin clung to his saddle-horn and looked down to see both lassos vanish underneath the murky water.

The zombie head lay floating on the mud.

"Rescue me!" Martin shouted to Happy, and he jumped back into the muck and seized the zombie head.

Happy and Princess Bogzma slammed their padded paddle-ends into each other, but Happy was stronger. Princess Bogzma almost tipped over, and Happy used her upset to seize Martin, who was clutching the zombie head, and tossed him up to his saddle.

Happy and Princess Bogzma broke free. Princess Bogzma managed to paddle herself around, and headed toward her side, where Grand Witch Dorkey was holding out a fresh, clean lasso. Yet Happy pushed forward, closer to their side. King Bury A. Bunny, the dogwood treeman, was paddling as hard as he could, Trick-Tok holding tight to his lasso, dragging Stabbing behind them. Brain was roaring, chasing them, within easy reach of Stabbing, but trying to get closer.

"The Shantdareya Skullcrackers score!" Evilla shouted, and Martin glanced to the far end. Crusto had managed to pull ahead of King Ghastoria by a dozen feet, and Veils had drug Sir Green Friskers across the goal line, into the end zone. Instantly her lasso opened, and Sir Green Friskers spread out to float ... until King Ghastoria could reach him.

The crowd was cheering loudly.

"That's the first point of this game and the first point ever by novice Veilscreech Hobbleswoon!" Evilla shouted.

"It's Veils ...!" Veils shouted angrily at Evilla, yet she was barely heard over the roars and hoots of the cheering monsters in the stands.

Chapter 7
Rompday / Monday

Challenges become personal ...

With Veils on her saddle, and no one nearby, Crusto stuck his paddle in his mouth and used both webbed hands to paddle through the end zone. He widely circled King Ghastoria, then headed to center, veering toward the Shantdareya side.

Having lost his lasso, Martin wondered what he could do, even with the zombie head. Yet Happy seemed intent on intercepting King Bury A. Bunny, the dogwood who looked white no longer; thickly covered in mud. Brain looked no cleaner, and approached from close behind.

King Bury A. Bunny plowed onward, but Happy cut him off. They met with paddles fighting, and Happy's long body moved to block his passage, preventing King Bury A. Bunny from circling away. Moments later, Brain converged on them; King Bury A. Bunny struggled, yet was pummeled on two sides by Happy and Brain. Knocked about, the treeman flailed ... and Trick-

Tok struggled to hold on. Close up, Trick-Tok looked like a robot; predominate on his chest was a clock with moving arms. Gears and pulleys made up his joints. In all other respects, he resembled a Flunkie, just made of burnished copper and brass. Trick-Tok and Stabbing were both busy blocking each other's casts, while Martin kept one arm up, blocking anything cast at him.

However, before Trick-Tok toppled, King Bury A. Bunny fell into Brain and smacked him in the arm with the wide, flat end of his paddle, shaking him so hard Stabbing fell off his saddle. Martin gasped, knowing what would happen; enemy Bigs could only be hit by the red, padded handles.

Z-z-z-z-z-zap!

King Bury A. Bunny and Trick-Tok burst with the crackles of electricity and a bright yellow glow, which dropped both of them into the muck. Brain roared in triumph, but Happy reached out, stabbed his paddle into the mud beneath Stabbing, and flung him up onto Brain's head. Stabbing landed on one foot, did a flip, which flung mud everywhere, and landed on his saddle with practiced ease. His flip had flung off much of the mud caking his fur.

A lasso fell over Martin; Grand Witch Dorkey had tossed a clean lasso to Jackal Pumpkinshread, and he'd ridden Princess Bogzma right up behind them. Instantly she began paddling to turn around, and Happy started his small circle, but he couldn't turn easily and his bulk was blocking Brain. Martin toppled and splashed, yet managed to keep his fingers closed upon the zombie head. By the time Happy managed to start the chase, Martin was fifteen feet away, skimming atop the muck with his feet wide.

"Martin the Magnificent goes for a ride!" Evilla laughed. "No one's there to block ... looks like the next score's on a human ...!"

"Martin, drop the zombie head!" Stabbing shouted.

Guffaws burst from the crowd as Martin struggled, helpless and soaked to the bone, yet he dropped the zombie head, leaving it behind; carrying it across their goal line would give their opponents two points. He struggled to pull free of the tight lasso, yet he couldn't. He watched Happy and Brain chase after him, feeling embarrassed.

Stabbing had managed to keep hold of his lasso, and he cast several times, but Jackal Pumpkinshread clung with his feet, riding backwards on his saddle and blocking Stabbing's every cast. They drew closer to the goal line.

"The Flying Munchers score on a human!" Evilla laughed. "Game is tied, one up!"

The lasso around Martin loosened as they crossed the goal line. Seeing Happy paddling toward him, Martin spread out, but Stabbing shouted for Brain to block Princess Bogzma, who hurried along through the end zone as fast as she could.

Letting his feet sink deep to keep his head above the surface, Martin sank halfway under the muck before

Happy paddled near. Roughly Happy seized Martin by one arm and pulled him up.

"You need to warn me when someone's sneaking up behind us!" Happy growled. "If you don't have a lasso; look around!"

"Sorry ... I will!" Martin shouted back, and he sat back onto his saddle and looked around. "Brain and Stabbing are following Princess Bogzma!"

"Let's go help them," Happy said, and he started to circle toward them.

"Veils is getting yelled at by Rude and Grand Wizard Bastile Wraithbone!" Martin said. "They seem to be arguing. Crusto's turning ... he's coming toward us."

About halfway between the edge of the pitch and Happy, Veils held up her new, clean lasso.

"Martin, catch ...!" she shouted.

Veils flung her coil of rope at Martin, but it fell short. Seeing it start to sink, Martin jumped off his saddle and landed feet-first in the muck, grabbed the lasso, and a moment later Happy plucked him off the surface and set him back on top.

Martin quickly coiled his new lasso. It was coated, wet and slick, but better than not having any. As he coiled it, he sluiced it off as best he could.

"Princess Bogzma is taking a big risk," Evilla said. "The referees are watching their game clocks; staying in the end zone for more than three minutes is a zap! Brain and Crusto are converging on her, hoping to gang up and yo-yo Jackal Pumpkinshread ... and here comes rescue!"

Martin looked around.

"King Ghastoria and King Bury A. Bunny closing from behind!" Martin shouted.

Happy paddled faster, having circled to turn around and exit the end zone.

"How far back?" Happy asked.

"About twelve feet," Martin said.

"Keep your eyes on them!" Happy shouted, and he focused on moving forward, kicking his legs underwater so hard he widened his lead, although his increased jostling almost unsaddled Martin as lassos flew at him. Frustrated, Martin blocked with one arm and wrapped the back end of his rope around his saddle horn several times, then held onto the rope to keep Happy's efforts from dislodging him.

"They're falling back!" Martin shouted.

To his surprise, Happy turned to the left and Martin wondered why ... until he spied the zombie head floating on the muck. Happy stopped paddling just long enough to shove his paddle under it, and with a mighty flick he flung it up into the air. The zombie head flew toward Crusto and splashed right behind him. With ease, Veils cast, caught the zombie head with her lasso, and reeled it in.

"They didn't follow us!" Martin shouted, looking behind.

Ahead of them, Princess Bogzma had made it all

the way to the edge of the pitch and finally pushed her way across the goal line, back into play. Jackal Pumpkinshread was twirling his lasso, ready to throw, but Stabbing was waiting on him to cast at Veils, and he knew it. Brain and Crusto converged on Princess Bogzma ...

Suddenly Veils screamed, so loudly and unexpectedly it rose even over the cries from the stands. All eyes glanced at her.

Stabbing cast and caught Jackal Pumpkinshread, who's attention had been distracted by Veils' scream. Princess Bogzma turned her paddle to attack Brain, yet Crusto struck her from behind.

"Stabbing ....!" Veils shouted.

"Throw it ...!" Stabbing shouted.

They were only six feet apart; Veils easily tossed the zombie head. Stabbing caught the head in one hand, holding his rope wrapped around his saddle-horn, and Brain paddled across the goal line ... dragging Jackal Pumpkinshread.

"Double-score for the Shantdareya Skullcrackers!" Evilla shouted. "Skullcrackers take back the lead, three to one!"

The crowd exploded in cheers. Stabbing lifted the zombie head high, showing it off to the crowd; monsters roared, shrieked, and howled with delight.

Princess Bogzma rescued Jackal Pumpkinshread, who was caked with so much mud he didn't look thin anymore. Together they started back across the end zone, toward their own side of the pitch.

"King Ghastoria and King Bury A. Bunny are moving toward our goal line!" Martin said.

"They're forming a screen to protect Princess Bogzma as she emerges," Happy said, circling widely.

The game seemed to be restarting; both sides regrouped and faced each other. Yet, as the Skullcrackers started forward, the Flying Munchers started paddling along the side of the pitch, past Grand Witch Dorkey and her spare Flunkies, who tossed new, clean lassos to each of them. Then they headed toward mid-field.

"Where are they going?" Crusto asked. "We're winning; they should be pressing us."

"Beware of tricks," Happy said. "Brain, follow us! Stay together!"

Several minutes passed as everyone paddled to mid-field, then the Flying Munchers turned to face their chasers. Slowly they spread out.

"Match them!" Crusto shouted. "Don't let them surround and flank us!"

They spread out. Before Martin and Happy stood the dogwood, King Bury A. Bunny, with Trick-Tok on his saddle. Slowly King Bury A. Bunny started paddling backward.

"Watch the others!" Happy shouted as he advanced. "Don't let them flank us!"

Happy and Martin crossed the mid-field, then suddenly Princess Bogzma and King Ghastoria converged on Brain. Both threw at Stabbing, but he jerked to the side so hard, to keep from getting caught, he almost toppled himself. Crusto paddled to assist, and Veils managed to lasso Sir Green Friskers, but he was heavier and she couldn't pull him from his saddle. She wrapped her rope around her saddle-horn and Crusto spun and began paddling away, toward the goal line; eventually the slack would tighten and Sir Green Friskers would be pulled off. Yet Sir Green Friskers unexpectedly ignored them and flung his whole lasso atop Stabbing, who was foundering in the muck as Brain reached to pick him up.

Both stopped and stared at Sir Green Friskers; Smalls simply didn't disarm themselves in Marsh Paddle Rider ...!

Jackal Pumpkinshread cast his lasso and caught the zombie head Stabbing was trying to hold above the waterline as Brain reached down. The lasso tightened, and Jackal yanked the zombie head out of Stabbing's hands.

Instantly Princess Bogzma and King Ghastoria began backing away, toward their own goal line.

"They're leaving Sir Green Friskers lassoed by Veils!" Martin said.

"That's crazy!" Happy shouted. "He'll drown!"

"Crusto's dragging him to score!" Martin continued. "Their Bigs aren't even trying to follow him ...!"

King Bury A. Bunny kept paddling backwards, across mid-field, and to their amazement Trick-Tok opened a little door on the side of his metal body, reached inside, and drew out a roll of paper.

"It's a spell ...!" Happy shouted, and he started to paddle backwards.

"What can it do?" Martin asked.

"Anything ...!" Happy shouted.

Trick-Tok began to read, although Martin couldn't hear the words as the crowd rose to its feet.

The roar of the crowd drowned out Evilla's loudspeakers as Trick-Tok read the scroll while all their treemen backed up.

Suddenly a fierce, cold gust of wind blew across the pitch. A white fog filled it, frosting everything with a wintry glistening.

As he finished reading, Trick-Tok's magic scroll froze, and the yellowed parchment became thickly layered in an inch of ice. It cracked into a hundred fragments and broke apart in Trick-Tok's hands. The frozen fragments fell to land on the watery pitch.

The white fog blew up into the air in a solid, curving column and streamed down, striking the pitch beside Crusto. The mud frosted over where it hit. The white fog spread out, covering the entire Skullcracker side of the pitch. It flowed around Crusto and Brain's waists and frosted the surface of the muck into a bright winter white. Then the white fog slowly vanished, seeping down inside the frosted mud.

The mucky Shantdareya half of the pitch froze into solid ice.

Crusto and Brain stood trapped, waist-deep in hard, glacial ice ... encased, unable to move. Atop them, Veils and Stabbing cried out. On top of the ice, Sir Green Friskers lay, half frozen ... laughing.

"A Winter Wonderland spell ...!" Evilla shouted. "Half of the pitch is frozen, trapping Brain and Crusto in solid ice! Two Smalls and all three Bigs of the Flying Munchers are safe ... and converging on Happy Lostcraft and Martin the Magnificent!"

Not frozen in ice, Happy turned his head and glanced up at Martin.

"Defend yourself ... and hold tight!" Happy growled. "We're on our own! This is going to get ugly!"

Martin glanced around. Evilla seemed pleased, yet the crowd looked shocked, some laughing, others stunned.

Trapped in the ice, Crusto struggled to turn around, found he couldn't move, and started hacking at the ice with his paddle. Brain roared and began punching the ice so violently Stabbing jumped off his saddle onto the hard, frosty surface. Veils also jumped down, but she slipped on the ice and fell.

Except for Sir Green Friskers, all the Flying Munchers paddled toward Martin and Happy as fast as they could.

Happy reared, kicking his caked forehooves in the air above the mud. Martin clung low and tight, unable to flip his lasso with both hands holding on. Happy leapt over the mud, splashing back into the muck only two feet in front of King Bury A. Bunny. With his paddle inverted, Happy slammed his red padded handle down through his thinnest branches onto King Bury A. Bunny's leafy head.

The dogwood crumpled, staggered, and then fell backward, splashing into the mud. Trick-Tok cried out and jumped off his saddle, landing in the muck beside his fallen mount, avoiding being knocked underwater by the wide, leafy hair.

Princess Bogzma paddled to aid them. She reached Trick-Tok, scooped him up with her paddle and tossed him to King Ghastoria. King Ghastoria caught him in midair and lifted him to his empty saddle, where Sir Green Friskers had previously sat.

While Princess Bogzma righted King Bury A. Bunny, King Ghastoria aimed his path straight at Happy and Martin. Trick-Tok lifted and whirled his muddy lasso over his head.

"Both referees are lifting wands ...!" Evilla shouted. "Happy's attack was unexpected ... but did he break a rule ...?"

Martin glanced at the referees yet tried to focus on Trick-Tok. No zaps came, yet Martin thought a penalty may be less painful than what was about to happen.

King Bury A. Bunny looked unsteady, yet once on his feet, Princess Bogzma left him to recover. On his saddle, Jackal Pumpkinshread lifted his lasso, laughing wickedly at Happy and Martin.

Two mounts and riders against one, Happy began

paddling backward. The Flying Muncher Bigs paddled closer, glaring at him; Happy's surprise attack wouldn't work twice. Happy reared again and jumped away, along the edge of the pitch. His move dislodged Martin, yet Martin clung to the rope-end around his saddle-horn and managed to climb back on. Happy's leap had earned one advantage; only two Bigs were converging on them, yet they couldn't afford to get trapped in a corner by the Flying Muncher's goal line.

Princess Bogzma and King Ghastoria paddled after them, widening their angles. Jackal held the zombie head under one arm. Happy paddled toward their goal line, hoping to get ahead of them, yet they circled, determined to close off all possible escapes.

"Halftime ...?" Martin asked.

"Fifteen minutes away ...!" Happy said.

"Attack one ...?" Martin asked.

"The other will catch up while we fight," Happy said.

"Can you jump ...?" Martin asked.

"Between them ...?" Happy asked. "We'll get pinned ...!"

"Better there than here," Martin said, looking behind them at the goal line.

"I can't tire myself out jumping through this mud," Happy said. "Defend yourself!"

Happy charged Princess Bogzma. Jackal Pumpkinshread spun his lasso and cast. Martin blocked it, but then Happy and Princess Bogzma began trading blows, and both Jackal Pumpkinshread and Martin struggled to hold on. Martin threw his lasso over Jackal Pumpkinshread, but they were too close and he couldn't let go of his saddle to choke up on his rope.

A lasso flew over Martin and tightened. Having come up from behind on King Ghastoria, Trick-Tok yanked Martin off his saddle. Laughing, Jackal tossed the zombie head to Trick-Tok, and with ease King Ghastoria pulled Martin across the nearby goal line.

"Double-score!" Evilla cried. "Tied game! Three each!"

As they'd scored, the lasso around Martin opened, dumping him free on the mud. Princess Bogzma and King Ghastoria both paddled away, out of range. Martin stretched out on the surface, yet he was half-sunk before Happy reached him. Happy looked furious, but he gently lifted Martin back to his saddle.

"We've got two and a half minutes to exit the end zone," Happy snarled.

"What happens then?" Martin asked.

"We get zapped," Happy said. "That's at least four zaps before halftime ... if we sit here."

"Then what ...?" Martin asked.

"If we don't survive the zaps, then we drown," Happy said. "Every time we leave the end zone they'll gang up on us ... and double-score."

"We let them win ... or we die ...?" Martin asked.

"We don't let them win," Happy said. "We can take one zap, no more, and then we'll be too weak. We'll wait until the last moment, then exit."

Princess Bogzma paddled back and took her place on one side. King Ghastoria took his place on her other side.

"Two Bigs against one!" Evilla cried, the crowd on their feet.

Happy could cross the goal line back into play, but he and Martin wouldn't get far.

Veils and Stabbing were standing on the edge of the frozen ice, stomping at the ice to break it apart and kicking off large chunks, yet they'd never clear all of it. Behind them, Crusto was still trapped, his paddle broken, using his sharp claws to rake the icy surface. With his massive fists, Brain was furiously pounding the ice, occasionally lifting out a large chunk and hurling it away. Yet he'd never free himself in time.

At the last second, Happy carried Martin out of the end zone. Princess Bogzma and King Ghastoria began converging.

"Can we go back across their goal line ...?" Martin asked.

"Not without getting zapped," Happy said as "To avoid all zaps, we'd have to let them double-score three times," Happy snarled. "They've tied the game. I intend to keep their scoring down to one more ... and they're going to have to earn it."

Martin clung tight to his saddle, raising his lasso. As Jackal and Trick-Tok approached, three lassos began to spin.

Happy tried to circle around to gain time, but they cornered him. Heavily splattered, Grand Wizard Bastile Wraithbone and Rude came running up to the edge near them.

"Happy, let's use our spell ...!" Grand Wizard Bastile Wraithbone shouted from the edge.

"No!" Happy cried. "We'll need it later!"

"Happy, be sensible!" Rude shouted. "We need you alive ...! There's more to this season than one game ...!"

"Quit disturbing me ...!" Happy snarled.

Pushing closer, Princess Bogzma and King Ghastoria quit paddling. They and Happy raised red, padded oar-grips, and faced each other. Martin spun his lasso, ready to defend against two, but they just kept twirling. The two groups met.

Happy fought like a berserker, slamming into both Princess Bogzma and King Ghastoria as he was knocked aside, getting hammered by both. Trick-Tok fouled Martin's lasso, yet Martin blocked both their casts. He didn't cast; Skullcrackers couldn't score across a frozen goal line; he only used his lasso to block.

At times the Smalls were close enough to strike each other, yet Martin had learned not to punch in his first game: he'd get zapped for fighting.

Minutes passed in a furied, painful tumult. Finally Martin was lassoed by Trick-Tok after Jackal Pumpkinshread fouled his block. Yet Martin clung to his saddle, struggling even as King Ghastoria moved away and Trick-Tok tightened his rope on his saddle-horn. However, Martin's strength couldn't defy a living tree; Martin was pulled off.

Martin fell onto the muck. Happy was busy pummeling Princess Bogzma, who was keeping him occupied. With the zombie head in Trick-Tok's arms, King Ghastoria again dragged Martin across their goal line.

"Another double-score!" Evilla said, but her voice trembled.

Many in the crowd jumped to their feet, but mostly fell silent, simply staring aghast.

"This is a fierce battle, totally one-sided," Evilla said. "Happy Lostcraft and Martin the Magnificent are putting up a ferocious defense against insurmountable odds ... and here comes King Bury A. Bunny, back into play, having finally righted and recovered ... even though Sir Green Friskers is out until the ice melts. That's three Bigs against one! How much more punishment can Happy Lostcraft survive ...?"

Barely a sound came from the crowd.

"Martin is free, floating on the surface in the end zone," Evilla said. "Happy is paddling to rescue him, but he's staggering, barely able to walk. How much more of a beating can our Charming Centaur endure ...?"

Happy reached Martin right before his face went under, but he could barely lift him. Martin grabbed his thick arms and held on just enough to keep from sinking completely under.

"Happy, it's not worth it ...," Martin said.

"We've done ... all we can," Happy stammered. "We delayed them ... they won't score again."

"How ... how long?" Martin asked.

"Two minutes have passed," Happy said. "Five more minutes remain."

"We'll do it," Martin said.

Martin took Happy's hard, thick hand in his small, weak grip, and pulled himself up. Together they waited.

"What're they doing?" Evilla asked as the seconds passed. "It's almost been three minutes! They're both going to get ... zapped."

Happy lifted Martin up, holding him against his chest. Martin put one arm around Happy's neck ... both waiting.

Utter silence fell over the stadium. Outside the end zone waited three treeman and two Flying Munchers, motionless, staring, disbelieving. Inside the end zone stood Happy holding Martin ... as the last seconds ticked past.

"Score is five to three," Evilla said in monotone.

Neither Martin nor Happy moved. The referees glanced at each other and raised their wands almost reluctantly. They took aim.

Z-z-z-z-z-zap!

The crackle of both lightning bolts filled the air, the only sound in the stadium save for Happy and Martin's screams. Yellow lights blasted and burned.

Both Happy and Martin crumbled, almost falling unconscious. Happy staggered, yet remained standing, holding Martin up. But neither looked like they could endure another zap.

The stadium stood frozen, Martin barely able to see the stands clearly. Martin had already endured one zap before the Winter Wonderland spell ... and the half wasn't over.

Slowly, one minute passed ... and then another. Happy didn't move. Another three minute mark approached.

In silence, the referees took aim.

Z-z-z-z-zap!

Unbearable pain ... both Martin and Happy screamed. Happy staggered, and almost fell. Martin clung to him, barely conscious.

The final minute passed lasting eternities.

A lonely horn blew, clear and loud.

Halftime had come.

No more zaps ...!

Reeling, Martin tottered in Happy's arms. His head fell back ... and then everything went black.

Chapter 8
Rompday / Monday

Horrible halftime ...

"Martin ...? Please, wake up!"

Murder's voice seeped into Martin's awareness.

"Let him sleep," Crusto said. "He needs it."

"He deserves to be awake," Happy said. "He earned it."

Martin opened his eyes. He was lying on his back, looking up at stars dimmed by the lights of the noisy stadium.

"The ... the game ...?" Martin asked.

"We've only moments before halftime is over," Grand Wizard Bastile Wraithbone said. "However, for you, this game is done."

"No ...!" Martin tried to shout, but the effort weakened him.

"Martin, we've done our part," Happy said, although his frown couldn't be deeper ... or his voice more pained. "It would be ... dishonorable for us to demand to play injured ... while healthy players stand idle."

"Rude and Snitch are playing in your places," Murder said.

"Call everyone ... to me ... before halftime ends," Happy said.

Grand Wizard Bastile Wraithbone called them to circle around Happy. The Smalls were already mounted, Rude on Snitch, Veils on Crusto, and Stabbing on Brain.

"Martin kept up a constant watch for me, alerting me to the movements of every enemy," Happy told them. "It helped me know what's going on. Every Small should do the same."

Small heads nodded.

"I also ... tried something new," Martin said. "Even when I didn't have someone lassoed, I wrapped the tail end of the lasso tight around ... my saddle-horn. Holding onto the rope, rather than the horn, helped me stay on ..."

"We'll try both," Rude promised.

"Veils," Grand Wizard Bastile Wraithbone said, "I know this is your first game, but if Martin wasn't injured, then Rude would be taking your place. I'm not just your grandfather, I'm your team wizard; you take orders like every other member of this team ... or you don't play!"

Veils frowned but nodded, flashing a dark glare at Martin. He wondered why ...

"The game's about to restart!" Evilla said over the loudspeakers. "This match is red hot, much like me, your ever-sexy announcer, the gal with the tremendous ... fan-base! So sit up and stare all you want ... at the game ... during the fabulous second half! It's sure to be the height of excitement ... and I love to feel excited!"

"Take your places!" Grand Wizard Bastile Wraithbone said. "Crusto, try to get to the zombie head first!"

The Bigs turned around, facing the pitch. Martin tried to rise.

"Stay with me," Murder said to Martin.

"We're losing ...!" Martin frowned.

"Only by two ... because of your and Happy's sacrifice," Murder said. "If anyone else had been trapped alone by that ice-spell, then we'd be losing by a lot more."

"Let the mayhem resume!" Evilla shouted.

Snitch, Brain, and Crusto jumped in. Rude, Veils, and Stabbing clung to their saddles. Their splashes slopped mud onto everyone beside the pitch, but they were already so muddy no one cared.

"Rude Stealing is returning to play!" Evilla said. "He's technically still on injured reserve, but after the noble, unbelievable endurance of Happy Lostcraft and Martin the Magnificent, it's no surprise they're taking a well-deserved break."

Martin glanced at Murder and she smiled.

"No other monster has ever done what you two just did," Murder said appreciatively.

"Happy did it ... I just went along," Martin said.

"We had little choice," Happy said. "A true champion does what he must ...!"

"Happy, lean over here," Murder said. "Martin wanted me to give you a message ... from his sister, Vicky."

Despite his stern demeanor, Happy leaned down and let Murder kiss him. Both of them smiled ... then turned their heads to see Martin watching them.

"Do you mind ...?" Murder asked, and Martin quickly looked away.

"Spread out wider!" Grand Wizard Bastile Wraithbone shouted to the players on the pitch. "Snitch! Listen to Rude!"

Although pained, Martin wrenched himself up and walked to stand by the muddy edge.

The Winter Wonderland spell had ended; the ice and every trace of frost was gone, vanished during halftime. Crusto had his paddle in his mouth and was digging through the muck with his hands, but as he reached the zombie head, Princess Bogzma approached from the other side. He took out his paddle and used it to toss the zombie head all the way to Stabbing. It splashed near Brain; Stabbing used his lasso to loop and rein it in. Meanwhile, Crusto and Princess Bogzma raised their red-tipped paddles, and Veils and Jackal Pumpkinshread began twirling lassos.

"Crusto gets the zombie head and passes it to Stabbing!" Evilla shouted. "Princess Bogzma doesn't look happy. On the sidelines, King Bury A. Bunny is sitting this half out, still recovering after that horrible smash from Happy, and Trick-Tok has also left the game, citing mechanical error. Yet look who's on in their place: that Wondrous Willow Queen Fried-Lice, and pretty Jelly Ajambi, here to clean up all competition in her first game ever! They're both fresh and ahead by two points, but the Flying Munchers are facing last season's champions ... and as always, just like being alone with me, anything can happen!"

Martin laughed and glanced to see Evilla, whose black and white zebra stripes were unsurprisingly dotted with brownish blobs of dripping muck. Grand Wizard Bastile Wraithbone paused to stare at Martin.

"Sorry," Martin said. "I think she's funny."

"Quite amusing ... always ... and very pretty," Grand Wizard Bastile Wraithbone said. "She's the perfect distraction ... and many games have been lost because their wizard or players became distracted by her outrageousness."

Martin took his meaning and concentrated on the game.

"Stabbing!" Grand Wizard Bastile Wraithbone cried. "Behind you ...!"

"Crusto and Princess Bogzma are backing away; no mid-field battle right now," Evilla said. "Yet Stabbing Kingz and Sir Green Friskers are twirling their lassos as Brain Stroker and King Ghastoria face off beneath them. Looks like we've got the first challenge of the second half!"

Stabbing and Sir Green Friskers both cast ... and their lassos struck each other and fell. They reeled them in as their Bigs neared, paddles raised. Their Bigs came together, fighting hard.

"The battle has begun!" Evilla cried. "Stabbing Kingz has the zombie head, and they're close to the Skullcracker's goal line, but Sir Green Friskers isn't resting on his two-point lead! And here comes Crusto, closing fast! Princess Bogzma is chasing in his wake, but he'll be in the thick of it before her!"

On the far edge of the pitch, Grand Witch Dorkey was shouting, yet even her loud, resonate voice failed over the roars, hoots, and screeches of the cheering monsters in the stands.

As Crusto neared, Veils cast and looped Sir Green Friskers from behind. Startled to find himself entrapped, he fell off his saddle, helpless as Crusto backed up. Then Crusto resumed his course. Furious, Sir Green Friskers raised a fist and shook it at Veils, but Stabbing dropped his lasso upon him as he lay in the mud, looped his raised arm, and Sir Green Friskers was roped twice.

"Release!" Veils cried, and the loop of her lasso loosened, as Stabbing held the zombie head.

King Ghastoria attacked Brain, but at Stabbing's direction, the huge ogre only defended himself and began backing toward the goal line. Helpless, Sir Green Friskers was drug across by a lasso tight around his arm.

"Double-score to the Shantdareya Skullcrackers!"

Evilla shouted. "Tied game, five up! Grand Witch Dorkey isn't happy! Her incredible Winter Wonderland spell should've given her more points, but Happy made her unhappy! Now she's facing a serious challenge from a vastly more-accomplished team!"

Martin couldn't believe how often Evilla commented on the plays. While on the pitch, he must've drowned out her chatter without even being aware he was ignoring her.

"⟨...⟩eatest strength of the Flying Munchers has alw⟨...⟩ the amazing spell-casting ability of Grand W⟨...⟩key, which they needed to win this game!" ⟨...⟩uted. "They've cast their only spell. If they ⟨...⟩ today, their odds of making it to the Regionals ⟨...⟩ greatly diminished!"

Rude wasn't as healed as he'd claimed. Facing Jelly Ajambi atop Queen Fried-Lice, he was quickly pulled off his saddle and dragged across their goal line. Yet Veils and Stabbing kept tossing the zombie head back and forth, using it to score, so their frequent double-scores more than made up for Jelly Ajambi's singles.

While Grand Wizard Bastile Wraithbone kept yelling at Veils and Stabbing, helping them to score points, Martin walked unsteadily to the other end of the pitch to help Rude. Rude gnashed his teeth and grimaced every time he was dropped into the mud, yet he never cried out. Snitch got angry and started using his red paddle handle on Queen Fried-Lice, tired of being poked by her. Snitch knocked her backwards so many times Jelly Ajambi had to stop looping Rude, clinging onto her saddle with both hands and feet to keep from being dislodged.

Rude had dropped his lasso, and Martin threw him a new, clean rope, and he finally managed to loop Jelly Ajambi. Yet Snitch wouldn't stop attacking Queen Fried-Lice, not until he'd knocked her over.

"Timber ...!" Evilla shouted as Queen Fried-Lice toppled onto her back, raising a huge splash of mud. "There goes Queen Fried-Lice, bless her old heart, knocked flat by Allfed Snitchlock, the strongest troll in the league! Listen to that troll-roar of triumph! Rude Stealing has Jelly Ajambi caught, but he can't seem to make his mount grasp that they need to head toward their goal line. Ha! Troll-strengths are in their muscles, not their minds! Wait ...! It looks like Allfed Snitchlock has finally grasped what Rude is shouting. He's turning, starting to drag Jelly Ajambi! And there goes Queen Fried-Lice, slipping underneath the mud! Will she go under ...? Are we looking at Jelly Ajambi for the last time? No, she's managed to roll over! Those long treegirl arms ...! She's righted herself, but she's too far behind to rescue her Small!"

Martin shouted encouragement, running along the mud-splattered edge, yet his cries were mostly lost in the cheers of the crowd. He hated not playing in the second half, watching but not being able to physically assist. Rude must've felt this helpless throughout the Finals while his broken leg healed ... as Murder was feeling it now.

Helplessness felt frustrating ... but occasionally it was part of being an athlete. Somehow he had to make it up to Rude and Murder, to find a way to make them feel included. He owed both of them that much.

Remembering his other plan, Martin raised his voice and began to sing. To his delight, his other team members heard him, and joined in.

"Here we come!

Clinging on bad trees!

Giving stupidest looks cause ...

We're all covered with fleas!

Hey, hey, we're the Flunkies!

Beasts say we Flunkie around!

But we're too busy itching ...

To drag our enemies down!"

The crowd fell silent to listen ... and then burst into laughter. Soon they picked up the chorus and sang along, their voices ringing out and filling the stadium to the coast.

Hearing the song, the tantrums of Flying Munchers became hilarious. They screamed, shouted, and gestured threateningly both at the Skullcrackers and the singing crowd.

Furious, their concentration became spoiled, and they began to ignore the game ... which the Skullcrackers eagerly capitalized on.

Two short toots finally filled the air; the warning horn blew; the game was almost over.

Stabbing and Veils celebrated the end of the game by jointly dragging Jackal Pumpkinshread across the goal line for the final double-score.

The horn finally blew for the end of regulation.

"The Shantdareya Skullcrackers win!" Evilla shouted. "Final score: fourteen to eight! Not unexpected for the winners of last season's Finals, but a clear disappointment for Grand Witch Dorkey! To make it into the Regionals now, she'll have to beat the Greasy Golems now ... without a spell! But, for all the filth, they did play a strong, clean game! Let's hear a big cheer for the Flying Munchers and the land of Bogz...!"

Monsters whooped, hollered, and applauded, yet their treemen ... now mostly treewomen ... crawled out of the muddy pitch frowning and looking dispirited.

Martin ran to join the other Skullcrackers as they climbed out of the mud, every monster on their team delighted to be finished with Marsh Paddle Rider.

However, as they hugged and congratulated each other, Martin spied the zombie head floating alone on the murky pitch, dropped and forgotten. Martin picked up a clean rope, ran around to the end zone, lassoed, and drug him in.

"Are you all right?" Martin asked, pulling the zombie head from the muck and wiping his face clear.

"Thanks, I'm fine," the zombie head said. "This mud is actually good for my rotting complexion, but I can't open my mouth ... Marsh Paddle Rider may look fun, but you don't want to taste it."

"I'll get you cleaned up," Martin promised.

Soon, Grand Wizard Bastile Wraithbone had them all gather to face Evilla, Martin still carrying the zombie head.

"Here they are, the game winners!" Evilla shouted, wiping away mud trying to drip down from her hair onto her face. Martin was amused to see her splattered all over. "What an overwhelming victory! Were you surprised by Grand Witch Dorkey's Winter Wonderland spell?"

She shoved her microphone at Stabbing, but Rude stepped forward, although he still seemed shaky and looked like he needed his cane.

"Grand Witch Dorkey is a powerful and deeply-respected magician, as everyone knows," Rude said. "Her chilling spell literally froze us in our tracks ... and could've cost us the game. Luck went against her, I'm afraid."

"That's right!" Evilla shouted, pulling back her microphone. "Happy, we were all shocked and impressed with your handling of being trapped, unaided, against all three Flying Munchers' Bigs. How did you endure the pummeling ... and two zaps?"

She shoved her microphone at Happy, who seemed displeased to speak to her.

"Centaurs fear no challenge or pain!" Happy growled angrily.

"Well, I fear both!" Martin said, stepping forward to rescue Happy, and Evilla turned her microphone to face him. "Happy Lostcraft showed great courage, worthy of any true centaur. He inspired me ... and I'm proud to have endured those zaps with my friend!"

"Thank you, Martin the Magnificent!" Evilla said. "Tell me, Martin, what do you think of the recent ruling of the Grand Council of Wizards ...?"

"Evilla, this is a festive occasion, and we are too covered with mud for serious conversation," Grand Wizard Bastile Wraithbone interjected, stepping forward and stealing her attention. "We are delighted to have won, having faced such a talented and formidable team, led by a truly wise and respected witch. Now, I think we'd all like to get cleaned up so we can celebrate properly."

Evilla obviously wanted her interview to last longer, but when Grand Wizard Bastile Wraithbone turned away from her, every Skullcracker did likewise.

"Before the next game, let's see if we can pry a few words from Grand Witch Dorkey about her chances in the rest of the Locals ...!" Evilla said, and she jumped off her stand and headed off in the opposite direction.

They left the stadium and returned to the outdoor shower, where everyone but Grand Wizard Bastile Wraithbone washed off the mud as best they could. Grand Wizard Bastile Wraithbone was almost as muddy as the rest of them but he waved his wand and quietly cast a cleaning spell upon himself. Martin also washed the zombie head, getting all the mud out of his matted hair, and he seemed to enjoy it.

"I've got two more games tonight of Marsh Paddle Rider, but I appreciate this," the zombie head said.

"Who's next?" Martin asked.

"The Greasy Golems face the Roaring Giants," the zombie head said. "That should be a horrible match ... those teams really hate each other. Then the Gorgedown X-Lorecists face the Knights of the Unliving Dread; that game may last past dawn."

"I wish I could stay to watch," Martin said, looking up at Grand Wizard Bastile Wraithbone.

"How will you explain to your parents why they can't wake you up tomorrow morning?" Grand Wizard Bastile Wraithbone said. "You know the rules; you have to allow for your life in the human world."

"I know," Martin said, and he handed the zombie head to Murder and picked up his mostly-clean sneakers.

Grand Wizard Bastile Wraithbone waved his wand and a tiny, warm whirlwind enveloped Martin. When it vanished Martin was clean and dry.

"Until tomorrow night ...," Grand Wizard Bastile Wraithbone said, and he raised his staff again.

Chapter 9
Smashday / Tuesday

Enemies are revealed ...

"Take your new school-things inside and get them ready," Martin's mother shouted as all four boys got out of the car. "You're not going to like waking up early Monday morning."

Martin frowned and helped carry a bag. He and each of his brothers had gotten spiral notebooks, pencils, pens, and a new backpack to carry their books in. They'd wanted electronic reader-pads like Vicky used, but their mother insisted they were too expensive.

School ... Martin hated the idea of classes starting. He used to hate the start of school because his mother wouldn't let him play sports. Now he feared school would interfere with the only sport he cared about: the Grotesquerie Games.

Martin put his school supplies in his room, then returned to the living room and sat with his brothers playing Alien Slaughter.

"No exercising today?" Martin's mother asked.

"I need a rest," Martin said, still recovering from his first round of Marsh Paddle Rider.

"You should rest more," Martin's mom said. "When school starts, you'll need all the rest you can get."

"Indeed I will," Martin said gloomily.

Martin fell into Happy's arms and was instantly set onto his feet.

"Well ...?" Martin asked.

"The Greasy Golems won," Stabbing scowled.

"We expected them to, didn't we?" Martin asked.

"The Roaring Giants almost beat them," Stabbing said. "Their spell was killer ...!"

"They summoned a Thundercloud Giant," Grand Wizard Bastile Wraithbone said. "Very dangerous ... and it almost failed, which would've been disastrous."

"Not disastrous for us!" Stabbing laughed. "Half of the stands emptied when it appeared."

"Thundercloud Giants are savage and, if not appeased, can turn their lightning bolts on anyone ... even the crowd," Murder said.

"Evilla broadcast the whole first half from under her stand," Stabbing said.

"Grand Wizard Risk Master-One must've been working on that spell from the day the Roaring Giants were put out of last season's Regionals," Grand Wizard Bastile Wraithbone said.

"What's a Thundercloud Giant?" Martin asked.

"Imagine a massive thundercloud assuming the shape of a giant ogre," Grand Wizard Bastile Wraithbone said. "Twice as mean, vengeful, and not particular about who it targets, Thundercloud Giants hover over the pitch for an entire half and rain lightning bolts at anyone ... worse than penalties earn."

"It's like referees gone mad," Murder said. "Endless zaps."

"Powerful ones," Happy said. "Worse than we suffered."

"The Roaring Giants took the risk and won their reward," Rude said. "They cast their spell moments after the match started ... and it lasted until halftime. They double-scored five times before the Greasy Golems made their first point."

"How did the Greasy Golems not lose?" Martin asked.

"Maxivoom Snydho and the others fled their half of the pitch, where most of the bolts landed, so they couldn't score," Murder explained. "The first half was almost over when Maxivoom Snydho jumped off his mount onto Fame La Frankenstein, Ruddy's Big, and openly taunted the Thundercloud Giant. Of course, jumping onto another team's Big is a foul.

Three lightning bolts flew ... from both referees and the Thundercloud Giant. However, Maxivoom Snydho jumped off, into the muck, at the last second. Fame La Frankenstein was stuck; her scream deafened the stadium. Ruddy Max-Scowall fell off her into the muck, crisped, barely able to move.

"Fame La Frankenstein and Ruddy Max-Scowall were Grand Wizard Risk Master-One's best players on this pitch," Rude said. "Both had to be carried out of the muck or they'd have drowned."

"In those last moments, no one was safe from the Thundercloud Giant," Stabbing said. "Every player on both teams got badly zapped ... and several bolts landed in the stands. But halftime calmed quickly. The Thundercloud Giant dispersed, and in the second half, the Greasy Golems played with ruthless abandon. They pulled every trick you could imagine ... even abandoning Smalls of the Roaring Giants in their end zones, and then blocking their Bigs when they tried to rescue them."

"A petition is being written to make that a foul," Grand Wizard Bastile Wraithbone said. "I'll vote for it; that practice should be banned."

"I think the whole game should be banned," Martin said. "I never felt so dirty ...!"

"It's a popular game with the fans," Rude said. "Only the players hate it."

"And the coaches, referees ... and Evilla," Murder said.

"So we and the Greasy Golems remain undefeated, and the Flying Munchers and the Roaring Giants have one loss each," Martin said. "Who else is there ...?

"The Gorgedown X-Lorecists defeated the Knights of the Unliving Dread," Stabbing said.

"The Knights of the Unliving Dread are a

formidable team, but the Gorgedown X-Lorecists beat them soundly," Murder said. "They're now our bigger threat."

"We need to beat both of them ... and neither used a spell in their first game," Rude said. "Doubtless they're saving their magic for the Greasy Golems ... or us."

"Us," Happy said. "We face the Knights of the Unliving Dread next Rompday. The Greasy Golems face the Flying Munchers. The Roaring Giants and the Gorgedown X-Lorecists face each other."

"Both the Flying Munchers and the Knights of the Unliving Dread have one loss," Martin asked. "After Rompday both may be out ... right?"

"No, that's how the Finals work," Rude shook his head. "In the Locals, each team plays every opponent, and those with the best scores move on to the Regionals."

"So ... we've played one game ... and have four more?" Martin asked.

"Exactly," Rude said. "We have one slight advantage for ties. If we win the most games, we move on to the Regionals. If another team wins more games than we do, then we're out. However, if we tie, then the team with the best record moves on, and the other gains a chance at a wildcard. As we are last season's champion, we beat the Greasy Golems even if we tie."

"How many wildcard spots are there?" Martin asked.

"Three to five, usually," Rude explained. "The

Grand Council of Wizards decides how many wildcard spots to assess each season, and the teams with the best records get them."

"Enough talk," Grand Wizard Bastile Wraithbone said. "It's time we show Martin what we'll be facing next."

Together they marched out to view the tall, new pitch.

"Martin, welcome to Butterfly Noose Swinger," Grand Wizard Bastile Wraithbone said.

"Butterfly Noose Swinger ...?" Martin asked, looking up.

The stands on both sides of the stadium were raised, although not as high as with Net-Door Maze. Grand Wizard Bastile Wraithbone led them up the stairs onto the stands, from where Martin could get a better view. On the highest level was a raised metal framework of many horizontal squares. From the ceiling framework hung a hundred long, green, small-leafed ropes, looking like vines, each ending in a noose. The countless rope-nooses hung a foot over the tops of thin brick walls, eight feet tall, which enclosed tiny square rooms with no doors.

"Don't be alarmed; those nooses never tighten," Murder said. "They're there to help you."

"Help me ... what ...?" Martin asked.

"Swing," Stabbing said. "Smalls swing on the vines and drop the zombie head in those big bowls on each end." Stabbing pointed out both raised golden bowls, each five feet in diameter.

"Can we walk on the wall-tops?" Martin asked.

"Yes, while they're there," Stabbing said.

"No doors divide those brick walls," Rude pointed out. "Bigs knock them down ... sometimes while Smalls are standing atop them. Both teams knock down the walls near their golden bowl to make it more difficult for the other team to score. Very quickly the only way to score is to swing."

"You can't swing directly into another Small," Murder said. "That's a foul. But you can grab the vine an opponent is swinging on and try to jerk it away, and make them fall."

"You don't want to fall," Rude said. "Smalls have gotten stomped by Bigs ... or had broken walls topple upon them."

"If you fall, one of our Bigs will toss you back up, or there's an unbreakable stair in each corner which ascends to the vines," Murder said. "Get up quickly; the floor-level is dangerous for Smalls."

"So ... that's it?" Martin asked.

"Oh, no," Stabbing smiled, and he pointed to a series of thick, large red pads encircling the pitch. "You have to avoid the nets."

"Nets ...?" Martin asked.

"Giant butterfly nets," Rude grinned. "Bigs carry butterfly nets, and if they catch a Small, then they dump them out onto those thick red pads on the sides."

"Bigs also fight with the nets, to keep the other Bigs

from netting their Smalls," Murder said. "However, no Big can catch two Smalls in a net, so when they get one, they have to leave play to dump their Small off-pitch."

"That delays the Bigs," Rude said. "Also, when left alone, the zombie head floats at noose-level, and when you score, it falls off-pitch. Then it reappears somewhere in the middle."

"That's enough rules for now," Grand Wizard Bastile Wraithbone said. "He won't understand the nuances until he's tried it. Get Martin swinging."

They descended the stone steps back to the ground, then the Smalls ascended the circular iron stairs in the closest corner. The brick walls were only three inches wide, yet looked hard and sturdy. The hanging green ropes were stout and strong, the leaves too small to bother them. Veils set one foot in a noose and swung on it, caught another vine, and swung away.

"It's like Tarzan," Martin said.

"What's Tarzan ...?" Rude asked.

"A series of great books ... and many movies," Martin said, and he grabbed a vine and swung as Veils had.

Swinging was fun. The framing above them consisted of five feet wide squares. A vine hung from every crossing, so it was hard to swing without hitting another vine, and there was always one close enough if you wanted to switch. The thin walls were easy to land upon if your grip was failing. Martin swung from vine to vine for about half an hour before Stabbing swung past, reached out, and touched him.

"Now, Martin, try and tag me!" Stabbing laughed.

"Easy ...!" Martin laughed.

However, keeping up with Stabbing wasn't easy. Randomly swinging was fun, but trying to keep up with somebody else was nearly impossible. Soon all the vines were swinging, and you had to catch them while they were moving. Also, when the person ahead of you grabbed a vine, it often arced them in a different direction. Martin had to frequently stop on a wall, or swing to his vine's fullest extension, and then swing back, to chase his quarry.

"This is impossible!" Martin said.

"Now you're getting it!" Rude shouted, swinging close. "Let's switch. You try to escape, and Stabbing and I'll chase you."

Martin took the lead, but he didn't get far before Rude swept past close to his right, touched him, and then Stabbing almost swung into him. He kept grabbing different vines to suddenly alter his direction, yet he couldn't escape for long.

Suddenly he swung past Veils, who was standing on a wall, just holding a vine. She reached out and grabbed the vine he was holding, and jerked it from his hands. Martin fell, crashed into a brick wall-top, then toppled down onto the dirt.

"What are you doing?" Rude shouted angrily at Veils. *"We're teaching him to swing first!"*

"That's what any opposing player would do!" Veils

shouted back.

"He's not ready for that!" Stabbing sneered. "You could've seriously hurt ...!"

"Is he a player ... or not?" Veils demanded.

Martin looked up at Veils, and to his surprise, she looked down upon him with a glare of absolute loathing.

What had he done to infuriate Veils?

Chapter 10
Smiteday / Wednesday

Unfair games ...

"What's wrong?" Vicky asked from the door to his bedroom.

Martin startled from his reverie, sitting alone on his bed.

"Nothing," Martin said.

"You're not exercising or playing video games," Vicky said. "Something's on your mind. Did Happy not like my kiss?"

"I gave it to Murder," Martin said. "She passed it on ... and Happy didn't look unhappy."

"I'll have to speak to Murder next time I visit," Vicky said.

"Don't blame her," Martin said. "I asked Murder ... I wasn't going to kiss Happy!"

"Murder and I are going to collude, not argue," Vicky said. "No man deserves kisses from both of us ... not even a centaur. Now, what's up ...?"

"Veils," Martin said. "She's angry at me."

"Why ...?" Vicky asked.

"I don't know," Martin said.

"Did you ask her?" Vicky asked.

"No," Martin answered. "She didn't look like ... she wanted to talk."

"Whatever your first mistake was, that was your second," Vicky said. "Without communication, disagreements never get better."

Martin fell into Snitch's hands.

"Hi, Snitch!" Martin said.

He glanced around; they were alone. Usually someone was with Snitch to make sure he held his arms out at the right time ... and didn't eat whoever he caught. Yet Snitch seemed unsurprised; he was getting accustomed to Martin falling out of the ceiling.

Without even prompting, Snitch set Martin down.

"Thanks, Snitch!" Martin said. "How're you doing?"

Snitch looked puzzled.

"Is Snitch happy?" Martin asked.

Snitch shook his head and pointed at the door out of the locker room.

"Happy there," Snitch grunted.

Martin winced, realizing his mistake.

"Yes, Happy is practicing," Martin said. "Does Snitch feel good?"

Snitch smiled.

"Snitch break walls!" Snitch beamed. "No mud!"

"Breaking walls must be fun!" Martin said, although

he doubted if he'd ever be strong enough to shatter even thin brick walls. "I don't like mud, either."

"Go break!" Snitch urged.

"Yes, let's go break!" Martin said.

"Don't forget me," Murder's voice came from the girl's room, and she wheeled her chair out.

Snitch picked up Murder's wheelchair and carried her up the steps. Martin held the door for them.

"Were you hiding?" Martin asked Murder.

"Snitch has gotten used to catching you," Murder said. "I told him you were coming. I was watching, seeing if he could do it alone. I was glad to see him catch you."

"What if he hadn't caught me?" Martin asked.

"I was pretty sure he would," Murder said. "He likes you. Besides, I can almost walk now. If he failed ... well, you could borrow my wheelchair."

"Ha-ha," Martin pretended to laugh.

Snitch grinned; he liked laughter.

"Where's Veils?" Martin asked.

"Practicing, I suppose," Murder said. "She's been in a foul mood. She wouldn't even talk to me yesterday. Did you say something to her ...?"

"Not that I know of, but I intend to find out," Martin said.

Murder smiled as Snitch carried her around the corner where they could see Grand Wizard Bastile Wraithbone shouting instruction to the team from Evilla's raised platform.

Veils, Rude, and Stabbing were swinging on vines. Below them, half of the brick walls lay in piles of rubble, which Happy and Crusto were walking atop, facing each other with large butterfly nets. The Bigs wielded the poles of their nets like quarterstaffs, banging them together, long translucent webbing trailing one end as they fought.

Suddenly a solid wall behind them burst apart, its bricks tumbling down. Brain flew out of the rubble, wielding his own giant butterfly net, and Happy and Crusto broke off their fight to face him.

"Smash ...!" Snitch shouted joyfully, and he started to run toward the pitch.

"No, Snitch!" Murder cried. "Wait! Put me down!"

Snitch finally remembered he was carrying Murder, and set her down near Grand Wizard Bastile Wraithbone. Grand Wizard Bastile Wraithbone lifted up a huge butterfly net, but Snitch ignored it, charged forward, and smashed through a brick wall. Grand Wizard Bastile Wraithbone and Murder glanced at each other and shook their heads.

"Hello, Grand Wizard Bastile Wraithbone," Martin said.

"Good evening, Martin," Grand Wizard Bastile Wraithbone said. "Are you getting enough sleep?"

"Trying to," Martin said. "School starts next week."

"Excellent!" Grand Wizard Bastile Wraithbone said. "Nothing as important as learning! Now, get out there and get started."

Martin walked past him and Murder, out onto the pitch.

"Crusto, give me a lift?" Martin asked.

Overhearing, Happy attacked Brain fiercely, drawing his attention toward him. Crusto held out his butterfly net. Martin dipped both of his elbows into it, its strong wire circle pressed against his chest, and Crusto lifted him with ease. High up, Martin reached out with one arm, grabbed a swinging vine, stuck his foot in its noose, and released the net. He swung lightly, but by kicking his heels out and rocking his weight, he swung far enough to reach a second vine, which he caught and held until he could get his other foot in its noose. Then he swung to the top of one of the few remaining brick walls.

"Martin ...!" Rude cried as he swung past. "Help me catch Stabbing ...!"

Smiling, Martin joined in the chase. Both Rude and he cornered Stabbing, but the limber ratling swung out of their vise. Stabbing had tiny claws instead of fingernails and could cling to a vine quicker and better than Rude or Martin.

Martin landed atop a brick wall and then he spied Snitch charging at it. He grabbed the closest vine, and was barely off the wall before Snitch, laughing uproariously, burst through it. Bricks from the wall flew in every direction. Only Happy's voice rose above the loud crash.

"Snitch, no!" Happy shouted. "You don't need to

break every wall!"

Suddenly Rude swung close and grabbed the vine Martin was on. Their momentum jerked both to a sudden stop, yet Martin held tight, and then Rude let go.

"Much better!" Rude said. "You're getting into the swing of it! Now do that to me!"

Martin chased Rude for five minutes, helped by Stabbing, who cut off Rude's every attempt to escape. Finally Martin managed to grab the vine Rude was on. Both jerked, rocked back and forth, and then hung suspended between both vines.

"Okay, time to learn something new," Rude said. "Veils, let's show him!"

Martin spied Veils swinging nearby; so far he'd only seen her from a distance.

"Use Stabbing!" Veils snapped.

"I want you," Rude said.

With a set frown, Veils swung to a rope swinging at a different angle, switched to it, and swung back toward them. His foot in a noose, Rude caught his rope between his neck against his shoulder, leaving both hands free.

Veils swung to a vine hanging right beside them, but as she reached for it, Rude grabbed the vine and pulled it back. Veils started to fall, but with his other hand, Rude reached out to her, and she caught his arm instead. If he hadn't caught her, she'd have fallen onto a pile of broken bricks.

Instantly Rude held the vine to Veils and let her

grab it.

"That's the real danger we face," Rude said to Martin. "Smalls can't fight, run into each other on purpose, punch or kick an opponent, but we can pull a vine away as another Small is reaching for it. Never let go of any vine until you have another firmly grasped!"

"Stabbing jumps from vine to vine," Martin argued.

"Stabbing excels at Butterfly Noose Swinger," Rude said. "You can do that, too, but be especially careful. The longer the half progresses, the more walls will be knocked down, and you don't want to land on broken bricks."

"The walls reform at halftime ...?" Martin asked.

"Well, yes ...," Rude said. "Sorry ... we should've told you."

"Not knowing what's about to happen is my biggest weakness," Martin said.

"We should take a break," Rude said. "I can go over the whole game from start to finish."

Martin glanced at Veils, who was swinging away.

"Yes, but I need to talk to Veils first," Martin whispered.

"Good luck," Rude said. "She hasn't spoken to anyone since Marsh Paddle Rider."

Martin swung after Veils, watching her progress by the movements of vines. When he caught up, he called to her, but she changed vines and swung away. Determined, Martin chased her for ten minutes before he caught the vine she was on.

"Let go!" Veils snapped angrily.

"What's wrong?" Martin asked.

Veils tried to kick him, but Martin shook hard on her vine, upsetting them both.

"Let me go ...!" Veils shouted. *"I'll ...!"*

"Not until you talk to me ...!" Martin shouted.

Hanging between two vines, pressed close, Martin was taken aback by the fury of her glare.

"Why don't you talk to Murder ...?" Veils snarled. *"Why don't you kiss her again ...?"*

Expertly Veils dropped off her vine and landed below with a roll, onto one of the few spaces clear of fallen bricks. Then she stormed away between broken walls.

Martin hung there, thinking through the sequence of actions Veils must've seen. Then Martin let go of Veil's vine and swung away.

"Happy ...!" Martin cried. *"Happy, I need you!"*

Martin drug Happy off to the side for a brief conversation, then they both walked back to rest beside Rude.

In detail, Rude went over every aspect of Butterfly Noose Swinger, which Martin listened to intently. Then Rude confessed that his arms were sore and he was done swinging, and Martin and Happy walked back onto the pitch together.

Until they were broken, each brick wall enclosed a room ten feet square, with one green rope hung above each corner, one center on each wall, and one hanging over the middle. Martin found a standing wall to hide behind, and Happy nodded to him and went hunting.

Minutes later, Happy came trotting back, holding out his large butterfly net. Trapped in his net hung Veils.

"Let me out ...!" Veils screamed. *"Let me out ... or I'll ...!"*

Martin stepped out from behind the brick wall. When Veils saw him, she fell silent, then struggled even harder. She tried to jump out of Happy's net, but he shook it and fouled her attempts.

"Happy ...!" Veils screamed angrily.

Happy held out his net so Veils hung right in front of Martin.

"I didn't kiss Murder," Martin said calmly.

"Liar ...!" Veils screamed. *"I saw you ...!"*

"That kiss was from my sister Vicky," Martin said. "She asked me to give it to Happy, which I did ... through Murder."

Veils glared, and then she twisted around to look at Happy.

"It was a good kiss ...!" Happy grinned.

Veils jerked back to face Martin, who stared at her defiantly. The webbing between them was white, fine as spun silk, with an open weave like a tight fishing net, entrapping, yet flexible.

Suddenly Veils threw herself against the side closest to Martin and punched hard. Despite the net, her fist landed square on his nose and struck hard.

Bleeding, Martin flew back and fell down.

"That's enough talking," Happy declared, and he swung Veils away from Martin and began to trot in the opposite direction. Veils, still trapped in his net, bounced and struggled uselessly.

"Let me out right now ...!" Veils shouted.

Chapter 11
Stompday / Thursday

Pains of swinging ...

"How did you get a bloody nose?" Martin's mother asked.

"Tripped ... into a door," Martin lied.

Her eyes narrowed as she looked at him.

"Not while you were exercising ...?" she asked.

"Believe me, I wasn't exercising," Martin said.

Martin dabbed at his nose with a bloody paper towel, wishing the red flow would stop for good. It hurt, but it'd be worth it if Veils wasn't angry at him anymore.

"You need haircuts before school starts," Martin's mother announced to Martin and his brothers. "Your father will be taking you on Saturday morning; you can't go to school on your first day looking ratty."

Martin smiled, wondering what Stabbing would think of her description.

After bowls of cereal, their parents left for work. Martin and his brothers played tanks, driving massive treaded vehicles with turrets around hills and through cities, constantly shooting at each other. Martin knew he should be exercising, but his hands and arms were sore from hanging on vines.

Much later, Vicky woke up and came stumbling out of her room looking haggard.

"Rough night ...?" Martin asked her.

Vicky paused to stare at him.

"It was ... Murder," Vicky said. "I feel like someone's been Stabbing me ... and I could've used some Brain."

Martin nodded, yet kept playing with his brothers, who looked confused by Vicky's answer.

She pointed at the bloody paper towel in his lap.

"Rough night ...?" Vicky asked him.

"It was like ... being smothered by Veils," Martin answered.

Laughing, Vicky walked into the kitchen.

Crusto caught Martin, his webbed hands wide to avoid poking Martin with his claws, and then he set him onto his feet before Murder.

"Veils and I had a long talk," Murder said to Martin.

"Is everything ...?" Martin asked.

"We ... colluded," Murder smiled.

Martin didn't trust the way she said 'colluded', but unlike Veils, who was two months younger than he was, Murder was a dryad, much older than she looked, and as tough as a tree-trunk. What Murder chose not to tell him he'd never learn.

Crusto carried Murder in her wheelchair, and gently set her beside Grand Wizard Bastile Wraithbone at the edge of the pitch.

"Last night of practice," Grand Wizard Bastile Wraithbone said to Martin. "Do you feel ready?"

"The Knights of the Unliving Dread won't know what hit them," Martin said.

"Wonderful!" Grand Wizard Bastile Wraithbone said. "You'll be practicing the full game today. Be careful ... and don't fall!"

Martin walked out onto the pitch, then had to jump aside as Snitch backed through a wall, net-pole fighting with Brain.

With ease Crusto snagged the back of Martin's collar and lifted him up to the top of a wall. Most of the walls remained unbroken save for one wide section near the far side of the pitch.

Veils flew past, releasing one vine only to jump through midair to the next. A second later, Stabbing came chasing after her, only a swing behind. Rude came right behind, and Martin swung to follow them.

However, as Martin reached for a vine, a circle of white webbing flashed before his eyes. It swooped to fill his vision and caught him, its metal circle bumping into his shoulder. Before Martin realized what had happened, he was upside-down, trapped in Crusto's net.

Helpless, Martin hung in the silky weave, struggling yet trapped.

Crusto carried him over to a thick red pad and

dumped him onto it. The red pad wasn't as soft as it looked, yet Martin quickly bounced to his feet.

"Be careful on those pads," Murder said to him. "Bigs dump Smalls fast so they can get back into the game. Not all Smalls are dumped on their feet."

"Take the stairs," Grand Wizard Bastile Wraithbone told Martin. "Never run blindly onto the lower pitch; Bigs are usually looking up. Smalls get stepped on."

Martin ran to the corner and up the steep, circular stairs. No Bigs were around; rather than swing, Martin ran along the tops of the brick walls. Veils almost hit him as she swung past.

"Martin, that's dangerous!" Veils shouted at him.

"Smalls get fouled if they purposefully swing into each other," Martin said.

"Accidents happen!" Veils shouted, swinging away. "Always be reaching for a vine!"

Martin jumped at a vine, caught his foot in its noose, and swung after Veils.

He saw Rude kick at Happy's net as it rose toward him, and to Martin's surprise, Rude momentarily balanced on the edge of Happy's net just long enough to grab another vine. Nets were flashing up from the remaining walls like fish jumping out of a lake ... more like wide-mouthed sharks jumping to swallow live bait. The Bigs seemed to be purposefully leaving some walls intact so they could hide behind them, then net a Small as they swung over.

Brain caught Martin next, and dumped him on his head on a red pad. Happy dumped Stabbing almost on top of him. Both rolled onto their feet and jumped off the pad.

"Watch this," Stabbing said.

Stabbing ran to the edge of the pitch, looked about, and then shouted.

"Snitch, up ...!"

Darting between Happy and Brain, Stabbing ran to Snitch, who paused just long enough to lower his net. Stabbing ran to grab it, and Snitch flung him up and to the side. Stabbing held out his hands, slapping several vines as he flew past, before he seized one, and his momentum instantly swung him on that vine.

Martin wanted to try it, but he didn't want to risk Snitch's troll-strength on his first attempt.

"Brain, up ...!" Martin shouted.

Martin ran onto the pitch at Brain, grabbed his net, and the next thing he knew, he was sailing through the air. He had his choice of vines, yet he chose the first, just to be safe. His initial swing was a near-miss of Rude, who twisted to avoid a collision.

"Careful there ...!" Rude called.

"Sorry ...!" Martin shouted.

They practiced for two hours until everyone was sore, and then Grand Wizard Bastile Wraithbone called for a break. The Smalls gathered and sat on the edge of a red pad. The Bigs stood around them, all were too winded for talk. Murder rolled her wheelchair closer with five waterbags in her lap, and she handed three to the Bigs and two to the Smalls.

"The Knights of the Unliving Dread aren't slouches," Murder said. "Grand Wizard Gorge Roamer is sure to use a spell against us, and Judge O'Death and D'Wain Bones are vicious."

"Who are they?" Martin asked.

"Judge O'Death is a banshee, about Veil's size, and as fast as Stabbing ... with longer claws," Murder said. "She likes to rip vines right out of opponent's hands. D'Wain Bones is a skeleton; no flesh, so he's incredibly light, can flit from vine to vine, and falls don't hurt him. He's their best at scoring, and he's been known to stuff the zombie head inside his rib cage so he can use both hands."

"Don't forget Swill Crocodile," Crusto hissed with a scowl.

"Swill Crocodile is a lizardwoman," Murder told Martin. "She and Crusto have an ongoing rivalry, and she's just as fast and strong. If she gets you in her net, be careful; Swill Crocodile dumps Smalls hard."

"Snarl HardBan is their only troll," Happy said. "He's almost as strong as Snitch and his temper is even worse."

"The hardest task is guessing what type of spell they'll use," Grand Wizard Bastile Wraithbone said. "Some spells are designed to improve scoring, others to delay opponents, and some to take out key players."

"The problem is finding a spell that gives only your

side an advantage," Rude said. "In Marsh Paddle Rider, if the whole pitch had frozen, then both sides would've been stuck and no one could score."

"They have just as many extra Bigs and Smalls as we do, so it's unlikely they'll choose a damage-spell," Crusto said.

"We're similar teams," Happy said. "They have a minotaur, a cyclops, a satyr, and a gnome."

"Watch out for the gnome ... he bites," Stabbing said.

Martin expected everyone to laugh at Stabbing's joke, but no one did.

"He ... bites ...?" Martin asked.

"Everything he can," Stabbing assured him.

After their rest, Grand Wizard Bastile Wraithbone brought out the zombie head, who smiled when he saw Martin. They greeted each other warmly. However, the zombie head complicated everything. Swinging from vine to vine was easy and fun, but holding the zombie head occupied an arm, so you only had one free arm for swinging ... and while switching vines. The nooses that never closed became essential, as you had to support your weight on one foot so you could switch to another using only one hand.

Martin's first attempts succeeded, yet Happy and Crusto stayed underneath him, ready to catch him if he fell. Martin swung much slower holding the zombie head. Rude showed him a few tricks, like holding the vine in the crook of his neck and shoulder while he switched to another vine.

"You'll get used to it," Veils said.

"This's why scoring is hard," Stabbing said. "The Small carrying the zombie head is slowest, and other Smalls aim swings to block their path."

"Whenever possible, toss the zombie head to Stabbing," Rude said. "He's best at this game, and then swing beside him to block opposing players. But you need to practice scoring, so head for that bowl."

On each end of the pitch was a five foot in diameter raised golden bowl, which was easy to drop the zombie head into, but Martin hesitated.

"What's wrong?" Veils asked. "Throw it in!"

Martin swung to the top of a nearby wall, then turned the zombie head to face him.

"Does it hurt?" Martin asked the zombie head.

"Falling into that metal bowl ...?" the zombie head asked. "Of course it hurts! Wouldn't it hurt you?"

Martin stared at the wide golden bowl.

"Rude, could we put a pad in there ... or at least a few blankets?" Martin asked.

"I don't see why not ...," Rude said. "You keep practicing. I'll ask Bastile ..."

Stabbing grabbed the zombie head and headed off, Veils on one side of him, Martin on the other. Stabbing was almost as fast with the zombie head as without it, and he struggled to keep up. Yet Stabbing shouted directions at Martin and Veils, and they matched him, pretending they were shielding him from enemy players.

Then Stabbing had Veils pretend to be an enemy, and he circled the pitch twice with Martin trying to keep Veils from getting close enough to grab Stabbing's vine or snatch the zombie head from his grasp.

When Rude returned, Martin was given the zombie head and told to score. Stabbing alone blocked his path, yet Martin circled him and let him swing past, then swung ahead of him. When Martin reached the wide golden bowl, he spied its bottom layered in old blankets. Both he and the zombie head smiled, and Martin tossed the head in with ease.

"Much better!" shouted the zombie head as they swung away.

A moment later, a bright flash came from mid-pitch, and the zombie head reappeared, hovering beside a vine.

"Get him, Martin, and score!" Rude shouted.

Martin swung past and caught the floating zombie head, then clung to the vine he was on until it reached its zenith and began to swing back.

While the others flew at him, Martin swung away on another vine, headed back toward the padded bowl. They easily caught up with him, as he was slower when carrying the zombie head. Stabbing protected him as Veils and Rude tried to block him. Martin tossed the zombie head into the bowl, and it laughed as it dropped onto soft blankets.

They practiced passing the zombie head back and forth, which was difficult. Each vine was swinging, and trying to pass the zombie head to a teammate who was moving, often at a different speed or in a different direction, seemed nearly impossible. Also, vines no one was using hung or swung in the path of your throw, so anything but short tosses were likely to be deflected.

Martin once failed a catch; the zombie head plummeted toward a pile of broken bricks. Martin cried out, but the zombie head vanished before it hit, and with a flash, it reappeared, floating near mid-pitch.

"The zombie head can't hit the ground," Rude explained. "The same thing happens if the zombie head is in your hands when you get caught in a net; it vanishes almost instantly."

"The zombie head always stays in play," Stabbing added, and he threw the zombie head off the pitch at Grand Wizard Bastile Wraithbone. It neared his purple wizard's hat ... then vanished, and reappeared in the center.

Martin nodded. Inside he was smiling; never had he felt so prepared for a match.

Chapter 12
Rompday / Friday

Butterfly Noose Swinger ...

Instead of exercising or playing video games, Martin spent the day reading one of Vicky's books. He wanted to be fully rested for the game... and he was curious about the worlds Vicky visited.

Zantheriak was much more dangerous than Heterodox. Martin read about half of her book, exploring star systems where space elves suspected evil Slurks were building a hidden base. They found it when a single blast from a proto-plasma cannon took out half of their shields. Instantly they fled, chased by three Slurk Scavenger ships, until they could restore their shields, and then they turned, circling a small moon, and began a deadly ship-to-ship battle. Two of the Slurk Scavenger ships were destroyed, and the last flew back toward their new base.

Damaged, the space elves flew into an asteroid field to hide their change of direction, then headed back to their home world, Zantheriak, to alert their fleet.

Their captain was distressed. A friend of the space elves, a mysterious woman who could appear and disappear at will, had invented the proto-plasma cannon and given it only to the elves. The Slurks had never had one before, and the elf captain wondered how they'd gotten their hands on one .... how many cannons they had ... and how their fleet could attack a hidden base defended by multiple proto-plasma cannons.

Although engrossed in the story, Martin wondered if the mysterious woman, who could appear and disappear at will ... *was his sister, Vicky.*

Snitch caught Martin as he fell into the locker room. The whole team was there.

"Ready to play ...?" Grand Wizard Bastile Wraithbone asked him.

"There'll be no victory to Knights!" Martin smiled.

Smiles broke out on most faces. Brain looked confused, but Crusto patted his arm.

"No victory for the Knights of the Unliving Dread," Crusto explained to Brain.

"Smash walls ...!" Snitch roared.

"Violet and black!" Grand Wizard Bastile Wraithbone told Snitch. "Remember, violet and black!"

Happy held up a huge violet and black jersey and showed it to Snitch. Seeing it, Snitch growled menacingly.

"That's right, Snitch!" Grand Wizard Bastile Wraithbone said. "Snitch has eaten and we're ready.

Let's go."

They headed out onto the starlit pitch where the crowd was already cheering. Monsters of all kinds filled the stands on both sides, hooting and howling, many in Shantdareya purple while a few wore violet and black. Before them, on her stand, stood Evilla wearing a deep burgundy dress with a tight miniskirt. Her thick hair was bright magenta.

"Greetings and beatings!" Evilla shouted into her microphone. "Yes, it's me, Evilla, your gal gorgeous, bringing you a night of unrivaled excitement ... and a match between two great teams! And here comes the home team, last season's victors, who last week grounded the Flying Munchers, Grand Wizard Bastile Wraithbone and the Shantdareya Skullcrackers!"

The crowd cheered and several rose to their feet. Martin was getting used to the crowds now, and this time he noticed many waved excitedly at them, and a few of his teammates waved back. One squid-like creature, wearing an Evilla t-shirt, waved four tentacles at Martin and cheered him by name. Martin blushed and waved back, used to getting attention for being the only human in their games.

"Welcome, Brain Stroker, the Opulent Ogre, and that troll who rolls over every opponent, Allfed Snitchlock! Here's Happy Lostcraft, that Galloping Juggernaut, and Rude Stealing, finally back from injured reserve in the last game! The Dazzling Damsel, pretty Murder Shelling, is still in her wheelchair, but rumor has it she's healing well. And here's Stabbing Kingz, the Gatling Ratling, and Crusto Fernwalker, who's renewing a true rivalry tonight when he faces his Fellow from Below, the lovely Swill Crocodile, who'd like nothing better than to take a bite out of Crusto. And, here's sweet little Veilscreech Hobbleswoon ...!"

"It's Veils ...!" Veils shouted angrily.

"As you know, Veilscreech Hobbleswoon proved herself a valuable Small last week, in her first game," Evilla said, looking right at Veils and waving her hand. "I'm sure Veilscreech Hobbleswoon is a name none of us will soon forget!"

Veils hissed in disgust.

Martin grinned, certain Evilla had heard Veils correct her.

"Lastly, of course, comes that Entrant from Earth, the Highlight of Humanity, the Mulberry Mayhem, Martin the Magnificent!"

Martin shook his head, wondering how Evilla made up all these silly names.

"And here comes Grand Wizard Gorge Roamer and the Knights of the Unliving Dread!" Evilla cried, waving to the other side of the stands. "Leading the pack is the Saucy Skeleton D'Wain Bones, who's dead-set to win every match! Beside him is that Beautiful Banshee, the Screaming Dream of countless fans, the fabulous Judge O'Death! Behind them is that Slammin' Satyr, Merry Leastfan, whose brutal butts take every advantage! Beside her is everyone's favorite Thumpin' Troll, Snarl

HardBan; I pity any Small he nets! Look! Riding on Snarl's shoulder is that Gnawing Gnome, Teeth Slain, known in every game as Mighty Bitey! Sly Cyclops, Junkish Ridgelay, comes next, and beside her is that Minotaur of Mastery, Pranked Oak, whose horns have punctured the reputations of many opponents. And, lastly, here she comes, the Sweetness of the Sea, that Darling of the Deep, the lovely Swill Crocodile, to face her nemesis, Crusto Fernwalker! This famous Reptilian Rivalry will be played out tonight, before our eyes, lizardman against lizardwoman, both deadly, both sexy, and we can only wonder who'll come out on top!"

Crusto sighed heavily, shaking his head.

The Knights of the Unliving Dread were hidden from view by the brick walls, so Martin couldn't see them, but the crowd on the far stands rose and cheered.

"As you know, Grand Wizard Join A. Fussygo was the first coach of the Knights of the Unliving Dread, but he was lost after his foolish challenge to Grand Wizard Gorge Roamer in a Deadly Duel of Dominance," Evilla said over her loudspeakers. "Grand Wizard Join A. Fussygo, wherever you are, we hope you're safe and come back soon! Now hold on to your frosty Manticore Mints and Toasted Dragon-Toes! I'm about to get heated up ... and so is our match, the exciting second round of the Locals of the three hundred and fifteenth season of the Grotesquerie Games!"

Martin tried to ignore the cheers of the crowd. He had to focus on the game. As Rude had explained,

Snitch, Brain, and Crusto stepped forward, and he, Veils, and Stabbing stepped back.

"Our referees are moving into place!" Evilla said. "I see wands and staffs raised, two ... three ... four! That's it! Here's the horn! Let the mayhem begin!"

As the horn blew, Martin dashed ahead, Veils and Stabbing beside him. He aimed at Crusto, while Veils aimed at Brain, and Stabbing aimed at Snitch. Each Big was holding out a butterfly net. As they reached them, all three nets rose; Smalls flew up into the upper pitch, swatted by vines. Martin grabbed one, swung to another, got his foot in place, and swung toward the right. As planned, Veils grabbed a vine, long after Martin had begun his first swing, and she headed off to the left. Stabbing aimed himself at the zombie head, not grabbing a vine until the last second before his momentum failed.

A pale skeleton, only three feet tall, appeared on the far side, hurtling forward. Both reached the zombie head simultaneously, but Stabbing's claws snagged it and tossed it to Veils. She took off, and Martin hurried after her. He'd been heading toward the Knight's end, designated to delay them from scoring if they'd gotten the zombie head first.

"Stabbing gets to the head first and passes to Veilscreech Hobbleswoon!" Evilla cried, and the monsters in both stands roared in delight, although they were hard to hear over the deafening crashes of brick walls being broken apart by Bigs beneath the vines.

"Veilscreech is headed toward the goal, but Judge

O'Death is closing fast!" Evilla shouted. "Judge O'Death cuts her off, but here comes Stabbing and D'Wain Bones!"

Suddenly Martin saw a vine move near him, and a tiny figure came swinging into view. It was short, the smallest Small Martin had ever seen, yet it had wiry muscles, big eyes, and an even bigger mouth filled with massive, chomping teeth. It's motley skin looked similar to Rude's goblin light-green, yet it had curly brown hairs spouting all over it, although not as thick as Stabbing's fur. It swung forward as if aimed at Martin.

Martin wondered what it was doing; Smalls couldn't fight or collide.

Was it intending to foul him ...?

Suddenly it flew off its vine, high through the air, almost hitting the framework holding up the vines. It grabbed onto the vine Martin was holding, a foot above Martin's hands. With alarming fervor, it sank its teeth into the vine Martin was swinging on, and only too late did Martin realize what it was doing. He reached for another vine ... and then the vine he was holding snapped ... bitten through.

Martin dropped, slammed into the top of a wall, and almost fell into a room.

"Mighty Bitey drops Martin the Magnificent!" Evilla shouted over the stadium. "Teeth Slain swings free! Is Martin trapped? Not yet, but maybe ...!"

Martin looked down; if a Small fell into a room without any broken walls then they'd be stuck there until one of his Bigs could rescue them. Straining, he clambered up on top of the thin brick wall, then grabbed a vine. Teeth Slain was swinging a circle around him, laughing.

"Veilscreech Hobbleswoon scores!" Evilla cried. "Judge O'Death looks furious ...!"

A flash illuminated nearby; the zombie head appeared. Teeth Slain swung for it, and Martin did too, but the toothy gnome was closer. Martin aimed toward their goal-bowl; as Teeth Slain grabbed the zombie head and swung to score, Martin was halfway between him and their end of the pitch.

"Teeth Slain has the head, but Martin is defending!" Evilla shouted. "Stabbing is hurrying across the pitch, but too far away! Teeth isn't waiting for Stabbing to catch up. Martin is swinging back and forth, ready for anything. Teeth is aiming straight at him, Martin moves to block ...!"

Twice Martin cut off Teeth Slain, making him veer in another direction. Then Stabbing appeared, and Teeth flung the zombie head over Martin's reach ...

"Teeth Slain shoots ... grazes Martin's vine ... he scores!" Evilla shouted.

Teeth Slain laughed uproariously and gnashed his huge teeth.

"Back ...!" Stabbing shouted, and Martin followed him as he hurried toward the center, leaving Teeth Slain behind.

Another flash illuminated the vines, and Martin saw

the zombie head appear about twenty feet away from where it had last appeared. Stabbing aimed at it, but D'Wain Bones was swinging to reach it, too. D'Wain Bones reached it first, but Stabbing cut him off. D'Wain's next swing slammed right into Stabbing, who was knocked aside, and only kept from falling by one hand.

"Foul ...!" Evilla cried.

Twin lightning bolts erupted from the wands of the referees, arcing across the pitch toward D'Wain Bones. The swinging skeleton screamed and thrashed in the yellow voltage, then fell into an unbroken room, taking the zombie head with him.

"D'Wain Bones is trapped!" Evilla shouted. "Somewhere in the middle; that'll clear out some of these walls! Nice move by Stabbing Kingz! And there's the zombie head ... appearing near Martin the Magnificent ...!"

With a flash, the zombie head appeared nearby. Martin veered right past it, snatching it in the crook of his arm. Continuous crashes from below sent bricks flying up to their level, but Martin ignored them and swung toward Stabbing.

Behind Martin came Teeth Slain, getting close, when suddenly another figure came swinging at him; the banshee Judge O'Death. She resembled Damhell Hairy; thin and ghoulish, but without the long drape of blonde hair Damhell had. Yet she looked just as bloodcurdling, like a specter from a grave restored to living flesh. Both she and Teeth were swinging towards Martin faster than he could manage while carrying the zombie head.

"Stabbing ...!" Martin cried.

"Throw ...!" Stabbing shouted.

Martin flung the zombie head, getting rid of it only a second before Judge O'Death swung to block him, swiping a clawed hand at the zombie head as it flew between vines trailing black greasy hair. Stabbing had grabbed a vine at one extreme of its swing, swung wide, caught the head in mid-swing, and held on as the vine arced back and flung him towards the Shantdareya golden bowl. Judge O'Death swung to chase him, but Stabbing tossed the zombie head onward to Veils, who caught it and carried it away.

As D'Wain Bones was still trapped, the Skullcracker Smalls had a numeric advantage, so as they blocked, no one could catch up with Veils. Those behind swung toward center, watching to see where the zombie head would reappear after Veils scored. Stabbing and Martin joined them, ready for anything.

"Veilscreech Hobbleswoon scores again!" Evilla cried. "And look! Big Junkish Ridgelay has reached D'Wain Bones, who's been trapped since the first goal! How she found him with only one eye is anyone's guess. The cyclops is lifting D'Wain on her net ... and both teams again have three Smalls in play!"

The crowd cheered.

"Here comes Allfed Snitchlock, smashing walls with

abandon!" Evilla cried. "Brain and Crusto reached the area before the Knight's goal-bowl and have cleared out the walls near it, and Snarl HardBan and Swill Crocodile have done the same on their side. There are no supports remaining near any goal-bowl, but the Bigs have yet to meet."

Martin looked down and saw the she-cyclops looking up at him, her net ready and a snarl on her face. Martin was glad he was out of her reach. Yet the crashes of walls as Snitch approached sent bricks flying and deafened everyone.

"Junkish Ridgelay is moving back!" Evilla shouted, and several Bigs looked up at her. "Sorry about that, folks, but I can't announce without the players hearing me as well. Apparently Junkish Ridgelay doesn't want to match one-on-one against Allfed Snitchlock, and who can blame her? Yet she's taking a different route, opening up the pitch, clearing out space for the Bigs to meet!"

With a flash, the zombie head appeared midway between Judge O'Death and D'Wain Bones. Instantly the skeleton swung away from it, toward their golden bowl, while Judge O'Death raced toward the head. Martin swung to get ahead of D'Wain, but Teeth Slain came flying overhead, aiming for Martin's vine, and Martin jumped to another before his was bitten in half.

Judge O'Death seized the zombie head and chased after D'Wain Bones, finally tossing it to him. He was ahead of Martin when he caught it, yet he swung noticeably slower holding the head. Watching everyone converge behind him, Martin managed to cut D'wain off. Yet D'Wain Bones dodged, then swung straight at him. Martin determined to block.

A metal loop trailing a white weave fell over D'Wain Bones.

"Crusto nets D'Wain Bones ... carrying the zombie head!" Evilla cried.

Teeth Slain hissed angrily, and everyone swung toward the center. Behind him, Martin saw Crusto run off. D'Wain Bones cursed, trapped in Crusto's net, and with a flash, the zombie head vanished out of D'Wain's hands.

Another flash popped the zombie head dead center, and Veils was closest. She swung toward it, and every Small oriented on her. Martin took a deep breath as he swung to block for her; Butterfly Noose Swinger reminded him of basketball, a fast, high-scoring game where endurance was tested as much as skill.

Veils seized the zombie head and swung back as Stabbing hurtled toward her. Judge O'Death was closest, and approaching fast, but rather than cut her off, Stabbing swung ahead of Veils, and she tossed the zombie head to him. Then she cut off Judge O'Death, who trailed only one swing behind. Stabbing had a clear path to their bowl and he was the fastest swinger on the pitch.

Ignoring Evilla's commentary, Martin glanced down to see the pitch. Snitch had broken through, clearing a line from one goal to the next, and wide gaps showed at each end. Brain was running beneath him, while Snitch was net-battling the other troll, Snarl HardBan, near their goal line. Crusto came running in from the back, having dumped D'Wain Bones on the red pads on their side of the pitch. Yet that meant Stabbing was trying to score in the open, with Junkish Ridgelay and Swill Crocodile both trying to net him.

"Stabbing is driven back!" Evilla cried. "He's still got the zombie head, but nets block his path. Judge O'Death is racing to catch him as Veilscreech Hobbleswoon hurries to help. Martin and Teeth are holding back, waiting for the zombie head to reappear. There's a lot of walls down ...! Stabbing shoots! No! Swill Crocodile catches the zombie head on its way to the bowl ... without standing in the foul zone! As you know, goal tending was outlawed only three seasons ago! All three Knights are ganging up against Allfed Snitchlock! They've driven him back through a wall! But here comes Brain Stroker! Swill Crocodile is struck from behind! The lizardwoman falls! Junkish Ridgelay attacks Brain Stroker, cyclops against ogre, while the trolls battle behind him! Swill Crocodile is rising to her feet, and here comes Crusto Fernwalker! The rival duel begins!"

The flash was right next to Martin; he seized the zombie head and swung away. Teeth Slain swung to cut him off, but Martin circled widely in the other direction.

D'Wain Bones was swinging straight toward him, yet

Stabbing was hurrying back. Returned to the game, D'Wain Bones would reach Martin first, Teeth Slain trailing right behind him, while Martin swung slower, carrying the zombie head.

Martin grabbed a new vine and changed course just as D'Wain Bones swung at him. Martin cut to the inside, then spied Judge O'Death and Veils both racing toward him. Suddenly his vine shook, and Martin looked up to see Teeth Slain gnawing at his only support almost near the top.

He tried to jump to another vine, but Teeth Slain was watching and jumped to the vine ahead of him. The vine shook as Teeth grabbed it ... and Martin's hand closed on nothing. He fell, slammed into the side of a brick wall, and dropped. A flash of light stole the zombie head from his hands a second before he crashed down onto the hard dirt floor. He struck feet-first and rolled, but he still hit hard ... and slammed into a wall before he stopped.

Aching, Martin lifted his head and looked around. He was surrounded by four tall, unbroken brick walls.

"Martin the Magnificent is trapped!" Evilla shouted.

Martin threw himself against a brick wall, hoping to break it, but with no success. He stopped to catch his breath. He was out of the game ... until he was rescued.

"Judge O'Death snatches the zombie head!" Evilla shouted. "Lucky girl, it appeared right in her path! She's headed to score, D'Wain Bones and Teeth Slain blocking for her, Stabbing Kingz and Veilscreech

Hobbleswoon outnumbered and far behind. Judge O'Death swings right to the last vine, no Bigs beneath her! She drops it in; Judge O'Death scores! The game is tied!"

Martin snarled, looking up at the swaying vines, wondering when someone would come looking for him.

"The Skullcrackers fall back, taking places, and none of the Knights Smalls' are near the center!" Evilla cried. "D'Wain Bones and Teeth Slain are headed to mid-field, but there's the flash! Veilscreech Hobbleswoon grabs the zombie head! She and Stabbing Kingz are off!"

Frustrated but helpless, Martin flexed his arms, trying to relax. The best he could do was sit tight and rest, prepare himself to rejoin the game when he could.

"Every Big is fighting, and few walls remain near them!" Evilla shouted. "What's this? The Knights' Smalls have fallen back, waiting for the zombie head to reappear, but Stabbing Kingz and Veilscreech Hobbleswoon have veered to one side! They're not scoring! Smart move! They need Martin the Magnificent back in play to win. They're yelling at Crusto, who fights back ... yes! Crusto Fernwalker has broken off with Swill Crocodile and started running. He's smashed through two walls! He's reached the path back to Martin, but Swill Crocodile is trying to net Stabbing Kingz and Veilscreech Hobbleswoon instead of chasing him. The odds favor her; all the walls around both scoring areas are gone, so Swill Crocodile only has to maneuver around the other Bigs. But Judge O'Death and D'Wain Bones are swinging toward them!"

Martin clenched his teeth, wishing he could see.

"What's this?" Evilla asked. "Stabbing Kingz has the zombie head ... and he's jumped down onto the head of Allfed Snitchlock, who's dueling Snarl HardBan! Stabbing Kingz is riding dueling trolls! Is he mad? And here comes Swill Crocodile, swinging her net!"

"No! Stabbing Kingz passes to Veilscreech Hobbleswoon, then jumps onto Snarl HardBan! Swill Crocodile has netted Allfed Snitchlock's head, a clear foul, and he's roaring in anger! Snarl HardBan swings his net at Stabbing Kingz, but Stabbing jumps back into the vines! Snarl HardBan has netted his own head, and here come the bolts!"

Z-z-z-z-z-zap!

Electric crackles filled the air; the referees had struck.

"Swill Crocodile is zapped!" Evilla shouted. "She's hit, she falls ...! Stabbing is swinging away, and here comes Judge O'Death and D'Wain Bones!

"Veilscreech Hobbleswoon swings to score! She shoots ... Veilscreech scores! Skullcrackers pull ahead!"

Martin wanted to cheer, yet the brick walls infuriated him. Finally he heard a voice.

"Crusto! Over here!" Stabbing called, pointing.

Moments later, Stabbing swung overhead.

"Get in a corner and shield yourself!"

Martin backed into a corner and raised his arms to

shield his face. Loud crashes came nearer, and finally one wall before him burst apart. Crusto broke through, paused to shake off the mortar-dust, looked around, and then lowered his net to Martin. Martin seized it, then was lifted back up to the vines.

"Martin the Magnificent is back in play!" Evilla shouted. "This game is far from over!"

Chapter 13
Rompday / Friday

Deadly Swinger ...

Butterfly Noose Swinger was a calamitous game. The Knights scored twice more, but so did the Skullcrackers. The score approaching halftime was 5 - 4.

Right before the horn blew, Teeth Slain jumped onto the vine over Stabbing, trying to bite it in half. However, Stabbing bounced upwards on his vine, flipped a coil skyward, and looped his coil around Teeth Slain's neck. Caught in the vine when Stabbing's weight dropped, Teeth Slain choked and writhed, trapped in the coil.

Things nearly got deadly, but Judge O'Death and D'Wain Bones came charging at Stabbing, determined to free their teammate. Both slammed into him; Stabbing was knocked off his vine. Teeth Slain was freed, yet both referees raised their wands, and Judge O'Death and D'Wain Bones were blasted. They jerked spasmodically as the yellow bolts zapped them, but only Judge O'Death held on. D'Wain Bones fell onto a pile of broken bricks and didn't get back up.

"Swing to score ...!" Veils shouted at Martin, and he swung over the fighting Bigs, who'd spread their battles across half of the pitch, and Veils swung close behind him and tossed him the zombie head. Martin didn't catch it, only helped it along with one hand, and the zombie head flew from him, past several swinging vines, toward the blankets inside the wide golden bowl.

"Nice move!" the zombie head complimented Martin as it flew.

"Martin scores!" Evilla shouted, and the horn for halftime blew.

At Crusto's prompting, Brain and Snitch helped Veils and Martin down while Crusto ran to find Stabbing. Both teams exited the pitch and gathered on opposite sides.

"Are you injured?" Grand Wizard Bastile Wraithbone asked Stabbing.

"No," Stabbing said. "Judge O'Death kicked me; her foot hurt more than the fall."

"She's a mean player," Veils said as Murder forced a waterskin into her hands, then passed more around.

"Do any of you want a break?" Grand Wizard Bastile Wraithbone asked. "Rude and Happy can substitute ..."

Every player shook their head.

"D'Wain Bones looked hurt, and I think Stabbing twisted Teeth Slain's neck," Rude said. "Also, Brain's net struck Junkish Ridgelay in her one eye, so I suspect she's out as well. Their replacements will be rested ..."

"They only have one extra Small, so they can't replace two," Murder said. "Drink, all of you!"

"I could replace Brain," Happy said. "We need Snitch for Snarl HardBan, and I know Crusto won't leave the field while Swill is playing, but centaurs match against minotaurs better than ogres."

"I agree," Grand Wizard Bastile Wraithbone said. "Brain, you took out the cyclops, so Happy will play the second half. Anything else?"

"Yes," Martin gasped. "Snitch ... was having too much fun. He broke through, then he was unprotected. They ganged up on him."

"Snitch, stay near Crusto and Happy," Grand Wizard Bastile Wraithbone said.

"No," Martin said. "They should stay with him. Their Bigs drove to clear out our scoring area while we did the same to theirs. Then the fighting broke out near theirs, and we had to score over their fighting, where we could get netted. Attack their Bigs right away, and then run back; let them chase you. We need the Bigs fighting where our nets can block their team from scoring."

"They haven't used their spell yet," Grand Wizard Bastile Wraithbone said. "We need to be careful."

"They're two points behind," Rude said. "They'll use their spell in the second half."

"I'll take point," Veils said. "If I see anything that looks like a scroll, I'll swing to stop them ... even if I have to foul them."

"You take care, too!" Grand Wizard Bastile Wraithbone said to Veils. "We know it's coming. Be prepared for anything."

The referees waved their wands and the broken walls restructured themselves. A hundred conversations muted Evilla's endless chatter as the crowd readied for the game to resume.

Brain wasn't thrilled at being left out, but unlike Snitch, Brain understood that Happy hadn't had a chance to play yet. They lined up as before, except with Veils aimed at Happy.

"Here we are again, my favorite sweeties!" Evilla said as she bounded back up onto her stand with a dramatic, bouncy leap. "As expected, the Shantdareya Skullcrackers are in the lead, and keeping up with them has been touch and go for the Knights of the Unliving Dread ... and as many of you know, there's nothing this gal likes more than a little touch and go! But the fans back in FollyGood are rooting for their team, and Knights never disappoint! Neither team has used a spell this season, and the Knights have to defeat at least one of the top two teams, the Skullcrackers or the Greasy Golems, to have a chance at moving on to the Regionals. But good Knights always have a sweet surprise hidden somewhere ... just like me ... that might yet leave us disbelieving this evening! So suck down a can of Crud Lite and gobble some delicious Deep-Fried Gopher Guts, because the second half is about to begin!"

The crowd cheered and applauded. Both referees raised their wands and both wizards raised their staffs. The horn blew.

"Let chaos reign ...!" Evilla shouted.

Smalls ran at their Bigs and were catapulted into the high pitch. Vines slapped as they flew in separate directions, but Evilla's cry startled them.

"A scroll ...!" Evilla shouted. "Judge O'Death is unrolling a scroll ...!"

The crowd rose to its feet, ready for anything. Martin grabbed the next vine he touched, swinging to the top of a wall. Veils did the same, but Stabbing didn't stop, flying toward the zombie head.

Martin looked across the pitch and saw the grim banshee holding up a scroll half her height. She was clearly reading it, her fellow Smalls swinging beside her rather than moving forward. Martin tensed; something bad was about to happen ...!

Crashes of breaking walls drowned out whatever she was saying, but as she finished, a brilliant white light shined from Judge O'Death. Her scroll rose up into the air, caught fire, and then burst into a pink cloud that whirled around and around. As it swirled, it became perfectly round, solid, red, and thinned out. As it solidified and ceased to spin, everyone in the stands could see what it was.

"A Death-Wheel ...!" Evilla screamed. "But who is its target?"

As Martin watched, the spinning pink cloud

transformed into ... an old wooden cart's wheel, such as the pioneers used on horse-drawn wagons when they crossed western America during the Gold Rush. He'd seen wheels like that in every cowboy movie, but why ...?

The magic wooden wheel flew toward them, spinning like a Frisbee, swatting vines aside. Stabbing dropped below it, and Martin swung out of its path, yet he quickly realized it wasn't aimed at him. Stabbing barely jumped aside as it drove straight at him again, and then he flattened as it came flying back.

The crowd cried out, some with cheers, others angrily. Stabbing turned and ran across the tops of the brick walls, and then jumped high and pulled himself up onto a vine, letting the spinning wheel pass under him. It flew forward and turned in an arc. Stabbing ran from it again.

Martin stared at the spinning wheel ... no, it wasn't a wagon wheel! It was ...!

Stabbing dodged too late. The spinning wheel flew hard into Stabbing, who was knocked upwards by its impact, and as he fell, it swooped under him. He landed upon it, and a second later Stabbing was spinning atop it, around and around. When it finally slowed, Stabbing lay across it, not moving.

"Stabbing is caught by a Death-Wheel!" Evilla shouted. "That's it for Stabbing! He's out of the game!"

Martin stood flat-footed atop the brick wall. *Stabbing was out of the game ...?* That left only him and Veils to compete against three Knights' Smalls!

They were outnumbered ... for an entire half ...!

Apparently he wasn't the only one surprised; even the crashes of the walls had stopped.

"Veils swings for the zombie head!" Evilla shouted, and Martin glanced to see her swinging toward the floating head as fast as she could. Martin didn't bother swinging; he ran along the tops of the brick walls with ease; it was more dangerous but faster.

Veil's movement seemed to restart the game. The Knights' Smalls swung forward, and crashes resumed, louder than ever.

Veils grabbed the zombie head, and reversed her course as the Knights moved to cut her off. Martin ran to catch up with her, but he quickly neared an area where smashed-apart bricks were flying upwards, and he resumed swinging. He caught up with Veils, but the Knights were closer to her than he was.

"Martin, score!" Veils cried, and she tossed him the zombie head.

Martin caught the zombie head and swung as fast as he could. The Knights came on, Judge O'Death in the lead. Veils cut her off, but she couldn't stop them all. Teeth Slain and Merry Leastfan were swinging toward him.

"Behind you!" the zombie head shouted at Martin. *"Throw! Throw now!"*

Martin wasn't close enough for a guaranteed score, but he wouldn't get another chance. With all three knights close behind him, Martin threw ... and the zombie head hit the rim, teetered, and fell into the golden bowl.

"Martin scores!" Evilla shouted. "That's Skullcrackers winning, 7 - 4, but without Stabbing, can they keep it up?"

Martin turned to see all three Knights' Smalls staring at him.

"Are you surprised?" Martin asked them. "Don't you know why the Grand Council of Wizards let a human play here ... and continue to let me play ...?"

The expressions on their faces were priceless, even on big-toothed Teeth Slain.

"Don't you know?" Martin demanded. "Didn't you figure it out? Of course you didn't! That's why I'm here!"

Judge O'Death, Merry Leastfan, and Teeth Slain continued to stare at Martin.

"Monsters have many advantages over humans, but humans have only one advantage over monsters," Martin said. "Don't you see ...? Can't you see it ...? The one thing humans have is the one thing monsters can't see!"

"What ...?" Judge O'Death asked in a voice like a creaky coffin lid.

"I can't believe you don't see it!" Martin said, holding out one hand. "It's right here ... in my hands ... right now!"

Suddenly the zombie head flew over Judge O'Death, Merry Leastfan, and Teeth Slain ... and landed in Martin's hands. Without hesitation, he flipped it over his head, and the zombie head dropped into their wide golden bowl.

"Martin scores again!" Evilla laughed. "8 - 4!"

The crowd burst out in howls, snorts, guffaws, and chuckles. Judge O'Death, Merry Leastfan, and Teeth Slain turned around to see Veils, who'd retrieved the zombie head ... while Martin distracted them.

"Get to the head!" Judge O'Death shouted. "No more mistakes!"

Following her, Merry Leastfan and Teeth Slain raced Veils back to mid-field. The flash illuminated the high pitch, and the zombie head appeared to the left of all of them. Veils reached it first, but Teeth slain jumped to the vine above her, and as she hurried to change vines, Judge O'Death slashed past her, and used her long claws to snatch the zombie head from her grip. Martin and Veils tried to catch her, but Merry Leastfan and Teeth Slain blocked them both.

"Judge O'Death steals the zombie head and scores!" Evilla shouted. "8 - 5, a three-point game!"

Martin swung over Snitch, who was fighting Snarl HardBan, Happy fighting Pranked Oak, and Crusto fighting Swill Crocodile, all before the Knights' scoring area. Martin kept hoping one of them would net one of the Knights' Smalls, but their struggles were intense, flashing net-poles smacking like quarterstaffs. Martin considered jumping down on Snitch's head, as Stabbing had, but doubted if he'd survive the attempt. Unlike the other Bigs, who fought with speed and complex combinations of strategy, trolls simply slammed their net-poles together so hard they knocked each other backwards, often through a brick wall.

Yet Martin didn't stay to watch. He raced back to mid-field. Veils, Merry Leastfan, and Teeth Slain waited there. When the zombie head flashed into reach, Veils tried to snatch it, but Judge O'Death swept in while Merry Leastfan and Teeth Slain blocked.

The game became a rout. The Knights Smalls scored several more times, Veils and Martin unable to stop them. Then, just after Judge O'Death and Merry Leastfan both blocked her, Teeth Slain bit through a vine and dropped Veils into a sealed room.

"Veils is trapped!" Evilla cried. "Score tied at 8, and Martin the Magnificent faces the Knights of the Unliving Dread alone!"

Three to one, Martin was completely outmatched.

Fortunately, Crusto was beating Swill; she fell and dropped her net. Martin called to him, and Crusto instantly followed Martin to the room where Veils was trapped.

"Judge O'Death scores again!" Evilla cried. "Knights lead, 9 - 8!"

Ignoring the upper pitch, Crusto smashed through brick walls and finally lifted Veils to the vines. The Knights' Smalls were hurrying to score again.

"Martin, any ideas?" Crusto hissed anxiously. "Can you two win ... against three ...?"

Martin shrugged. Evilla cried out again.

"Judge O'Death scores! Knights ahead, 10 - 8!"

Martin glanced at the wheel, slowly spinning near one side.

"Is Stabbing dead ...?" Martin asked.

"No, asleep ... but nothing can awaken him until the end of the half," Veils said.

"Wait ...!" Martin shouted. "A sleeping death ...? A spinning wheel ...?"

"What ...?" Veils asked.

Martin glanced at Stabbing, then looked at Veils.

"How long have you known Stabbing?" Martin asked.

"What ...? Why ...?"

"How long ...?" Martin demanded.

"Since I was six!" Veils said.

"Do you like him?" Martin asked.

"Wha ...?"

"Just answer my question!" Martin shouted. "How much do you like him?"

"Stabbing ...?" Veils asked. "He's ... like ... an uncle ..."

"Family ...?" Martin asked.

"Of course!" Veils said. "All the Skullcrackers ..."

"This is important!" Martin snapped. "Do you love him ...?"

"Martin ...!"

"Answer me ...!"

Veils shrugged. "Of course ...!"

"You've got to kiss him!" Martin shouted.

"What ...?" Veils asked.

"It's a human story ... a spinning wheel ... sleep of death ... a true love's kiss awakens the sleeper!" Martin said.

"I know you didn't kiss Murder ...!" Veils said.

"If Murder were here, she'd do it!" Martin said. "But she's not! This story isn't our game; the details are different, but it's our only hope!"

"Just ... kiss him?" Veils asked.

"Now ... before we lose too many points!" Martin shouted.

Veils shrugged, then jumped for a vine and swung toward the spinning wheel supporting Stabbing.

Martin let her go. Judge O'Death was rushing to score again, but Crusto's net swung at her, driving her back. She tossed the zombie head to Merry Leastfan, who circled around. Crusto ran from one side to the other, but he couldn't block both Smalls. Eventually Merry Leastfan tossed the zombie head into the golden bowl.

"Merry Leastfan scores!" Evilla shouted. "11 - 8, another three-point game!"

Teeth Slain and Judge O'Death raced to get back to mid-field. Teeth Slain arrived first, and when the zombie head appeared, he raced to it, then tossed it to Judge O'Death.

Martin glanced over and saw a scene Walt Disney never imagined. Veils, the beautiful dark elf, had jumped onto the slowly-spinning wheel, leaned over the sleeping ratling, and kissed Stabbing's hairy muzzle.

Judge O'Death was swinging past him, and Martin couldn't watch any longer. Risking everything, he jumped to grab a vine, swung as hard as he could, and jumped through midair to grab the vine Judge O'Death was swinging to. He got there first, and if she ran into him, then she'd get zapped.

Holding the zombie head, Judge O'Death let go rather than get zapped. She dropped off her vine, half-bounced against the broken wall beneath Martin, and bounded with practiced ease to the rugged ground.

One wall of this room was shattered, bricks lay everywhere, and she fumbled for footing as the rubble beneath her shifted. As the zombie head had vanished, Judge O'Death jumped off the bricks, though the gap, and ran toward the nearest stairs.

Teeth Slain recovered the zombie head and started rushing forward. He wasn't as fast as Judge O'Death; Martin swung to cut him off.

"Teeth ...!" Merry Leastfan shouted, her voice sounding like a sheep bleating.

Martin looked behind him at Merry Leastfan. She was a satyr, like Caroling Jokers, with hard, curved ram's horns on her head, a furry, narrow body, and a mean expression.

"Catch ...!" Teeth Slain shouted, and he threw the zombie head to Merry Leastfan.

Suddenly, awake again, Stabbing swung between them. He caught the zombie head intended for Merry

Leastfan, flew past her, and circled around Teeth Slain.

"Stabbing Kingz is awake ...!" Evilla cried. "How's it possible ...? He has the zombie head ...!"

Martin turned to chase after Stabbing, but Veils stopped him.

"Martin, wait here!" Veils shouted.

Confused, Martin obeyed and only watched.

Teeth Slain chased Stabbing, but he had no hope of catching him. Stabbing swung to the gold bowl and dropped the zombie head in.

"Stabbing Kingz scores!" Evilla cried. "11 – 9 ...!"

"H-h-how ...?" Merry Leastfan stammered, staring at Stabbing.

Martin ignored her. When the zombie head flashed near them, Merry was opposed by Veils, and Martin grabbed it. He raced to score, and ended up facing only Teeth Slain, who'd swung to catch up, and tried to block him, yet Martin wasn't alone. He tossed the zombie head to Stabbing, who was right behind Teeth. Stabbing outdistanced all of them with ease, while Veils raced back to center.

"Stabbing scores again!" Evilla cried. "11 - 10 ...! Will the Skullcrackers catch up ...?"

The zombie head appeared near mid-field. Merry Leastfan raced to get it, but Veils flipped a vine at her head. It's noose caught on one of her horns, pulled her off her vine, and the satyr fell into an unbroken room.

"Merry Leastfan is trapped!" Evilla cried. "Despite their spell, the Skullcracker Smalls outnumber the

Knights!"

Judge O'Death swung into the thick of it, but she and tiny Teeth Slain couldn't compete against three. Judge O'Death sent Teeth to get a Big to release Merry Leastfan, but Swill Crocodile was down, Happy and Crusto combined were more than a match for the minotaur Pranked Oak, and Snitch and Snarl HardBan had pushed each other into another section of the pitch, intent only on continuing their fight.

Without Merry Leastfan, Judge O'Death and Teeth Slain couldn't equal Martin, Stabbing, and Veils. When they did get the zombie head, either Happy or Crusto broke off from their joint pummeling of Pranked Oak to swipe at the Knights' Smalls with their net.

Happy captured Teeth Slain and slowly carried him over to the red pad. Judge O'Death was left alone. Her attempts to stop three Skullcrackers were pitiful.

Before the end of regulation horn blew, the Skullcrackers had scored four goals unopposed. The score was 14 - 11; the Knights had no hope of winning. Teeth Slain returned to the game, but Merry Leastfan got trapped again, and so their only objective became trying to pull vines out of a Skullcracker Small's grasp, hoping to hurt them. Yet the win was decided, and the Skullcrackers couldn't afford an injury; as the end of regulation sounded, the Skullcrackers stood back and let Judge O'Death reach the zombie head first, then let her score out of sympathy.

The final horn blew.

"Judge O'Death scores the last goal!" Evilla shouted. "Final score: 14 - 12 ...! The Shantdareya Skullcrackers win!"

The crowd cheered and many monsters jumped up and down.

"Wait, wait!" Evilla shouted. "It's not over! The referees are signaling ... it's a challenge!"

The crowd fell silent, aghast. All the players gathered on their sidelines, then followed their coaches to a council with the referees.

"Foul ...!" Grand Wizard Gorge Roamer cried. "Players can't use magic spells ... incantations not written by their wizard!"

The crowd fell silent. All strained to listen. Martin squeezed to the front; he'd never seen anything like this.

Grand Wizard Bastile Wraithbone waved his team back, then stepped forward to parley alone with both referees and Grand Wizard Gorge Roamer.

Veils was called forward to explain how she'd broken Grand Wizard Gorge Roamer's Death-Wheel spell. Finally Martin was called to join them, and he explained about the animated movie based on one of Mother Goose's most-popular fairy tales.

"The Death-Wheel spell was created by wizards ... who have visited Earth several times," Grand Wizard Bastile Wraithbone said. "Obviously someone got the idea for this spell there ... and assumed no monster would ever guess the spell's weakness."

"It's not fair ...!" Grand Wizard Gorge Roamer

shouted. "His players negated my spell through sorcery ...!"

"Veils kissed Stabbing," Grand Wizard Bastile Wraithbone said. "Exactly which no-kissing rule did she break ...?"

Speechless, Grand Wizard Gorge Roamer glared at him.

After hearing both wizards, the referees walked away for a moment, whispering to each other.

The crowd didn't like delays. Boos and catcalls filled the stadium. However, eventually the referees came back. Evilla gestured for silence and held her microphone down as the senior referee approached.

The crowd fell utterly silent.

"Veilscreech Hobbleswoon awoke Stabbing Kingz with a kiss," she said. "No second spell was cast; the only spell that was cast was later broken by its own weakness, not by another spell. There's no rule against players kissing one another, and until the next meeting of the Council of Grand Wizards, and unless they make a rule about kissing during matches, the outcome stands."

The crowd cheered again.

"You cheated me ...!" Grand Wizard Gorge Roamer shouted at Grand Wizard Bastile Wraithbone. *"I challenge you ... to a Duel of Dominance ...!"*

To everyone's surprise, Grand Wizard Bastile Wraithbone didn't react, but stared at his fellow wizard with his eyes narrowed. Then he lifted his staff into the air and slammed it down.

With a blast that startled everyone, the magic staff of Grand Wizard Gorge Roamer shot up out of his hand and into the sky like a rocket on the fourth of July.

"My dear, honorable, and ancient fellow conjuror, Grand Wizard Gorge Roamer," Grand Wizard Bastile Wraithbone said firmly. "I appreciate your anger and frustration at this moment, but I beg you not to surrender to base foolishness. I wield the magic staff of Master Grand Wizard Borgias Killoff, the most powerful staff of the most powerful wizard.

"Lucky for you, I've no desire to duel with any of my brothers or sisters, even though my victory is assured. We of the Wizard's Council mustn't disgrace our status with public brawls, so I ask you to petition our council, and there state your case fully. I myself promise to ask the council to vote on any new measures you suggest to avert this dispute in the future.

"For now, the referees have made their decision, and I'm going to depart with my team in peace." Grand Wizard Bastile Wraithbone paused and looked high up into the sky. "Happy, Grand Wizard Gorge Roamer's staff will drop back down in a few moments. Will you please wait here ... and see it is safely caught and returned to him?"

Happy nodded, and Grand Wizard Bastile Wraithbone politely bowed to Grand Wizard Gorge Roamer, then turned and led his team back to the locker room.

Chapter 14
Smashday / Saturday

New challenge ...

"Martin, could you come with me?" Vicky asked.

"I'm playing!" Martin snapped, and instantly he regretted it. He wasn't angry at Vicky; he'd taken her book to the barbershop and had wanted to keep reading it, but his father insisted he keep his brothers quiet by making Martin play video games with them.

"I hate to be Rude," Vicky said with great emphasis. "I won't be Stealing you for long."

To his brothers complaints, Martin dropped his controller and followed Vicky down the hall. Her bedroom looked the same as always, yet sitting on her bed was ... a goblin!

"Rude ...!" Martin whispered.

"I found him in your room," Vicky said.

"I've been sent to invite you both to a very elegant evening tonight ... usual time," Rude said.

"Aren't we going to practice ...?" Martin asked.

"You already know the next game," Rude grinned.

"Net-Door Maze ... so Grand Wizard Bastile Wraithbone thought we should relax for one night."

"I'd be delighted," Vicky said.

"Good, because the whole team wants you there," Rude said to Vicky. "Dress nicely; Murder chose Medusa Manor, the finest restaurant on Heterodox."

"How did the games go?" Martin asked.

"Plenty of time to talk tonight," Rude said. "I've got to get back into your room and go home."

"Check the hall and open your door," Vicky told Martin.

Martin looked out.

"Mom's door is open, but I can't see her," Martin whispered, then he crossed the hall and opened his door.

Moments later, a pair of bare, light-green, hoary feet shuffled across the hall and into Martin's bedroom. Above the feet floated a blanket draped around a figure, upheld by Vicky. As soon as Martin closed his door, she dropped the blanket.

"Thank you for showing me how your computer works," Rude said to Vicky.

"My pleasure," Vicky said.

"See you tonight," Martin said.

Rude clapped his many-ringed hands. A soft hum, like a swarm of bees, filled Martin's room, and then a bright flash blinded them all. When Martin and Vicky blinked their eyes open, Rude was gone.

"Dinner at Medusa Manor ...!" Vicky grinned, but

Martin eyed her slyly.

"In Zantheriak, are you ... the mysterious woman ...?" Martin asked.

"I'm glad you're reading," Vicky smiled. "But if you're going to be a serious reader, then you'll learn soon enough: there's always a mysterious woman."

With a laugh, Vicky walked back to her room, leaving Martin's question unanswered.

Martin fell into Crusto's hands, and right beside him, Vicky fell into Happy's arms.

"Sister ...!" Snitch grinned widely.

"Snitch remembers you!" Murder exclaimed.

"Of course he remembers me!" Vicky said as Happy set her on her feet, and she hurried over and gave Snitch a big hug. Snitch bent down to allow her hug, closed his eyes and smiled.

Crusto set Martin down. Martin stared, too stunned to speak. They weren't in a locker room, but in an austere, ornate lobby.

Snitch was wearing long black trousers and an immense long-sleeved black jersey with a cheesy dark purple suit-front with a red bow tie printed upon it. Yet the rest of their formalwear wasn't fake. Grand Wizard Bastile Wraithbone wore a robe of dark purple crushed velvet and a matching pointed hat, both trimmed with real gold. Rude, Stabbing, Crusto, and even Brain were wearing dark purple tuxedos. Happy wore a tuxedo over his human half with a gold-trimmed dark purple drape elegantly covering his equine half to his four knees. Sitting atop his back was Murder, not in her wheelchair, dressed in a beautiful dark purple gown that fell to her ankles and glittered all over. Upon her green feet she wore sleek dark purple high heels.

"Hello, Martin," Veils said.

Martin's jaw dropped. Veils was wearing a sparkling dress like Murder, incredibly elegant, and Martin was reminded of Yuck Wand DeSnarlo, the older version of Veils who'd helped them win last season's Finals.

Martin nodded to her; his voice seemed to have stopped working.

"Martin, Vicky, may I introduce you to my beloved, Miss Theater," Rude said, gesturing to a tall, elegant woman in a dark, rose-colored dress. She wasn't a goblin; she had light blue skin and dark blue hair; a naiad, a spirit of the waters.

"My friends call me Terri," she said, nodding gracefully.

"Our pleasure," Vicky replied.

Martin nodded, still unable to speak.

"I believe we're ready to be seated," Grand Wizard Bastile Wraithbone said to the maître d'.

The maître d' summoned a waiter, who escorted them into a grand dining hall. On each side, a ramp gently sloped downward to a raised stage on which a trio of monsters were softly playing musical instruments. On both sides of each ramp were flat levels, on which elegant dining room tables were set with gleaming china plates and sparkling, polished silverware. Small vases held flowers on every table between tall candelabras, and monsters sat around each table, laughing, talking, and eating.

Martin gazed at the dim, elegant room in shock. Never had he been inside such a formal, highbrow setting, not even in the human world.

Their waiter led them down the ramp to a table with a 'Reserved' sign, which he removed. He held out a chair, and Crusto lifted Murder down and sat her upon it. Then the waiter held a chair for Terri, who thanked him as she sat, and then he did the same for Vicky, who thanked him most graciously. Veils seemed as surprised as Martin when the waiter held out a chair for her. Yet she stepped forward, thanked the waiter, and sat in the chair as gracefully as Terri and Vicky. Finally the waiter held the chair on the far end for Grand Wizard Bastile Wraithbone, who thanked the waiter most respectfully, then seated himself in a lordly fashion.

From a side table, the waiter lifted a stack of tall menus and waited for the men to seat themselves. As before, most of the seats were raised, with low stools for Snitch and Brain. Happy stood, as centaurs always did, at a place-setting right beside Vicky.

The waiter handed a menu to each. Snitch turned his upside down, looked at it curiously, and Crusto stopped him before he bit it.

"Murder, this place is lovely," Vicky said.

"Indeed," Terri added.

"Thank you," Murder said. "Medusa Manor is my favorite."

Martin glanced at his menu and almost gagged. Appetizers included Toad Tar-Tar, Snail Soup, Basilisk Baste, and Wasp Crisps. Entrées were Marinated Musk Ox, Planked Python, Roasted Rambutan, and Seared Saucy Shark. Desserts were Caramelized Sapota and Frosted Fairy Fricassee.

"Looks delicious," Crusto said.

"Indeed," Rude smiled, looking at Terri.

Terri lightly cuffed his arm.

The waiter asked for their drink orders, and Veils spoke at once.

"I'd like to try a Velvet Rainbow," Veils said.

"That would be for me," Murder said firmly. "Veils and Martin would like Pixie-Slushes."

"Very good, madam," the waiter said, and Veils scowled.

"Such lovely music ...!" Grand Wizard Bastile Wraithbone commented after their waiter had hurried off with their drink orders.

Everyone turned to glance at the trio of musicians. On a tall stool before a harp sat a pale woman who was obviously a vampira, dressed all in black with long, sharp fangs. Beside her stood a fully-bandaged mummy playing a violin, and what looked like a werewolf sat at a wide, gleaming black piano. Their music was gentle and sweet; everyone listened and enjoyed it.

Their drinks soon arrived. The Velvet Rainbow

had shades of colors cascading down its tall, thin glass. Grand Wizard Bastile Wraithbone got a Minnow Margarita, and Martin wasn't surprised to see tiny fish jumping out of its icy depths. Vicky had asked Happy to order for her, and both lifted White Whippoorwill Wines and clinked their glasses together. Crusto ordered Avalanche Ale for himself, Brain, and Snitch, and Rude and Terri each accepted three tiny shot glasses of Belladonna Bourbon. Stabbing accepted and sipped a mug of Naughty Nightshade, which frothed and churned, and a tiny black cloud hovered over his glass and hid his eyes as he drank.

"You look surprised, Martin," Stabbing said. "Didn't expect monsters to dine like this ...?"

"Stabbing, we should always arise to the elegance of our setting," Grand Wizard Bastile Wraithbone said. "There are all kinds of monsters ... in the same way there are all kinds of humans."

"More humans should enjoy places like this," Vicky said.

"Everyone should ... at least once in a while," Happy agreed.

"I hate to bring our discussion back to business, but Martin asked about the last games when I visited his world," Rude said.

"Good games!" Brain said, and Snitch nodded wholeheartedly.

"It was exciting and disastrous," Crusto said. "Greasy Golems beat the Flying Munchers badly. Your old friend, Maxivoom Snydho, seriously injured Jackal Pumpkinshread, and King Ghastoria suffered squashed roots from Ton Eat-oddly."

"Ton Eat-oddly is still playing?" Martin asked.

"Grand Wizard Crass Gopherly constructed a steel helmet that Ton Eat-oddly now wears," Crusto said. "It completely covers his life-word, which golems need to stay alive ..."

"You can't beat him by changing his life-word again," Stabbing said to Martin, "... which makes him nearly invulnerable."

"The Flying Munchers had two spare Bigs and two spare Smalls," Crusto continued. "Now they're down to one each ..."

"But they can still play," Stabbing interrupted.

"The Roaring Giants beat the Gorgedown X-Lorecists," Crusto said, and then he paused, staring at Stabbing as if daring him to interrupt him again, but Stabbing took a drink and hid his eyes. "Their best Big, Meercreeds Microfridge, was seriously injured by Jolt Huge. Meercreeds Microfridge will be out for at least the next game, which means they have no spare Big."

"It's also bad luck for us," Grand Wizard Bastile Wraithbone said. "In the first round, the Flying Munchers used their spell against us. The Roaring Giants likewise used their spell against the Greasy Golems. However, then the Greasy Golems got the Flying Munchers, who'd already used their spell, while we suffered the spell of the Knights of the Unliving

Dread. Both us and the Greasy Golems are saving our spells for when we face each other, which leaves the Gorgedown X-Lorecists as the only other team who hasn't used their spell ... and we face them next."

"By the end of the Locals, we'll have faced four spells, while the Greasy Golems faced only two," Rude said. "Unfair ... but it's luck of the draw."

"The Gorgedown X-Lorecists are a tough team, and Grand Wizard Will-Pester Batty is no slouch at magic," Murder said. "But let's worry about that tomorrow."

"I agree," Grand Wizard Bastile Wraithbone said. "In this setting, let's discuss something other than work."

"If I may ask, since I know little of your world, what do you do?" Vicky asked Terri. "Are you an actress?"

"Despite my name, I've nothing to do with any stage," Terri said. "I manage the library of the Grand Council of Wizards, caring for their books."

"A librarian of Heterodox!" Vicky exclaimed. "I read voraciously, so that sounds exciting to me. What kind of books do you have?"

"I'm afraid that's confidential," Terri said. "Wizards are understandably particular about who they allow to read their spellbooks."

"Don't you read them?" Vicky asked.

"I've ...," she glanced at Grand Wizard Bastile Wraithbone, "... had a book or two fall open in front of me. Never on purpose, of course."

Grand Wizard Bastile Wraithbone smiled at her.

"Does that make you a Grand Witch?" Vicky asked.

"You needn't answer if you don't want to."

"I'm ... hardly grand ...!" Terri smiled.

Their food arrived, served on silver platters. Appetizers of Basilisk Baste and Wasp Crisps were set in the middle for everyone. Martin got a Marinated Musk Ox steak, which most of the men did, but Crusto ordered Planked Python and Grand Wizard Bastile Wraithbone and Vicky ate the Seared Saucy Shark. Terri also had the Planked Python, and Murder smiled at her Roasted Rambutan.

As they ate, new topics arose and died. Stabbing knew all the local musicians and he, Terri, and Murder discussed their favorite local bands. Grand Wizard Bastile Wraithbone told of a wise lizardwoman who'd agreed to teach reading and writing to all the children of Shantdareya in a nearby lagoon, and he expressed his hopes of acquiring books for the children to read.

Vicky offered to help, telling everyone about the numerous used bookshops she haunted, and how countless books could be bought there for cheap. Vicky and Martin laughed when Happy asked how many gold coins it would cost to buy a hundred kid's books. Then they apologized and explained that one gold coin could buy more than a hundred used books. Delighted by this news, Grand Wizard Bastile Wraithbone reached into his robe and pulled out a large gold coin, which he passed to Vicky.

"You'll have to come to my college to get them," Vicky said. "Martin will have my new address, and I'll let him know when I have them."

Martin smiled, but he didn't feel like talking. He was wearing his best Easter Sunday clothes, yet felt underdressed. Also, he didn't know what to say to Veils, who looked so pretty she took his breath away. Yet, just as they were about to serve desserts, a familiar voice spoke behind them.

"Well, tighten my corsets!" Evilla said. "What a pleasure to run into my favorite team!"

Everyone looked up. Evilla was dressed in pure black, yet her dress was nothing like she wore when announcing the games. It looked elegant, yet also like a spider had spun its black silk right onto her, clinging so tightly it revealed her every curve.

"What a delightful coincidence!" Grand Wizard Bastile Wraithbone said. "This is twice I've taken my team out for dinner, and both times you've managed to find us ..."

"Well, I've been accused of being a stalker before, but never so nicely!" Evilla said. "You all look lovely! And, of course, you know me ... looks are what I collect. Any chance of collecting a few quotes for next week's game?"

"I'm afraid not," Grand Wizard Bastile Wraithbone said. "If you will excuse us ..."

"Oh, I'll excuse anything ...!" Evilla said.

Everyone looked exasperated. Crusto sighed heavily.

"Evilla, might I have a quick word with you ... in

private?" Martin asked.

"Oh, of course ...!" Evilla said, breathing heavily and fanning herself. "I've never been asked out by ... by a human before ...!"

Most of the Skullcrackers glared at Martin, yet he stood up, gestured, and followed Evilla away from the table. She led him to a secluded corner in the back.

"How would you like to interview me?" Martin asked.

"An exclusive ...?" Evilla's eyes widened. "How could I refuse ...?"

"I expect payment in return," Martin said. "Not money; I want something else."

For a moment, Evilla looked worried, but then she smiled and waved her hand.

"Seriously," Martin said before she rattled off more nonsense.

Evilla's foggy expression suddenly hardened, and her airy demeanor evaporated.

"What do you want?" Evilla asked in a very different, business-like voice ... not at all the playful demeanor she usually showed.

Martin's eyes widened; he didn't know Evilla had a serious side.

"I want you to stop calling Veils by her given name," Martin said. "Call her Veils."

"But Veilscreech Hobbleswoon is such a unique name," Evilla said. "The fans love it."

"She doesn't," Martin said.

"I won't call her Veilscreech Hobbleswoon anymore," Evilla promised. "Can we schedule our interview for tomorrow night?"

"Stompday, if Grand Wizard Bastile Wraithbone allows it," Martin said. "But I get to say what the interview is about ...! I don't want you starting false rumors ...!"

"Martin, I know what everyone thinks of me," Evilla said, and she lowered her voice. "In fact, I pretty much know everything ... even about your misty conversation with Master Grand Wizard Borgias Killoff ...!"

"Ummm .... Who ...?" Martin pretended not to know ... or show how amazed he was.

"He does masquerade as Grand Wizard Veinlet Prize ... to keep his secret from Grand Witch Maim La Nuormal," Evilla whispered.

"How do you know that ...?" Martin whispered.

"Some idiots try to act smart, but they're not," Evilla whispered to Martin. "Not everyone who acts stupid is. I've learned from him that you can keep secrets, and I'll trust you to keep mine because I need to know certain things from you. Believe me; I keep secrets very close. Because of my public persona, no one ever guesses I know anything."

"Why do you ...?" Martin asked.

"I like the job," Evilla said. "Yet, before I get back to it, I wanted to tell you how impressed I was at your willingly taking those two fouls during the first game. I expected nothing less of Happy ... he's proven himself many times. You're just a boy ... but a very impressive boy."

"Thank you," Martin said, and Evilla sighed a deep breath.

As if putting on a mask, Evilla suddenly smiled and looked vacuous, and Martin almost laughed. He held out his arm, and she acted as if he were honoring her above all else. She took his arm and let him escort her back to their table.

"Thank you, Martin ... Mr. Magnificent!" Evilla breathed when they returned to his team, and she extended her hand. "What a perfect gentleman!"

Martin had seen enough old movies to play this part; he took her hand in his and softly kissed it.

Evilla looked as if she were about to swoon, then sighed, blew him a kiss, and wandered back up the ramp.

Martin sat back down and smiled when he saw everyone staring at him ... especially Veils.

"We just talked," Martin assured them.

"About what ...?" Veils demanded.

"About you," Martin said.

Veils startled.

"What about her ...?" Grand Wizard Bastile Wraithbone asked.

"Evilla's agreed to not call her Veilscreech Hobbleswoon anymore," Martin said.

Veils looked shocked, yet Stabbing and Rude laughed, and Grand Wizard Bastile Wraithbone held up both of his many-ringed hands and softly applauded Martin.

Everyone but Veils joined in.

Chapter Chapter 15
Smiteday / Sunday

Practice and Planning ...

After church Martin went outside to exercise in the backyard. The day was still hot, but overcast and cloudy; summer was drawing to a close. Tomorrow school started and he'd lose his days in the yard.

Net-Door Maze; it was the only game Martin had ever watched rather than play; the Grave Gutters had defeated the Barkrover Bullies and forced them out of the Finals. He'd watched from the stands as they'd rearranged the walls of the maze, and then run through enemy territory to try to score ... without getting trapped in rooms by self-locking doors.

Smalls fought with nets made of rope. Bigs fought with nets made of chain. People got hurt playing this game, even powerful Bigs like Jackknife Illson and the massive Slug Gormet-Wreather.

Martin would have to be careful ... and be ready for anything.

Martin fell into Happy's hands. As he was set onto his feet, Martin glanced around. Murder wasn't there.

"Martin, I wanted to thank you for bringing Vicky," Happy said.

"Rude invited her," Martin said. "It's not like I could keep her away."

"I've said what I wanted to," Happy said. "Let's go out to the pitch."

Together they walked out. As Martin had expected, the stands on both sides were raised fifteen feet into the air so everyone in the stadium could look down onto the pitch.

The pitch was a huge building, filled with moving walls, with wide open doorways on each end. The only way to win was for Smalls to find the zombie head and carry it outside your opponent's door. But that meant crossing past three enemy Bigs in narrow hallways ... and not getting squashed.

Rude was standing beside Grand Wizard Bastile Wraithbone who was standing beside ... *Murder* ...? Yet, as they neared, Martin saw Murder had her wheelchair nearby and was standing using crutches.

"Getting a fresh perspective?" Martin asked.

"I'm sick of sitting," Murder said.

"Welcome back, Martin," Grand Wizard Bastile Wraithbone said. "The others ran off that way; you'd best hurry if you want to catch them."

"I'll take him," Happy said, and he held out a hand to Martin.

Martin swung onto his back, and Happy broke into a gallop. Within a minute, they closed on Snitch, Brain, Crusto, Veils, and Stabbing, who were running toward a distant post. As they caught up, Happy helped Martin off without slowing down. Martin ran beside them, noticing all of them were sweating and gasping.

The post, when they reached it, was buried in sand. They'd arrived at a beach, looking at the sea. Yet Crusto didn't stop; he led them onto the sand toward the water.

"Get as far out as you can!" Crusto cried. "Don't let the water touch you!"

They spent almost an hour getting soaked. Crusto was best, chasing the retreating waves farther than any of the others dared, then running back when a wave splashed in. However, even he couldn't predict every wave, and sometimes others got in his way and blocked his retreat.

Running back and forth, Martin realized why; they were training racing short distances and then suddenly changing direction. Sand made their transitions and take-offs harder, so this was the perfect place to train. Sometimes someone would slip, or the wet sand collapsed beneath their feet, and more than once Martin joined those who fell and had a cold ocean wave splash over them.

Drenched, they all ran back without a break, clothes, hair, and fur dripping. By the time they made it back, Martin was one of those gasping, barely able to stand.

"Drink water," Grand Wizard Bastile Wraithbone ordered them, although several had to catch their breaths first. "When you're ready, Rude has a lesson for you."

Five minutes passed before Rude began. He was standing beside a wooden tripod on which was a poster-sized pad of paper. The first page had been drawn on with colored markers.

"As you know, the tops of each door-frame is color-coded, so the crowd can see what they are, but not the players," Rude began. "Maroon doors start opened, but automatically close behind you, and then stay locked for ten minutes. If there's no other door in the room, you're trapped. Pink door-frames show open doorways; no doors at all. Red doors are like maroon doors, only they don't automatically close when you step through them. You can leave them open, but once closed, they're locked for ten minutes."

Rude pointed at a door drawn of each color, then at drawn walls with colored stripes.

"The two main doors are marked yellow. On their tops, the outer walls are black, but we won't be able to see those marks from the pitch. Outer walls are solid and unmovable. Walls that can't be moved are marked purple. Walls that can be moved are marked blue, but they can't be pushed past a door in another wall. Walls that can be pushed past a door are marked green; they can permanently block any closed door."

Rude flipped the page to the next.

"These are the secret symbols we'll use," Rude said and he went through each one; a seven-pointed star, a pentagram in a circle, crossed lightning bolts, a perfect snowflake, a flaming skull ...

"Wait a minute," Martin said. "These are pretty complicated ..."

"We have to keep them secret," Rude said. "We don't want Gorgedown X-Lorecists knowing our designs."

"Those take too long to draw and have no relation to their meanings," Martin said.

"Martin, could you suggest better?" Grand Wizard Bastile Wraithbone asked.

"I don't want to ... force my ideas," Martin said.

"Show us your ideas and we'll let Rude choose," Grand Wizard Bastile Wraithbone said.

Martin shrugged. He got up and stood before the tripod. Rude gave him a pen, and Martin stared at the options. Then he drew a rectangle taller than it was wide.

"Tall rectangles are doors," Martin said. "We don't need to mark doorways without doors. Doors that automatically close and lock we cross with an 'X'. Doors that lock only when you close them we cross with a horizontal line. Normal doors we mark with a vertical line."

Martin drew an example of each. Then Martin drew another rectangle, wider than it was tall.

"Wide rectangles are walls," Martin said. "We don't

need to mark yellow walls; you can see the grounds outside through the door. Walls that don't move get an 'X'. Walls that can't block a door are split by a vertical line. Walls that can block a door are split by a horizontal line."

"It's so simple ...!" Murder exclaimed. "So quick and obvious ...!"

"Rude ...?" Grand Wizard Bastile Wraithbone asked.

"Easy to remember," Rude nodded appreciatively. "Easy to draw and understand ... but won't the other team figure them out?"

Martin smiled.

"We've got marking pens of many colors," Martin said. "We give each Small two different colors ... and the Gorgedown X-Lorecists will waste their time wondering what the different colors mean. Also, you can draw other symbols next to our rectangles, like circles and triangles. We know the weird symbols mean nothing, but they'll waste time trying to figure them out."

A brief pause followed ... and then laughing started.

Rude flipped to the next page on his tripod, showing a complex floorplan drawn in colored walls and doors.

"Consider the classic arrangements of walls and doors," Rude said.

"Wait ...!" Veils said. "How many drawings are there?"

"Just the basic twenty-six," Rude said.

Everyone sighed and eyes rolled.

"Twenty six ...?" Murder exclaimed.

"As much as I hate to say it, there's no way we can learn and remember these strategies as well as Rude in the next few nights," Martin said. "While none of us want to be left out, I think Rude should play."

Surprised looks came from everyone.

"That means either you or Veils must sit out," Murder said.

"Neither of us wants that ... but it's best for the team," Martin said.

"That's the winning spirit!" Grand Wizard Bastile Wraithbone said.

When everyone had physically recovered, Grand Wizard Bastile Wraithbone lifted a blanket off a nearby pile of nets they'd use in the game. Curious, Martin tried to lift a net made of chain. Veils saw him and laughed.

"That net weighs more than you do!" she chuckled.

"I just wanted to examine one ... before I get hit by it," Martin said.

"The goal is to not get hit by it," Stabbing said. "I've been hit ... and it took me out of the game."

The Smalls took nets of rope and practiced throwing them, trying to entangle each other. They'd briefly played with nets before, but only for an hour, and they'd covered nothing but the basics.

"Net-fighting isn't about strength or speed," Stabbing said. "Nets are about timing and dodging. If you block your opponent's net with yours, then yours will be

blocked. The best net-fighters counter-time each other
... try to get their opponent to commit, then dodge ... and
counter-attack while their opponent's net is out of
position."

Crusto led Happy, Brain, and Snitch into the main
room inside the building and practiced. Their chains
simultaneously crashed and rang, frighteningly loud.
Despite Veil's comment, Martin believed each chain-net
weighed about fifty pounds, which became deadly when
swung in the hands of a Big. No Small had skin tough
enough to survive a blow ... which gave Martin an idea.

Stabbing and Rude trained Martin and Veils outside
the building, off the pitch. They practiced for an hour,
swinging their rope nets, which weren't soft but didn't
hurt badly. Martin was amazed at how difficult it was to
throw off an entrapping net; it caught on everything, even
folds of clothes, and getting entangled was far easier than
getting un-entangled. Also, each net bore a five-foot
rope from which it could be held once thrown. Stabbing
got Martin entangled, then drug him in a wide circle, and
escaping a net while being drug was almost impossible.
Yet this also gave Martin an idea.

As they finished practice, Martin kept his ideas to
himself, but they were all he could think about. He just
wasn't sure he'd thought them through completely and
didn't want to say anything until he was sure.

When he arrived for practice tomorrow, he'd be
ready to prove his theories.

Chapter 16
Stompday / Monday

New Ways to Play ...

Waking up for the first day of school: *nightmare!* Martin felt awful; he'd only fallen asleep a few hours before, then he had to scarf down breakfast and run to catch his bus.

Paying attention enough to find his new classes, open his new locker, and choose desks without walking into walls, which would be highly embarrassing, proved hard. Martin was so groggy he wanted to droop his head onto his desk and ignore whatever his teachers were prattling about.

He knew most of the faces he saw. A lot of friends whom Martin hadn't seen since the end of Spring greeted him cheerily, and he was glad to see them again. Yet he couldn't stop yawning.

When Martin finally woke up, sitting in his desk after lunch, things got worse. He couldn't keep his mind off the Grotesquerie Games and the ideas he'd had. He knew what he wanted to do and it wouldn't be hard. He just had to do it before he fell asleep.

However, he hadn't counted on homework. Three different teachers assigned him a chapter to read, and he had a list of ten basic multiplication and division problems to solve ... showing his work. He started reading one chapter on the bus ride home ... and almost missed his stop.

Martin's brothers wanted him to join them shooting zombies, but Martin focused on his homework, and when his parents got home, they shut off the zombies and made his brothers start their homework.

"Do as Martin says," his father told his brothers. "Next week, he'll be in charge."

"What ...?" Martin asked.

"Vicky is leaving on Wednesday ... going to college," his father said. "You'll be in charge from now on."

It'd been a long time since Martin screamed as he plummeted, yet despite going to bed early, he was sound asleep at midnight. He startled awake as he smacked into Brain's hands.

"Martin ...?" Brain asked.

"It's all right," Martin said. "I was asleep. Sorry."

"Asleep ...?" Brain asked, as if this was unthinkable. "At night ...?"

"Yes," Martin said, yawning widely. "School kept

me awake all day."

Then he saw the shoelace tied to his wrist, and as he'd hoped, the other end was still tied to the large bag; *it had worked!* He untied and opened the bag. His belongings were still in it.

Beside the pitch, Murder balanced on her crutches again. She and Grand Wizard Bastile Wraithbone were standing before Snitch, holding up a large sickly-green and red jersey.

"Only swing chains at players wearing this!" Murder shouted at Snitch, pointing at the jersey. "See these colors? This is green ... and this is red. Hit anyone wearing these colors!"

Both Murder and Grand Wizard Bastile Wraithbone nodded to Martin and glanced at the bag he was carrying, then returned their attention to Snitch. Martin picked up a rope net, and Brain picked up a chain net, and both walked toward the pitch.

Crusto and Happy were slowly chain-dueling, only for practice. Rude, Stabbing, and Veils were running at them from behind, then leaping onto them or darting around them, staying close, but dodging to avoid their swinging chains.

"Wait a minute, Brain," Martin said.

From his bag, Martin untied his shoelace, restrung it on his shoe, and then opened his bag. Out of it he pulled his hard-plastic skateboard pads, which he strapped on. Practice stopped while everyone looked at him.

No one asked, but when he had it all on, helmet, vest, kneepads, elbow pads, and forearm and shin shields, he walked forward bravely.

"What's this ...?" Crusto asked.

"A test," Martin said, and he held out his arm. "Lightly, very lightly, swing your chain net at me."

Crusto glanced at Happy, then at the other Smalls, and finally lifted his chain net. He didn't swing, only wafted it gently at Martin.

The chains bounced off his pads.

"I didn't even feel that," Martin said.

Reluctantly, Crusto wafted his net harder. The chains struck with no effect.

"Still fine," Martin said.

Leaving Murder talking to Snitch, Grand Wizard Bastile Wraithbone came over to watch.

With a deep, worried exhalation, Crusto lightly swung his chain as he would at another Big, just slower. The linked chains hit hard, moving Martin's arms.

"I felt that," Martin said, "but it didn't hurt."

"It's like ... Ram-armor!" Stabbing said.

"Ingenious ...!" Rude said.

Warily, but with increasing strength, Crusto swung his net. Finally he slammed Martin to the ground, but Martin immediately stood up, ready for another.

"That sorta hurt, but it wouldn't stop me," Martin said.

"Do you have more of these?" Veils asked.

"No, and we wouldn't want them," Martin said.

"Armor has advantages and disadvantages. I can take a pounding I couldn't before, but I'm heavier, slower, and have more edges for nets to catch on. We don't want to be specialists like the Flying Munchers. With this, one of us can take a pounding the others can't. The other Smalls need to score, and the job of the one wearing the armor is to give them every chance."

"Can you jump in it?" Rude asked.

"Let's find out," Martin said.

Martin vaulted onto Happy's back, bounced to Crusto's shoulder, then jumped wide and landed with ease onto Brain's head ... although he was still in range of Crusto's swinging chain. Brain caught him as he dropped down.

They practiced for a while, and then Martin offered to let Veils try wearing his armor.

"No," Rude said. "I'm mostly healed, but I'm not going to be winning any races. Veils is fast. Let me be the slow one."

"I want to try it sometime," Veils argued.

"They're mine," Martin assured her. "You can keep them here."

Rude loved the velcro straps, and soon stood in Martin's skateboard armor, flexing to test his ability to move. Happy tested him, slowly increasing the strength of his swings as Crusto had. Rude was nearly the same height as Martin, a little thinner, yet he was tougher, having been playing the games for years. Happy tried a side-swing that swatted Rude ten feet backwards, yet he rolled to his feet barely stunned.

"Martin, this is brilliant!" Rude said.

"I had another idea, but it won't work," Martin said. "We'd need new outfits."

"Why ...?" Stabbing asked.

"Some human athletes wear slick, skin-tight clothes ... especially for those who move very fast," Martin said. "It cuts down on friction ... air resistance ... and lets them move faster. I thought, if we had better outfits, maybe we could un-entangle ourselves better ... have fewer edges for nets to cling to ..."

"No net has ever caught on my jersey or fur, mostly on my claws," Stabbing said. "However, I've had nets catch on my necklace and earring ..."

"We removed our jewelry for Trip-Hook Roller because metal conducted electricity," Happy said. "We could do that here ... remove anything a net could snag on ..."

"Martin, if we wore skin-tight outfits, could we jump farther ... stay in the air longer?" Veils asked.

"I think so ...," Martin said.

"Different outfits for different purposes," Rude said. "Assign tasks to each Small ... and dress them accordingly."

"Martin, I like these ideas," Grand Wizard Bastile Wraithbone said. "Perhaps we should ..."

He broke off to the sounds of sharp footsteps approaching. Evilla came walking around the stands wearing a black dress, with hair to match, and a flowing purple cape that matched the Skullcracker's jerseys.

"Ah, I believe Martin has an appointment," Grand Wizard Bastile Wraithbone smiled. "I can delay it, if you wish ..."

"No, I promised," Martin said, and he stood up and walked to face Evilla before she started talking to everyone.

"Martin, so lovely to see you!" Evilla said airily.

"Good evening, Evilla," Martin said.

"Before we begin, could I speak to the whole team?" Evilla asked.

"They're busy, and I don't have much time," Martin said. "I thought you wanted an exclusive ...?"

"Oh, you do know how to manipulate me!" Evilla laughed. "And ... you know how much I love being manipulated ...!"

"I know you use your looks and persona to manipulate others," Martin said.

"Don't you like me?" Evilla asked.

"Actually, I do," Martin said. "But I know little about you ..."

"What's there to know?" Evilla asked, and she winked. "Perhaps we should talk somewhere more ... intimate."

"In the stands," Martin said.

"Surely we could find somewhere more ... private," Evilla began.

"The stands," Martin said flatly.

Evilla's smile faltered for a second.

"Anything for you ...!" Evilla forcibly smiled.

Evilla led the way, and to Martin's annoyance, she climbed up to the first level, then continued to climb a dozen steps before she gestured for Martin to sit on a seat. He did, and to his surprise, Evilla sat right beside him and draped a long, slender arm around his shoulders.

"Must you ...?" Martin asked.

"My reputation demands it," Evilla said, yet she'd dropped her high, airy voice, although she kept her bright smile. "You wanted our interview where everyone can see us ..."

"Yes, to avoid misperceptions ...," Martin said.

"Sports is misperceptions," Evilla said. "I'm part of those perceptions ... chosen to keep all Heterodox interested. What good would our games be if no one watched ...?"

"On Earth, people pay to sit in stadiums," Martin said.

"Here, monsters who used to fight and eat each other sit together and share exciting experiences," Evilla said. "Sports brings monsters together and helps them get over their differences."

"Our sports do that, too," Martin said.

"Your presence is adding to that," Evilla said. "The human world was hated until you arrived. Monsters cursed it."

"Why?" Martin asked.

"Because of all your sophisticated toys, the countless

technologies we don't have," Evilla said. "Humans hate us. Whenever a monster has gone to your world, they seldom survived to return."

"My world doesn't know about yours," Martin said.

"That's probably for the best," Evilla said.

"Actually, there's a lot here I wish my world had," Martin said. "We have people who still fight over land and resources."

"Are we the people ... and you the monsters?" Evilla asked.

"I wouldn't want to be quoted saying that," Martin said.

"Oh, I'll make up some amusing quotes to entertain the crowd," Evilla said. "It's about you, your intentions, that I wanted to talk."

"What about me?" Martin asked.

"Do you feel the Grand Council of Wizards is using you to suit their purposes?" Evilla asked.

"I know they are," Martin said. "If my presence helps civilize Heterodox, then I support their goals."

"How long are you thinking of staying?" Evilla asked.

"I've ... never thought about it," Martin said.

"You're human," Evilla said meaningfully. "You'll grow ... soon you'll be too big to be a Small, yet you'll never be heavy enough to be a Big."

"Some humans are," Martin said, yet his voice dropped. "Not many."

"Have you ever considered staying here ...

permanently?" Evilla asked.

"Wow ...," Martin said. "I've not thought that far ahead ..."

"Will you stay as long as you can play?" Evilla asked.

"I hope so," Martin said. "I love it here."

"You seem to be fond of Veils ...?" Evilla asked.

"That's personal," Martin warned.

"My favorite type of question ...!" Evilla smiled. "And ... I heard you kissed Murder ...!"

"That was just ... friendly," Martin said. "Not what I want you talking about ..."

"This is just between us," Evilla said. "Look ahead a few years ... maybe a century; do you see Heterodox becoming like Earth?"

"I hope not," Martin said. "I mean, you could use more technologies, but monsters don't fight wars anymore. Everyone seems happy."

"You've seen little of Heterodox," Evilla said. "Imagine you're a monster and appear at a human sporting event; would whatever they see teach them everything about humans?"

"Hardly," Martin said. "I see your point."

"I asked you here to explain that point," Evilla said. "You need to understand what Heterodox is really like."

"What's the problem?" Martin asked.

"How long before our monsters get bored?" Evilla asked. "The Grand Council of Wizards has civilized them by providing for their needs ..."

"Now that their needs are met, the monsters don't know what to do with themselves?" Martin asked.

"Exactly," Evilla said. "Our society is evolving. I want to make sure we're headed in the right direction. Both you and I are part of our evolution. We have a responsibility for what Heterodox will someday become."

"How can we fulfill that responsibility?" Martin asked.

"If the Grand Council of Wizards asked you to provide them with advanced human technologies, would you?" Evilla asked.

"I don't know," Martin said. "It depends on the technology ..."

"Don't," Evilla said. "To appreciate something, it's best if it's earned."

"You want monsters to develop their technologies independently?" Martin asked.

"Selectively," Evilla said. "Let monsters learn to care for themselves ... and each other ... before they start squabbling over luxuries."

"You're not at all like I thought you were," Martin said.

To his embarrassment, Evilla hugged him tightly, pulling him against her voluptuous figure. She smiled brightly and rested her head against his. Martin struggled, wondering if every Skullcracker was watching him writhe.

"Smart people choose the image they want to

portray ... and work to maintain that image," Evilla said. "I want to make sure the popular images on Heterodox remain positive."

"Me, too," Martin said. "Too many humans choose bad role models ... characters they think will make them look cool, tough, or important."

"Role models never work in the long term," Evilla said. "You can't be someone else."

"I figured that out long ago," Martin said. "Actually, my sister helped me understand it."

"Martin, I need you," Evilla said. "I need you to be more than another athlete. I need you to be a great role model."

"On Earth, the best athletes are," Martin assured her.

Evilla smiled and hugged him again ... tightly.

"Martin ...!" Grand Wizard Bastile Wraithbone called up to him, as if on cue.

"Let's go down," Evilla nodded to Martin.

"Thank you," Martin said. "Evilla, I ... consider you a friend."

"Time for me to put on my act again," Evilla smiled, and she leaned over and kissed Martin's cheek.

Martin grimaced, and then maintained his frown all the way down the steps to Grand Wizard Bastile Wraithbone. One glance proved the whole team was watching, and he didn't want to smile ... not with Veils glaring at him.

He didn't need another bloody nose!

"I'm sorry to interrupt, but Martin has to spend his daytime in school today, which I believe starts in a few hours ...," Grand Wizard Bastile Wraithbone said.

"Not to worry," Evilla smiled. "We were just finishing ... with everything we can do in public ...!"

She wrapped her arm around Martin and again hugged him tightly.

"Excellent," Grand Wizard Bastile Wraithbone said. "Evilla, always a pleasure ...!"

"Oh, Grand Wizard Bastile Wraithbone ...!" Evilla blushed and held out her hand. "Consider me at your beck and call ... anytime!"

Grand Wizard Bastile Wraithbone didn't take her hand. He reached out and plucked Martin from her grasp.

"Come, Martin, you need to say good-bye before you go," Grand Wizard Bastile Wraithbone said.

"Of course," Evilla said. "Have fun learning today ... and remember what you've learned tonight."

"I will," Martin said, and when she extended her hand to him, Martin smiled and kissed it.

Evilla sighed dramatically, then turned and headed back the way she'd come, toward the backside of the stands. With matching smiles, Martin and Grand Wizard Bastile Wraithbone walked back so he could say good-bye.

Everyone was staring at him ... especially Veils.

"I'll try to keep practicing at home," Martin said, trying to change the unspoken subject, the reason for their stares.

"We'll keep practicing," Grand Wizard Bastile Wraithbone said. "You need to focus on learning. I appreciate your zeal, but we can't allow you to ruin your life on Earth for the sake of our games."

"I understand," Martin said, and as if he meant to prove his point, he yawned loudly.

"Say good-day," Grand Wizard Bastile Wraithbone told Martin, and he lifted his staff and wiggled his many-ringed fingers.

"Good-day!" Martin said to everyone.

Chapter 17
Rompday / Tuesday

The Net-Door Maze ...

Few inanimate objects deserve as much hatred as alarm clocks. Martin's arm shot out from under warm blankets, slapped the snooze button, and then vanished back inside.

Martin's mother's voice shouted and his bed suddenly shook. Without awakening, Martin climbed out and started to dress for school, then realized he'd put on his purple jersey. Exchanging it for a t-shirt, Martin stumbled into the kitchen and grabbed the first box of cereal he saw, not bothering to look what type it was.

"What's that ...?" his mother asked, and she came over and sniffed him. "You smell like a stable! If you're going to exercise, you need to bathe before you go to bed!"

Martin lifted his hands and sniffed them; the unmistakable scent of Happy Lostcraft filled his nose.

"Yes, mom," Martin said.

He had to wake up! He had a game tonight!

Milk. Spoon. Chew.

Hours later, Coach Anderson, Martin's gym teacher, had an obstacle course set up; run and jump over three-foot walls, climb through six tires, run across ten tires on the ground, climb a rope, and finish with a long-jump. Martin managed all with ease and ended up scoring in the top five, the other four being well-known jocks much bigger than him. On the way back to the locker room, Coach Anderson asked Martin if he'd like to try out for any of his teams.

"My mother wouldn't allow it," Martin said.

"You have a father, don't you ...?" Coach Anderson asked.

"Yes, but he wants me to wait until I'm in high school ...," Martin said.

"Well, I'll talk to him," Coach Anderson said.

Martin spent the rest of the day worrying. He couldn't attend school, practice sports after school, do all his homework, get enough sleep, and play in the Grotesquerie Games. What would he do if his dad agreed ...?

Crusto and Happy both jumped to catch Martin.

"Snitch, you missed him!" Murder shouted as voices rose in alarm.

"We shouldn't have distracted him," Grand Wizard Bastile Wraithbone said. "It's all right, Snitch; Martin's safe. Ignore the empty jersey. Wait until we're on the pitch."

Martin had half-landed with his feet touching the ground, and Happy and Crusto righted and steadied him. Blinking his eyes as he awoke, he looked around. Everyone looked ready to play ... except ...

"Like it ...?" Veils asked.

Martin stared. Veils was wearing a skin-tight, purple spandex Olympic skier's outfit with jagged black stripes.

"Well ...?" Veils asked. "Will this cut down on wind resistance?"

Martin swallowed hard, stared at her sexy outfit, and then nodded.

"Un-undoubtedly ...," Martin stammered.

Veils smiled wickedly, then assumed an exaggerated, dramatic pose.

"Will it keep you from thinking about Evilla during the game?" Veils asked in a gasping, airy voice.

Martin froze ... and everyone laughed.

"Let's ... go win!" Martin said, again hoping to change the subject.

Still laughing, they headed out together.

Cheers rose as they stepped out into the moonlight, starlight, and torchlight. Monsters jumped, shouted, and waved purple pennants.

"Here they are, the Shantdareya Skullcrackers!" Evilla cried into her microphone, atop her high, raised stand. Martin glanced at her; Evilla was wearing shiny gold with flaming red hair today ... and Veils elbowed him hard.

"We need to win ...!" Veils hissed.

"I-I'm not ... I intend ...!" Martin stammered, but Veils grabbed his arm and pulled him toward the pitch.

"Led by the ever-dignified Grand Wizard Bastile Wraithbone, the Shantdareya Skullcrackers remain undefeated!" Evilla said. "Here's the ever-popular Allfed Snitchlock, the Traumatic Terror, and Brain Stroker, ready to clot every opponent's path. Happy Lostcraft is our Super-Centaur, and few think or swim as deeply as Creepy Crusto Fernwalker! Poor Murder Shelling is still on crutches but hopes to play in the Regionals. That's Rude Stealing wearing what appears to be human armor, with the Righteous Ratling, Stabbing Kingz, and my favorite player, Martin the Magnificent! Oh, and look; it's pretty Veilscreech Hobbleswoon sporting a sexy new look! Actually, she and I had a long talk, and she thinks her full name is too formal for our tough, exciting games! Therefore, monsters of all kinds, I give you the newest member of the Shantdareya Skullcrackers, that pretty Vixen, Vibrant, Volatile, Vivacious Veils!"

Martin burst out laughing as the crowd cheered and applauded. Veils looked shocked, and angrily raised her fist, but Crusto seized her wrist.

"You wanted a different name," Crusto said.

"Not ...!" Veils started, but half the team was chuckling.

"You need to be specific when you ask for what you want," Murder said.

Veils glared at Martin.

"I didn't suggest that ...!" Martin defended.

Veils scowled and turned away.

"And here come the visitors!" Evilla cried. "Help me welcome the Gorgedown X-Lorecists! Leading them is the honorable Grand Wizard Will-Pester Batty, that Mad, Eerie Enchanter. First comes that Fem-Fatal, She-Ogre Hell N. Bursting! And standing on her shoulders is that Premier Possessor, your favorite Shadow Demon, J-Stone Swiller! And here's that Wholloping Were-Bear, Baregone Slayman, every opponent's hairiest problem! Here's your Imperial Imp, Cheater Blasterone ... he's suffered five zaps this season and only played two games! Here's my favorite Gregarious Gargoyle, Crude Old Swindler; I'll never play poker with him again! And the league's most Likable Lich, Robber Slybonds! Lastly comes Wrong Saber, that Towering, Fiery Pit Fiend! I don't see Meercreeds Microfridge; that Sneaky Shapeshifter's on injured reserve, having borne the revenge of the Roaring Giants just last week! Yet here they are, to challenge last season's winners: the Gorgedown X-Lorecists!"

The crowd roared, hooted, and squawked with delight.

Martin's eyes widened. Never had he seen a team more demonic-looking. He'd never seen a she-ogre before, and Hell N. Bursting looked like she could pick Brain up and throw him across the pitch. J-Stone Swiller was tiny with devilish-red skin and short, stubby horns, wearing a long black robe under his sickly-green and red jersey, looking oddly formal for a player in any game. Baregone Slayman looked like a real Kodiak bear on two legs, thick black fur, muzzle full of teeth, and claws that could shred bark off trees. Cheater Blasterone was also a Small, a thin, shadowy wisp with an evil grin, and Crude Old Swindler looked like the meanest gargoyle ever carved onto any cathedral. Robber Slybonds wore a concealing hood, yet looked like a corpse whose skin had withered away, and Wrong Saber stood as tall as Snitch, as muscular as Happy, and resembled every fantasy drawing Martin had ever seen of a powerful, fiery, muscle-bulging devil.

"Here we are, two great teams to meet in that challenging puzzle that tears players into pieces, that captures all into capitulation, Net-Door Maze, in the Locals of the three hundred and fifteenth season of the Grotesquerie Games!" Evilla shouted.

The crowd cheered.

"Ropes and chains; you can tell this is my favorite game!" Evilla smiled, striking another pose to the delight of her fans. "Locked doors, bindings, and inescapable traps; what a wonderful way to spend an evening! And I'm glad you're here to share this adventure with me ... may it last all night! So cozy up ... preferably by me ... with overflowing tankards of Chameleon Caffeines, flagons of Cannibal Cola, and a bowl of Sugar Skunks ... and hold tight, because it's about to get ram-m-m-m-m-m-bunctious!"

"Martin, hang back," Grand Wizard Bastile

Wraithbone said. "With Rude in, and Veils wearing her new outfit, I want her in the first half. You'll replace her in the second half. Snitch is waiting, too. He'll go in with you."

Martin frowned yet nodded; no one could play all the time. Stabbing had the most experience. Rude knew the strategies. Veils had her new outfit. Neither he nor Veils had played an entire season, so it was fair they each shared one half.

Murder stood beside him, leaning on her crutches; if not playing was frustrating for him, she must be feeling tortured.

Stabbing, Rude, and Veils carried their rope nets to the entrance to the Net-Door Maze building. Dragging noisy chain nets, behind the Smalls walked Brain, Happy, and Crusto.

"Get ready for excitement!" Evilla cried. "I see raised wands and staffs! Here comes the horn! Let the mayhem begin!"

The Shantdareya Skullcrackers ran through the wide doorway outlined in yellow into the maze.

"Hey, we can't see the other team!" Martin objected.

"If you try, you'll be zapped," Murder said. "Even Grand Wizard Bastile Wraithbone isn't allowed to see; that's the point of the maze!"

"Smalls are testing the doors, peering through them!" Evilla cried. "Will they suddenly shut? Will they lock? We'll see ...!"

Stabbing, Rude, and Veils each took a different wall, examining its doors, stepping through each to test them. Then Stabbing and Rude came back and drew marks on the wall on both sides. Veils closed a door behind her and didn't reopen it.

"A red door!" Grand Wizard Bastile Wraithbone scowled.

"Must be," Murder agreed. "She would've reopened it if she ... *Snitch, no ...!*"

"No, Snitch!" Grand Wizard Bastile Wraithbone called. "Stop! Come back! Stand by me!"

Snitch hesitated, looking as if he wanted to run onto the pitch, but Martin was sure four Bigs in play would be a foul. Reluctantly Snitch came back and stood by them.

Crusto and Happy ran to the walls, pressing against them, seeing if they would move.

"Moves!" Happy shouted, and he marked it with a red pen.

"Moves!" Crusto shouted, and he marked his wall with a blue pen.

"Brain!" Stabbing's face appeared in a doorway. "Brain, this way!"

Brain ran through the door, following Stabbing as he vanished.

"Stabbing is exploring closest to enemy territory, so Brain is going to protect him," Grand Wizard Bastile Wraithbone said to Martin. "But he won't be going far; it's part of Rude's strategy."

Trying to watch, Martin waved away a dragonfly

buzzing near him, yet both Crusto and Happy vanished through other doors Stabbing and Rude had marked as safe.

"Hell N. Bursting is moving a wall!" Evilla shouted. "It's unusually early for that, but I'm sure she's got a reason. J-Stone Swiller is running about, testing doors, and ... Baregone Slayman is trapped! Those maroon doors are treacherous! Bigs don't usually risk untested doors! The Gorgedown X-Lorecists must have something devious planned!"

Snitch looked ready to run onto the pitch again; Martin circled Grand Wizard Bastile Wraithbone and grabbed Snitch's littlest finger.

"Wait for halftime!" Martin told Snitch. "We go in together, you and me!"

Snitch grunted softly, staring longingly into the empty pitch. They could see nothing but empty walls and doors.

"Vivacious Veils is trapped!" Evilla cried. "That's ten minutes she's out of the game, locked behind a maroon door! Stabbing Kingz is moving deep, but so is Robber Slybonds! It looks like both teams have big surprises planned!"

Martin glanced behind him and up at the crowd. The raised stands were so high he had to rise onto his toes to see more than the first few rows leaning over to look down. The monsters looked delighted, fixated on the game, waving pennants of their team's colors ... mostly purple, as this was a home game. Others had hands, claws, pincers, and tentacles full of small boxes of Devilish Demon Drops, greasy bags of Manticore Meatballs, Kamikaze Kobold Knishes, and tall cups of frosty Slug-Sting Shakes or Larva Lemonade. The larger monsters bounced excitedly on their low chairs, the smallest standing on their high seats, all with horns, feelers, and antennas rising over bulging eyes, fanged mouths, suckers, and unnerving, clicking pincers. Yet few looked down at Martin; all were watching the game.

Martin envied the fans. They could see how the doors were marked, peer into hidden rooms and corridors, observe the players advance toward each other from a perspective Martin wasn't allowed.

"Baregone Slayman is freed!" Evilla cried. "Vivacious Veils is still stuck, only a few minutes left for her. Oh! Cheater Blasterone, that impetuous imp, is trapped! That's bad timing for the Gorgedown X-Lorecists!"

Martin understood; soon the Smalls would regroup to compare notes.

"First sight!" Evilla cried. "Robber Slybonds opens a door and sees Stabbing! Both raise nets, swinging them over their heads! Robber Slybonds is advancing, Stabbing moving back. Yet both are in range ... who will cast first?"

Martin squeezed on Snitch's littlest finger, although he doubted if the huge troll noticed.

"Stabbing's net is caught on an open door!" Evilla shouted. "Robber Slybonds is charging ... Stabbing Kingz is running away! You can see what's about to happen ...! There ...! Robber Slybonds spies Brain Stroker! Brain's heavy chain net swings ... almost a hit! Robber Slybonds dodged ... now he's running back! Brain Stroker is chasing him, followed by Stabbing! Stabbing Kingz knew Brain was there! He lured Robber Slybonds into a trap! Now both are running, and Stabbing is getting his first view of the Gorgedown X-Lorecists side of the pitch! This may prove a major advantage!"

"Snitch, it's time to roar!" Grand Wizard Bastile Wraithbone said. "As loud as you can ... roar!"

Snitch looked down, a puzzled expression on his face.

"Roar for me!" Murder said to Snitch. "Show me how big and strong you are! Roar ...!"

Snitch took in a deep breath, and Grand Wizard Bastile Wraithbone and Murder both covered their ears. Martin did likewise.

Snitch rose to his full, impressive height, his massive fists clenched, and burst with a roar to startle and frighten most of the monsters in the stands.

"That must be their signal!" Evilla shouted when Snitch's roar concluded. "Yes! Stabbing Kingz and Brain Stroker are retreating! Now comes the thinking part of this game! Veils is released. She's running back, holding something high ... Yes! Vivacious Veils has the zombie head! We're facing an early start to the scoring!"

Soon all the Skullcrackers came running back into the main room, visible through the yellow-rimmed open doorway. Instantly they dropped to their knees and began drawing marks on the floor.

The crowd's cheers softened; nothing exciting happened while plans were made. Martin was glad Rude was out there; he'd be no use devising a maze-strategy to help them win.

Minutes later, Happy, Crusto, and Brain ran to the farthest wall and started to push it. They slid it back at least fifteen feet, then turned and ran through doors on the left side wall. Stabbing, Rude, and Veils stayed on their knees, pointing out details and arguing; Martin wished he could hear them.

"Be nice, monsters!" Evilla said. "Watch, but no signaling! Each team is on their own, and must discover the other team's plans only when they meet. That's when the thrills happen, and as you know, there's nothing I enjoy more than a night of tantalizing thrills! So calm yourselves with a fresh bag of Barbequed Battered Batwings, a Rancid Rum, and a shot glass of Never-Say-No New Eye of Newt! Keep your claws clenched, because the fun is about to begin!"

Stabbing got up and ran after Happy, Crusto, and Brain. He vanished through the red door but left it open. Rude and Veils kept arguing, pointing at their hastily-drawn map, and eventually Brain and Crusto came running back. Rude and Veils rose, joined them, and together they vanished through another door into the right side of the pitch. Then the whole wall began moving, pushed from the other side five feet into the large room.

"Both teams are rearranging the walls!" Evilla said. "The maze is taking shape, growing in complexity! I don't know how this is going to work out! Hallways are being lengthened! Key doors are being blocked! Look what's happening! I dare say no more! This will be an interesting half!"

Chapter 18
Stompday / Monday

A Nest of Nets ...

Stabbing and Crusto burst out of a door on the left side, crossed the big room at a run, and vanished into the door on the other side. Long minutes passed.

"The game is on!" Evilla cried as the crowd jumped to its feet, cheering wildly. "Look at them run! Never have I seen a more complex maze!"

The game went on, yet the main entrance stayed empty. Martin wished he could see his teammates, or even encourage them, but to no avail. The cheers of the crowd told him he was missing some exciting action.

Then the worst news of all reached his ears.

"The Shantdareya Skullcrackers are caught!" Evilla cried. "Hell N. Bursting and Crude Old Swindler have moved a long wall sideways, cutting the Skullcrackers in half! Stabbing Kingz, Happy Lostcraft, and Crusto Fernwalker are cut off, trapped in a room without doors! All of the Gorgedown X-Lorecists are converging on Brain Stroker, Rude Stealing, and Vivacious Veils, two to one!"

Martin's jaw fell. *They were in trouble ...!*
Veils could get hurt ...!

"The Gorgedown X-Lorecists built a trap for the Skullcrackers!" Evilla shouted. "Happy Lostcraft and Crusto Fernwalker are pushing walls, trying to find an opening! Brain Stroker is swinging his chains over his head, but he's alone facing Hell N. Bursting, Baregone Slayman, and Crude Old Swindler!"

"Martin, grab Snitch!" Murder shouted. "Snitch, grab Martin!"

Martin hadn't even noticed he'd started forward, but suddenly the huge hand of Snitch circled around him and picked him up. Martin struggled, yet no human could out-muscle a troll.

"Veils jumps into the thick of it!" Evilla screamed. "Vivacious Veils has jumped ... I don't believe it! Vivacious Veils jumped four times, once atop the center of each swinging chain net! She's passed overtop both the Bigs and Smalls of the Gorgedown X-Lorecists! Vivacious Veils has the zombie head ... and she's running to score!"

The crowd went insane. Screams, roars, shouts, bellows, and caws of every description deafened Evilla's loudspeakers. Martin writhed against Snitch's grip, yet couldn't break free.

"J-Stone Swiller, Cheater Blasterone, and Robber Slybonds are chasing Vivacious Veils!" Evilla cried. "Their trap exposed a mostly-clear route ... if Vivacious

Veils can find it in time! Will she get trapped? No, she sees the yellow door! Three Smalls on her tail, only paces away ... Vivacious Veils scores!"

Cheers burst from the stands.

"Bigs are dueling!" Evilla shouted. "What's this? Brain is going after Hell N. Bursting! Ogre against ogre, him against her! That hallway's too narrow! Chain nets are flying! Oh! Hell N. Bursting catches one against her face! Hell N. Bursting is down! Brain is raising his net again! No! Baregone Slayman's chains knocked down Brain!

"Rude Stealing is fleeing backwards! Wait, he stopped! He's taunting Baregone Slayman! That were-bear means business ... he's chasing Rude! Rude Stealing runs ... it's a long way back! Looks like he's going all the way! He's in the main room. Baregone is chasing him! Can that human armor endure a chain net? Are we going to see a death ...?"

Rude ran across the big room and vanished through the first door Veils had first tried. The huge, hairy bear chased after him. However, suddenly Rude jumped out of the door and closed it behind him.

"It's a red door!" Evilla shouted. "Goblin Small Rude Stealing traps werebear Baregone Slayman!"

Veils came running around the outside of the building.

"Veils, wait!" Grand Wizard Bastile Wraithbone shouted. "Delay! Another minute ...!"

Martin glanced up at the game-timer; Veils had fifty

more seconds before she had to enter the pitch ... or she'd suffer a foul. She bounced from foot to foot, eager to rejoin, as Rude ran toward the door back to Brain, but suddenly the huge gargoyle came through, spreading his wide batwings to block Rude's path.

"Crude Old Swindler blocks Rude Stealing!" Evilla shouted. "He's swinging his net ... but not advancing! Crude Old Swindler is defending the door! Brain Stroker is down, Hell N. Bursting standing over him, and the Gorgedown X-Lorecists Smalls are searching the pitch, looking for the zombie head! Where will it appear?"

"Veils, now ...!" Grand Wizard Bastile Wraithbone shouted, and Veils charged inside.

"Lucky break! The zombie head appeared right in front of J-Stone Swiller! The Gorgedown X-Lorecists have the advantage! Everyone is running to score!"

Veils ran to Rude, but neither could do anything. Crude Old Swindler was guarding the only door accessing their sole route through the maze, shaking his clanking chain net. As they watched in horror, J-Stone Swiller came running out from behind the gargoyle carrying the zombie head. They moved to cut him off, but the gargoyle charged them, swinging his net, aiming at Veils. Rude jumped in front of her, and the net of chain crashed down upon him.

"Rude blocks for Veils ... Rude is smashed!" Evilla cried. "J-Stone Swiller scores!"

Skullcracker screams rose and were lost among the

exultation of the crowd. The gargoyle raised his chain net again, then glanced at the referees.

"Wands are pointing!" Evilla cried. "Will Crude Old Swindler risk a zap for striking a prone opponent? No, he's stepping back, away from Rude Stealing! Veils is running to help ... what's this? Rude is standing up!"

The crowd gasped. Rude looked shaky, but Veils grabbed and supported him. They backed away from the gargoyle lest it attack again.

"Only two Smalls of the Shantdareya Skullcrackers remain against all of the Gorgedown X-Lorecists!" Evilla cried. "J-Stone Swiller runs around the outside ... Cheater Blasterone and Robber Slybonds are already fanning out, looking for the zombie head. Where will it appear? Happy Lostcraft and Crusto Fernwalker have moved every wall and still haven't found a combination to let them escape! Will they be trapped until half-time?"

Suddenly the red door burst open and the huge bear ran out, swinging his chain net.

"Baregone Slayman is free ... and Robber Slybonds finds the zombie head!" Evilla cried. "He and Crude Old Swindler are swinging their chain nets, chasing ... No! Rude Stealing and Vivacious Veils have run inside and closed the red door! They've trapped themselves ... to spare them from the chains of Baregone Slayman! That's ten minutes they're out, and only nine minutes left before the end of the first half! But how many times can the Gorgedown X-Lorecists score ...?"

To Martin's disbelief, Robber Slybonds scored, then Cheater Blasterone scored another, and J-Stone Swiller scored again.

Finally the horn blew.

"Half-time!" Evilla shouted. "The Gorgedown X-Lorecists are slaughtering the Shantdareya Skullcrackers, 4 - 1!"

The hometown crowd was angry, shouting nastily and calling names. Snitch released Martin, who stomped to face Grand Wizard Bastile Wraithbone.

"Veils could've been killed ...!" Martin shouted.

"Rude almost died," Grand Wizard Bastile Wraithbone said, his voice just as distressed.

"Martin, calm down," Murder said. "All doors and walls open at half-time to free trapped players; look, here they come."

Veils and Rude came walking out of the building, looking furious. Rude looked battered but otherwise fine.

"Don't lose your heads!" Grand Wizard Bastile Wraithbone warned them all. "This game isn't over! Most scores in Net-Door Maze happen in the second half ...!"

"Usually ...!" Veils snarled.

"We're down by three," Murder said. "We haven't lost yet."

"I don't know what happened," Rude said, waving a dragonfly away.

Stabbing, Happy, and Crusto came stomping out.

Happy and Crusto had Brain slung over their shoulders, helping him walk. Brain was limping, and looked sore and beaten.

"The referees released us," Stabbing said.

"They knew our plan!" Happy snarled. "There's no other way ...!"

"Rude's plan was great," Crusto hissed. "We blocked their main route, then opened the right-side wall. Somehow they cut us off. If that was pure chance, it was the luckiest break I've ever seen!"

"What's our plan for the second half?" Grand Wizard Bastile Wraithbone asked.

"Rude has it all planned," Stabbing said. "We close off the route we used and switch to the left wall, then cut back to center. They shouldn't be expecting that."

"What if it doesn't work?" Happy snarled.

"It has to ... or we're out of the Regionals," Murder said.

"Rude ... are you all right?" Martin asked.

"It was ... touch and go," Rude said. "Thanks, Martin. If not for your armor, I'd be dead."

"Or I'd have gotten chained," Veils said. "Thanks, Rude."

"Can you play ...?" Grand Wizard Bastile Wraithbone asked.

"I can ... but if I get hit again ...!" Rude shook his head.

"Rude is out," Grand Wizard Bastile Wraithbone said. "Stabbing, can you lead the team?"

"Veils and I studied his map before we scuffed it out," Stabbing said. "We can execute Rude's plan, but if anything goes wrong, if we need to invent a new plan ...!"

"We must prevail!" Grand Wizard Bastile Wraithbone said. "Rude, give Martin his armor. Martin, don't take chances, but help our Bigs, especially Snitch. We need to trap their Bigs, and without Brain ...!"

Half-time was almost over before Martin finished putting on his armor.

"Martin, Veils, find the zombie head," Stabbing said. "I'll lead the Bigs. We plug up their route first, then open the new path for us."

Martin nodded, picked up his rope net, and went to stand before the pitch. Stabbing stood on one side of him, Veils on the other. Happy, Crusto, and Snitch stood behind them, their chain nets clanking.

The horn blew.

"Let the chaos continue!" Evilla shouted.

Martin ran inside and to the right, Stabbing and Veils to the left. All their Bigs chased after them, leaving Martin alone. He ran through the red door, careful not to close it behind him, and began searching every room. He avoided any door marked as maroon, but dashed through every other opening.

"Martin ...!" the zombie head called.

The zombie head was floating at Martin's chest-height in the center of a small room.

"There you are!" Martin shouted, and he ran in and

grabbed him.

"Good to see you ... usually!" the zombie head said. "Strangest game I ever saw ...!"

Carrying the zombie head, Martin ran back into the main room and found Stabbing and Veils on their knees over the floorplan, which they'd redrawn.

"I got it!" Martin cried, showing off the zombie head.

"Good!" Stabbing said. "They're closing all access to these rooms, then we'll open a path to score ..."

"We must score quickly and get the zombie head again!" Veils insisted.

"I'm rooting for you, but I can't control where I appear," the zombie head said.

"Every bit helps!" Martin said.

Happy, Crusto, and Snitch came out the door. Crusto had Snitch stick his hand back inside and shove hard at a wall beside the door. Then Snitch yanked his arm out and Happy slammed the door shut.

"No one's coming in from that side!" Crusto said, and he scuffed his foot across the drawn floorplan.

"Let's go!" Stabbing said, taking off running.

They ran through the main door on the left, then hurried to the doors they'd blocked. Stabbing directed from memory, and Happy, Crusto, and Snitch hurriedly moved more walls. They exposed two doors they'd blocked, then found small rooms with doors carefully marked. Happy, Crusto, and Snitch expanded these rooms into narrow hallways.

"This is the outer wall," Stabbing told Veils, pointing at a wall. "We need to open this wall another ten feet, then block the route forward, and clear a path toward the center."

"What if they blocked the center?" Happy growled.

"According to Rude, there's always one path that can't be entirely blocked," Stabbing said. "We'll have to find it ... fast!"

Holding the zombie head, Martin stood back. The walls moved slowly and took a great deal of muscle; all the Smalls working together probably couldn't move one. Yet slowly their path opened up.

"We're almost through!" Stabbing said. "Veils, clear Martin's way. Martin, if Veils gets ahead of you, throw the zombie head to her. I'll try to distract ... and shout if I get in the clear. Snitch, you stay with Martin! You understand? Stay with Martin!"

"Martin ...," Snitch nodded.

"Good!" Stabbing said. "Get ready; there's no telling where they are."

Happy and Crusto pushed the last wall aside, and Stabbing jumped forward and opened the door.

Crash ...!

A chain net smashed against the door as it opened, almost striking Stabbing.

With cries of fury, Crusto charged through the door, swinging his chain net. Happy charged right behind him, swinging his net, and Stabbing jumped onto Happy's back, swinging his rope net. Veils ran next,

Martin carrying the zombie head behind her, and Snitch smashed through the doorway so hard his shoulders left cracks in its frame.

Utter chaos reigned. Hell N. Bursting, Baregone Slayman, and Crude Old Swindler were fighting Happy and Crusto. Snitch roared and ran into the fray, his swinging chain net striking the gargoyle and knocking him into the huge bear.

Stabbing was already trapped in a rope net. Veils tossed her net completely over J-Stone Swiller's head, which looped around the head of Cheater Blasterone, who was standing behind him. Veils yanked hard and pulled both down.

Martin ran forward, net in one hand, zombie head in the other. Before him stood Robber Slybonds, the skin-shriveled corpse, the lich, swinging his rope net over his death's head skull.

Martin didn't have time to play safe. He feinted, then flung his net. Robber Slybonds ducked his throw, then threw his; Martin dodged aside, purposefully aiming his path. Robber Slybonds had stepped atop Martin's fallen net, and Martin suddenly yanked with all his weight. Shrieking in fury, Robber Slybonds tripped and fell, and Martin abandoned his net and ran, both hands gripping the zombie head.

The long path led them to the main room of the Gorgedown X-Lorecists. Martin lowered his head and dashed for their yellow-rimmed door, deafened by the chaos behind him. He didn't dare pause to look behind.

"Martin the Magnificent scores!" Evilla cried. "Two to four, yet the Gorgedown X-Lorecists are still in the lead!"

"Bye ..!" the zombie head said, and with a flash of white light, it vanished from Martin's hands.

Martin ran around the outside as fast as he could. The zombie head wouldn't reappear until he entered the other door and they couldn't wait a second longer than necessary. Heavy footfalls pounded in his wake, and Martin glanced back to see Snitch running only a few paces behind him. He grinned; Stabbing had told Snitch to stay with Martin ... and he'd probably need him when he reentered the pitch.

"Vivacious Veils has trapped J-Stone Swiller!" Evilla shouted. "Stabbing is still entangled, but Happy Lostcraft and Crusto are facing three: Hell N. Bursting, Baregone Slayman, and Crude Old Swindler ...! The Gorgedown X-Lorecists are driving them back ...!"

It was crazy! Martin thought. The Gorgedown X-Lorecists had all been there ... waiting ... as if they knew where ...!

"Martin ...!" Rude shouted as he dashed around the corner.

Rude tossed him a new rope net. Martin caught it and ran inside, Snitch right behind him. He headed to the open door, seeing nothing in the main room but the dragonfly hovering low in the middle.

Martin skidded to a halt. The dragonfly was hovering ... right over the scuffed map they'd drawn on the floor. He ran toward it, raised his net, and swung ...!

Too late the dragonfly tried to escape. Martin's thick rope net crashed down on it. When Martin yanked his net back, there it lay ... on the stone floor ... stunned but not splatted ...!

Unusually tough for a dragonfly ...!

Martin reached down, grabbed the stunned dragonfly, and lifted it to stare at it. He squeezed his hand, trying to crush it ... but he couldn't ...!

"Snitch ...!" Martin cried. "Open your mouth! Now! I need you to eat something ...!"

Snitch hesitated, looking confused. Martin ran to him, holding the dragonfly tightly.

"Snitch, open your mouth ...!" Martin cried.

"What is this?" Evilla asked. "Martin is trying to feed Snitch ... in the middle of a game? The Skullcrackers don't have time to waste ...!"

Snitch opened his huge mouth. Martin drew back to throw ...!

Suddenly the dragonfly swelled, expanded, and grew large. Inside Martin's grip it shifted its shape ... to something humanoid. Where Martin had been squeezing a tiny dragonfly, suddenly he found himself holding the throat of a slick, gelatinous man who looked like he was made of thick maple syrup.

"Meercreeds Microfridge ...!" Evilla cried. "That's Meercreeds Microfridge, the demon shapeshifter ...! That's four Smalls on the pitch for the Gorgedown X-Lorecists ...! What's going on here ...? Referees ...!"

A moment later, a huge yellow zap of lightning struck, hitting Martin, Meercreeds Microfridge, and Snitch ... and the walls, doors, and floor. The entire pitch and everyone on it twitched, zapped. Martin cried out, but it was the lightest zap he'd ever felt, more like lightning bolts from Trip-Hook Roller than a punishment from the referees, probably because it was so diffused.

"The referees stopped the game ...!" Evilla cried. "There's going to be an investigation ...!"

The referees turned their wands on themselves. They levitated upwards and floated towards the Skullcracker main room. Martin saw them clearly for the first time; one looked like a blonde alien and the other had insectoid features.

"He was that dragonfly!" Martin shouted at them, still holding Meercreeds Microfridge by his slimy, gelatinous throat. "He's been buzzing around us the whole time, spying on our strategy!"

"Martin ...!" Grand Wizard Bastile Wraithbone shouted. *"Release Meercreeds Microfridge ...! Now ...!"*

Martin released his grip. The oily demon stepped back, his expression terrified, looking up at the two referees, both of whom were floating toward him.

"Martin, take Snitch and go get the rest of our team," Grand Wizard Bastile Wraithbone said. "Take everyone outside and stay by Murder and Rude. I'll talk to the referees."

Martin knew better than to refuse. He grabbed

Snitch, pulled, and finally led him through the nearest door, following the route they'd opened.

"The referees are gathering with Grand Wizard Bastile Wraithbone and Meercreeds Microfridge!" Evilla announced. "Grand Wizard Will-Pester Batty is walking around the pitch to join them! This will be a serious council! The last Grand Wizard accused of cheating was the infamous Prank N. Strain, who lost his team and was banished from the Grand Council of Wizards! Will we witness a duel? What will happen now ...?"

When Martin led Snitch into the Gorgedown X-Lorecists' main room, he found every player on both teams standing still, just staring at each other.

"Master Bastile wants us, all the Skullcrackers, to gather by Murder and Rude," Martin said, pointing at the big door. "This way."

Without a word, everyone exchanged glances, and then Crusto and Happy led the way out their yellow-lined door and around the outside. Veils, Stabbing, Martin, and Snitch followed. His last glance at the Gorgedown X-Lorecists showed them looking horrified and ashamed.

They gathered together, all of the Skullcrackers, while Grand Wizard Bastile Wraithbone conferred with the referees, Grand Wizard Will-Pester Batty, and Meercreeds Microfridge. No one could hear anything over the angry catcalls from the crowd.

Everyone looked furious, and only Grand Wizard Will-Pester Batty spoke loudly.

"I didn't ...!" Grand Wizard Will-Pester Batty shouted. *"I'd never ...!"*

At a wave of a referee's wand, the stands fell silent, every monster still as if stricken. No one outside the pitch spoke.

Finally both referees came walking out, off the pitch. They walked around the corner and headed toward Evilla's stand.

Striking Meercreeds Microfridge with his staff, Grand Wizard Will-Pester Batty forced him back, and both vanished through the left door Martin had taken.

Grand Wizard Bastile Wraithbone calmly walked out of the building, a serious frown on his face. Several opened their mouths to ask, yet Grand Wizard Bastile Wraithbone waved for silence, then closed his eyes and leaned on his staff.

"Here's the chief referee," Evilla said into her microphone. "Let's hear what's happened."

A woman's voice Martin had never heard before came over the loudspeakers.

"This game is ended," the insectoid referee said. "An accusation of cheating has been made, and sufficient evidence exists to support it. Pending a higher ruling, the Gorgedown X-Lorecists are hereby banned from all games for the rest of the Locals, and all points they scored tonight are forfeit. Grand Wizard Will-Pester Batty may appeal this ruling to the Grand Council of Wizards, but no further discussion will be allowed today. The Shantdareya Skullcrackers are declared the winner.

Final score: 2 - 0. Please turn off this sound system and clear the stadium immediately, promptly, and with as little argument as possible. This concludes all business and all discussion for this game. Thank you."

Loud boos and catcalls followed this announcement, but Grand Wizard Bastile Wraithbone finally opened his eyes and obediently headed toward the locker room. Every Skullcracker followed.

A New Perspective ...

After dinner, in Vicky's bedroom, she and Martin spoke in whispers.

"Banned ...?" Vicky asked.

"Permanently," Martin confirmed. "Meercreeds Microfridge won't even be allowed inside any stadium ... ever again. We discussed it in the locker room until half-time of the next game. That's why I got home so late ... and then I couldn't sleep."

"You need sleep," Vicky insisted. "I know what it means to be half-asleep in school because of Zantheriak. You can't afford that. Heterodox will always be there, but you need to focus on here, too. Lack of sleep means you won't pass tests ..."

"I stayed awake today, but it was hard," Martin said. "I'm not sure if I'll remember what we covered."

"Take copious notes so you can review them later," Vicky said. "So, do you think the X-Lorecists players knew ...?"

"Not all of them," Martin said. "You'd think a female ogre, a shadow demon, a werebear, an imp, a gargoyle, and a lich couldn't look innocent ... yet they did. But someone knew ...!"

"How embarrassing!" Vicky shook her head. "They've lost their whole season ... and maybe their careers ...!"

"There'll be a hearing," Martin said. "I don't know if they use truth spells, but I'd be surprised if they don't have them ..."

"The defendant is also a wizard," Vicky said. "Magic and science have different, but similar, weaknesses."

"It's hard to feel sympathy for them," Martin said.

"How would you feel if you were falsely accused of cheating ...?" Vicky said. "I feel sorry for the other players. We can't decide their guilt or innocence; never assume either until you have strong evidence."

"I'll try," Martin said. "Tonight, I'm going to bed early."

"Excellent idea," Vicky said.

Martin fell into Snitch's hands, then was lowered to the floor. Around him stood the whole team. Rude and Brain were covered in bruises, and the rest looked unhappy.

"Grand Wizard Will-Pester Batty has refused a formal hearing with the Grand Council of Wizards," Grand Wizard Bastile Wraithbone told Martin, and from their lack of reaction, Martin guessed everyone else already knew. "A formal hearing could've cleared him. However, Grand Wizard Will-Pester Batty departed for Gorgedown Valley ... and is blocking all attempts at communication."

"What will happen to him?" Martin asked.

"A hearing shall convene with or without him," Grand Wizard Bastile Wraithbone said. "Under pressure from the rest of the team, Meercreeds Microfridge has agreed to testify. He claims his teammates knew nothing, although they were suspicious when Grand Wizard Will-Pester Batty's strange instructions worked so well."

"Brain ...?" Martin asked. "Rude ...?"

"We'll be fine," Rude said. "We've already enjoyed some healing spells. We just need a few days rest."

"The Gorgedown X-Lorecists are out for the season," Grand Wizard Bastile Wraithbone said. "If they do play next year, Grand Wizard Will-Pester Batty won't be coaching them. If he confesses to cheating he'll receive the same lifetime ban as Meercreeds Microfridge."

"What about the other games?" Martin asked.

"The Greasy Golems easily beat the Knights of the Unliving Dread," Happy said. "Maxivoom Snydho scored almost every point. Then the Flying Munchers beat the Roaring Giants, but it was a near miss. Sir Green Friskers, Trick-Tok, and Princess Bogzma ganged up on Cleave Revile in the last few minutes and trapped him halfway through a doorway as Queen Fried-Lice moved its wall; Cleave was crushed ... and almost died."

"In their first attempt to score, Sir Green Friskers and Trick-Tok netted Ruddy Max-Scowall, their best Small, and tossed him into a locked room with Princess Bogzma, who chain-netted him," Stabbing said. "He needed a healing spell and was still out for the rest of the game."

"We face the Roaring Giants next," Murder said. "Bad for us ... they've lost twice and are itching for a victory."

"Worse for us: the Greasy Golems were supposed to play the Gorgedown X-Lorecists on Rompday," Veils said. "Now, our worst threat gets a free week to rest and practice."

"The Knights of the Unliving Dread face the Flying Munchers, but they're both out of the Regionals," Stabbing said. "The Knights have lost three and the Munchers have lost two; impossible to move on from there."

"Our next match is Savage Sumo," Crusto said. "Martin, this is a game like none you've seen. It's a series of individual contests, not a team competition. Before play, each team chooses three Bigs and three Smalls. No one else can play. The field is a raised stone circle over a deep lake. One-on-one, each Big must face each of the other team's Bigs, and try to toss them off the stone circle down into the water. If one remains dry while their opponent plunges, the winning team get two points and their opponents get none. If both plunge, each team gets one point. After the round-robin of Bigs, Smalls contest. After the round-robin of Smalls, the Smalls of each team must face each other once more, but they don't win by tossing the other off. This time the zombie head sits in the center, and on each side hangs a basket. The team with the most points gets their basket lowered five feet, within easy range, and the other team's basket is raised five feet; otherwise both are ten feet above the platform. If both competitors fall into the lake, the next pair of Smalls compete. If three matches of Smalls fail to produce a victor, then the Bigs do the same. The game ends when one team gets the zombie head into their basket. If the zombie head falls into the lake, then the match is over."

"Savage Sumo," Martin said. "They play sumo in our ... in the human world. I can research it ..."

"Please do," Rude said. "We need every advantage we can get."

"Group strategies won't help here," Happy said. "Even if we win every match, we still have to basket the zombie head ... or lose."

"That sounds like basketball ... in my world," Martin said. "I've played of lot of that ..."

"Wait until you see the pitch," Rude said.

Together they walked outside ... slowly, as Murder walked on her crutches.

"Good thing we're not facing the Greasy Golems

this week," Stabbing said. "Size matters in Savage Sumo
... and Maxivoom Snydho is the heaviest Small ... and
Ton Eat-oddly is the heaviest Big."

They emerged from the locker room into a stadium
Martin almost didn't recognize. The stands were now
circular, wrapping tightly around a concrete-edged lake.
In the center of the lake rose a thick pillar supporting a
round platform of flat stone, twenty feet in diameter, ten
feet from the outside edge of the lake, and ten feet above
the water. On each side stood a twenty foot tall, narrow
stone pole with a basket on its side. Over one basket
was a purple flag. Over the other basket was a flag of
pink and orange stripes.

"Pink and orange ...?" Martin asked.

"The Roaring Giants' colors," Murder said.

On each side was a slanted wooden ramp, leaning
away toward empty air. Happy grabbed and rotated the
closest ramp with ease, turning it so it touched the
platform, and all the Smalls climbed up its steep slope.

Crusto was right; Martin had never played a game
like this. Up here, teamwork wouldn't matter. This
would be player against player ... with no backup.

Martin stared at the empty stands, imagining them
filled with monsters ... whose attentions wouldn't be
diffused by multiple, simultaneous confrontations.

Twenty feet in diameter: the circle was too big for
human sumo, huge for smalls, but would be tight for
Bigs. Two trolls would barely have enough room.

He glanced down at the water; he wasn't afraid of

splashing in or getting wet. He was afraid of failing ... with every eye watching him.

"Rude and Stabbing!" Grand Wizard Bastile Wraithbone shouted from below. "Show Martin how it's done."

"We stand back," Veils said to Martin. "We mustn't interfere."

Stabbing and Rude faced off, pacing each other around the circular stone platform. Martin and Veils edged away whenever they came close, but a full minute passed before they stepped close enough to touch each other. Each made numerous grabs at the other's arms, but none succeeded. When they finally grabbed each other, they began wrestling like kids, pushing back and forth.

Suddenly they simultaneously tripped. As they rolled over and over, Martin stared, confused. He was no expert on sumo, but he was certain human professionals didn't wrestle like that.

Stabbing's longer claws clung better, and finally he ripped Rude's jersey. Rude's longer legs triumphed; he kicked Stabbing over the edge. The ratling fell out of sight. A second later, a loud splash sounded. Rude jumped to his feet.

"That's how you do it," Veils said.

Martin looked down over the edge at Stabbing, soaking wet, climbing out of the pool. He didn't know what to say.

"Martin and Veils!" Grand Wizard Bastile

Wraithbone said. "Give it a try."

Rude grinned at him, then stepped back, giving them room.

With one glance, Veils jumped at Martin, catching him unprepared for her attack. She pushed him hard, near to the edge, but he easily circled until she was pushing him toward center, which nullified her attack. He kept circling backwards, then braced his feet and pushed back against her.

Veils was fast and agile. She kept altering her angle of attack, but she was physically smaller; an inch shorter and thinner. Yet she was strong for her size. Martin resisted her pushes, then twisted and let her slip past him, bent low. As she flailed, he bent over her back and wrapped his arms around her waist. Then he lifted her, holding her aloft upside-down, her back pressed against his chest. Veils elbowed his ribs and kicked at his head, but he simply carried her to the edge. Yet he couldn't drop her, especially not on her head. Martin stepped backwards and set her down.

"You have to drop her off ...!" Rude instructed.

"I got that ... but ...," Martin stammered.

"What's going on up there ...?" Grand Wizard Bastile Wraithbone asked.

"Enough ...!" Happy and Crusto shouted together, and both looked at each other.

"Let Martin speak," Crusto said, and Happy nodded in agreement.

All eyes looked up at Martin, standing on the edge

of the platform.

"Well ...," Martin fumbled for words. "It's nothing ... just what my dad taught me ..."

"What was that?" Crusto asked, speaking loudly despite his native hiss.

"We ... humans ... I'm ... not supposed to ... hit girls," Martin said.

The monsters exchanged confused looks.

"Why not?" Crusto asked.

"Well ... not always, but among humans, guys are usually ... stronger," Martin said. "Picking on someone weaker isn't considered ... proof of strength."

"*Weaker ...?!?*" Veils screamed. "*Is that what you think of me ...?*"

"Veils, we must consider every new concept before we judge," Crusto said. "We know little of humans ... or their ways."

"Martin, are you saying women are ... not equal?" Murder asked.

"No, that's not what I mean ...," Martin said. "I ...!"

"Careful, Martin," Happy warned. "Off those crutches, Murder can beat you one-on-one at any game."

"Exactly!" Martin said. "That's precisely what I'm trying to say ...!"

They all fell silent and stared at Martin.

"Murder could crush me at anything ... at any time," Martin said. "Instead, she's taken it easy on me ... taught me slowly ... until I was trained enough to compete. Why ...?"

The monsters glanced at each other.

"Because there's no sport in destroying a player who can't ... or doesn't know how ... to play," Murder answered.

"That's it: sport!" Martin said. "Why compete when the outcome is obvious ...?"

"I see," Happy said. "It's not you shouldn't go easy upon someone because they're a girl. It's you shouldn't use overwhelming strength to harm the weak."

"Yes," Martin said. "It's about having strength, but not misusing it."

"I can agree with that," Murder said.

"Well, I don't ...!" Veils shouted, and she pushed Martin a step back from the ledge and stood between him and the others. "Don't you dare treat me like I'm weaker than you! I'm as tough as you are ... *and I expect to be treated like it!"*

Martin stared at her and sighed heavily.

"If you insist, I'll respect your wishes," Martin promised Veils.

"I insist ...!" Veils shouted, her face so close their noses nearly bumped.

Martin nodded, grinned, ... and pushed her off the ledge.

All the way down Veils screamed in outrage ... until she splashed.

A New Perspective ...

The next day Martin stayed awake through school. He paid attention, took notes, and underlined important facts he felt certain would be on a test.

Veils had been furious with Martin, but Murder had taken him aside and complimented him on his philosophy of restrained strength.

"A truly strong person doesn't need to constantly prove themself," Murder had insisted.

At lunch, he sat with his oldest friends, who wondered why he wasn't joining them in their favorite new online game. Martin told them he was exercising every evening rather than fighting virtual monsters. He didn't tell them he was resting so he could fight real monsters.

Martin arrived home to find Vicky's suitcase and three sealed boxes beside the front door.

"Vicky ...!" Martin called.

Vicky came out of her bedroom ... not carrying a

book.

"When do you leave?" Martin asked.

"Dad's driving me tonight, when he gets home," Vicky said.

The TV turned on; Tom, Terry, and Ron were beginning an army game, its preview blaring explosions.

"I'll miss you," Martin said.

"I'll miss you," Vicky said, and she lowered her voice. "Of course, I'll be visiting you more often than the others."

"I'd love for you to come see me play," Martin said. "Well, maybe not this game ..."

"You'll do fine," Vicky said. "I'd rather watch you play the Greasy Golems ...!"

"You just want to see Maxivoom Snydho," Martin snickered. "You'll hate him."

"Then I'll love watching you beat him," Vicky said. "Just do me a favor ... keep reading. I like the idea of having a smart brother."

Martin nodded to their brothers crowded on the couch, controllers in hand.

"They'll be smart someday," he said.

"We can only hope," Vicky said. "And who knows? Before the Regionals begin, maybe you can visit me in Zantheriak."

"Me ...?" Martin asked. "What would I do? I know nothing about spaceships ...!"

"I didn't either ... until I started reading about them," Vicky said.

"Could you leave me a book ...?" Martin asked.

Vicky smiled. "Look on your nightstand; I left you three."

Martin fell into Happy's hands with a plastic bag of papers looped on his wrist.

"Excellent!" Rude said, eyeing the bag as Happy set him on his feet.

The whole team was gathered around him and a wide table was set up. Martin spread out his papers and Grand Wizard Bastile Wraithbone leaned over them.

"I spent all evening researching Sumo, Wresting, and Ultimate Fighting," Martin said.

"I'm no wizard," Rude said. "What do these say?"

"This is a list of the best qualities of wrestlers," Martin said. "Agility, quickness, balance, flexibility, coordination, endurance, strength, aggression, discipline, and a winning attitude."

"With those skills anyone could win," Murder said.

"These describe specific strikes," Martin said. "Kicks, kneeing, and elbowing. Punches are feints, slaps, piledrivers, and jabs. This drawing shows the correct standing position."

Martin pointed to a drawing and all leaned over to look at it.

"This describes clinches ... what they call holds," Martin said. "Its purpose is to gain full-body control over your opponent. It says controlling your opponent is the key to victory."

"Control is always best," Happy said.

"This describes grappling," Martin continued. "When either opponent hits the ground, both fighters seek the dominant position. In some human sports you can't strike while grappling."

"Why not ...?" Stabbing asked.

"Sportsmanship," Martin said, and several heads nodded.

"On Earth ... my world, sumo is Japanese for wrestling, and it ends when one opponent forces the other out of the ring or down to the ground. Jujitsu is an ancient style of wrestling that focuses on throws, pins, chokes, and joint locks. Those styles were refined by the Samurai."

"What's Samurai ...?" Veils asked.

"Ancient professional fighters," Martin answered.

"I prefer my techniques," Stabbing said. "Tripping, knocking over, hair-pulling, eye-gouging, choking, and finger-locking."

"In most human sports, those aren't allowed," Martin said.

"We're not playing a human sport," Rude said. "When you wrestle monsters, be prepared for everything."

"Martin, I'm not sure you should wrestle," Murder said. "No offense, but you don't have claws or rugged skin that can endure deep punctures."

"Veils doesn't either," Martin argued.

"One Small must sit out," Crusto said. "I'll sit out

for the Bigs; Snitch, Brain, and Happy outweigh me, although hooves aren't best on flat stone. I don't do this gladly; I do it for the team. One of you must join me."

Martin and Veils glanced at each other.

"We need the best wrestler," Grand Wizard Bastile Wraithbone said. "We must have our own Smalls' competition. One must prevail and one must step aside. The victors must play."

"Let's go over these papers tonight," Happy said. "We'll have our competition tomorrow."

Hours passed as Martin read and tried out numerous sumo techniques, even those with Japanese names: Yori-Kiri, Oshi-Dashi, Uwate-Nage, Tsuri-Dashi, and Soto-Gake.

Martin also read to them the names of Judo techniques: Nage-Waza, Yoko-Sutemi-Waza, Osaekomi-Waza, Shime-Waza, and Kansetsu-Waza. The Bigs liked Nage-Waza, the throwing techniques, while the Smalls preferred Shime-Waza, the choking techniques.

The new tricks delighted Snitch. He didn't understand the moves, but after watching Brain, Happy, and Crusto demonstrate them, he managed to repeat the simpler moves. So great was his strength that they struggled to restrain his enthusiasm ... to not be thrown into the stands.

Stabbing wrestled Martin and taught him how to defend himself, especially his eyes, from creatures with claws.

"Fouls do exist," Murder warned. "When an

opponent is down, you can't jump up and stomp on them. You can't bite or use poison. Use of wings and tails are forbidden. Vampires can't use mesmeric gaze."

"Do the Roaring Giants have vampires?" Martin asked.

"Yes," Stabbing said. "Pettyer BloodBowels is a vampire, as bloodthirsty as any undead."

"They also have a dark elf," Veils said. "Ruddy Max-Scowall, and he's fast and agile."

"Don't forget their goblin, Gale Bunnygut," Rude said. "She's their biggest Small ... and no slouch at sneaky tricks."

"Fame La Frankenstein is one of their Bigs, and she's almost as unbreakable as a golem," Happy said. "Rue Gland Cultster is a she-cyclops, and she's just plain mean. Join Huge is almost as strong as Snitch; he got him name by crushing two Smalls together until they became permanently affixed."

Martin shuttered to think about it.

Another hour they practiced, all of them, even Snitch, taking splashes into the water. The techniques on the papers worked, and Brain and Happy were amazed at how they could turn Snitch's great strength against him.

Then they took a break. Martin and Veils kept darting looks at each other; Martin didn't want to hurt Veils but he didn't want to be left out of the game. He hoped Veils felt the same way, but from her glares, he suspected she'd like nothing better than to prove she was a better wrestler than he.

Only one of them could play ...!

He wished Vicky hadn't left for college. She'd tell him how to fight Veils fairly without giving up every advantage he had. *Would Veils hate him if he beat her? What if he hurt her? How could he live with himself if he hurt Veils?*

"The Roaring Giants used their spell against the Greasy Golems," Grand Wizard Bastile Wraithbone said. "A nasty Fire-Face spell; Ton Eat-oddly wasn't affected, but Maxivoom Snydho was dancing around, jumping into the mud and sticking his head underwater to extinguish himself. Yet we're safe; this will be our first game where no one can cast a spell on us."

"And our last," Rude said. "The Greasy Golems have a bye, and they're saving their spell for us."

"The Roaring Giants are out of the Regionals," Murder said. "They have two losses; with their bye, the worst the Greasy Golems can end up with is one loss."

"That means they have nothing to lose," Stabbing said. "We defeated them last season. They're playing for their reputations ... and revenge."

Soaking wet, Martin asked Grand Wizard Bastile Wraithbone to dry him off early. Grand Wizard Bastile Wraithbone obliged, suggesting that he should go home and get some sleep before school. Martin promised he would, but insisted on talking to Murder first.

"Murder, could you ... take a short walk ...?" Martin asked.

On her crutches, she nodded and headed toward the door to the locker room, Martin beside her.

"I need some advice," Martin said.

"Veils ...?" Murder asked.

"I don't want to hurt her," Martin said.

"I doubt she'll be so generous," Murder said. "She wants to play."

"If I use my full strength, I might hurt her," Martin said.

Murder nodded and led Martin to the wall beside the stands.

"The solution is simple," Murder said, leaning against the wall.

Carefully balancing, Murder removed and rested one of her crutches against the wall. Then, with her free hand, she suddenly grabbed Martin by his neck and shoved him hard against the wall, her strong grip squeezing his throat, cutting off his breath.

"This isn't a dinner party," Murder said. "Veils is a competitor, the same as you. She's a girl; she's not as strong as you, but she's a dark elf, faster and more agile. Those skills give her advantages you don't have. She'll dodge anything you can dish out. She'll also work to negate your strength. She knows you like her, and that you don't want to hurt her. She'll use that against you. If you hurt her for no reason, then I'd be angry, but you're competing; you need to win. You want advice? Fight her as you'd fight me. I think of you as my friend, teammate, and student; I'd be furious if you dishonored me by treating me like an inferior. I wouldn't give you one break, and if we were fighting, I'd use every trick I know, physical and psychological, to beat you. Veils will, too. Your only prayer is to do the same."

Murder released Martin, whose face was red from lack of oxygen, and he coughed and gasped.

"Thank you, Murder," Martin wheezed.

"Anytime," Murder said.

Chapter 21
Stompday / Thursday

A New Perspective ...

School was boring, yet Martin managed to clear his mind and focus. Worrying about his upcoming match with Veils wouldn't help ... and might hurt his chances. Besides, if he didn't get good grades, his parents might start wondering why.

When he and his brothers got home, Martin was in charge. He missed Vicky, and sat playing video games with his brothers until his parents came home. After dinner, he hid in his room, finished his homework, and then fell asleep reading one of Vicky's novels.

Awakening as he dropped, Martin fell into Happy's hands. The centaur set him down before Murder.

"Are you ready?" Murder asked.

"Ready to win," Martin said.

"That's the attitude we need," Happy said.

Together, the three of them walked out to the pitch.

"Martin, just in time," Grand Wizard Bastile

Wraithbone said. "I've decided I want all of the Smalls challenging each other, not just you and Veils. Go on up. I'll call the matches."

Martin frowned and walked up the ramp. On the platform, Stabbing, Rude, and Veils met him with silent nods. Grand Wizard Bastile Wraithbone, Murder, Brain, Happy, Crusto, and Snitch mounted the stands to see clearly.

"Veils and Stabbing ...!" Grand Wizard Bastile Wraithbone called to them, and he held up a small, dark wand. "I'm going to be your referee. I want a clean fight. If you commit a foul I will zap you."

Rude stepped back to the edge, giving them as much room as he could, and Martin did the same.

Veils and Stabbing faced each other, staring intently. Slowly they circled, and Rude and Martin matched their movements to give the opponents as much room as possible.

Stabbing charged, grabbed Veils, and as their arms locked on each other, he shoved her backwards. She resisted and turned to the side, circling to avoid the edge. Stabbing tried to twist her back, attempting to hip-throw her toward the ledge. However, Veils jerked in the other direction, flailed wildly, and finally pulled free. Then she was on the inside; she jumped to push Stabbing backwards, but he dodged low, and she toppled over his extended left leg. She grabbed, tripped Stabbing, and fell atop him; they grappled, but neither could roll the other off the edge without also being pulled over. As if by unspoken agreement, they kicked apart and jumped to their feet.

Martin noticed scratches on Veils' arms; Stabbing wasn't treating her like a girl. He was doing his utmost, and Veils was matching his determination. He felt foolish for worrying about hurting her; if she won today, Martin felt certain she'd find a way to triumph tomorrow. He trusted her that much. He just had to trust her enough to fight his best.

Veils and Stabbing ran at each other and slammed together. Stabbing was a few inches shorter yet heavier, or perhaps he just looked thicker because of his fur. Neither was knocked backwards, and Stabbing punched her ribs as Veils slapped his face, once with each hand.

Stabbing shoved with both hands, yet Veils sidestepped and pushed; Stabbing half-tripped, stumbled toward the edge, and almost fell over, flailing his arms. Veils tried to turn her momentum in time to push him off, but he recovered and circled back.

Martin and Rude shifted aside to avoid fouling their combat. Veils regained her balance and they inched off the middle-ground, hands extended to catch the other. Eyes locked, they slipped into range.

Both feinted several times, trying to draw the other into committing or over-extending, but neither did. Finally Stabbing feinted, then jumped to his hands and swept his legs hard against hers. Veils tripped, and Stabbing jumped atop her. She tried to push him off, but he rolled her completely over and against the edge.

Looking over the edge, Veils shoved her hand into Stabbing's mouth and screamed. Yet he only turned his head; he hadn't been biting her; she'd been hoping for a foul. Yet no zap came, and Stabbing inched her closer, hanging her over the edge.

She was clinging, struggling to pull him off with her; better both players fall than allow yourself to splash alone, but Stabbing played smart. She was only being held atop the platform by clinging to him.

Suddenly Stabbing shook himself, flailing as wildly as she had, and she lost her grip. Stabbing rolled toward the center, leaving her nothing to hold on to, with half of her weight over the edge. With a cry of frustration, Veils dropped from the platform ... down to splash into the cold water.

Grand Wizard Bastile Wraithbone and their teammates in the stands cheered and applauded. Stabbing stood up and bowed to their accolades.

A minute later, Veils came stomping up the ramp, drenched and angry. She walked to the edge closest to Grand Wizard Bastile Wraithbone, standing beside Stabbing.

"Very good, both of you," Grand Wizard Bastile Wraithbone said. "Stabbing, Veils almost had you at one point. What did you do wrong?"

"I charged with my arms too far forward," Stabbing said. "If they'd been wider, she wouldn't have slipped past me."

Every teammate nodded.

"Veils, why did you lose?" Grand Wizard Bastile Wraithbone asked.

"I didn't jump his sweep," Veils said. "Once I was down, I let him get one hand around the back of my neck."

"And he used that to roll you over," Grand Wizard Bastile Wraithbone said, and then he looked at Murder and the Bigs.

"Veils, you're too stiff," Happy said. "You could've twisted free if you were looser. Be strong, but flexible, not rigid."

"Lower your stance to reduce your center of gravity, which will help you turn sharper," Murder said. "A high body height takes longer to reverse momentum. If you'd ducked, you might've dunked him."

Veils nodded her dripping head. No one else spoke, so she and Stabbing stepped back. Rude stepped forward, and Martin looked at him.

"Good luck!" Veils whispered to Martin, and although soaking wet, she leaned close and kissed his cheek.

Startled, Martin stepped forward and braced himself for Rude's attack, arcing his back to lower his center of gravity, yet he could still feel the soft touch of Veils' lips on his cheek.

Why had she kissed him ....?

Suddenly Rude charged. Martin fumbled to block his assault, yet was grabbed, lifted into the air, and dropped over the brink. He saw the water approach and gasped a shallow breath ...!

Splash!

His match had lasted only seconds. Feeling idiotic, Martin swam to the edge and pulled himself out. Then he walked back up the ramp, soaking wet, and stood beside Rude at the edge of the platform.

"Martin, what happened?" Grand Wizard Bastile Wraithbone asked.

"Veils kissed me ... right before the match," Martin said, blushing scarlet. "She obviously wanted to distract me ... and she succeeded."

Everyone laughed. Martin blushed and struggled to not look at Veils, but he couldn't resist. She beamed a wide grin at him. Martin's cheeks glowed bright red.

"Congratulations, Veils ... on your victory," Murder said.

Everyone laughed again.

"Veils, why did you cause Martin to lose?" Grand Wizard Bastile Wraithbone asked. "Did you think he could beat Rude?"

Veils stepped up beside Martin.

"When competing, a good player takes every advantage," Veils said.

Martin didn't look at her again, but the smugness in her voice made him want to push her off the platform.

"You're twelve years old ... and my granddaughter," Grand Wizard Bastile Wraithbone said, his tone deeply parental. "Find other methods for taking advantage."

"I'm saving my other methods for my match against

Martin," Veils said.

Martin clenched his teeth; *did she have other methods ... or was she just trying to psyche him out again?*

Smiles stretched every face. Crusto, Happy, Murder, Brain, and even Snitch were chuckling. Martin flushed, embarrassed.

"Rude didn't tire himself," Crusto said. "Let's see if Veils can charm him."

"Very well," Grand Wizard Bastile Wraithbone said. "Veils against Rude."

Martin stepped aside as Veils and Rude stepped to opposite sides of the platform, then faced each other. Slowly they circled, and then both ran at the other.

At the last second, Veils threw herself down, against Rude's bare shins. He stumbled, tripped over her, and fell face-flat onto the smooth stone platform. Instantly Veils rolled out from under him, jumped onto his back, and wrapped her forearm around Rude's neck.

Veils had Rude in a choke-hold ...!

Calmly, as if she wasn't there, Rude stood up, and then he rose up onto his toes. He was taller; with her grip tight around his neck, Veils hung down his back, her feet dangling. He grabbed her arm with both his goblin hands, releasing her pressure enough to inhale deeply, and then he jumped backwards ... horizontally ... onto his back. At the last second he stuck out his elbows, catching himself so he didn't land flat, crushing Veils beneath him. Yet she smashed down hard against the stone and lost her grip.

Rude rolled off her, then stood and reached down. Prone, Veils lay coughing, still reeling from her impact with the smooth stone surface of the platform. Rude helped her to her feet, then stepped behind her, slipped his hands under her armpits, and lifted her with ease. He carried her to the edge of the platform and held her out over the water. He waited until she was done coughing.

"Are you okay?" Rude asked.

"Yes," Veils confessed.

Rude dropped her. Without a cry, Veils fell and splashed.

Martin grinned. If she'd beaten Rude then he'd have to beat Stabbing just to match her.

After dragging herself out of the pool, Veils walked slowly up the ramp, dripping wet, and walked to stand beside Rude.

"Veils ...?" Grand Wizard Bastile Wraithbone asked.

Veils took several breaths before she replied.

"Rude ... countered my strategy ... and I didn't have a counter for his," Veils said.

"You should have," Murder said. "If he'd dropped his full weight upon you, as he would've against an enemy player, he'd have hurt you ... possibly put you out of competition."

"Suggestions ...?" Grand Wizard Bastile Wraithbone asked.

"You allowed him to stand up," Happy said. "If you'd wrapped your legs around his, you may have delayed his counter."

"Tactics need to be as flexible as a player," Crusto said to Veils. "When you commit yourself to one strategy, you lose."

"Rude ...?" Grand Wizard Bastile Wraithbone asked.

"I'd have had trouble if she'd wrapped her legs around mine," Rude said. "I need to think of a way to counter that."

"And never wait until they're breathing better before dropping them over the edge!" Stabbing laughed.

"Excellent points," Grand Wizard Bastile Wraithbone said. "All right; Martin against Stabbing."

Martin turned to face Stabbing, who had a rat-like smile on his rat-face. They approached each other warily, both crouched low. Suddenly Stabbing screamed, a shrill, high-pitched cry, and charged forward. Martin waited, letting him gain momentum, then dodged to the side, avoiding collision. He gained the inside, yet as he charged, arms wide, Stabbing shoulder-rolled under his left arm and flipped to his feet in a single flowing leap. Then Stabbing unexpectedly came at him from behind, crouched low, arms wide, and pushing.

Martin spun, pinned on the outside only three feet from the edge. He tried to run to the side, circling, making Rude and Veils circle to stay out of his way. Yet

Stabbing side-stepped masterfully, not letting him back inside.

Martin pressed Stabbing, trying to force their fight back to the center, away from the edge. However, Stabbing met his momentum, tripped him, and they fell grappling. Martin grabbed Stabbing's right arm to try and twist it. Yet Stabbing held his left hand over Martin's face, wiggling his sharp claws inches from Martin's eyes.

"If I was an enemy, you'd lose ... right now!" Stabbing hissed.

Stabbing released him and jerked free, then rolled off to one side. Instantly Stabbing attacked, sliding Martin, who was still on his back, across the stone. They were three feet from the edge, but the smooth platform was now wet. Stabbing slid Martin inches from the edge.

Martin resisted, clinging on as best he could, trying to keep Stabbing from pushing him off. He couldn't get up; any attempt would leave him completely vulnerable to Stabbing's push. He pressed his hands flat against the stone, scrabbling with the toes of his sneakers, yet he couldn't get the upper hand. Stabbing pushed Martin against the edge so Martin's leg hung half over the edge.

Rather than fall, Martin dropped bodily onto the platform. His whole body had more friction than just sneakers; he had to stay on. Stabbing would have to roll him off ... with Martin clinging to him.

Stabbing pushed low and hard. Despite every attempt to hold on, Martin's left hand lost contact and stretched out in midair over the long drop.

In desperation, Martin shoved his right hand under Stabbing and pushed up. Stabbing was providing all the forward motion he needed; Martin's hand caught Stabbing's stomach and pushed upwards. Bent over double, Stabbing was suddenly lifted off his feet, and Martin flipped him ... overtop his prone form, and Stabbing flew out over the edge.

Stabbing fell, but he caught his claws on Martin's belt and jeans, and clung tight. Martin struggled to not be pulled off, but the wet platform was slick. Stabbing jerked hard, his whole weight hanging off Martin ... and both toppled and splashed into the water.

Even before he surfaced, Martin smiled. *He'd fought Stabbing to a double-splash!* Now he didn't have to beat Veils; if they also double-splashed, then Martin would win.

But if he fell, and she didn't, then they'd be tied ... with her beating him.

"Thanks for not blinding me," Martin said as they sloshed up the ramp.

"You needed to know," Stabbing said. "Ruddy Max-Scowall won't be so nice."

Veils glared at him when they climbed to the platform, yet Martin met her stare undaunted. He and Stabbing walked to the edge of the platform.

"Stabbing ...?" Grand Wizard Bastile Wraithbone asked.

"I've never seen that attack," Stabbing said. "If I'd

pushed harder and gotten lower, or dropped suddenly, I might've countered it."

"Very good," Grand Wizard Bastile Wraithbone said. "Martin ...?"

"Stabbing spared my eyes," Martin said. "After that ... I couldn't match him. What I was trying wasn't working, so I tried something new ..."

"Is there any way you could've kept from being pulled in ...?" Grand Wizard Bastile Wraithbone asked.

Martin shrugged.

"Attack the hands clinging to you, not your opponent's body," Murder said.

"Precisely," Grand Wizard Bastile Wraithbone said. "Still ... well done!"

"Martin double-splashed because Stabbing took pity on him!" Veils complained.

"And Martin lost to Rude because you kissed him," Grand Wizard Bastile Wraithbone said. "These things happen ... not only in practice. Very well; Martin against Veils."

"Martin hasn't recovered from his last fight!" Rude said.

"Games don't always allow time to rest, " Grand Wizard Bastile Wraithbone said. "Martin has the points advantage. Begin."

Martin moved to one side, opposite Veils.

"Don't worry," Martin said to Veils. "I'll take it easy on you."

Veils' eyes glared.

"You don't expect me to believe that ... do you?" Veils demanded.

Martin frowned, hiding his smile. *No, he hadn't expected Veils to believe it. He expected it to infuriate her ... and it did.*

With a savage cry, Veils charged. Martin waited, then ran at her. Their impact knocked both of them back, but he was heavier ... and physics works the same in any world. Veils came at him again, grabbed his arm, and flipped him over her shoulder; a judo throw. Martin kicked out his heels to absorb the crash as he landed on his back on the hard stone, and the rubber soles of his sneakers took most of the impact. Veils raised an elbow and dropped onto Martin, but he caught her elbow in his hand and twisted; she fell onto her shoulder, and the side of her head smacked onto his chest. Martin rolled away and got to his feet, yet Veils flipped to her feet with a dark elf agility he couldn't match.

Again Veils charged. She was trying to give him no time to recover his breath. He reached for her, yet she grabbed his forearm and ducked under his arm, coming up behind him. She clung to his arm and lifted it as high as she could. Martin cried out and struggled against her arm-lock, yet he couldn't break free.

With no recourse, Martin twisted his torso, which hurt his arm even more, but he reached back with his free arm, circled her head, and closed his grip. She had him in an arm-lock. He had her in a head-lock. They were stuck together, and that was Martin's key to victory.

Not releasing her, Martin began backing up, pushing her toward the edge. She pushed against him, but she was smaller, lighter, barefoot, and the platform was wet; they slowly neared the dangerous ledge. She wrenched his arm higher, forcing tears from his eyes, but he kept pushing. She could release his arm, but that wouldn't free her. Martin didn't need to win outright ...

They inched backwards ... and her heels inched over the edge. Veils screamed furiously and clung tight.

Martin jumped backwards. Together they dropped over the brink and plummeted toward the water.

Martin smiled as he fell; he'd won!

Chapter 22
Rompday / Friday

Savage Sumo Bigs ...

"I talked to your dad," Coach Anderson said.

Martin looked up at his gym teacher.

"Yes ...?" Martin asked.

"Unfortunately, no," Coach Anderson said. "Do you think you could ...?"

"I've been fighting this war for years," Martin said.

"You've got talent," Coach Anderson said. "You're not big, but keeping the other team from scoring is just as important."

"I was hoping ... in high school they have pole-vaulting," Martin said. "That's fun."

"You can pole-vault ...?" Coach Anderson asked.

"I've ... tried it," Martin said. "If my mom knew, then I'd never do it again."

"I'll work with you," Coach Anderson promised. "Even if I can't have you for a team, I'll make sure you're top of my class."

Martin fell into Brain's hands, before all of them, and together they walked out to face the cheering crowd.

"Here come the Shantdareya Skullcrackers!" Evilla shouted over the loudspeakers, and the crowd went wild.

Martin stared at the stands, which were packed; fur, scales, armored plates, feathers, and leathery wings pressed together, all cheering and applauding.

"Large crowd," Martin commented as they stepped toward the pitch.

"Savage Sumo is a crowd-favorite," Rude said. "It holds the record for 'most deaths'."

Martin frowned.

No one had told him that!

"Grand Wizard Bastile Wraithbone leads his team to the pitch!" Evilla shouted, and Martin glanced up at her. She was wearing pure white today, standing like a snowbank of white fur with tights and hair to match. She waved at him; he nodded to her.

"Here she is again, Vivacious Veils, the Darling Dark Elf!" Evilla said, making Veils groan. "Beside her is Brain Stroker, the Ornery Ogre! And that Mountain of Muscle, Allfed Snitchlock! Happy Lostcraft, the Clever Centaur, follows, beside Crusto Fernwalker, the Smasher from the Sea! Here's Stabbing Kingz, who Brings the Stings, and Rude Stealing, the Clobbering Goblin, who looks fully recovered! Murder Shelling is still on crutches, I see, but look who's with her! It's every monster's favorite human, Martin the Magnificent!"

They stepped up onto a raised level before the

stands that allowed them a view of most of the platform. Evilla paused to let the crowd finish applauding, then continued.

"While we're waiting, I had another private interview with Martin the Magnificent this week," Evilla said.

The eyes of every teammate flashed to Martin, yet he shook his head.

"Never happened," he whispered.

"I asked Martin, straight out, why he thinks humans should be allowed to play," Evilla said into her microphone. "His reply astounded me: Evilla, he said, in our history, humans have done so many terrible things, I sometimes wonder whose world has the real monsters! Having seen both worlds, I can honestly say Heterodox is best!"

"I never said that!" Martin scowled, but only his teammates heard.

The crowd applauded, approving the false quote. Martin shook his head; no one would believe he hadn't said that ... although it might be true.

"At last, here they come!" Evilla shouted. "From Deutsch Deathhol, the Roaring Giants! Grand Wizard Risk Master-One is leading them! And there she is, the Patchwork Princess, Fame La Frankenstein! And there's her beloved sadistic sister, Rue Gland Cultster, whose one eye sees every chance to maim and kill! Behind them is that Toll-Taking Troll, Join Huge, back to challenge Allfed Snitchlock at last! I can't wait for that match! And here's the Deadliest Dark Elf to ever play, Ruddy Max-Scowall, who only smiles when he wins! Beside him is Magic-Hands Cleave Revile, the High Elf with the wizard's touch! He probably won't play today, yet he was never really a player, more of a healer, keeping his teammates in the game! Three complaints have been filed against him, but the Grand Council of Wizards has yet to kick him out! And here's the last two Smalls, that Gobbling Goblin Gale Bunnygut and that Dapper, Deadly Blood-Drinker, Pettyer BloodBowels, who enjoys every bite to the last drop!"

Cheers and some boos came from the crowd, and Martin stared at them, glad the stone platform was held up by only one pillar, which let him see them all. They wore pink and orange jerseys, yet they looked tough and ready.

Grand Wizard Risk Master-One looked aged, gray, and even older than Grand Wizard Bastile Wraithbone. Fame La Frankenstein was no slender Bride of Frankenstein; she was massive, hulking, and stitched together, a reanimated corpse if ever Martin had seen one. Rue Gland Cultster was a She-Cyclops, as big as Jackknife Illson, and she also wore spiked leathers and an eye-guard of steel bars. Join Huge was a troll as big as Snitch and looked excessively angry. Ruddy Max-Scowall was the tallest Small he'd ever seen, a dark elf like Veils ... but bigger, stronger, and with more experience. Gale Bunnygut was another goblin, shorter but clearly heavier than Rude. Pettyer BloodBowels was a sleek, fanged vampire with white skin and slicked-back black hair, and Martin was suddenly glad biting was a foul.

Martin stared at Cleave Revile; he'd never seen a high elf before. He and Ruddy Max-Scowall could've been matching salt and pepper shakers, one white and one dark. His teammates hadn't described him probably because they knew he wouldn't play.

"So ... let's get ready for the Romp on the Rock!" Evilla said. "Here we are in the fourth round, asking who will win the Locals of the three hundred and fifteenth season of the Grotesquerie Games? I'm so excited I'm baking, and you know how I cook: I pour the spice of excitement into every recipe!"

She spun around, showing off her buxom figure in her white tights ... and the crowd cheered louder.

"So sit back, those of you who like to snuggle ... leave your names at the gate where I can find them ... and order up a pitcher of Heavenly Hemlock to go with your Choke-Down Caramels and Pooka-chips with Double-spiced Doppelganger Dip! Get set ... because the deadliest game of all is about to begin: Savage Sumo!"

The same two referees as last game came out, lifted their wands, and each levitated themselves up onto a tiny stand atop one of the tall narrow stone poles which held the baskets, into which the zombie head had to be thrown. Over one basket a purple flag still hung. Over the other basket hung a flag of pink and orange stripes.

The game wasn't over until the zombie head went through one of those hoops.

"What will the order of pairing be?" Evilla asked. "Hold on ...! Looks like we're starting! Staffs are up! Wands are raising ...!"

From the wands of the referees came a sparkling silver mist, such as a Disney fairy might trail, and the two mists flew toward each other. Where they struck, a spinning ball of light appeared, and from it beamed two spotlights, one onto a player of each team.

"First up: Happy Lostcraft will face Rue Gland Cultster!" Evilla cried. "It's a centaur-cyclops challenge!"

Happy nodded to his teammates, then stepped toward the ramp, the spotlight following him. In its light, Happy clip-clopped up the ramp and onto the platform. The crowd cheered all the way. Happy placed one hoof onto the platform, and then waited for Rue Gland Cultster to place one foot on the other side.

"That's it!" Evilla shouted. "The game has begun! Let's start the slaughter!"

Happy and the she-cyclops stepped out onto the stone platform, and both ramps swung away. The spotlights stayed on them, yet they both paused and glared at each other. Then they charged and met in the middle. Instantly they locked arms around each other's torsos; Martin might've thought they were hugging if they weren't straining so hard. Happy had greater total bulk, but Rue Gland Cultster had a thick body and arms bulging with more muscles than Happy's human half.

She threw him down, onto his side, but he pulled her down with him and flipped her, and then rolled over and kicked her away with four hooves. She slid to the edge, yet the platform's surface was dry; she didn't fall over. Both jumped up, the crowd going wild.

Evilla was commenting on the match, but the cheers of the crowd drowned her out.

Rue Gland Cultster charged and punched a meaty fist at Happy, yet he caught it with one hand and redirected it as he dodged. Then he slammed into her with his horse-body, and she was knocked backwards.

As Rue Gland Cultster staggered, suddenly Happy reared. His front hooves stomped into her steel-bar eye-patch six times, one hoof after another, in rapid succession. Rue Gland Cultster was driven backwards. She raised her arms to shield her face.

Happy spun, raised his horse's rear and, tail flapping, he mule-kicked as hard as he could right into her stomach. Rue Gland Cultster fell back, her heels over the edge, flailed, cried out, and fell to splash into the water.

"Two points to Happy Lostcraft!" Evilla shouted. "Skullcrackers score first!"

The crowd cheered and pennants waved as the ramps rotated back. Martin stared at Happy as he walked back down the ramp, while Rue Gland Cultster sloshed out of the water and stormed back to her side. Martin had never seen Bigs wrestle and couldn't believe how dangerous they looked.

As Happy returned to the Skullcrackers, the magical spotlight on him faded. The wands of the referees sent out two new silvery mists, which joined the flashing circle of light and beamed two new spotlights down.

"Allfed Snitchlock and Fame La Frankenstein!" Evilla said. "A troll against a manufactured monster of beauty!"

Fame La Frankenstein stomped up the ramp in one spotlight as Snitch trooped up the other, the snarl on her face not looking even slightly pretty. She was thickly built, although not as big as Snitch. She walked without grace, stomping mechanically, and reached the top, placing only one foot on the platform. Snitch arrived shortly after; Crusto had delayed him until Fame La Frankenstein was near the top. He stomped right out onto the platform.

"Let the mayhem begin!" Evilla shouted.

The two ran at each other. She dodged to avoid a collision, then dropped and grabbed Snitch's leg. She pulled to lift it, trying to throw him off-balance, but Snitch hammered his elbow down onto her head.

She crumpled, stunned. He grabbed her thick arm and spun, using one of the throws Crusto had shown him. Fame La Frankenstein flew tumbling toward the edge, yet stopped rolling before teetering over. She avoided falling, but in the time it took her to recover and jump up, Snitch had drawn back his arm. His hard backhand swat knocked her clean off the platform. She flew upwards, over Evilla, and landed in the stands atop a family of gelatinous blobs, which splashed in every direction.

The monsters cheered, even those who'd fled to avoid being crushed or splashed.

"Snitch stands Fame La Frankenstein!" Evilla cried. "But is she ...? Yes, she's moving ... and looks to be all in one piece! That's good, because she's got a lot of pieces and we've got a lot more game to play! Shantdareya Skullcrackers lead, 4 - 0!"

Wands raised, mists sparkled, and new spotlights beamed.

"Join Huge and Brain Stroker!" Evilla shouted. "The Roaring Giants have lost every match! Can they keep up?"

"Remember, slowly!" Crusto whispered, and Brain nodded, then headed toward the ramp.

Brain was big, but Join Huge was massive. Brain walked up the ramp slowly, letting Join Huge reach the top first. However, before he walked out onto the platform, a whistle blew from below, and Join Huge stopped, stared down, and then put one foot on the platform.

"A foul if you walk on before the match starts?" Martin asked Rude. Rude nodded affirmatively.

Brain reached the top and walked out to face the troll.

"Begin!" Evilla shouted. "Let's see some savagery!"

Join Huge roared so loudly it drowned most of the cheers. Brain roared back, and the two charged. Martin feared this was a mistake, and was horrified to see Brain instantly knocked flat as the monstrous troll batted him down, then tried to stomp his leg. Brain kicked back and tried to stand, but Join Huge grabbed and lifted him off his feet. He raised him high, ready to throw him off, but suddenly Brain hammered a piledriver punch straight down on top of Join Huge's head. The troll staggered and dropped Brain ... Brain fell on top of him.

Hanging onto the troll's side, Brain locked his legs around the huge waist, one arm hooked around his neck, and was punching his troll-face at will.

From his feet, Join Huge dropped onto his shoulder, which Brain was pressed against. The whole platform shook and Brain was smashed between the hammer and anvil.

"That's going from top to bottom!" Evilla cried. "Can Brain Stroker survive?"

Join Huge climbed to his feet, looking down at Brain, whom Martin could barely see. Again Join Huge tried to stomp, but Brain rolled away from him. He tried to jump to his feet, but a giant troll fist smacked down on him, and then two massive hands pushed him off.

Brain stumbled over the edge and dropped to the water right in front of them. His splash drenched their whole team, Evilla, and several rows of stands.

"Brain Stroker drops into the drink!" Evilla cried, shaking off the water, flinging drops from her hair. "The Roaring Giants aren't out of this yet! Score is 4 - 2!"

Crusto, Happy, and Snitch helped pull Brain from the water. Martin had never seen Brain look so weak and battered. He crawled out soaking wet and managed to stand only with help, shaking his head and holding one hand splayed against his chest. Even for an ogre, he looked pale.

"We'll examine him," Crusto cut off Martin's step forward. "You have a game to play."

The spotlight on Brain faded and the referees raised their wands again. New spotlights shined down.

"Allfed Snitchlock faces Rue Gland Cultster!" Evilla cried. "Troll against She-Cyclops!"

To Martin's horror, Rue Gland Cultster walked up the ramp as slowly as Snitch. When she reached the top, she waited, not placing one foot on the platform, while Snitch walked out onto the stone with both feet.

Z-z-z-z-z-zap!

Both referees shot electric bolts at Snitch, and he lit up, then fell forward, onto his knees, smoking. Rue Gland Cultster charged out while he was down and began pummeling him.

Enraged, Snitch grabbed both of Rue Gland Cultster's legs and yanked them out from under her. She fell hard onto her back. He staggered to his feet, then roared down at her. Yet she rolled away, jumped to her feet, and charged him again. Snitch hammered both fists down on her, and the she-cyclops collapsed at his feet. Snitch raised his massive foot to stomp her.

"Snitch, no ...!" Martin shouted. *"Push her off ...!*

Push her off ...!"

His voice barely seemed to rise above the cheers of the crowd, but Snitch turned his head and looked down.

"Yes, push her off ...!" Crusto shouted, and he gestured pushing with both hands.

Martin did likewise, and soon every Shantdareya player, even Grand Wizard Bastile Wraithbone, was shoving both hands at an imaginary opponent.

"What's this?" Evilla cried. "The Skullcrackers want Allfed Snitchlock to spare Rue Gland Cultster! They may regret that later; she hasn't faced Brain Stroker yet, and he took several bad punches!"

Some of the crowd booed, but Snitch drew back his foot, and instead of stomping her, he kicked her hard. Rue Gland Cultster rolled to the edge and laid there like a lifeless lump. Unlike the crowd, the Skullcrackers kept shouting encouragements, gesturing pushing, and Snitch looked confused. Finally he kicked her again, lightly, yet Rue Gland Cultster limply rolled off the edge and fell.

"Victory to Allfed Snitchlock!" Evilla shouted over the splash. "Skullcrackers lead, 6 - 2!"

The crowd seemed angry; they hadn't come to watch kindness and generosity. Yet Crusto, Happy, and Grand Wizard Bastile Wraithbone smiled at Martin and nodded their thanks.

Rue Gland Cultster didn't surface. Join Huge and Fame La Frankenstein ran to the water's edge, staring down into it.

Splash ...!

Crusto dove into the water, and a moment later, Rue Gland Cultster broke the surface, pulled by Crusto. Join Huge and Fame La Frankenstein grabbed her and pulled her out.

"Crusto Fernwalker saves Rue Gland Cultster!" Evilla cried. "She doesn't look like she'll be playing any more today, but we could've had a death ...! A Roaring Giant was spared by a Shantdareya Skullcracker! Will wonders never cease ..?"

The crowd booed and catcalled. Evilla looked at them and frowned.

"Well, that's what happens when you let a human on your team!" Evilla said.

The jeers turned to laughter ... and the crowd slowly calmed.

"You did the right thing, telling Snitch to push her off," Crusto said to Martin after climbing out of the pool.

"So did you," Martin replied.

"I'm proud of both of you!" Grand Wizard Bastile Wraithbone said.

Martin went back to stand where he could see atop the raised level and spied Veils making Brain drink water. It was too noisy to talk; Veils nodded to him and Martin nodded back.

New spotlights beamed.

"Happy Lostcraft faces Join Huge!" Evilla shouted. "Will the Skullcrackers regret their compassion ...?"

Fearlessly Happy walked up the ramp. Join Huge came up the other, and the same whistle blew as he reached the top. Then another whistle blew ... from Happy's lips. Happy reached out one foreleg and set a hoof on the platform. Join Huge seemed to recognize this action and did the same. Then both stepped out to meet the other.

Happy met the massive troll's charge head-on. He tried two moves from Martin's printouts: Harite and Hiki-Taoshi. Harite was a series of rapid open-hand slaps to the side of the face used to distract the troll. Hiki-Taoshi grabs an opponent's arm and pulls him to the ground, which usually stops a charge. Yet human sumo wrestlers never faced a troll; Join Huge punched his troll-hard fist into Happy's equine ribs and knocked him aside.

Happy broke free and raced around the tight circular platform, making Join Huge spin to follow him. Finally he attempted a mule-kick, as he had against Rue Gland Cultster. But Join Huge caught his back legs and lifted them high, forcing Happy's human-half flat against the stone platform. Yet, braced by his strong hands and forefeet, Happy pulled free and kicked hard, striking his face. Join Huge fell back, but not over the edge.

They charged each other, and Happy used Harite again to confuse the troll, who was trying to bodily-lift him. Enraged, the troll forgot the rules, opened his mouth, and bit hard on Happy's arm.

Z-z-z-z-z-zap!

Happy throat-punched Join Huge to free himself an instant before the bolts struck. The massive troll trembled as he illuminated, but he didn't fall. Despite smoking from two bolts, Join Huge punched Happy in his human torso, and Happy staggered, dropping to the knees of his forelegs. Suddenly Join Huge grabbed and lifted Happy high over his head, preparing to throw him into the stands.

Unexpectedly, Join Huge stopped and lowered Happy, looking at him confusedly. Happy looked helpless, clutching his chest. The crowd was shouting cheers, calling for blood. Yet Join Huge carried Happy to the edge, held him out, and gently dropped him.

"Happy Lostcraft takes a bath!" Evilla shouted. "Join Huge wins! Score, 6 - 4!"

Happy wasn't unconscious; as Crusto stepped to jump in, Happy waved him back, then swam for the side. Crusto and Snitch helped pull him out, and Happy shook off like a dog, flinging water on all of them, although his expression still looked pained. Then he looked over to see Join Huge walking down the ramp, the spotlight still on him.

"Join ...!" Happy shouted, and he stepped toward him.

Join Huge stopped and stared. Happy faced him proudly, then bowed slightly. The troll looked confused, but slowly, unsurely nodded his head at Happy.

The spotlights faded, then returned. Everyone knew what was coming.

"Brain Stroker faces Fame La Frankenstein!" Evilla said. "Now we'll see some serious savagery!"

Brain Stroker rose and left Veils, walking up the ramp. Fame La Frankenstein reached the platform when he did, and both stepped out at the same time.

"Both look damaged!" Evilla said. "Will the beatings of trolls decide this match?"

Brain Stroker and Fame La Frankenstein looked evenly matched; he was shorter and stouter, and she was taller and built to be sturdy. They circled each other, seeking advantages.

After several feints, Brain Stroker charged Fame La Frankenstein. She punched at him, but he dodged and grabbed her arm, attempting to throw her over his shoulder.

She resisted, wrapping her other long arm around him from behind, her hand on his chest. Fiercely he pulled, his strength against hers.

Stitches ripped and broke. Brain spun unexpectedly as she fell to her knees. Then both realized what had happened. Brain held up his prize as if astounded by it; *Brain held aloft the torn-free arm of Fame La Frankenstein!*

"Brain Stroker rips Fame La Frankenstein apart!" Evilla shouted, and the crowd went wild, cheering and jumping up and down. "Fame La Frankenstein must've suffered serious damage when Allfed Snitchlock hurled her into the stands! Don't worry! Girls like her can fall to pieces and come back stronger!"

Fame La Frankenstein roared in fury and charged. Brain Stroker swung her arm like a club, and struck the side of her head, yet she didn't seem daunted. She punched with her only remaining fist, then kneed Brain. He crumpled beside the edge, looking as damaged as she. Fame La Frankenstein drew back a foot to kick him over the edge.

Straining on the edge, Brain Stroker swung the severed arm low and knocked aside her knee while her other leg was raised to kick. She tilted, and bodily fell on top of him. As he slipped over the side, Fame La Frankenstein fell with him.

"Brain Stroker and Fame La Frankenstein splash together!" Evilla shouted, and the crowd cheered.

Both teams ran to help their players out of the water. However, after they climbed from the water, Brain held out her thick, meaty arm. Fame La Frankenstein accepted its return.

"Score is 7 - 5, Skullcrackers in the lead," Evilla said. "What new thing will we see next?"

The new spotlights shined.

"Happy Lostcraft faces Fame La Frankenstein!" Evilla shouted. "Join Huge just pummeled Happy Lostcraft, but he looks able to compete! Yet Fame La Frankenstein has been disarmed ... will she dare play ...?"

The crowd fell silent as Happy Lostcraft climbed up the ramp, spotlight on him. Yet the other ramp remained empty. The cheers of the crowd lessened in anticipation.

"Grand Wizard Risk Master-One is coming

forward!" Evilla said. "He's signaling! Fame La Frankenstein is out of the game! Happy Lostcraft wins by default! Wait! What's this? Grand Wizard Risk Master-One is calling to the referees! What's he saying? Rue Gland Cultster is also too injured to compete! Brain Stroker wins by default! The Shantdareya Skullcrackers widen their lead by two wins, 11 - 5!"

"The Roaring Giants Bigs can't win!" Evilla continued. "Yet they have one chance left to ease the reputations of their Bigs! Hold tight for the Champion Match of Master Monsters, troll against troll: Allfed Snitchlock faces Join Huge!"

The crowd's cheers rose again, and both monstrous trolls ascended the ramp. Fortunately, Snitch had to wait for Happy to dismount, and the Roaring Giants blew their whistle again to remind Join Huge to wait, not to place both feet on the platform until Snitch joined him.

"Allfed Snitchlock walks out to fight Join Huge!" Evilla shouted. "This rivalry has lasted three years! Its victor may decide little on the scoreboard, but will change who's regarded as the mightiest monster in the Grotesquerie Games!"

Martin watched in horror as Snitch and Join Huge ran forward two steps; the stone circle was too small for them. Their thick bodies smacked together so hard every flag in the stadium fluttered. Neither tried fancy moves, but met each other grunting and straining in a colossal struggle of pure muscle. Both looked equal for height and mass, and each bulged muscles only years of combat with equals could evoke. The trolls pushed, with irresistible weight and strength, yet neither moved the other an inch.

"Troll Titans Tussle!" Evilla shouted. "This grudge match is for the title of Strongest in the League! Cheer for your champion!"

Cheers escalated.

Slowly Join Huge was pushed backward, yet then he twisted their positions, rotating Snitch so he was closest to the edge. Oblivious, Snitch kept pushing, and soon they returned to the center.

The grunts of the trolls rose over the cheers of the crowd. They kept trying to push each other backwards ... and then both trolls fell onto their side. The *crash!* as they landed shook the stands, and the stone platform wobbled. Strikes began, punches, elbows, and knees. Join Huge rolled on top, slamming monstrous fists downwards. Snitch struggled to block and eventually got both feet pressed against Join Huge's chest. Snitch kicked, and Join Huge flew straight up into the air, flailing wildly. Snitch rose to his knees, and as Join Huge descended, Snitch punched upwards. Join Huge flipped before he smashed to the ground, cracking the stone platform, and lay gasping. Snitch rose in fury, grabbed him and lifted. Although he strained to do it, Snitch lifted Join over his head and aimed at the stands.

Join Huge wasn't finished; he punched straight down on Snitch's head. Snitch roared and dropped him, kicking his massive knee upwards into Join Huge's back as he fell. The troll cried out as his spine bent, and he collapsed to the platform ... unmoving ... right next to the edge.

Snitch roared in triumph, then raised a thick foot to kick Join Huge off the edge. But Join Huge grabbed his foot and twisted. Snitch toppled, and looked like he was going to trip over his opponent and fall off. Instead, Snitch crashed atop him shoulder first. The cracked stone platform broke, and a four-foot wide section underneath them shattered, crumbled, and fell, dropping both trolls with it. Together Snitch and Join splashed into the water.

"Allfed Snitchlock and Join Huge fall together ... with part of the stone platform!" Evilla cried. "No one has ever broken the platform before; this is unprecedented! Yet the Shantdareya Skullcracker Bigs triumph, 12 - 6! This gives the Skullcrackers the lower net for the third match ... odds are definitely in their favor! Yet only sinking the zombie head wins! Which will prevail? Stay with me to the end ... and hopefully much later ... and we'll watch the victory together!"

Savage Sumo Smalls ...

Martin had never seen a crowd of monsters look so happy or cheer as loudly.

"Join Huge fails to steal the title of strongest troll in the league!" Evilla announced. "Allfed Snitchlock reigns supreme! Yet this game isn't won! There're more kicks, punches, and clinches to come, and as you know, clinches are my personal specialty ...!"

Martin shook his head and tried to ignore her playing to the audience. He needed to listen to his teammates.

"Grand Wizard Risk Master-One and Cleave Revile are healers!" Veils said. "Why didn't they fix Rue Gland Cultster or Fame La Frankenstein?"

"Winning the Bigs round isn't key to victory," Rude explained. "Bigs help decide who has the easiest throw to win the game. The key is the Smalls; this is where the game gets vicious. If a Small gets hurt in the round-robin, then they can't play in the final round ... where one throw of the zombie head wins the game. They're saving their healing spells for their Smalls."

"We can't afford an injured Small either," Grand Wizard Bastile Wraithbone said. "Fortunately, we haven't had to use a healing spell, but I always keep one ready."

"Take care to not get hurt," Crusto said. "These matches decide the order of who plays in the final match. Everything in this game comes down to the throwing match."

Murder brought water and made them drink. She was only using one crutch; she was quickly healing, and Martin smiled to see it. Yet halftime wouldn't last ...

The crowd cheered and Martin glanced up. Although wet, Evilla was posing in her skin-tight white outfit, decorated with white fur, and her snow-white hair made her gleam in the starlight. She looked very different than she usually did, almost angelic, yet Martin knew her appearance was as fake as her persona. Still, the crowd of monsters cheered and clapped hands, claws, pincers, and tentacles.

"The best of the game is about to begin!" Evilla shouted into her microphone. "So grab what you want most ... a big bag of Poltergeist Pretzels, I mean, and munch away! The Slamming Smalls of the Roaring Giants and Shantdareya Skullcrackers are about to collide!"

Martin laughed ... and Veils glared at him.

"Keep your mind on the game ... not Evilla!" Veils

snapped at Martin.

She was right, Martin knew. She was also still angry at being left out of this game. Yet ... no point arguing with her.

"The referees are signaling!" Evilla cried. "Wands are up! Waiting on the wizards ...!"

Grand Wizard Bastile Wraithbone looked up and lifted his magic staff, and the wizened Grand Wizard Risk Master-One did the same. The horn blew.

"That's it!" Evilla cried. "Time to restart! Let the chaos continue ...!"

The referees sent streams of silvery mist to join again. The brilliant ball of light shined over the broken platform, and two beams of light streamed down.

"Stabbing Kingz faces Ruddy Max-Scowall!" Evilla shouted. "Ratling against dark elf! This is a beginning of bruises!"

Stabbing climbed the ramp and placed one foot onto the platform. Ruddy Max-Scowall walked up to face him. Both were wiry and slim, yet Ruddy Max-Scowall was a head taller and held himself as if to exemplify a lofty appearance despite the pink and orange stripes of his jersey.

Both charged at each other, but at the last second, Ruddy Max-Scowall jumped high, completely over Stabbing's head. Stabbing checked his dash before he ran over the edge, and spun to face his opponent. Ruddy Max-Scowall charged from behind, hoping to push him off. Yet Stabbing jumped sideways, caught his claws on Ruddy's jersey, and whipped around him. On the edge, Stabbing tried to push the dark elf off, but Ruddy dodged, rolled head over heels and bounced up, landing on his feet on the other side of the platform.

Martin watched fascinated; both Stabbing and Ruddy Max-Scowall were more dexterous than he. They darted around the platform, bouncing like super-balls, each trying to gain the upper hand. Yet suddenly Ruddy Max-Scowall slipped and fell. Stabbing jumped at him, throwing himself low. He slid across the wet pitch, feet first, and kicked Ruddy Max-Scowall as he tried to rise. Ruddy Max-Scowall slid across the platform toward the broken edge, clawing at it. When Stabbing rose and walked over, he found Ruddy Max-Scowall hanging over the edge, clinging to the rough, cracked edge by his hands and one foot.

Stabbing raised his arms, then swung them down in opposite, circular movements, and swatted Ruddy's hands off the rocks.

"Ruddy Max-Scowall takes a bath!" Evilla cried. "That's two points to Stabbing! 14 - 6!"

"What happened ...?" Martin asked.

"You haven't been up there," Happy said. "It started dry and smooth, but the top of that platform is now mostly water and blood, with lots of shallow cracks. Stabbing has toe-claws, which gives him better traction."

New spotlights beamed down.

"Rude Stealing faces Gale Bunnygut!" Evilla shouted. "Two Goblin Grapplers! Who shall swim?"

Rude Stealing walked up the ramp at the same time as Gale Bunnygut. They looked similar, although where he was bald, she had a long, beautiful fall of shiny red hair. They approached each other warily, circling. She charged in first, but Rude employed a Nodowa, a throat-thrust with open palm. Gale Bunnygut's chin flew up and she stumbled backwards. She came at him again and Rude employed the Soto-Gake, the outside leg trip, wrapping his leg around hers as he pushed. She fell, clawing to try and drive him back.

Martin was impressed; Rude was always the most-studious of his teammates. He must've studied Martin's printouts deeply ... even in daytime.

Rude dropped on top of Gale Bunnygut, executing all three techniques of Katame-waza: Kansetsu-waza, locking her joints, Osae-komi-waza, pinning her in place, and finally Shime-waza, his arm around her throat. Gale Bunnygut tried to gasp, unable to breathe, and finally she weakened and passed out.

"*A death ...!*" Evilla shouted. "I think Gale Bunnygut is dead ...! The referees are signaling; this match is over ...! There's Cleave Revile, the high-elf healer, running up the ramp! But is there anything left to heal ...?"

Rude stood up and stepped back as Cleave Revile reached Gale Bunnygut. The high elf dropped to his knees to examine her ... yet Rude looked down and shook his head.

Cleave Revile closed his eyes and bowed over her

still form.

Barely aware what he was doing, Martin dashed up the ramp. Martin reached the top and kneeled over Gale Bunnygut, pushing Cleave aside. Gale wasn't breathing and her green skin was darkening. Martin grabbed her chin and pulled her mouth open, then reached inside and flattened her tongue.

"Hey ... leave her alone ...!" Cleave Revile began.

"Spells can't heal the dead," Rude said, resting a hand on Cleave's shoulder. "Let him try!"

Martin pinched her long nose and pressed his mouth to Gale Bunnygut's green lips. He blew hard, forcing his breath into her. Then he stabbed three fingers into her chest, feeling for the joint where her lowest ribs met in front. Inches below there, Martin placed both hands and began thrusting, repeatedly using his whole body weight.

"What's Martin doing ...?" Evilla asked as the crowd fell silent. "First, he kisses her ... and now ...?"

"Rude, do what I did!" Martin said. "Squeeze her nose and breathe into her ... fill her lungs with air!"

Rude didn't wait for an explanation. Cleave Revile objected, but both ignored him. Martin kept going ... and began to sing.

"Ho ... ho ... ho ... ho! Come back to life! Ho ... ho ... ho ... ho! Come back to life!"

"Is that a spell?" Cleave Revile asked.

"A song," Martin said. "I can't remember the right words but it's the timing I need. Help me!"

Cleave Revile began singing along with Martin, and Rude kept doing mouth-to-mouth resuscitation. Finally Gale Bunnygut coughed.

"She's alive ...!" Rude gasped.

"Quick! Use your healing magic!" Martin shouted.

Cleave Revile held his hands inches over Gale Bunnygut, and suddenly a blue-white light glowed from him. The lights engulfed Gale Bunnygut ... and she rose into the air, floating off the wet stone platform.

The healing lasted minutes, and the crowd fell silent, watching in amazement. When the blue-white lights faded, Gale Bunnygut lowered to the platform and opened her eyes.

"She's alive ...!" Evilla shouted. "Martin the Magnificent, Rude Stealing, and Cleave Revile have brought Gale Bunnygut back to life ...!"

Cleave Revile looked shocked.

"It's not magic, it's medicine," Martin said. "CPR: I'll print out articles describing it in detail ... and have Grand Wizard Bastile Wraithbone share them with the whole wizard council."

"You'll ... give us this technique ...?" Cleave Revile asked.

"Every human athlete knows how to do this," Martin said. "Every monster athlete should, too."

Cleave Revile forced his hands under Gale Bunnygut's back, Rude took her head, and Martin grabbed her feet. Together they lifted and carried her down the ramp. Gale Bunnygut objected and tried to stand, but Martin ordered her to lie still, and Cleave Revile repeated his order.

Once Gale Bunnygut was settled among her teammates the old, gray-bearded wizard stepped toward them.

"Martin the Magnificent, you have my personal thanks," Grand Wizard Risk Master-One half-bowed to him. "This is a miracle!"

"Many humans know CPR," Martin said. "To us, Cleave's magic would be the miracle."

"I understand," Grand Wizard Risk Master-One smiled. "I objected to your playing in our games. I'm sorry. Perhaps ... together we're best."

"Together's always best," Martin said. "I don't know how powerful Cleave's magic is. Humans restored by CPR need to rest ... it's important."

"She's out of the game," Grand Wizard Risk Master-One said. "We're just glad we didn't lose her."

Martin nodded, then circled the pitch to rejoin the Skullcrackers. Rude went to talk to Evilla.

"Martin didn't do magic," Rude said into Evilla's microphone. "He used a human medical technique ... and he's promised to provide details of it to all of us soon, so every monster can save another."

The crowd applauded appreciatively.

"The best of both worlds!" Evilla shouted. "A death ... and a resurrection ...! This is another Grotesquerie Games first ...! You witnessed it! And that's two points to Rude Stealing! 16 - 6! And pretty Gale Bunnygut is out of the game!"

Martin startled as a thin spotlight fell on him; he'd almost forgotten ...

"Martin the Magnificent, Giver of Life, faces Pettyer BloodBowels, the Bringer of Undeath!" Evilla shouted. "The game is still on!"

Martin tried to focus back on the game as he climbed the ramp. Pettyer BloodBowels was waiting for him at the top, one foot on the platform. Pettyer BloodBowels looked like a small vampire, thin and fanged with slicked-back black hair. Martin nodded to him and walked out.

"Martin, I thank you for what you did, but I can't go easy on you," Pettyer BloodBowels said.

"It would be unsportsman-like for me to expect you to," Martin said.

They faced each other, circling. Martin glanced down at the surface, which he'd barely noticed while Gale Bunnygut was unconscious. The whole top of the smooth stone platform was ruined. Two wide cracks crisscrossed it, deep gouges that appeared to be from the spikes of Rue Gland Cultster's armor dotted it, and four feet of stone was broken off one side. Yet most of it was smooth stone slick with water and blood, divided by tiny, jagged cracks.

He was wearing sneakers. Pettyer BloodBowels wore long black trousers and his colorful jersey, but no shoes. Martin charged him, caught his arms, and pushed him backwards.

Both struggled, but slowly bare feet slid ... more than Martin's sneakers. Pettyer BloodBowels seemed to realize he couldn't win this way; suddenly he kneed Martin in the chest and dropped onto him as he bent over. Martin slipped and Pettyer flipped him as he fell, landing hard on his back.

"Pettyer BloodBowels flips Martin the Magnificent!" Evilla cried. "Vampire over human!"

Martin kicked hard and rolled away, but ended up close to the edge. Pettyer BloodBowels dropped low and pushed with both hands. Fearing he'd topple, Martin grabbed the vampire's thin arms and clung tight. Pettyer BloodBowels stopped pushing.

"Let go ...!" Pettyer hissed.

"Stop pushing ... or we both fall!" Martin snarled.

Slowly vampyric fingers crawled up his arms, like spiders toward Martin's face. Martin struggled, but he couldn't gain ground. His hands were still clenched around Pettyer BloodBowels's arms; if he let go, he'd fall. Yet the vampire's greater strength was evident.

Vampyric fingers reached his eyes and hovered menacingly. Vampires didn't have long, thick claws like lizardmen, sharp, curled claws like ratlings, or short, stubby claws like goblins, but they had long, thick fingernails sharpened to points. Those dangerous points stopped only inches from Martin's eyes.

"Your call ...," Pettyer BloodBowels warned.

Martin sighed. *He could try to pull them both over the edge, but it might cost his eyes.*

"You win," Martin sighed, and he let go.

Martin fell the long drop to splash deep. Frowning, he paddled to the surface, not hurrying; he had no desire to hear Evilla announce his failure.

Crusto and Happy reached down and lifted him out with ease.

"Smart choice," Crusto whispered, and Happy nodded in agreement.

Martin blushed, ashamed.

"16 - 8!" Evilla shouted, and then the twin spotlights beamed. "Rude Stealing faces Ruddy Max-Scowall! Goblin against dark elf!"

As they walked up opposite ramps, Martin looked from one to the other. Rude and Ruddy were equal in height. Ruddy Max-Scowall was more agile, and Rude heavier, yet Rude had been studying human martial arts for most of two days.

As they ran together, Ruddy Max-Scowall dodged Rude's attempts to slap him. Rude tried to knee him, but had his leg swept aside. Rude punched and grabbed at his arms, but Ruddy Max-Scowall jumped out of range and counter-attacked with lightning speed. Yet their battle stayed in the center; neither was forced toward an edge.

Ruddy Max-Scowall kicked high; Rude caught his leg and yanked it up. The dark elf fell on his head, then flipped over and kicked Rude with his other foot. Rude fell back.

Martin frowned. Human strategies depended on

targets you could reach. Ruddy Max-Scowall was clever; he'd watched Rude fight Gale and wasn't going to give Rude the chance to choke him out of the game.

Rude charged to seize hold of his opponent, yet Ruddy Max-Scowall spun and back-flipped over him. Rude managed to grab onto his arms while he was in midair, yet Ruddy Max-Scowall finished his jump, landed on his feet, and dropped onto his back, dragging Rude forward. He caught Rude's chest with both feet and kicked hard. Rude flew over him.

Kicked far over the edge, Rude flew past the lake below ... and every Skullcracker cried out. Evilla screamed and jumped out of the way ... and Rude crashed down atop her raised stand.

Martin ran with the others. Rude was hurt again. Grand Wizard Bastile Wraithbone examined him carefully.

"No badly broken bones ... but a few may be cracked," Grand Wizard Bastile Wraithbone said. "I could heal him now, but even so, he won't play again today."

Brain and Crusto lifted Rude and laid him over Happy's back. They carried him back and set him down.

"Are you in pain?" Murder asked Rude.

"Not ... too bad," Rude hissed between clenched teeth. "Heal me ... tomorrow ... in case someone else needs ...!"

Grand Wizard Bastile Wraithbone nodded.

New spotlights suddenly shined down.

"Stabbing Kingz faces Pettyer BloodBowels!" Evilla cried. "Ratling against vampire ... 16 - 10 ... and each team is down one Small ...!"

Stabbing and Pettyer BloodBowels both climbed their ramps and walked out to face each other. Pettyer BloodBowels was taller, stronger, and had vampyric strength. Stabbing had dexterity, claws, and strategy.

Both approached slowly, neither flinching. Stabbing Kingz and Pettyer BloodBowels reached out and grabbed each other's arms. Both shifted, pushing, pulling, and twisting to one side, then the other.

Suddenly Stabbing dropped low, slipped between his legs, and jerked his hands up, still clenching an arm. Pettyer BloodBowels flipped and landed facing the edge, and Stabbing pushed him hard. Pettyer twisted, turning aside, but Stabbing matched him, and gave him no chance. Stabbing gave one last shove, and tried to yank his hands free, but as Pettyer went over, he wrapped one leg around Stabbing's knees, tilting both their weights over the edge.

Suddenly Pettyer BloodBowels transformed, but Stabbing grabbed him by one wing and drug him down.

"Stabbing Kingz takes Pettyer BloodBowels down with him!" Evilla shouted. "They splash together! One point each! 17 - 11!"

Martin watched as Crusto and Happy went to pull Stabbing out while Pettyer flew up, spraying water as he flapped. Then the spotlight shined on him.

"Martin the Magnificent faces Gale Bunnygut!" Evilla said. "Is she really out of the game ...?"

Grand Wizard Risk Master-One raised his staff and motioned it side-to-side.

"Gale Bunnygut yields!" Evilla said. "Martin the Magnificent scores two! 19 - 11!"

"Martin's tied with Rude!" Veils said. "If Rude can't play, Martin takes his place in throwing order!"

The referees waved their wands and the mists restored the bright light over the platform.

"Stabbing Kingz and Gale Bunnygut!" Evilla said. "Again ...? Yes, Stabbing Kingz wins by default! Two points to Stabbing Kingz! 21 - 11!"

Moments later, the spotlights switched targets.

"Rude Stealing and Pettyer BloodBowels!" Evilla said. "Will we have a match?"

Grand Wizard Bastile Wraithbone raised his staff and waved it side-to-side.

"Rude Stealing is unable to compete! Pettyer BloodBowels gains two! 21 - 13! A lot of injuries today ... but there's only one pair left: Martin the Magnificent and Ruddy Max-Scowall!"

"Martin, you don't have to fight!" Veils said. "Stabbing's won the most; even if you win, you won't beat him. Stabbing and Pettyer BloodBowels will fight first in the finals, no matter what. If they both fall, then you and Ruddy Max-Scowall fight! There's no other way!"

"I want to fight ...!" Martin said, looking at Rude.

"Martin, no," Rude gasped, and he glared at him. "If you get hurt, and Stabbing doesn't win, we lose. To fight when there's no need ..."

"Rude is right," Grand Wizard Bastile Wraithbone said. "Martin, we need to win. One fight is not the game. But if you can't play, Ruddy Max-Scowall gets a free shot to win the game."

Grand Wizard Bastile Wraithbone waved his staff again.

"No match!" Evilla shouted. "Two points to Ruddy Max-Scowall, 21 - 15, but the finals are decided: at five points each, Stabbing Kingz challenges Pettyer BloodBowels in the Throwing Round... for the win!"

Chapter 24
Rompday / Friday

Savage Sumo Finals ...

"Second halftime," Murder explained. "Fifteen minutes."

"It's all up to you," Happy said to Stabbing.

"You double-splashed against him once," Crusto said. "We can't afford that now."

"His vampyric strength is greater, but you're more agile," Murder said.

"Rude and Ruddy ...!" Martin said.

"What ...?" Murder asked.

"Rude and Ruddy; strength against agility!" Martin said. "Ruddy won by fast strikes and retreats, in and out, making Rude play his game."

"What do you think?" Happy asked Stabbing.

"It might work," Stabbing said.

"Don't forget the zombie head," Murder said. "Our basket will be lower, but you can't let him grab it and shoot."

"If either of you shoot and miss, your match is

over," Crusto said. "You have the better shot, and you're a better match against Ruddy Max-Scowall than Martin is against Pettyer BloodBowels. If you can, we need to win this now."

Stabbing nodded.

Veils stepped forward and kissed Stabbing's cheek. "For luck ...!" she said.

Stabbing grinned at her ... and she handed him a waterskin.

Stabbing drank while they all watched.

"Give him a moment ... and some space," Grand Wizard Bastile Wraithbone said, and they all turned and walked a few paces away, even Snitch.

As they walked away, Grand Wizard Bastile Wraithbone stayed and spoke to Stabbing alone. Only Rude overheard, since he wasn't yet able to move. A minute later, Grand Wizard Bastile Wraithbone came over and joined the group, leaving Stabbing alone with Rude, who laid beside him but didn't speak.

"Stabbing needs to focus," Grand Wizard Bastile Wraithbone said. "He'll do his best."

"He's got good skills and a plan," Murder said reassuredly.

The rest held their tongues, each with private thoughts.

"I'm so excited I've got the shivers!" Evilla cried to the crowd, startling them from their reverie. "Who's your favorite player ...? Shout their name ...!"

The crowds shouted many names, yet Martin was

too nervous to listen. This game had lasted hours, and all they'd decided was how high each basket would be, and in what order they'd fight to shoot. It was still anyone's game.

He'd only fought one match, which he'd lost, and if he fought again, he'd be facing the dark elf that had beaten Stabbing.

"We're getting ready to start!" Evilla said. "The preliminaries are done, and both teams are hungry for victory! The Roaring Giants are out of the Regionals, but nothing would make them happier than to end their season with a victory against last season's champion, the undefeated Shantdareya Skullcrackers! The Skullcrackers will be facing the Greasy Golems next week and a loss today would make their situation desperate. The zombie head is in the center, waiting to decide the game! So, players, take your places!"

With whispered well-wishes, Stabbing mounted the ramp and made his way up. On the other ramp, the vampire Pettyer BloodBowels walked up. He'd recombed his hair after his swim. Both climbed with a confidence Martin wished he had.

Referees and wizards raised wands and staffs. The horn blew.

"Let the mayhem begin!" Evilla shouted.

Both combatants stepped out onto the cracked, broken, slippery platform. Stabbing and Pettyer BloodBowels circled each other, watching warily. Martin climbed up onto the stand beside Rude, rose up on his toes, and spied the top of the zombie head, sitting dead-center on the platform, waiting to be grabbed.

Martin glanced at the baskets. The basket under the purple flag was only five feet above the platform, while the basket under the pink and orange flag was fifteen feet above the platform; mostly thanks to their Bigs, Stabbing had the easier throw. Yet neither player could throw until their opponent was pacified ... or they'd never sink a basket.

Both players feinted, then they ran together. However, Stabbing dropped low to the side and tripped Pettyer BloodBowels, who fell sprawled atop the zombie head. Stabbing hammered a fist onto his back, then jumped away as Pettyer BloodBowels took a swipe at him.

The match went as planned. Stabbing kept darting in close, striking where he could, then darting out, avoiding Pettyer BloodBowels's attacks. Pettyer kept trying to pin him, but every Small knew how to slip past an opponent, although several times Pettyer BloodBowels grabbed Stabbing's arm. Stabbing always twisted away, and finally Stabbing took advantage of his frustration. Instead of fleeing, Stabbing grabbed the hand reaching toward him and slammed his boney shoulder into Pettyer BloodBowels' chest. He didn't knock him down, but managed to twist his arm into a goose-neck hold, his hand bent forward, his elbow trapped in the crook of Stabbing's arm. With the slightest pressure on the back of his hand, his wrist bent too far. Stabbing dropped Pettyer BloodBowels to his knees, crying out in pain. They'd all practiced this judo hold, and tested it on each other, but most had assumed the odds of managing it in a game were nearly impossible.

The crowd cheered madly. Stabbing had the vampire trapped in his hold, helpless, but he couldn't grab the zombie head and shoot with one hand. He tried to force Pettyer BloodBowels toward the edge, but the vampire resisted, despite obvious pain. Stabbing pressed down on the back of his wrist with both hands, making Pettyer BloodBowels scream, then dropped him to cringe on the platform. He released his foe, who crumbled onto the stone, then snatched up the zombie head and ran toward the purple flag. All he needed was to sink one basket.

The cries of the crowd warned him. Stabbing turned to see Pettyer BloodBowels leap at him, furious, fangs bared and snarling. Stabbing dropped the zombie head onto the platform and caught Pettyer BloodBowels' forearms, attempting to fling him off, but he only dropped him onto the edge with his head and both shoulders hanging over. Pettyer twisted and tried to dig in his vampire claws, fighting to pull Stabbing down with him.

Hanging mostly over the edge, Pettyer BloodBowels knew he wouldn't win. The zombie head was by their feet ...

Pettyer BloodBowels kicked hard. His foot

contacted the zombie head; it flew, skidding across the wet, cracked top of the platform. Stabbing tore free and jumped for it, but too late: as Pettyer BloodBowels fell off one side, the zombie head rolled off the opposite edge. Both dropped to splash into the water.

"The match is over!" Evilla shouted. "Neither side won!"

Every eye turned to Martin.

"Martin, it's up to you," Murder said, and then she turned to Rude. "Rude, if Martin pulls Ruddy Max-Scowall in, do you think you can make the shot?"

"I'll try, but Gale Bunnygut looks in better shape than me," Rude said, nodding to her standing on the other side of the pitch.

"If needed, I'll do what healing I can before your match," Grand Wizard Bastile Wraithbone said.

"Very well," Murder said. "Martin, you have one goal; don't lose. If you think he's going to win, do what Pettyer BloodBowels did; kick the zombie head off the platform in any way you can. Can you do it?"

"I will," Martin said.

The ramp suddenly looked higher than ever.

"In the finals, Martin the Magnificent meets Ruddy Max-Scowall!" Evilla cried. "Dark elf against human: who will you bet on? Will the Giants regret more human surprises? Will the Skullcrackers go down in defeat? Squeeze me tight 'cause I'm about to burst!"

On the way up, Martin reminded himself how appearances mattered in combat. He rose up to his tallest as he reached the top, and placed one foot on the platform with a determined pose. On the other side appeared Ruddy Max-Scowall, who was taller, darker, and had elf-points on his ears. He looked threatening.

"Let the battle begin!" Evilla cried.

Soaking wet, the zombie head sat back in the center of the pitch. As Martin and Ruddy Max-Scowall stepped onto the platform, the zombie head raised its eyes and looked at Martin. Yet Martin had to stay focused, keep his gaze on his foe.

Ruddy Max-Scowall circled, placing Martin closest to the broken edge. Martin knew his position was more precarious there, but the stones beneath his sneakers had the biggest cracks; he'd have better traction than a barefoot dark elf.

Ruddy Max-Scowall stepped toward the zombie head ... and Martin matched his move. The dark elf stepped over the zombie head, then swung a kick at Martin's knee. Martin's fist swung to block, a Karate Kid move, although he couldn't recall if it was wash the car or sand the deck. He blocked, then tried a kick of his own.

Ruddy Max-Scowall dodged back, and then he kicked ... the zombie head! It flew up into Martin's hands, then was knocked out of his grip as he looked at it, not at his opponent. Ruddy Max-Scowall elbowed his face and knocked him backwards. Blinded, Martin grabbed at anything, clung on and pulled himself forward; *if he was going over the edge then he'd take*

Ruddy Max-Scowall with him ...!

He kicked, hoping to make contact with the zombie head, but he couldn't see it. Suddenly he was flung to the side, stumbling over his own feet. He fell, and Ruddy landed atop him.

Staggering, Martin got a foot against Ruddy's chest, and kicked. Ruddy fell backwards, yet he immediately came back low, hands extended to push Martin off. Martin struggled, grabbed his hands and yanked, determined to pull both of them off. They fought on the broken edge, strength against strength.

Martin managed to open his eyes and see clearly; the zombie head was near the broken edge. If he could reach it, then he could easily kick it off. Yet it was inches beyond his reach.

Ruddy Max-Scowall was holding him over the edge, fighting to tear free of Martin's grasp without pulling him back onto the platform. Martin clung tight, determined to end this ...!

Ruddy Max-Scowall's knee hammered into Martin's ribs. Martin reeled, and then Ruddy Max-Scowall dropped his forehead to slam into Martin's face.

Martin suffered the head-butt, yet flashing stars filled his vision. He couldn't see ...!

Ruddy shifted his hold, slapping at his stunned opponent. Martin lost his grip.

Martin fell.

Splash ...!

Ruddy Max-Scowall hadn't fallen with him ...!

Martin swam to the surface and looked up. He was right underneath the pink and orange flag.

He'd failed ...! His only hope was that an agile dark elf, with a virtual free throw, might miss the basket!

Martin saw bare toes on the edge of the platform above him. He saw the zombie head in Ruddy's hands. Their basket was ten feet over Ruddy's head. *Could he make it?*

The crowd fell silent in anticipation.

The zombie head flew high.

It landed in the basket.

"The Roaring Giants win ...!" Evilla cried.

Cheers burst from the crowd.

Martin released the side and let himself slip back underwater.

He'd failed!

He'd disappointed everyone!

He'd lost the game!

A clawed hand covered in fishscales shot into the water and grabbed him. By his jersey, Crusto drug Martin up to the surface, and Happy grabbed his arm. Together they pulled him from the water like a limp fish.

Ashamed, Martin looked down. He could say nothing.

Happy and Crusto carried him back to the team.

"It's all right, Martin," Grand Wizard Bastile Wraithbone said. "We haven't lost the Locals yet."

"We'll beat the Greasy Golems!" Murder said. "We

got into the Finals as a wildcard; if we have to, we can do it for the Regionals as well."

Martin wasn't consoled. From the stands above them came boos and catcalls, complaints from Shantdareya fans angry that they'd lost. Never had Martin felt so miserable.

"A valiant victory!" Evilla was shouting. "Against all odds, and without spells, the Roaring Giants defeat the undefeated Shantdareya Skullcrackers, who must now face the truly undefeated Greasy Golems! And here comes our final basket-sinker, that Champion of Dark Elves, the Pride of Deutsch Deathhol, Ruddy Max-Scowall! Let's hear from him on his amazing victory!"

"Can we go inside?" Martin asked.

Grand Wizard Bastile Wraithbone nodded.

Together they slunk back toward their locker room. As they neared the door, an angry, fur-covered fan threw an empty cup at them. Snitch reached up, plucked the fan from his seat, and tossed him into the water under the broken platform.

They entered the locker room in silence.

"Let's not wallow in pity," Murder said. "We ...!"

"No," Grand Wizard Bastile Wraithbone said. "We can't deny our feelings or they'll take root inside us. Let's let it all out ... tonight ... and get rid of it."

"That's best," Rude said. "Bottling up feelings just make them come out at the worst of times ..."

"This is the worst of times ...!" Stabbing snapped.

"Yes, but time continues," Happy said. "We feel

bad now, but this moment will pass. We've one week to prepare for our toughest opponent."

"Martin, you didn't let us down," Crusto said. "That could've been any of us, and we all have games our skills aren't suited for. Next week will be a different game."

"Half the blame is mine," Stabbing said. "I should've beaten Pettyer BloodBowels."

"Martin, you scored more points than I did," Rude said. "I shouldn't have let Ruddy Max-Scowall kick me ... or land onto Evilla's stand. I let myself get hurt."

"The least you could've done was land on Evilla!" Stabbing hissed, and weak laughter followed.

"Martin, we'll just have to practice harder for next week," Veils said.

"Indeed we will," Grand Wizard Bastile Wraithbone said. "Until then, I'm sorry, Martin, but this is the longest game you've ever played. The Knights of the Unliving Dread still have to play the Flying Munchers, and if the Greasy Golems had an opponent, they'd be playing into daylight. You have school in a few hours. I have to send you home."

"No, tomorrow's Saturday; no school," Martin said. "Yet ... there's nothing I can do here. I'm so sorry. Send me home; it's what I deserve."

"I need to dry you off first," Grand Wizard Bastile Wraithbone said.

Martin nodded. Grand Wizard Bastile Wraithbone raised his staff and wiggled his fingers while everyone watched in silence.

Martin dried off completely, yet he had never felt so miserable.

Chapter 25
Smashday / Saturday

Defeat runs deep ...

Martin slept late, then got up and went to brush his teeth. In the mirror he saw a frightening sight; his right cheek was bright with a swelling bruise ... from Ruddy Max-Scowall's forehead.

How could he explain this to his parents?

Martin turned on the tap and splashed some water onto the bathroom floor. Quietly Martin reached over and locked the bathroom door. Then, gritting his teeth, Martin jumped up high and bodily crashed down onto the bathroom floor as hard as he could land, shaking the whole house.

"What ....?" Martin's dad cried. *"What was that ....? Who ....?"*

Martin cried out as if in pain. Footsteps echoed, coming closer. The doorknob rattled.

"Who's in there?" his dad called. "Martin, is that you?"

Martin let out a loud, piteous groan.

"Martin, open this door!" Martin's dad shouted.

Slowly Martin reached up and flipped the lock. The door flew open ... and smacked him on his head.

"What happened ...?" his dad demanded.

"Water ... on the floor ...!" Martin grimaced, and he pointed to the wet puddles.

"You slipped ...?" his dad asked. "Stand up. Let me see ... Oh, my ...! What did you do ...?"

Martin pointed to the edge of the bathroom sink, gasping as if pained.

"Well, you've certainly done it now," his father said. "Your gym teacher wants you to play basketball ... and you can't walk into a bathroom without slipping ...!"

Pulled to his feet, Martin was drug out of the bathroom, across the hall, and into the living room.

"Who spilled water all over the bathroom floor?" his father demanded of his brothers. They all looked surprised, shaking their heads. "Look what happened to your brother! If I have to tell you again ...! If I catch anyone making a mess ...! Ron, go clean that water off the floor! Now! Before your mother gets home ..!"

Martin spent the whole day feeling awful. He felt like he'd betrayed his team. He hated Savage Sumo, the most barbaric game he'd yet played. He hated Ruddy Max-Scowall, the brutal dark elf. He hated the Roaring Giants. He even hated Deutsch Deathhol ... and he didn't even know what or where it was.

Mostly, he hated himself.

He played a single-POV shooter against his brothers and died a dozen times in an hour. He went out into the backyard, but only sat on the swing, too angry to exercise.

Food tormented his stomach. Nothing on TV amused him. Vicky's books looked accursed; he wouldn't even touch one.

Vicky; he wished he could talk to Vicky. She'd know what to say ...

When his mother saw him, she raged, screaming at him for not being more careful. According to her, he could've somehow lost an eye.

Martin didn't tell her how close he'd come to losing both eyes ... to the thick, sharp fingernails of a vampire. Yet, by then his father had calmed down, and he took her into their room to talk.

Martin couldn't blame her; he'd been careless ... and let a dark elf push him off the platform.

Now he was telling another lie to his parents.

Martin consoled his conscience. He couldn't tell them the truth; he's tried to explain about Heterodox and the Grotesquerie Games after he'd broken his arm in the Finals, and they hadn't believed him then ...

The day lasted an eternity and the evening lasted even longer. He dreaded facing his teammates ...

What could he say to them ...?

They could lose the Locals!

Their whole season could end in one game!

No one caught Martin. He fell hard onto the stone floor, then had to pick himself up. The locker room was empty. He checked all the stalls, and even knocked on Murder and Veil's locker room door, but no one answered. He walked up the stairs and out onto the pitch.

The stone platform was gone. Inside the lake swirled a powerful whirlpool, the churning water circling endlessly, sucking everything down.

Jeers and catcalls made him turn around. The stands were full of monsters, snarling, scowling, bearing fangs, tusks, and pincers, angrily shaking claws, tentacles, long insectoid limbs, and large, hairy paws knotted into fists. Wings rose menacingly. Horns, feelers, and spiked ridges rose over heads. Furious purple eyes stared down.

Their hate stung Martin. They shouted horrible things, blaming him, and he stuttered, unable to speak. The stands rose higher, and a fierce wind blew him back. He fell into the whirlpool, spiraling around its vortex, about to be dragged down to its eternal depths.

Martin awoke as he fell into Crusto's hands. They were in the locker room, and Murder was with him.

"Feeling better?" Murder asked.

"No," Martin said angrily.

"Losing is part of every competition," Crusto said as he set Martin down. "You can't always win ... no matter how hard you try. All of us have lost at least one game, and felt it was our fault, but we can't let one loss make us lose forever. Either quit ... or help us win the next game."

"Crusto, can I talk to Martin ... alone?" Murder asked.

Crusto nodded, and then he stomped his webbed feet up the stairs and out the door.

"He's right," Murder said. "Players don't win or lose; teams do."

"I feel awful," Martin said.

"Good," Murder said. "No real athlete could lose a competition and not feel bad ... it would mean they didn't care about the game."

"I let everyone down," Martin said.

"Stabbing and Rude feel the same way," Murder said. "They both faced Ruddy Max-Scowall ... and Rude lost to him, too. If they'd taken him out of play, then you wouldn't have had to face him. We could've trained you harder. No one player bears all the blame."

A silence fell.

"Admit it," Murder ordered. "Agree with me ... or call me a liar."

Martin swallowed hard.

"I agree," Martin said. "But I could've ... fought harder ...!"

"Yes, but that's true for all of us ... in every game," Murder said. "Look what you did: you saved a life. None of us could've done that."

"Yes ... and we could've lost because of that," Martin said.

"Personally, I'd rather lose than feel guilty for killing an opponent," Murder said. "You think losing a game hurts? Think how bad Rude would feel if Gale Bunnygut had died ... because he'd choked her to death. Others have died in these games, and I can tell you: losing a game is nothing compared to that feeling."

Martin shrugged; he understood her words, yet he couldn't imagine feeling worse than he did.

"Martin ...?" Veils voice came from behind him.

Martin turned to see Veils come out of the girl's locker room.

"I'll leave the two of you to talk," Murder said.

Murder grabbed a cane, the sleek black cane Rude had used, and walked out leaning heavily on it, without crutches. Martin watched her go, then closed his eyes. He didn't want to talk to Veils.

Slowly, soft arms wrapped around and held him tightly. Martin gritted his teeth ... yet he didn't push her away.

Her head pressed against his shoulder.

Long moments passed; Martin had no idea how long ... *minutes ... or hours?* He'd lost track of time, feeling her hold him. Slowly he embraced her back, and they held each other in silence.

"Martin, have you ever gone sledding?" Veils finally asked.

This was such a strange question Martin stammered.

"S-s-sledding ...?" Martin asked.

"Riding a sled," Veils said. "On ice. Our final game

is ... Hell Hockey."

Holding his hand, Veils took Martin out to see the pitch. The stadium was round no more, and no lake or platform stood in its middle. Instead, a small ice arena lay before them, all inside a short, two-foot wall. The frozen rink was composed of two joined circles, outlining a vast, icy figure eight.

Snitch, Brain, Happy, and Crusto stood outside the short wall on opposite sides, two on each circle, holding large hockey sticks. However, no puck was in sight. Flying across the ice were Stabbing and Rude, both on tiny racing sleds, wooden slats with metal rails and raised ends, skidding around the circles dangerously fast.

As each Small reached a Big, a hockey stick was lowered behind them, swung, and struck the raised back of their sled, speeding the Small onward.

"Hell Hockey," Veils said. "A fast, high-scoring game ... and a dangerous one."

As Martin watched, Stabbing swirled around one circle, skittering against the short wall, propelled by the hockey stick of Brain. When he reached the end of one circle, Stabbing's path straightened out. He shot across the open space into the next circle. Then Stabbing met its short wall and skidded along it, circling in the opposite direction.

Martin saw the danger. When sledding in a figure eight, at the cross-point, collisions were likely.

"This isn't good," Veils said. "When sleds collide, weight matters. Maxivoom Snydho is the heaviest Small in the league ..."

Martin understood.

"And spells will be cast," Veils said. "Neither we nor the Greasy Golems have used a spell. They saved the best teams for the last game, we're sure to get hit."

"By what ...?" Martin asked.

"Who knows ...?" Veils answered. "Grandfather is working on several scrolls ... we don't know which we'll need."

No one waved or said hello. Veils took Martin over to Snitch, showed him a line of unused sleds, and pointed out the only two controls on the sleds ... a steering bar and a brake, which dropped iron spikes into the ice beneath the sled.

"How do we win?" Martin asked.

"There's a goal box on each end," Veils said. "Throw the zombie head inside the box as you slide past it. Then the head reappears in the middle ..."

"Where the sleds collide," Martin finished.

"Just practice steering today," Veils said. "Try to not collide."

Each took a sled and carried it to Snitch. Martin laid face-down on his sled and slid his hands inside the little metal shields protecting the steering bar. Then Snitch picked up his sled, with Martin on it, and set both onto the ice; not against the wall, where Rude and Stabbing slid past at irregular intervals, but closer to the center of one circle, where they just missed him. He turned Martin's sled to face the direction they were travelling, then put his hockey stick behind Martin. Martin lifted his feet to rest inside the raised back of his sled. Snitch waited for Rude and Stabbing to pass, and then gave Martin a hard, sudden shove.

Martin slid across the ice, twisting his steering bar to keep from ramming into the wall, yet his momentum was fierce. He scraped hard against the low fence. Yet he made it halfway around the circle, seeing Rude and Stabbing quickly catching up with him. Then Crusto's hockey stick whacked him from behind. He slid along faster, completing the circle and sliding across the open middle.

Rude was right behind him; the front of his sled bumped against Martin from behind. They approached Brain, and he ignored Martin and swung to hit Rude's sled. Accelerated, Rude slammed into Martin and knocked him forward. By the time he'd circled to where Happy was standing, Martin was flying across the ice, struggling to keep control.

Veils mounted a sled; soon four figures were flying around the figure eight. Each struggled to not run into the others ... and Martin knew what would happen if they did ...

Not if ... when they collided ...!

Chapter 26
Smiteday / Sunday

Visit from a friend ...

When they returned from church, Martin spent the day reading Vicky's book and the evening shooting at aliens ... who bore a striking resemblance to Vicky's evil Slurks. Martin felt like he was one of the space elves, a defender of Zantheriak, fighting the immortal scourge of the galaxy. The virtual Slurks even had a hidden base, and Martin blasted it with an electron death ray that strongly resembled a proto-plasma cannon ... which Vicky claimed to have invented.

He wondered about the similarities. No doubt the inventors of this game had grown up watching the same movies and TV shows. He wondered if any of them had ever visited Zantheriak ... or Heterodox.

"Look out ...!" Tom shouted from the recliner.

"Here they come ...!" Ron shouted from the other side of the couch.

Martin turned his powerful weapon toward the approaching fleet of enemy ships, wondering if he was blasting apart the origin of Slurk Scavenger ships ... and if he shouldn't go with Vicky to fly on spaceships and shoot laser pistols.

So many different stories ... generation after generation ... all with similar technologies ... or magic ... used against similar enemies ... how could they not all be related?

Martin awoke as he dropped into Brain's hands. Murder was there again, watching as Brain set him down.

"Feeling better?" she asked.

"No ... not as badly," Martin said.

"We all get angry," Murder said. "Yet anger is our deadliest enemy. Anger clouds your thinking so you make bad choices, which often leads to losing."

"I didn't get angry ... I lost," Martin said.

"Your strategy didn't work," Murder said. "Stabbing succeeded because you gave him a winning strategy ... and he followed it. You were outmatched; you needed a strategy that gave you the advantage."

"I'm not sure if any strategy would've worked," Martin confessed.

"Then you've no reason to berate yourself for losing," Murder said.

Murder used her cane, but she also held onto Martin's shoulder, straining to support herself. Yet she was obviously in pain.

"Brain, pick her up," Martin said.

"No, I ...," Murder began.

"Are you enjoying the pain ... or are you too smart to listen to good advice ...?" Martin asked.

Murder sighed. Brain picked her up, carried her out to the pitch, and set her in the front row of the stands.

Rude and Stabbing were both expert sledders. Despite being sore from Savage Sumo, they demonstrated moves Martin would've never attempted on his own. Both could turn their sleds so hard they returned to their own circle rather than transfer to the other, but it was difficult. If you turned too lightly, you'd slam headfirst into the sharp joint ... and fly over the short wall to land on your face. If you turned too fast, you'd flip your sled and crash into the wall, and the next person whizzing around the circle would likely plow you down.

Martin and Veils attempted to match their tricks at slower speeds with limited success.

The sleds grated against the wall as they circled, but you could use that friction to slow yourself down if you wanted to ... which let you time your crosses to cause or evade a collision. If you turned just right, staying inches from the wall, then you circled much faster. Their sleds' runners cut grooves in the ice. Yet the sleds were light; Rude and Stabbing could jump, pull their sled up and out of the grooves, and cut across the middle of a circle. Martin and Veils took a long time to learn this technique.

Because of the raised back end of the sleds, where

they got slapped by the hockey sticks, they had to ride with bent knees, their feet up in the air. It was dangerous, but you could drag a toe on the ice to help you to turn ... or to prevent a tight turn from flipping you over. However, other sleds could crash into you, and extending a leg was risky.

Martin's shoes proved an advantage even greater than Stabbing's claws.

"I have an idea," Martin said. "We need some ... metal spikes."

When Martin explained his idea, Happy galloped back to their locker room and returned with two thick rolls of athletic tape and three quivers of arrows. Martin took off his shoes and taped three arrows to each of his feet, their points extending an inch beyond the edges of his toes. He wrapped his feet like he was foot-binding himself, and ended up with feet like a mummy ... with three long, sharp, metal toenails.

Laying down on his sled, Martin held tight as Crusto started him around the circular rink with a strong push. When Martin dropped a foot to the ice, arrows scraped deeper and stronger than toes, claws, or even sneakers could.

"This is perfect!" Grand Wizard Bastile Wraithbone said. "We should all ... *Grand Wizard Veinlet Prize ...!*"

Everyone stopped and looked up. To their amazement, Grand Wizard Veinlet Prize was calmly walking toward them.

"Impressive!" Grand Wizard Veinlet Prize said, eyeing Martin's taped feet with arrows sticking out of them. "Another ... human invention?"

"Actually, I just thought about it," Martin said.

"You honor us, brother Grand Wizard Veinlet Prize," Grand Wizard Bastile Wraithbone said. "Welcome to our practice."

"Oh, I won't interrupt for long," Grand Wizard Veinlet Prize said. "I wish my team was playing Hell Hockey; I'd show them this trick. Yet I wished to have a ... brief, private conversation with Martin, if you would allow it. I shan't keep him long, my brother."

"That would be up to Martin," Grand Wizard Bastile Wraithbone said, and everyone looked at Martin.

Martin looked at his feet.

"I really can't walk wearing arrows on my feet," Martin said. "If you'd allow Snitch to carry me, I'd ... welcome a brief conversation."

"Of course," Grand Wizard Veinlet Prize said. "Shall we walk this way?"

Martin had Snitch lift him and walk beside Grand Wizard Veinlet Prize, whom Martin knew was really Grand Master Wizard Borgias Killoff. Martin waited until they were far apart enough that his companions couldn't hear.

"So, how is Grand Witch Maim La Nuormal?" Martin asked.

"The Queen of Wanderlost is as beautiful as always," Grand Master Wizard Borgias Killoff said. "She

341

wonders greatly about my relationship with you."

"Still keeping secrets from her ...?" Martin asked.

"Only when I must," Grand Master Wizard Borgias Killoff said.

"I hear you're putting on plays, and you've set up contests for storytellers ...?" Martin asked.

"It's been a rousing success," Grand Master Wizard Borgias Killoff said. "The monsters love them, and I offer valuable jewels to the winners."

"Are they becoming more civilized?" Martin asked.

"Civilized behavior requires a standard against which it can be measured," Grand Master Wizard Borgias Killoff said. "Until now it's been eating from a pantry, not killing and eating each other. However, I believe a common theme is being effected."

"What theme?" Martin asked.

"The same theme that exists in the human world," Grand Master Wizard Borgias Killoff said. "The heroes of popular stories are always noble, willing to sacrifice themselves to help others, while the villains are greedy and care only about themselves."

"That's true on Earth," Martin said.

"True on all worlds," Grand Master Wizard Borgias Killoff said. "The kindhearted gain life-long friends. The greedy gain vast possessions. Each wants what the other has, and only by choosing a balance can anyone have the best of both worlds ... but those with a balance only average at both and excel at neither."

"Everyone needs to know what they need to be

happy," Martin said.

"Exactly," Grand Master Wizard Borgias Killoff said. "Yet I didn't come to talk to you about theater and civil philosophies."

"What do you want?" Martin asked.

"I'd like some advice," Grand Master Wizard Borgias Killoff said. "You're clever, and I'm too close to the situation to trust my own judgment."

"What about?" Martin asked.

"Grand Witch Maim La Nuormal, of course," Grand Master Wizard Borgias Killoff said. "I'd like to end my charade. I can keep this appearance, as she likes it, but I'd prefer to announce my true self and resume my title and duty as leader of the Grand Council of Wizards."

"Tell her the truth," Martin said.

"I've misspoken," Grand Master Wizard Borgias Killoff said. "What I meant to say was that I'd like to end my charade ... without losing her affections or getting myself murdered."

"That's a lot to ask," Martin said.

"Hence my dilemma," Grand Master Wizard Borgias Killoff said.

Martin thought about it.

"The best advice I can give is: don't ask me," Martin said. "I'm only twelve. I've never been in a relationship. However, I know someone who has: Vicky, my sister. She wants to come to watch our match against the Greasy Golems ... and she's not part of this world, so she can keep your secret."

"Excellent!" Grand Master Wizard Borgias Killoff said. "That was what worried me; you and I are the only ones who know my true identity, and I want to keep it that way until I decide how to tell Grand Witch Maim La Nuormal."

"Always glad to help," Martin grinned, glad he hadn't divulged that Evilla knew his secret, too.

"As I said, heroes always help those who need it," Grand Master Wizard Borgias Killoff said. Then he looked up at Snitch. "Your troll won't remember any of this, will he?"

"Unlikely ... and not for long," Martin said. "I need to get back to practice."

"Good luck on Rompday," Grand Master Wizard Borgias Killoff said. "Oh, speaking of that: Maxivoom Snydho has sworn vengeance against you for putting them out of the last season's Finals."

"I'm not surprised," Martin said.

"A wise person would find a way to take advantage of that," Grand Master Wizard Borgias Killoff said.

Martin smiled in agreement.

Chapter 27
Stompday / Monday

Devious magical cunning ...

"No!" Ron shouted. "I want cereal!"

"You'll ruin your dinner," Martin said. "Mom and dad will be home soon."

"Vicky let us ...!" Ron shouted.

"Vicky let you have carrots and celery," Martin said. "You can't eat a meal ...!"

"You're not my boss!" Ron shouted. "I'm hungry!"

Tom and Terry rose to their youngest brother's defense.

"We're allowed to eat after school!" Tom argued.

"We won't last until dinner ...!" Terry insisted.

"No!" Martin shouted. "I'm in charge! You'll do as I say!"

Martin fell into Crusto's hands. Only Grand Wizard Bastile Wraithbone was with him.

"Thank you, Crusto, and welcome back, Martin," Grand Wizard Bastile Wraithbone said.

Crusto set Martin onto the floor, then nodded and walked off, up the stairs and out the door. Martin turned to face Grand Wizard Bastile Wraithbone.

"Obviously I wished to speak to you," Grand Wizard Bastile Wraithbone said. "I wanted to ask you about your conversation with Grand Wizard Veinlet Prize."

"He asked for my help ... with a personal problem," Martin said.

"Indeed ...?" Grand Wizard Bastile Wraithbone asked. "I thought he and Grand Witch Maim La Nuormal were getting along quite well."

"They are, but not as 'well' as he'd like," Martin said.

"I see," Grand Wizard Bastile Wraithbone said. "And ... did you help him?"

"I pointed him to someone who knows far more than I do about relationships ... someone whose advice would be better," Martin said.

"Might I ask ...?" Grand Wizard Bastile Wraithbone asked.

"My sister, Vicky," Martin said. "However, the subject of his problem was told in confidence."

"That's none of my concern," Grand Wizard Bastile Wraithbone said. "For the sake of the team, I had to ask."

"We didn't discuss the games," Martin said. "Wait; he told me Maxivoom Snydho has sworn vengeance against me."

"That's a worrisome statement," Grand Wizard Bastile Wraithbone said.

"Yes, and he said something else," Martin said. "A wise person would find a way to take advantage of Maxivoom Snydho's hate."

"We must endeavor to be wise," Grand Wizard Bastile Wraithbone said. "We defeated Grand Wizard Veinlet Prize's team, the Grave Gutters, in the last game of the Finals. Who would've thought he'd say anything to aid us ...?"

"When a good man asks a favor, he repays his debt," Martin said. "I can't say for sure ... but I think you and Grand Wizard Veinlet Prize may have a lot in common ... more than you know."

"You call Grand Wizard Veinlet Prize a 'good man'...?" Grand Wizard Bastile Wraithbone asked, seeming astounded. "Do we share any similarities you could elaborate upon ...?

"Not without revealing private confidences," Martin said. "However, I personally think your long-term goals for Heterodox are ... similar."

"Perhaps he and I should speak confidentially," Grand Wizard Bastile Wraithbone said.

"Together's always best," Martin smiled.

Side-by-side they walked out to the pitch. Everyone was on the ice or beside it. Murder was shouting instructions while Bigs hurled Smalls around the figure eight. To Martin's surprise, she was holding the zombie head in her lap, and both were watching the sledders.

Stabbing squeezed his brake, scraping into the ice to slow his sled, trying to avoid a collision with Veils. She slowed just as much. The resultant collision occurred, but it was softer, driving them both in opposite directions, back onto the rinks they'd just circled. However, Rude had been hastening to catch up with Veils. Rude yanked on his brake to slow his sled and still collided into Stabbing from behind.

Veils laughed at both of them.

Martin grabbed a sled from the pile and carried it to Snitch as Rude and Stabbing ganged up on Veils. By then she was careening almost out of control, trying to escape from Rude, who was chasing her, and Stabbing, who was timing his midfield-crosses to collide with her. Veils evaded as best she could, yet every time they crossed the center was a near-collision. Murder was yelling at all three of them.

Finally Veils tried to beat Stabbing's speed across the center ... and failed. He slammed into her from the side, and Rude collided with both. Veils' sled flipped onto its side and skittered across the ice. Veils went sliding, spinning around inside one circle, unable to stop herself.

"Dig in with your toes!" Murder shouted.

Veils did as Murder instructed and scraped to a stop. Martin noticed they all had three arrows thickly taped to each foot.

"Veils, get off the ice and back onto your sled!" Murder shouted. "Martin, I've got your arrows."

Martin left his sled by Snitch and went to get taped. Once the arrows were on his feet, he felt as if he were walking in steel-tipped snowshoes, yet he managed to get back to his sled and lay down upon it.

"Snitch, add Martin to the ice," Murder said.

Snitch stopped hitting sleds with his hockey stick long enough to pick up Martin's sled, with him on it, and lift it onto the ice. Then he gave Martin a sudden push ... directly across a circle. Martin twisted the steering bar yet slammed into the two-foot wall, then almost fell off when Brain slapped the back of his sled with his hockey stick and drove him onward. However, Martin wasn't going fast enough ... Stabbing smashed into his rear, and then Rude hit Stabbing. Martin was knocked forward, and steered around the circle ... but Veils skidded around Stabbing and Rude and came at Martin from the side.

Crash ...!

Jolted by the impact, Martin clung tightly and flailed his legs, one of which slammed into the wall beside him. She'd driven right into him, clinging just tight enough to keep from being knocked off.

"Hi ...!" Veils laughed at Martin.

"What was that for?" Martin asked.

"That's how you stop an opponent about to score," Veils said.

"Enough of that!" Murder shouted, and she held up the zombie head. "Stabbing and Martin are the purple team! Rude and Veils are the burgundy team! Get moving! I keep score!"

The Bigs got them moving, each Small circling fast. Grand Wizard Bastile Wraithbone waved his staff, and the zombie head floated out of Murder's grip to hover in the center.

Rude reached up and caught the zombie head first. He dropped it into the burgundy box as he passed it, and moments later it reappeared floating in the center. Stabbing grabbed it as he crossed the center and dropped it into the purple box. Only ten seconds had passed between scores.

Veils grabbed the zombie head, but missed her attempt to score. Her toss dropped the zombie head past the burgundy box, where it rolled across the grass and packed dirt.

In a flash, the zombie head vanished, then appeared just before Martin crossed the center. He reached out and seized it, then found his sled harder to steer with only one hand. His sled scraped against the wall and visibly slowed.

"Take your time!" the zombie head said. "Better to hold onto me than miss the box!"

Martin timed carefully, letting centrifugal force hurl the rotting head; he just had to release it at the right time.

He scored.

Veils missed grabbing the head when it reappeared, skittered sideways, and ended up trapped in the center, not moving. She put a foot on the ice and reached for the head.

"Veils, no ...!" Grand Wizard Bastile Wraithbone shouted.

"Get back on your sled!" Murder ordered. *"Are you crazy? Never get off your sled! It's dangerous!"*

Reluctantly, Veils laid back down on her unmoving sled. Then Stabbing came hurtling around the circle to the center, braking and veering; he hit her at an angle. His grazing impact knocked her forward and drove him back onto the same circle. Happy got Stabbing moving again, and on his next rotation, he veered across the center to hit Veils again, and knocked her into range of Crusto. Crusto tried to get her moving, but had to yank back his hockey stick as Martin came barreling around the circle and slammed into her from behind.

They continued practicing for several hours, then Murder called for a halt. Grand Wizard Bastile Wraithbone called them over to talk.

"We have to send Martin home early tonight," Grand Wizard Bastile Wraithbone said. "He has school in the morning and needs rest. Martin seems to have the basics, and we need to talk before he goes."

Everyone gathered around, Smalls walking on taped arrows.

"Now, with magic, timing is everything ... which is just as important as the spell," Grand Wizard Bastile Wraithbone said. "We don't know what they're planning; they may have numerous options or only one. They could plan something to dominate the game, or slow it, or to attack one player, and we won't know which until they cast it.

"They may want us to cast first. Some spells counter your opponent's spell, some seek to cause equal devastation, and some try to reverse the effects of a spell onto the team casting it. If we wait until they cast, we might be able to cast a spell to undo theirs, or they could undo ours. I'll decide when to cast as best I can, but it involves many factors. You must be ready at any time for spells to hit the pitch."

"Shout the instant you see a scroll," Murder instructed.

"Now, I've prepared four spells," Grand Wizard Bastile Wraithbone said. "The first is a Fog Cloud, which will cover their half of the pitch with a thick, white fog ... impossible to see through. This only lasts until the half is over. You'll be able to score easily and they won't, but if they get the zombie head, they'll try to keep it as long as they can."

All nodded grimly.

"The second is a Twisted Ramp spell," Grand Wizard Bastile Wraithbone said. "A solid purple ramp appears somewhere around the pitch. Those who go up that ramp will flip over and fly out ... either out of the arena or into the center of the other circle. If you see it, you must veer around it ... or you'll suffer the same fate."

"Pity we can't use both of those," Stabbing said.

"The third is a standard Fireball spell," Grand Wizard Bastile Wraithbone said. "Anyone caught in the blast will get badly burned, so we'll try to get as many of them as possible without hitting any of you. However, like lightning bolts, fireballs are unpredictable and hard to aim. Don't sled into flames."

"Avoid fire, even if you must crash into a teammate," Rude said. "I've gotten burned before."

"The last is a Magic Reversal spell," Grand Wizard Bastile Wraithbone said. "If they cast something dangerous at us, I may be able to negate it ... it depends on the type of spell they cast. Of course, we also have my healing spell."

"A good arsenal," Veils said. "But what if Maxivoom Snydho goes after Martin? Do we have any plan?"

"This is a game of collisions," Rude said. "We collide when they have the zombie head. They collide when we do. We try to upset each other's chances at scoring."

"We've got to think of something," Stabbing said. "Ram armor won't help this time."

"Martin, if ever we needed a human plan, this is it," Grand Wizard Bastile Wraithbone said. "Maxivoom Snydho has a terrible temper. If we can't nullify him, we won't win ... and either we win the Locals or we're out for the season."

Chapter 28
Rompday / Tuesday

Facing your enemy ...

School was a nightmare. Martin had managed to get some sleep, but he couldn't focus on lessons. He couldn't stop worrying about Maxivoom Snydho. Even in gym class he failed, not running as fast as he could and missing every cue. Coach Anderson asked him what was wrong, but his question just infuriated Martin. He could afford a bad grade more than he could afford to get killed by an angry wereboar.

In math, his teacher called on him to demonstrate multiplying fractions, but Martin couldn't do it. Humiliated, he stormed back to his desk and threw himself into his seat.

After school, the food-argument erupted as soon as the video games started. Martin shouted back at his brothers, refusing their every request. Shouts turned into screams, and Martin was soon unable to hear anything but an incoherent babble bursting from his brother's mouths. They weren't even making sense ...

just calling names, trying to make him angry ...

Make him angry ...?

Suddenly Martin laughed. His reaction surprised his brothers into silence.

"One small bag of popcorn," Martin said.

"For each of us ...!" Terry demanded.

"No, one for all three of you," Martin said. "I won't have any. I'll pop it and divide it into three bowls ..."

Five minutes later, Martin carried three bowls into the living room, set one before each brother, and they grabbed and stuffed their mouths as fast as they could, trying to keep their hands on their controllers.

Martin smiled; *he had a plan ...!*

Martin fell into Snitch's hands. The whole team was waiting for him.

"I'm ready," Martin said. "Where's Maxivoom ...?"

"Right outside," Grand Wizard Bastile Wraithbone said.

"Let's go get him!" Martin grinned wickedly.

The Smalls all had arrows taped to their feet, and waited while Martin took off his shoes and taped arrows to his. Then they wandered out, the Bigs carrying the Smalls. Evilla's voice rose above the cheering crowd as they stepped into the starlight.

"Here they come, the Shantdareya Skullcrackers!" Evilla's voice blasted over the loud speakers. "Down one game, they're fighting for their life tonight! Led by the always revered Grand Wizard Bastile Wraithbone, here

comes Allfed Snitchlock, recently re-proven the
Strongest Troll in the League, carrying Rowdy Rude
Stealing! Here's Brain Stroker, the Ultimate Cranium-
Strainium, carrying everyone's favorite Hidden Dagger,
Stabbing Kingz! What's that on their feet? Behind them
is Crusto Fernwalker, the Lizard who lays down the Law!
And here's Hammering Happy Lostcraft, the Stomping
Centaur, and the soon-to-be-off-injured-reserve
Murderin' Murder Shelling! On Happy's back rides that
Sucker-Punching Sweetie, Velvety Vivacious Veils! And
riding behind her is their Master-Strategist, that Wonder
of the Human World, Martin the Magnificent!"

As they had during the Finals, the crowd went wild.
This was the last game of the Locals and only the Greasy
Golems were guaranteed a spot in the Regionals or a
Wildcard.

"And here they are!" Evilla said. "From DeSpire ...
Grand Wizard Crass Gopherly leading his team, the
Greasy Golems! Here's that Wonderful Were-boar, the
Tusks of Terror, Maxivoom Snydho!"

The crowd cheered his name and he waved at them.

"And behind him is that Granite Gatling, Golem
Ton Eat-oddly, with that Rose of Ratling Beauty,
Crowscary Morguee! Following her is our favorite
Gruesome Gremlin, Flea Scarwart Monastary! We're
sorry to hear that sexy Pale Char is on injured reserve
after her sacrifice defeat of the Gorgedown X-Lorecists
... she's one brave goblin! And here are their Three
Triumphant Trolls, Joke CrampyLiar, Fart Hurlo Con-

well, and rookie troll Cats Grass!"

Pennants waved as the crowd went wild. Martin noticed many monsters in the stands wore Greasy Golem burgundy. They'd saved this rivalry for the final game to keep the excitement going.

"The Greasy Golems are undefeated!" Evilla continued. "Their path to the Regionals is guaranteed! They could take it easy, avoid risk of injury, and sail onwards. Yet they could also avenge their loss in last season's Finals and prevent a hated rival from reaching the next level! How hard will they play? We'll soon know ... in this last game of the Locals of the three hundred and fifteenth season of the Grotesquerie Games! So sit back with me, your Amazing, Amorous Announcer, your sexy Mistress of Mayhem, and share with me this Riotous Rivalry, the vengeful Greasy Golems against the surprising Shantdareya Skullcrackers! Grab a cool glass of Icy Inchworms, some Black Widow Brownies, Deep-fried Deviled Dodos, or a bag of Ghostly Gobblers, and let's snuggle down for a night we'll never forget!"

By agreement, Snitch and Veils stayed out for the first half; she'd take Martin's place for the second half, as he'd done for her in Net-Door Maze. Happy, Crusto, and Brain each picked up a Small on a sled and took their places around the pitch.

Crusto took center on one side, right between the circles. Ton Eat-oddly stood opposite; they would manage the dangerous crossing where sleds risked colliding. On Crusto's left was the troll Joke CrampyLiar, and to his right was Fart Hurlo Con-well. On Ton Eat-oddly's left was Brain and on his right was Happy. Each held a hockey stick and stood ready to get their teammates moving.

On the ice, right behind him, was his dreaded foe, Maxivoom Snydho. Before him was the female ratling, Crowscary Morguee. Between Rude and Stabbing was the small gremlin, Flea Scarwart Monastary.

"The ice is set!" Evilla cried. "Wands are raising! Staffs are raising! Here's the horn! Let the mayhem begin!"

Hockey sticks whacked the rears of six sleds and the game began. The sleds were hurled onwards and raced around the figure eight. Bigs were careful not to touch the sleds of another team, a fact they'd failed to explain, yet Martin was glad no Greasy Golem Bigs would be whacking his sled.

They circled the entire figure eight twice, avoiding collisions, and then the zombie head appeared, floating high over the center, too high to grab, but slowly descending.

Several hands reached for it, but Crowscary Morguee first snatched the zombie head out of midair. She headed to score, yet Crusto whacked Martin exceptionally hard, and he slammed into her rear. She fumbled the zombie head as she tried to score; it bounced off the side of the burgundy box and rolled away. Then it rose high, floated to the center, and slowly descended again. This time Stabbing grabbed it, and he slid to score. From Flea Scarwart Monastary, Stabbing suffered the same as Crowscary Morguee, being rammed from behind, but Stabbing didn't shoot; Stabbing circled to the center. He passed the zombie head to Rude, braking just before he crossed the center to block the enemy sled behind him, yet let Rude slide by. Rude scored easily, and with a flash, the zombie head appeared almost instantly in the center, as if it had fallen through a magic hole in the purple box. Flea Scarwart Monastary grabbed it and scored moments later.

Stabbing scored next, followed by Maxivoom Snydho. Martin pulled on his brake to slow down so he didn't shoot past the center until the head appeared, yet Flea Scarwart Monastary came speeding around the other circle, reaching for the head at the same time.

Their sleds crashed as both grabbed for the zombie head. Flea Scarwart Monastary snarled and gnashed his teeth inches from Martin's face, yet gremlins were small; Martin yanked the zombie head out of his hands. However, their collision sent each back around the circle they'd just traversed, so Martin couldn't score.

Just in front of Martin, Maxivoom hammered on his brake, making Martin run into him, but Stabbing jumped the ruts and came flying across the middle of the burgundy circle.

"Martin ...!" Stabbing called.

As he slid past, Martin tossed the zombie head to Stabbing, who masterfully skidded to slam into the two foot wall, ending his momentum, right in front of the burgundy scoring box.

A huge pile-up built; Martin crashed into the jumble, then felt three sleds run into him from behind. He couldn't tell who hit him last. Crusto or Fart Hurlo Con-well must've pushed someone, who turned out to be Rude, whose sled hit Martin's, which drove Stabbing into Brain's reach. Stabbing scored on his next circle, then jumped the track as Martin came hurtling around at him. Martin plowed into the back of Maxivoom's sled, and forced Maxivoom into the back of Rude's sled. Rude bounced forward enough that Happy could sweep him along, but Flea Scarwart Monastary was trapped in the center, blocking everyone's path.

Happy pushed hard; Rude crashed into Flea Scarwart Monastary and knocked him aside, and then Stabbing grabbed the zombie head and rejoined the action, reached by Crusto, with no sleds between him and the purple scoring box. Crusto dragged Stabbing into the Shantdareya circle and gently shoved him to score with ease.

The game got suddenly more complicated. Bigs got the sleds moving fast again, to which loud cheers arose from the monsters in the stands.

More collisions occurred, harder and with increased force, yet the Smalls had to be more careful; the faster they went, the more dangerous pile-ups were.

The zombie head appeared almost instantly after each score. Often it appeared overhead of a moving

Small, who couldn't grab fast enough to seize it. Yet when an attempt at scoring failed and the head bounced across the grass, it would float slowly up and then down into the center of the rink.

Scores for both teams happened with amazing rapidity. Collisions in the center occurred every time the zombie head reappeared there. Sometimes a risky skid stopped one sled, causing a pile-up, or someone's sled ran out of speed in front of an enemy Big, who would stand there and watch until one of their teammates slammed into them, knocking them farther along.

Maxivoom Snydho began targeting Martin, ramming into him for no reason. Martin decided it was time.

When next they approached, Martin aimed his sled into Maxivoom Snydho as hard as he could.

"One side, Hamhock ...!" Martin shouted.

Maxivoom Snydho looked shocked.

Their next time around, Martin pulled on the brake and dropped three foot-bound arrow-tips to scrape into ice. Maxivoom Snydho passed ahead, and Martin clipped his rear.

"You missed, Bacon-Bits ...!" Martin shouted.

On a subsequent pass, Maxivoom Snydho slammed hard into Martin and half-knocked him off his sled, which tilted onto one rail before he righted it. Stabbing came to his rescue; Maxivoom Snydho's impact had stopped him in dead center, and Stabbing rammed him from behind so hard Maxivoom Snydho was driven into the point where both centers joined, right at Crusto's feet. Ton Eat-oddly tried to reach over and swat him along, but Crowscary Morguee couldn't stop in time; she slammed into Maxivoom Snydho and bounced backwards on the ice. Another pile-up blocked everyone. When the zombie head floated down, Flea Scarwart Monastary grabbed it, yet he had no one to pass it to.

When he could, Crusto slapped Stabbing around the Greasy Golems' circle, past Fart Hurlo Con-well to Brain, who fired him right at Flea Scarwart Monastary. They crashed; the tiny gremlin's sled was knocked over and Flea Scarwart Monastary and the zombie head both went sliding across the ice.

Happy reached out with his hockey stick and pulled Martin's sled backwards, close enough for Martin to grab the loose zombie head. Then he pushed him onward. Martin didn't travel far but wrenched on his steering bar and used his arrow-tips to stay inside the Skullcracker's circle. Crusto sped him on, and Martin easily scored.

Bigs struggled to get the sleds moving again, yet another pile-up happened just before Martin slid in front of Brain. Brain whacked him hard; Martin's sled was the only one moving. He slammed into the pack, barely holding on as several Smalls lost hold and fell off their sleds onto the ice.

On the next lap, Martin got the zombie head, he jumped the tracks and cut across the middle behind Stabbing. He aimed straight toward the purple box and dropped it in. Then the zombie head appeared right over Stabbing, who grabbed it, but everyone crashed into him until no one was moving.

A whistle sounded; if there hadn't been a pile-up, Martin wouldn't have heard it.

"Greasy Golems lead, 18 - 16, and traffic has stopped again," Evilla shouted. "No one's hurt yet, but every pile-up is another chance! The referees are signaling a restart while Stabbing Kingz has the zombie head!"

Ton Eat-oddly whacked Crowscary Morguee, sending her into Stabbing, and Crusto shoved Rude into Maxivoom's rear, and then Ton Eat-oddly smacked Maxivoom into Stabbing. Soon all the Smalls were sliding around the figure eight again.

Another whistle sounded.

"Resume play!" Evilla shouted.

Stabbing scored. Instantly the zombie head reappeared, and Crowscary Morguee grabbed it and scored for the Greasy Golems.

Finally Martin got the zombie head, and was skidding to score when Maxivoom Snydho came flying across the middle of the circle, right at him. Martin slammed on his brake; Maxivoom missed him by inches and slammed hard into the two-foot wall, and then Crowscary Morguee's sled struck Martin's from behind. Martin crashed into Maxivoom, knocking him aside. With ease Martin tossed the zombie head into the purple box.

"Nice try, Pig-Puss ...!" Martin laughed.

Enraged, Maxivoom Snydho leaped off his sled and began punching Martin. Martin blocked as best he could, then shoved him back with an open palm. Maxivoom slipped on the ice, fell, and then two lightning bolts came.

Z-z-z-z-z-zap!

Maxivoom Snydho cringed and crumbled as the electric bolts stabbed into him, shaking his limbs. Martin caught some of the blast; Maxivoom still had a grip on his jersey, yet Martin was on his sled while Maxivoom was standing on ice. Martin felt a little sting pass over him, nothing worse. But Maxivoom ...!

"Maxivoom Snydho is down!" Evilla cried. "You can't start a fist-fight in Hell Hockey! Joke CrampyLiar is reaching over the pile-up to pull Maxivoom Snydho off the pitch before he gets sliced apart by sled-rails! The Greasy Golems are down one Small!"

"Martin, grab on ...!" Happy shouted.

Happy extended his hockey stick and Martin reached out and grabbed it, holding tight to his steering bar. Happy pulled Martin's sled toward him, and Martin tried to score as he slid past the purple scoring box, but another sled crashed into his, and the head rolled away. Then Happy sent him flying toward the center. Yet the zombie head appeared before he got there, and Flea Scarwart Monastary grabbed it.

The Bigs got the Smalls moving again, but the zombie head kept appearing in time for the Greasy Golems to grab it. Flea Scarwart Monastary scored twice, and Crowscary Morguee scored once, but at the next crossing, Rude slammed into Crowscary Morguee's sled, which crashed against Flea Scarwart Monastary's sled so hard it was knocked over. Flea Scarwart Monastary flipped, landed on Crowscary Morguee, and the airborne sled fell atop both of them.

Martin circled the Greasy Golem's loop, grabbed the zombie head, jumped the grooves, and scraped arrow-taped toes to make a sharp right turn, cutting across the middle of the purple circle. He turned hard and skidded to a stop near Stabbing, who had stopped right in front of the purple scoring box.

"Stabbing ...!" Martin called, and he hammered his brake to keep from plowing into his teammate, then handed him the zombie head.

"Passed to him by Martin the Magnificent, Stabbing Kingz scores again!" Evilla shouted. "Yet the Greasy Golems are right on their heels, 21 - 20! Flea Scarwart Monastary is headed toward the middle ... waiting for the zombie head to appear ...! He's got it, headed to score!"

"Happy ...!" Martin called, and he reached out a hand. Happy extended his hockey stick; Martin grabbed it with one hand and reached to Stabbing with his other. Stabbing held onto him, and Happy pulled them both in front of him, then Happy sent both of them on their way, Stabbing first.

"Flea Scarwart Monastary scores again!" Evilla cried. "Tied game! Yet Martin the Magnificent is approaching the center! Yes! Martin's got the zombie head! Fart Hurlo Con-well pushes Flea Scarwart Monastary onward, and Ton Eat-oddly pushes him again ...!"

Crusto caught his hockey stick behind Martin's sled and pulled him out of the way. Martin saw the tiny gremlin flying past him at incredible speed. Gremlins were small, but so were bullets, and any impact at this speed would be shattering.

One hand holding the zombie head, the other holding Crusto's hockey stick, Martin slid halfway off his sled. He heard rails scrape ice ... Rude and Stabbing shouted warnings ...!

Crowscary Morguee was aiming at him!

Crowscary Morguee slammed into him, but she wasn't going fast enough to injure. She tried to snatch the zombie head from his hands, but he held it tight.

Crusto pulled Martin away from her and sent him flying around the Shantdareya circle to score, which he did. Yet Crowscary Morguee came flying up behind him. Martin swerved and skidded with a toe down to get out of her way, but her two Bigs hastened her speed.

Suddenly Martin realized he wasn't her target.

"Stabbing ...!" Martin cried. *"Look out ...!"*

Stabbing saw her too late. He braced for the impact, but Crowscary Morguee jumped high, pulling her sled into the air with her. Crowscary Morguee and her sled's sharp rails slashed down.

Stabbing flipped his sled onto its side, hiding behind it ... and Crowscary Morguee's sled-rails sparked as they crashed onto the side of Stabbing's sled. Yet Stabbing's quick-thinking hadn't fully protected him.

"Ratling strikes Ratling!" Evilla cried. "That's a serious foul ... here comes the penalty!"

Z-z-z-z-z-zap!

Crowscary Morguee was blasted off her sled and fell twitching onto the ice. Martin wondered why she'd done it; both she and Stabbing were down, but Stabbing hadn't been badly hurt.

The horn blew once.

"Halftime ...!" Evilla shouted. "Crowscary Morguee pays the price for her foul, but she knew halftime was about to be called. Stabbing Kingz looks dazed; there's blood on the ice! Yet this grudge match is only half over! Martin the Magnificent made the last score of the half and gave the Shantdareya Skullcrackers' the lead, 22 - 21! But this game is too close to call, and both teams have spells waiting to be cast; the second half is coming! Will Stabbing play? Will Crowscary Morguee or Maxivoom Snydho return? Stay in your seats ... the exciting conclusion to the Shantdareya Locals is about to come!"

Chapter 29
Rompday / Tuesday

Defeat runs deep ...

Lifted off the ice by their Bigs and carried back, Smalls were all set down before Grand Wizard Bastile Wraithbone. He knelt to examine Stabbing, whose ribs were streaming blood. A long gash on his side matched one of the sled-rails of Crowscary Morguee.

"I can heal you," Grand Wizard Bastile Wraithbone said.

"N-n-no ...!" Stabbing gasped, pressing his furry hands against his wound. "That's what they want ... to force you to use your spell."

"I'll take Stabbing's place," Veils said. "We can't leave ourselves vulnerable to their magic."

"We're winning, but only barely," Grand Wizard Bastile Wraithbone said. "I've kept my staff ready, waiting for them to cast first, but ...!"

"Magic in the first half can be negated by magic in the second half," Murder said, handing out water bags. "Grand Wizard Crass Gopherly knows better than to waste his spell."

"We should've injured Flea Scarwart Monastary," Rude said, looking over at the far side of the pitch. Maxivoom Snydho is standing up, and Crowscary Morguee's no novice; she'll shake off one zap."

"That was clever, getting Maxivoom to foul you," Veils said to Martin. "It gained us the lead, but you almost got zapped ...!"

"It was a risk," Martin said. "Maxivoom's weakness is always his temper."

"Keep it up," Rude said. "In the meantime we've got to stay focused ...!"

Just then a surprise arrived; Grand Wizard Veinlet Prize came walking up ... with Martin's sister, Vicky.

"A wonderful first half!" Grand Wizard Veinlet Prize said. "Most impressive!"

"Your visit honors us, my brother," Grand Wizard Bastile Wraithbone said. "Welcome back, Vicky Mulberry."

"So glad to finally see a game!" Vicky said. "I just wanted to say hello and wish you well for the second half." She knelt beside Stabbing. "Are you all right?"

"Out of the game, but I'll live," Stabbing said. "Dirty trick, but I should've expected it from a fellow ratling. I'll pay her back someday!"

"Now isn't the time to worry about future rivalries," Grand Wizard Bastile Wraithbone said. "We've got to win this one."

"Martin, I wanted to thank you, and tell you what a

delight your sister is," Grand Wizard Veinlet Prize said. "I found her sitting in the very back row trapped between two hungry vampires, and insisted she come up front and sit by me. She's very insightful ...!"

"And I'm glad mom's not here to see this," Vicky said to Martin. "These games are far more dangerous than you described."

"I didn't want you to worry," Martin shrugged.

"Well, we can't disrupt your halftime with pleasantries," Grand Wizard Veinlet Prize said. "Good luck, Skullcrackers!"

"Play safe!" Vicky said, staring especially at Martin.

Vicky gave quick hugs to Murder, Happy, and Rude, and squeezed Veils' hand, and rested her palm against Brain and Snitch with a smile, then hurried back to the stands with Grand Wizard Veinlet Prize.

"As I was saying," Rude said. "Focus! We can't gamble on this game to be won by magic alone."

"Indeed not," Grand Wizard Bastile Wraithbone said. "Now, all Bigs switch sides at halftime; that's the rules. I see Crowscary Morguee standing, so it looks like we'll both field three Smalls."

"That's ... too bad," Stabbing said. "They don't have an ... extra Small."

"What if Grand Wizard Crass Gopherly waits until the last second to cast his spell?" Veils asked.

"I doubt that will happen," Grand Wizard Bastile Wraithbone said. "Grand Wizard Crass Gopherly wants to win, and last-minute spells are only useful if you're already winning or can win by just one more score. That won't work in fast-scoring Hell Hockey. We're playing a waiting game, he and I, but he won't wait too long. Yet I've got the staff of Master Grand Wizard Borgias Killoff; he knows my magic is more powerful."

"The game's about to ... resume," Stabbing groaned.

"We can't let them win by dirty tricks," Happy said.

"We can't let them win at all," Crusto said.

"Win ...!" both Brain and Snitch shouted.

"Yes, we must win," Grand Wizard Bastile Wraithbone said. "This is our last chance. Take your places ... and good luck!"

"Amazing action in the first half!" Evilla shouted into her microphone. "Shantdareya leads by one point, and Shantdareya's entrance to the Regionals is on the line! Maxivoom Snydho and Crowscary Morguee have been zapped, but both look recovered. Stabbing Kingz is out for the game, but pretty, Vivacious Veils is taking his place! My excitement is rising! I may need all of you to hold me for this second half ... and you won't hear me complain! So grab some Buttered Popcrud, a handful of Wolf Wafers, and a cup of Yodeling Yeti Yogurt! Get ready to watch the most fabulous thing you've ever seen ... standing on my announcer's platform ... and the second half of the last Locals!"

Martin, Veils, and Rude, their feet bound to arrows, were carried out to the pitch and set on sleds. Maxivoom Snydho, Crowscary Morguee, and Flea Scarwart Monastary came out and laid atop theirs, each between one Skullcracker. The Bigs circled and took their new places.

"The game's about to restart!" Evilla shouted. "Hold onto your fangs! Are we ready? Wands up! Staffs up! Let insanity prevail!"

With the horn, six Bigs lowered hockey sticks and swatted sleds. Smalls shot around the ice, steering through the figure eight. Everyone was careful to not crash; each wanted an equal chance to get the zombie head first.

"Half-wit human ...!" Maxivoom Snydho shouted at Martin as they whizzed a near-miss past each other.

Martin grinned; he was too smart to be goaded by name-calling.

"Boring boar ...!" Martin shouted when they passed again.

The zombie head floated high and descended slowly into the center where the sleds crossed.

Suddenly Maxivoom Snydho jumped high, caught the zombie head, and landed back on his sled. He dropped down, wildly steering to avoid colliding into the two-foot wall, scraping against it so hard Veils caught up and rammed him from behind, but he still managed to score.

"22 - 22!" Evilla cried. "Tied again!"

Rude grabbed the zombie head next and scored, and then Crowscary Morguee did the same. Then Maxivoom got it, but Veils slammed into the side of his sled, stole the zombie head from Maxivoom's hands, and tossed it to Rude, who flew past and scored.

Both teams were running up the score, but neither gained an edge. Martin took the lead; he rammed Maxivoom Snydho, who gave as good as he got on the next pass. Rather than cross the center, both careened back onto their own circles.

Martin wondered why no spell had been cast; some spells worked best at the start of a half, so they lasted longer. Yet he kept circling, accidentally ramming into Rude before him, and getting rammed from behind by Crowscary Morguee.

Flea Scarwart Monastary got the zombie head after a Greasy Golem score and tossed it into the burgundy box.

Then Veils made her first second-half score. Rude rammed Flea Scarwart Monastary, preventing both of them from grabbing the zombie head as they scraped rails though the center. Veils checked her speed, grabbed the zombie head, and scored again.

Crowscary Morguee slammed on her brake approaching the middle, grabbed the zombie head as it appeared, and tossed it to Maxivoom Snydho. Then Crowscary got rammed by Rude and Veils. Yet Maxivoom scored, and Ton Eat-oddly slapped Crowscary Morguee's sled so hard she was knocked off; her sled skittered sideways and blocked Rude and Veils out of the center, away from where the zombie head would reappear.

Happy and Crusto sped Martin toward the center,

but Fart Hurlo Con-well slapped Maxivoom Snydho to match him, and they crashed together so hard both sleds overturned and dumped their riders onto the ice.

"Getting dangerous out there!" Evilla laughed. "Will we see more blood on the ice? 25-26, Greasy Golems leading!"

Flea Scarwart Monastary flew through the center and grabbed the zombie head, but he had to veer around the pile-up and was forced back into the purple circle.

Both Martin and Maxivoom Snydho climbed to their feet and righted their sleds. Yet Maxivoom struggled; instead of feet, he had boar-hooves, which slipped easily on the ice. Martin tip-toed on the spikes of his arrows and propelled his sled faster.

"Boy-bumbler ...!" Maxivoom Snydho shouted at Martin.

"Flat-snout ...!" Martin shouted back.

Suddenly Veils came flying toward center, propelled by Brain and Crusto, and she jumped the ruts and aimed at Maxivoom Snydho, who was struggling to stand by his sled. The wereboar jumped high, barely avoiding her, and then slipped and fell onto his back atop his sled. Martin laughed at him.

"Human scum ...!" Maxivoom shouted.

"I saw you fly ...!" Martin laughed sarcastically. *"The swine flu ...!"*

"I'll get you ... and your ditzy dark elf!" Maxivoom shouted.

Martin's laughter ceased and he glared angrily.

"Oh, ho ...!" Maxivoom Snydho laughed. "No wonder you don't care about my insults! You care about her ...!"

"Stay away from her ...!" Martin shouted, and he began kicking his legs, scraping the ice with his arrowhead-toes, forcing his sled toward Crusto.

Martin finally reached Crusto, having watched Rude fly past him and score, although chased closely by Crowscary Morguee and Flea Scarwart Monastary. Crusto used his hockey stick to turn Martin's sled, then sent him flying after the others. Veils came right after, and she bumped Martin from behind, and Brain sent them both flying on. Martin tried to glimpse the scoreboard, but he couldn't, and the echoes of Evilla's loudspeakers were lost in the roars of the crowd and scrapes of rails on ice.

He caught up with Flea Scarwart Monastary, who was hot on Rude's tail. Together they barreled around the circle.

Crowscary Morguee scored and then veered off, and Rude caught the zombie head and steered unopposed to score.

Suddenly a burst of flames erupted before Martin. Too late to stop, he followed Flea Scarwart Monastary into the fire, which had engulfed the entire purple circle. But no player was burned! Red and yellow waves of heat flashed through the ice underneath them, and the frozen ice exploded upwards.

Martin flew upwards, out onto the shattered slew,

and then landed hard, rained upon by tiny ice fragments. His sled's rails struck the crusty mess as if he'd landed in a giant slushy. He sank deep and heard his rails scrape stone.

One last wave of heat flowed beneath them, and all of the ice melted ... *to water!*

Behind him, Veils swerved and swept around him, trying to stay on the icy burgundy circle, but Maxivoom Snydho rammed into her and knocked her across the center, off the ice, to splash into the water beside Martin.

"Grand Wizard Crass Gopherly casts a fireball!" Evilla shouted. "Not at the players ... at the Shantdareya ice! Their circle is melted! How can the Skullcrackers score now?"

The water was six inches deep, the same depth as their rails were high, so their sleds looked like little offshore docks, immovable platforms surrounded by water.

"Rude Stealing scores, but the zombie head appears center!" Evilla shouted. "Crowscary Morguee gets it! She's headed to score ... and Maxivoom Snydho is slowing, ready to grab the zombie head when it appears! Crowscary Morguee scores to tie the game!

"Shantdareya Skullcrackers are trapped in water! Is this the end of their season?"

"Hockey stick ...!" Martin called to Crusto.

Crusto held out his hockey stick as far as he could. Martin grabbed the very end of it and pulled, but even digging his arrow-tips into the top of his sled, he couldn't drag his sled's metal runners overtop stone ... in six inches of water.

"Maxivoom Snydho has the zombie head!" Evilla cried. "He's circling to score! Crowscary Morguee is setting up to get the zombie head again. Maxivoom scores! The Greasy Golems take the lead, 28 – 27!"

"What do we do?" Veils asked.

"Follow me!" Martin shouted, and he jumped off his sled, into the water, and pushed it toward the center.

Veils looked frantic, but she followed him through the over-her-ankles water, pushing her sled. Soon she and Martin were pressed against the watery edge of the ice, in the center.

"Maxivoom Snydho comes around!" Evilla shouted. "Crowscary Morguee grabs the zombie head ... she's about to score! She scores! 29 – 27! Only one team can score!"

"Don't count on that!" Martin snarled.

Martin jumped onto his sled, standing on it, and Veils did the same. Maxivoom Snydho was the heaviest, but Martin was taller. When the zombie head appeared, just as Maxivoom Snydho came flying toward it, Martin jumped up, grabbed it, and yanked it out of Maxivoom's reach.

"*Rude ...!*" Martin shouted. "*Catch ...!*"

Martin passed the zombie head across the circle like a basketball. Rude had been leading their pack; when their ice blew apart he'd landed right before the Skullcracker's purple scoring box. Flea Scarwart

Monastary was trapped only a few inches behind him, but he was short and out of position. Rude caught the zombie head and tossed it into the box.

"Rude scores ... on an arena with no ice!" Evilla shouted. "Yet the Shantdareya Skullcrackers are still losing, 28 - 29!"

Crowscary Morguee came flying at them, but Martin kicked the front of her sled to force her away, although her impact cracked the arrow shafts taped to his foot. Veils grabbed the zombie head and tossed it to Rude.

"Rude scores again!" Evilla shouted. "Tied game! Martin the Magnificent turns the tables on Grand Wizard Crass Gopherly's fireball spell! He melted their ice, but not the fire of their spirit!"

"Faster ...!" Maxivoom Snydho shouted at Ton Eat-oddly, and he repeated his command to Fart Hurlo Con-well. Crowscary Morguee skidded out of his way, and Maxivoom Snydho came flying around the circle dangerously fast.

The zombie head appeared, but Martin ignored it. Maxivoom Snydho was barreling toward center, his sled aimed to plow him down. Yet Maxivoom veered and jumped, his sled flew up into the air ... not at Martin ... *at Veils ... rails first ...!*

Veils screamed, but Martin threw himself forward and bodily slammed into the side of the airborne sled.

Martin was knocked off his sled, into the water, yet Maxivoom's path was diverted. His sharp rails tilted, he slashed past Veils. She dodged, yet he sliced a deep gash across the back of her forearm. Blood spewed ...!

Maxivoom Snydho flew past, and his sled splashed and crashed down into the shallow water, flipping over and throwing him off.

Despite his pain, Martin jumped up. He was bruised and battered, but Veils was badly cut. Blood gushed from her wound, which was too long to try and hold closed. She was lucky ... Maxivoom Snydho had tried to kill her ... but at this rate she'd bleed to death.

"Bastile! ..." Martin shouted. *"Heal her ...!"*

Martin stood up, soaked with water, and jumped out of the way as Grand Wizard Bastile Wraithbone's spell crossed the pitch. It struck Veils, a blue-white light that shined like a heavenly glow. It lasted long, and when it faded, Veil's arm looked healed. She wiped the blood away with her other hand, showing a long pink cut, partially healed over.

"Grand Wizard Bastile Wraithbone heals his granddaughter, Vivacious Veils!" Evilla cried. "Yet Crowscary Morguee scored while they were distracted, and she's grabbed the zombie head again! She's about to ... she scores! 30 - 29!"

Martin turned to face Maxivoom Snydho, who was still kneeling in the water, trying to stand, and laughing at him.

He'd tried to kill Veils ...!

Martin stormed toward him, splashing through the water, fists clenched.

"Martin, no ...!" Grand Wizard Bastile Wraithbone

cried.

Maxivoom Snydho looked surprised by Martin's approach, even more by the snarl on his human face, more twisted than any wereboar's expression.

Martin's first punch knocked Maxivoom Snydho backwards onto his sled, and then he jumped atop him and kept punching.

"Martin, no ...!" voices cried; Veils, Rude, Murder, Happy, and Crusto.

Z-z-z-z-z-zap!

The lightning struck and enveloped both him and Maxivoom Snydho. The pain was staggering, yet Martin didn't stop. Electrified, he kept punching Maxivoom Snydho.

Z-z-z-z-z-zap!

A second blast flew, and this time Martin couldn't see Maxivoom anymore; sparks flashed before his eyes, the whole pitch vanished. Martin was blinded as the charge burned through him. Yet he couldn't stop swinging his fists, even though he couldn't see his enemy anymore.

He'd tried to kill Veils ....!

Z-z-z-z-z-zap!!!

"Easy ...!" Grand Wizard Bastile Wraithbone echoed dimly in his ears, his voice muted by a loud, lingering buzz. "He's coming around."

Martin opened his eyes. The first face he saw was Vicky, looming over him, eyes bulging.

"Martin ...!" Vicky cried. *"Wake up ...!"*

A sea of faces swam before him ... human ... monster ... wizard ... *Veils.*

"Three zaps ...!" Murder's breathless tone sounded worried. *"He's lucky to be alive ...!"*

"Yet he kept fighting," Happy said. "This deed might be worthy of a centaur-song!"

"He lost his temper ... and control," Rude said. "Justified or not, he should've acted more civilly."

"He did it for Veils," Crusto said. "Any of us might've done the same."

"It was wrong!" Vicky insisted. "He knows better! Mother would ground him for a year!"

"The Grand Wizard's Council will decide this, both for Martin and for Maxivoom Snydho." Grand Wizard Bastile Wraithbone said, shaking his head. "We'll be lucky indeed if Martin isn't suspended from our games forever."

These words penetrated Martin's fog, yet he had a more urgent worry.

"Did ... did we win ...?" Martin asked.

"The Shantdareya Skullcrackers are headed to the Regionals," Grand Wizard Bastile Wraithbone said. "With you and Maxivoom Snydho out of the game, and Flea Scarwart Monastary in the wrong circle, Crowscary Morguee's ratling agility could almost equal a dark elf, but she had no one to pass the zombie head to, and we scored three times. Flea Scarwart Monastary ran to help, but was too short; couldn't reach the head first. When

Crowscary Morguee got it, Flea Scarwart Monastary had to push her sled to where Ton Eat-oddly could reach her. He spun her around the circle to score, yet we were ahead by two, and time was running out. Veils and Crowscary Morguee matched evenly ... both stood on their sleds in the center as the zombie head appeared, and each scored twice more before the horn blew. The final score was 34 - 32."

"We ... we won ..!" Martin gasped weakly.

"We may regret our victory," Grand Wizard Bastile Wraithbone said. "If it means you'll be suspended from the league ...!"

"I'll speak for him," Grand Wizard Veinlet Prize said, and Martin saw the tall, handsome wizard standing behind Vicky. "He fought to avenge an action that never should've happened. Maxivoom could've killed Veils ...!"

"Martin, no matter what they decide, you and I will discuss this in private ... later!" Vicky warned, her frown deeper than Martin had ever seen.

Martin swallowed and nodded.

"You're right," Martin said. "I should've let the referees handle it. Once Veils was safe ... she is safe, isn't she ...?"

Murder, Rude, and Stabbing stepped back. Before Crusto, Happy, Brain, and Snitch stood Veils. She was holding her wounded forearm, which bore a long, pink scar from the sharp rails of Maxivoom Snydho's sled, yet her face was beaming. Slowly she stepped forward, knelt beside Vicky, and looked down at Martin.

"I once said you weren't a monster," Veils said to Martin. "I'm sorry. I was wrong."

Veils bent and kissed Martin's cheek.

Chapter 30
Smashday / Wednesday

Accountability ...

Martin had barely gotten Tom, Terry, and Ron settled down, each with a small bowl of potato chips, shooting aliens on TV, when the phone rang.

"Hello ...?" Martin answered.

"Do you have any idea how angry I am with you ...?" Vicky asked.

"I think I do," Martin said.

"You're wrong," Vicky snapped. "You have no idea ... because you're only twelve. This is an adult angry, something you obviously can't know, since you still act like a child."

"I'm sorry," Martin confessed.

"Give me one reason why I shouldn't go before the Grand Council of Wizards, tell them I'm your sister and guardian, and ask them to ban you from their games forever."

"What ...?" Martin exclaimed. *"You can't ...!"*

"Can you stop me?" Vicky demanded. "Your

behavior was so abominable, so disgusting, they won't ask if I'm your real guardian or not; they'll use my plea as an excuse to ban you ... because of the damage you did to them."

"I damaged the Wizard's Council ...?" Martin asked.

"Look at what they're doing!" Vicky almost shouted. "Civilizing an entire world, a world once barbaric, and you go and exhibit barbarism in exact opposite of their goal! They need you to be a role model ... and you betrayed their cause!"

Martin hung his head. *Role model: wasn't that the same term Evilla had used ...? Exactly what Evilla had asked of him ...?*

"I did," Martin admitted.

"Children's stories are entirely about one child," Vicky said. "Heterodox is countless stories. There's the story of wizards trying to civilize monsters. There're stories of wizards trying to coach sports teams. There're stories of monsters trying to play in those teams. There're stories of monsters who aren't in any team, each trying to learn to be civilized, looking around them, wondering which examples set by others they should follow. If you want to be the hero, you need to stop looking only at your problems, and start realizing how many stories are out there, at least one for each wizard and monster, and every person on Earth, each with all the problems, dreams, and goals they have. You can be a good example for them; that's what heroes are, but you acted like a villain!"

"I didn't mean to ...!" Martin argued.

"Yours wouldn't be the first story of a hero gone bad," Vicky said. "But the choice is yours. You need to decide what kind of adult you want to be, and by that, what kind of role model you want to be. You need to see your story as one of many, all coexisting, everyone helping each other achieve their goals. Worlds are bigger than children think, even a world of monsters. Did you know that Heterodox is an English word, an adjective, a term used in psychology and philosophy? It means: 'not conforming with accepted standards or beliefs'. You can't go back if you can't abide by their standards. If you want to keep visiting Heterodox, you'd better start acting like the role model they need you to be."

"What can I do?" Martin asked.

"Write a letter of apology," Vicky said. "Leave it on your bed. Rude will drop in tomorrow, while you're at school, and carry it back. Grand Wizard Bastile Wraithbone will read it to the council, and if you can convince them, with honesty and sincerity, then they might not ban you."

"What should I write?" Martin asked.

"If you have to ask, you don't deserve to play in the Grotesquerie Games," Vicky said.

The next morning, Martin read his letter twice, before leaving it on his bed and going to school.

"Dear wise and most-honorable Wizards of the Grand Council of Heterodox, I wish to apologize for my inexcusable display of temper in my last game of the Locals on Shantdareya Island. At the time, my justifications seemed to warrant my outrageous behavior, yet I knew better, and I'm ashamed of what I've done. My only excuse, if any excuse may be offered, is that, among my own kind, I'm still a child. I'm still learning, as most inhabitants of Heterodox are learning, how to be the person I truly want to be. I know I made a mistake, and I only hope that you understand; mistakes are part of the path to growing. I hope you can forgive me, and allow me to continue to play in your games. I promise, upon my honor, such an event shall never happen again. My dream, and goal, is to be the type of role model others look up to, an example others are proud to follow. I pray you will assist me in this goal, and allow me to continue to play in your Grotesquerie Games.

Yours sincerely,

Martin Mulberry."

Chapter 31
Rompday / Friday *(... four weeks later ...!)*

The Unexpected Joining ...

Martin fell into Snitch's hands. Snitch was wearing his slick black pants and t-shirt printed with a formal shirt and red bow-tie. Snitch set him down, and Martin turned to look at Grand Wizard Bastile Wraithbone and his teammates, all dressed in their finest garb, with Murder on crutches, just as formal as at their elegant dinner at Medusa Manor.

"Here, change quickly," Vicky said, and she handed Martin a shopping bag. "Be careful with that; I rented it."

Martin hurried into a back room, changed, and came back out dressed in a black tuxedo with a bright silver vest and red bow tie.

"Wow!" Veils exclaimed, and then she paled and hesitated. "You ... clean up ... okay."

Veils was wearing her long purple dress again, and looked exceedingly pretty. Her arm wasn't bandaged, and the sore of her gash looked faded and mostly healed.

"You ... look ... so ...," Martin stammered to Veils, yet he could say no more. She frowned, but then Stabbing whispered one word into his ear, which Martin repeated. "... b-b-beautiful."

"Very beautiful," said Miss Terri Theater, the blue naiad, holding hands with Rude, dressed in a pale yellow gown that accentuated her light blue skin and dark blue hair.

"Thank you ... Terri," Veils said, still looking at Martin.

"Shall we go ...?" Grand Wizard Bastile Wraithbone asked. "It should begin soon."

Everyone nodded, and Grand Wizard Bastile Wraithbone led the way.

They entered a grand hall, much like a church, walked down the gentle ramp in the center, and filed into a row of seats near the middle. These seats were height-adjustable, like the seats in the stands of every stadium. Around them, in the crowded hall, sat every type of monster, and many looked down upon them from balconies, especially those who didn't sit, like centaurs, Happy Lostcraft among them, and some huge faces peered in through high windows: giants.

A familiar face, near the front, turned around, looked behind her, and waved at Martin: Evilla, dressed in her most elegant sparkling red dress ... with shiny purple hair. In the front rows sat many of the Grand Council of Wizards, more than Martin had thought there were. Grand Wizard Bastile Wraithbone nodded to his team, then walked up to join his brethren.

In the very front, off to the right, stood the pride of Lilliesput, the Grave Gutters: the great sphinx Slug Gormet-Wreather, brownie Jangelly Kurtails, naiad Barbaric Steal, the bigfoot Pansthorny Chopkins, yeti Bruise Clambell, banshee Damhell Hairy, minotaur Jerk Goldboom, and the satyr Caroling Jokers ... whose horns had cracked Martin's ribs in the last game of the Finals. Each looked amazing, in formal coats and gowns. Before them stood their leader, Grand Wizard Veinlet Prize, in a deep orange robe.

Soft music, playing from a huge pipe organ, suddenly swelled, and a procession began down the center. The Wonders of Wanderlost, the only all-female team, the Wild Wraiths, processed in single file, each wearing a flowing scarlet dress, and scattering flower petals. First came the tiny, enticing vampire, Fey Wraith, followed by the half-transparent shadow, Jailnet Lazy. Werewolf Lynn DaBlair-Witch followed her, trailed closely by the prettily-stitched Frankenstein's Monster, Death Wallache. The ogre Mykill Gouge led their Bigs, followed by the minotaur Don Alt-Pleasant and the massive dragling, Mad Eyelean Con, whose eyes glowed red and tiny flickers of flame smoked from her mouth. Only Fright Fried, the deadly ratking, who'd been banned from the games for purposefully injuring Murder, wasn't there.

The organ music swelled. Grand Witch Maim La

Nuormal came in, walking down the aisle wearing a black wedding dress with a twelve-foot train. She was carrying a bouquet of black roses and smiling brightly.

"So ... he finally told her," Martin whispered.

"No, he didn't," Vicky smiled.

"Tell her what ...?" Veils whispered, but Vicky shushed her.

"He asked me how to tell her, and I suggested he didn't," Vicky whispered in Martin's ear. "I told him to just propose; it's harder to dump a husband than a boyfriend."

"But ... she'll kill him!" Martin whispered.

"No one's that good at keeping secrets," Vicky said. "Most girlfriends know far more about their boyfriends than they think we do. I suspect she already knows."

"How ...?" Martin asked.

Vicky nodded to Veils.

"You beat up a wereboar for Veils," Vicky whispered. "Why don't you ask her that question?"

Martin glanced at Veils, who was sitting next to him, glaring at him for being left out of his whispered conversation with Vicky.

No ... he really didn't want to ask Veils ...!

"But why ...?" Martin asked.

"If she knows who he is, she must know what he gave up for her," Vicky whispered. "His identity, rulership of the Grand Council, and the most powerful wizard's staff; I hope I meet someone who would give up that much for me."

Martin subsided; he still felt chagrined to realize how many stories existed around him ... that weren't about him.

The wedding of Grand Wizard Veinlet Prize and Grand Witch Maim La Nuormal was a great event on Heterodox. Martin was glad to be there, and relieved that he and Maxivoom Snydho had each been given only one-game suspensions for their fist-fight on the melted pitch of Hell Hockey. He hoped his letter to the Grand Council helped sway their generosity.

The Regionals were coming soon ... and Martin couldn't wait to play again. He wanted to be a hero again ... and display to all Heterodox the qualities he now knew being a hero required.

THE END

Jay Palmer

ABOUT THE AUTHOR

Born in Tripler Army Medical Center, Honolulu, Hawaii, Jay Palmer works as a technical writer in the software industry in Seattle, Washington. Jay enjoys parties, reading everything in sight, woodworking, obscure board games, and riding his Kawasaki Vulcan. Jay is a knight in the SCA, frequently attends writer conferences, SciFi Conventions, and he and Karen are both avid ballroom dancers. But most of all, Jay enjoys writing.

JAYPALMERBOOKS.COM

Made in the USA
Columbia, SC
11 February 2024

31317892R00217